"I want to clarify. Until I tell you
I wish it, we will not…that is, we
won't actually—"

"Consummate our reunion?" He relished the abashed expression his bluntness called forth on her beautiful face, finding some kind of perverse pleasure in being outspoken about the act he wanted to enjoy with her desperately right now, but that he had decided to resist for both their sakes. By all the saints in heaven, he must be mad.

But then she surprised him again by echoing, "Aye. Consummate our reunion." She lifted her brow, her hesitancy seeming to dissipate in favor of that other, more defiant air of hers. That almost insolent look that attracted him like nothing else he'd ever known. "You give your oath that you will wait and not attempt to resume our relations fully, no matter how great the temptation, until I bid you take the liberty?"

He felt the right corner of his mouth quirk as it always did when he was thrown a challenge, even as the blood began to beat hotter in his veins. "Aye, lady; that is my offer and my oath. But I think it only fair to warn you about something."

"What is it?"

"You will have one week of grace—but after that it is not *I* who will have the most difficult part of this bargain."

Other AVON ROMANCES

A DANGEROUS BEAUTY *by Sophia Nash*
THE DEVIL'S TEMPTATION *by Kimberly Logan*
MISTRESS OF SCANDAL *by Sara Bennett*
THRILL OF THE KNIGHT *by Julia Latham*
TOO WICKED TO TAME *by Sophie Jordan*
WHEN SEDUCING A SPY *by Sari Robins*
WILD SWEET LOVE *by Beverly Jenkins*

Coming Soon

A WARRIOR'S TAKING *by Margo Maguire*
THE HIGHLANDER'S BRIDE *by Donna Fletcher*

And Don't Miss These
ROMANTIC TREASURES
from Avon Books

THE DUKE'S INDISCRETION *by Adele Ashworth*
THE VISCOUNT IN HER BEDROOM *by Gayle Callen*
HOW TO ENGAGE AN EARL *by Kathryn Caskie*

The
Templar's
Seduction

MARY REED MCCALL

AVON BOOKS
An Imprint of HarperCollinsPublishers

This is a work of fiction. Names, characters, places, and incidents are products of the author's imagination or are used fictitiously and are not to be construed as real. Any resemblance to actual events, locales, organizations, or persons, living or dead, is entirely coincidental.

AVON BOOKS
An Imprint of HarperCollins*Publishers*
10 East 53rd Street
New York, New York 10022-5299

Copyright © 2007 by Mary Reed McCall
ISBN: 978-0-06-117044-7
ISBN-10: 0-06-117044-5
www.avonromance.com

First Avon Books paperback printing: June 2007

Avon Trademark Reg. U.S. Pat. Off. and in Other Countries,
Marca Registrada, Hecho en U.S.A.
HarperCollins® is a registered trademark of HarperCollins Publishers.

Printed in the U.S.A.

10 9 8 7 6 5 4 3 2 1

For this last book in the Templar Knights trilogy, I'm going back to the beginning to dedicate this to all those who have helped me along the way in my writing career (listed in no particular order): John, Megan, and Rebecca; Pa and Ma; my mother-in-law, Norma, sister-in-law Judy, and brothers-in-law Richard and Donald; sisters Linda, Cindy, Susan, Sandy, Deb, and Carolyn, along with their husbands, significant others, and children; past and present members of Central New York Romance Writers; the many special teachers who have inspired and guided me in my love of literature and writing; all my "bosom friends"; my fantastic and talented agents Annelise Robey and Meg Ruley; and last but by no means least, my fabulous editor Lyssa Keusch. You've all been there for me in so many ways— and this one's for all of you.

Acknowledgments

An author's books don't end up on bookstore shelves without the efforts of many others who help in guiding it to its destination—and so in addition to some of those mentioned in the dedication, I'd like to thank:

All the men and women in Avon editorial, sales, marketing, art, and production departments who have worked with my books over the years. I am so grateful for your talents in the process of taking the raw pages that spill from my imagination and transforming them into a beautiful book.

The musical artists who continue to stir my emotions as I plot and write each of my books, including, for this story in particular, Faith Hill, Rascal Flatts, Evanescence, Chicago, Patrick Doyle, and Josh Groban.

And lastly, I'd be remiss if I didn't acknowledge a creative debt to the Templar Brotherhood and its knights, noble and true, who inspired this trilogy. May you live on in countless minds and imaginations for centuries to come.

Non nobis, Domine, non nobis, sed Nomini, Tuo da gloriam . . .

(Not for us, Lord, not for us but to Thy Name give glory . . .)

—Motto of the Knights Templar

The Templar Order had banished me, but that had not stopped my Inquisitors from exacting their due through endless, mindless torment. Aye, they made me pay for thwarting them, excusing their cruelty as necessary recompense for the sin of recanting my confession, given so glibly after the mass arrests in France.

When I was rescued from the hell of their dungeons and brought back to health through the efforts of my brother Damien and loyal friends Richard and John, I felt no comfort in it. Nay, I was a man without purpose. A man cut off from feelings of nobility, honor, even hope.

A man running, perhaps, from life itself...

—The letters of Sir Alexander de Ashby, the year of our Lord, 1315

The
Templar's
Seduction

Prologue

June 1309
Dunleavy Castle, the Lowlands of Scotland

"**T**he western wall is weakening, my lady, and may not withstand another assault of the trebuchet."

Muttering a curse under her breath, Lady Elizabeth of Selkirk stood to face the man who'd spoken—the castle steward, Edwin. She had not been bent in a position of prayer. Nay, she had been kneeling on the floor next to the pallet of one of Dunleavy's nearly three score of wounded men, doing her part to try to make him and the others here in the great hall more comfortable.

So many men, along with some lads now and a few women too. The siege had gone on too long to expect anything less, coming as it had on the heels of the English army's offensive against them last month. But their adversary this time was Archibald Drummond, the Earl of Lennox. He was a Scot and a neighbor to the north, and she hadn't expected him to attack.

"Shall I summon the captain of the guard for consultation?"

She shifted her gaze to Edwin's. "Nay, I would not call him away from his duty to tend to my questions, when you might be able to answer them as well."

Edwin tipped his chin, indicating he would oblige her if he could.

"Why do we not return fire with our own catapult to force him back?"

"It was smashed during Lennox's latest volley and will take until nightfall, at least, to be repaired." Edwin's voice was tight, though as always he wore his usual exterior of calm restraint. "The outer yard is in shambles; the wooden frame of the weapon is in splinters, and the stones used for ammunition scattered."

Elizabeth tried to hide her reaction to the news. Her gaze swept around the great hall, filled with men suffering burns, broken bones, cuts, and battered skulls. Men who had done everything she'd asked of them during the past four years, ten months, and five days since her newly wed husband and lord of this castle, Robert Kincaid, had joined in the war against his own English countrymen and been captured for his troubles.

They'd had but infrequent word of him since. He was still alive, so far as she knew, kept in miserable confinement in an English dungeon while the king's minions brought siege after siege against Dunleavy. They wouldn't succeed, by heaven. She'd sworn it to herself, her kin, and in her own mind at least, to Rob.

"My lady?"

Startled from her thoughts back to the here and now, Elizabeth shivered, gesturing for Edwin to move away from the rows of pallets with her, even as she nodded for Mariah to come and take her place tending to those in the makeshift infirmary. When she and Edwin had reached the corridor, she breathed in the slightly fresher air there.

"Something will need to be done, and quickly. We cannot wait until dark to return fire." She glanced away for a moment, frowning. "I will need to send word to Robert the Bruce, asking for his aid against this outrage. He will not look kindly upon Lennox for his siege against a Scottish castle whose lord suffers in English captivity."

"Lady, forgive me, but Lord Lennox asserted in his missive that he had received word of your husband's death at the hands of his English captors."

"It's a lie, else the English would have used it against us during their most recent assault against Dunleavy. They would not have remained silent if they'd had such a weapon to wield."

Edwin bowed his head in silence, though she could see he was holding back something more. Pompous and irritating as he could sometimes be, the steward was among her most loyal followers, and whether or not she'd have done so in other circumstances, she felt it necessary to hear anything he had to say in this desperate moment.

"Speak, Edwin, if there is aught else."

He paused before tilting his head in deference and murmuring, "I could not help thinking that if Lord Lennox genuinely believes your husband to be dead, he may perceive this siege as more than a stock conquest. He may consider it in truth an act of loyalty to Scotland."

"How so?" she scoffed.

"Pardon, my lady, but some believe your loyalties . . . *uncertain*. Having a Scot for a father does not alter the fact that your mother was of English blood. There are those who think it nigh impossible for you to remain firm in the face of continual attack by your mother's countrymen. Some fear you might choose a truce with the enemy over constant siege, and Lennox likely believes that reason enough for this aggression, even in Robert the Bruce's eyes."

"How convenient, then, that the earl never questioned my loyalty to Scotland when my very English husband fought by his side in the war for freedom five years past," she answered tightly. "Nay, the arrogant cur strikes now only because we are weakened by the previous assaults against us. The Bruce will take my side in this."

Edwin kept his eyes lowered, but his voice was sharp as he asked, "What do you suggest we do in the meantime, then? As you said, we cannot wait until nightfall to retaliate further, and Lord Lennox shows no sign of pulling his forces back." He lifted his gaze to her then, and the steeliness she saw there startled her. It was the first time she could remember seeing that look in her usually placid steward's eyes. "Might it not be better to at least *consider* forming an alliance with him, my lady, so that the next time the English—"

"I will not yield, Edwin, to him or to any man who comes with intent to beat down the walls of Dunleavy."

After a long, tension-filled silence, Edwin offered her a stiff bow, inclining his head in a manner that made it clear he disagreed and thought her foolhardy to continue as they were. But she was his lady, and in absence of her husband, she was in charge. He knew it and would not refute her outright.

She gritted her teeth. "We must do something, however, and it must be unexpected," she murmured, wrapping her arms around her middle. "Something we have never done before. It will be a risk, to be sure, but perhaps . . ." She let her voice trail off, lost in thought as this new plan began forming in her mind. Pushing herself away from the wall, she strode forward, unwinding her thick, honey-gold hair from its plait as she went.

"Where are you going, Lady Elizabeth?" Edwin called, exasperation coloring his voice as he hurried to catch up with her.

"To my chamber, to exchange this gown for one that is fresh and far more appealing."

"What?"

She glanced sideways at the steward as they strode onward. "I have not lost my wits, Edwin. The change of garments is part of the plan I am considering. But first I must ask another question of you. Have we a ready supply of pitch, still, in the storage chamber beneath the great hall?"

"Aye, my lady, but—"

"I want it brought up and heated in large vats. In the meantime, order a dozen men to dig a shallow trench the length of the outer yard, twenty paces inside the gate and curving forward to connect with the stone wall."

Edwin's brow furrowed, and in an uncharacteristic move, he grabbed her wrist, pulling her to a stop in the corridor.

She gave him a sharp look, and he dropped his hand.

"Pardon, my lady. I am only surprised by the order. Lord Lennox has never approached near enough to the gate to make pouring hot pitch effective against him or his men."

"Nay, he hasn't. But I am about to make it worth his while." Elizabeth clenched her jaw, welcoming the burning sensation. "I want the pitch spread along the bottom of the trench, not spilled atop Lennox and his men. I will be standing at the summit of the steps at the entrance to the great hall and visible to the earl and his men, when we raise the outer gate's portcullis. He will think himself the victor of this siege. Our archers will be hidden with bolts afire when the preening buffoon comes marching through the outer gate with his warriors in tow, expecting a pretty welcome from the lady he has defeated—"

"And we will ignite the pitch in the trench, giving them instead a wall of flame," Edwin finished for her, looking more than a little startled. "It will take them by surprise, for none would expect us to light such a fire within our own gates."

"Aye. It is a calculated risk, naturally, but the castle is unlikely to be in any real danger, for the stones of the outer yard will keep the flames from spreading to the masonry within the inner yard."

Edwin nodded in silence.

"They will be trapped as well," Beth added, "for the portcullis will be lowered at the moment the trench is lit." She allowed herself a grim smile. "It will be a welcome the likes of which Lennox has never experienced before, I'll warrant."

·

"That it will, my lady," Edwin said, still sounding somewhat shocked at the boldness of her plan. But the sharpness came back into his expression as he added, "Pray God naught goes awry, else we'll have opened our gates willingly to the enemy."

"I have faith in Him and the good soldiers of Dunleavy to see this through without falter." Elizabeth shifted the intensity of her stare to Edwin again, almost smiling to see him flinch a bit in response. "And I will trust you to begin the process of readying all, while I change into a gown that might help lull the earl more aptly to his doom."

"Aye, my lady," Edwin murmured, lowering his gaze from hers in the guise of another short bow, before he turned and set off to do as she'd asked of him.

"We must be ready within this half hour," she called after him.

He made acknowledgment of her command, but after he'd disappeared from sight, she paused for another moment, even knowing there was no time to waste in her preparations for what was to come. Taking a deep breath, she offered up a prayer. A solicitation to the Almighty for the success of her plan—and a swift conclusion to the deadly confrontation she was about to instigate with her new enemy by carrying it out.

Chapter 1

Two weeks later
Inglewood Forest, near Carlisle, northern England

He was going to hang at dawn.

Sir Alexander de Ashby tipped his head back against the oak to which his arms were secured and lifted his face to the afternoon sky. Squinting through the glare and trying to ignore the sting of the oozing cut on his brow, he looked to see whether this sturdy fellow had branches large enough to bear the rope that would end his miserable life once and for all.

Just then a puff of hot breeze ruffled the leaves overhead. It swirled through the treetops, dying away almost as soon as it began, but its action allowed the sun to stab into his eyes. It cut a direct path to the throbbing lump on the back of his skull—a parting gift from one of the half-dozen or so English soldiers who had beset him here a few hours ago.

The only soldier he'd left standing, damn it.

Tipping his chin back down, Alex closed his eyes and made an effort to think past the pounding in his head. He supposed the outcome of that little scuffle with the king's finest was why he'd be hanging come the morrow. He'd killed at least two of them, he knew, and the other three hadn't looked likely to get up for quite some time. But that sixth one . . .

A sharp pain suddenly streaked from his shoulders down his arms, as his bonds were yanked from behind.

"At attention, you mangy son of a mongrel bitch!"

Ah, yes, that sixth one . . .

Alex opened his eyes again to meet the hostile gaze of the one soldier who'd somehow gotten beneath his defenses. Instinctively he tightened the muscles of his stomach in preparation for the fist he expected to land there next. But this time the man didn't follow through with his usual blow. Nay, he was standing with his spine stiff as a blade, and his face, which was nicely marred with its own arrays of cuts and bruises, Alex noted with satisfaction, controlled. The soldier had shifted his gaze to a point just past Alex's shoulder, his entire demeanor professional.

In the next moment, Alex realized why.

Another man stepped into view from behind the tree. He was clearly the guard's superior, and by the quality of his clothing, he was also a man of title. Walking with slow, measured steps, he came around to face Alex. Then he just stood still. He did not speak as he perused Alex, from the tip of his scuffed boots, up his legs and torso, covered by a shirt ripped in several places, to the top of his head. As his chill blue gaze locked with Alex's own, his face remained impassive—but for the slight flare of his nostrils and the glimmer of something that filled the expressionless depths of his eyes for an instant before he mastered it.

Alex met that stare with cool insolence, allowing his lip to curl up on one side in mockery. The action was instinctive and the kind of thing that had landed him in trouble on many occasions before. But he didn't attempt to quell it. If he was being honest with himself, he knew he wouldn't have anyway, even if he'd still had something to lose.

The locked stare lasted for a count of eight or ten before the nobleman moved. Turning sharply on his heel, he stalked away a few yards to say something to the guard. Far enough that Alex couldn't make out his words. After a moment's hesitation, the younger man favored Alex with another biting glare before striding past him, his boots crunching on the accumulated twigs blanketing the forest floor.

And then the nobleman swung his gaze back to Alex and spoke directly to him.

"You seem to have cut quite a path of destruction through my men this morn, Sir—?"

"Alexander de Ashby," Alex answered without hesitation. It would serve no purpose to be hanged in anonymity, after all. There was always the chance that Damien might hear of the matter someday and have the peace of knowing what had become of him.

His jaw tightened as that thought of his younger brother swept through his mind; he forced himself to quash it, not wanting any inkling of weakness to be apparent in his expression as he faced this pompous English lord. Nay, he'd save any thoughts he might have of Damien and their difficult past for the lonely hours tonight, as he prepared for what would come at dawn.

"Sir Alexander," the nobleman intoned. His hands

were laced behind him, and he rocked back a bit on his heels, tipping his head to the side and giving a brief nod.

"And you are?" Alex asked, his disrespectful tone begging for reprisal, he knew. But to hell with it. That he faced death on the morrow didn't mean he had to cower like a dog in the meantime. There was naught this lord could do to him that the French Inquisitors had not already put him through during the nearly two years they'd held him as a Templar Knight in the hell of their prisons, except to hang him, of course. But even that would be over with soon enough.

The nobleman looked taken aback at first, but he recovered to answer in a clipped voice, "I am Roger de Gravelin, the Earl of Exford."

Alex felt a tiny shock go through him. The Earl of *Exford*? Even absent as he'd been from England during his time of service with the Brotherhood, Alex knew that name. The Gravelins had curried favor from the king and a good deal of power in the north for their commitment to England in her long-standing battles against the Scots. Lord Exford was likely the most powerful border lord in the realm.

That realization sank like a stone in his gut. Of course. He should have expected no less. It was his usual good fortune and a repeating cycle he could not seem to break, attracting the unfavorable attention of formidable English noblemen. Aye, he seemed to have a knack for flirting with danger, thumbing his nose at trouble by stepping directly into it . . . and then finding himself facing the far-reaching and usually painful wrath of some mighty lord for his efforts.

"Sir Stephen tells me that when you were apprehended, you were in possession of something quite valuable," Exford continued, clearly intent on gleaning information. "Something you attempted to sell to a goldsmith in Carlisle."

Stephen. Alex silently thanked Lord Exford for supplying him with the name of his guard, though it seemed unlikely that he would have opportunity to repay Sir Stephen for his less than hospitable treatment these past few hours.

"Something formerly protected by the Brotherhood of Templars," Lord Exford continued smoothly, bringing Alex's attention back to him with a gut-wrenching snap.

"Ah, yes," Exford murmured, a cold smile hovering on his lips, "I thought that might reclaim your wandering interest."

Alex didn't answer at first, instead taking a few beats to consider how anyone but another Templar Knight of the inner circle could know by sight alone the connection between the Brotherhood and the golden bowl he'd tried to sell at Carlisle . . . the bowl he'd stolen from his Templar brother-in-arms Sir John de Clifton several months ago, after John and their friend Sir Richard de Cantor had risked their own necks to rescue him from the Inquisition in France.

Bolstered by the knowledge that bitter thought inspired, Alex put on a show of innocent surprise. "And how, exactly, would I or any other mercenary knight in England be in possession of Templar treasure?"

"That is better answered by my captain of the guard, I think."

Alex did not have much time to weigh Lord Exford's enigmatic response; the still air seemed to waver as someone else approached, bringing with him a whiff of pomander—nutmeg chief among the scents combined in the hollow ball pendant. The punch of recognition that slammed into Alex as he caught sight of the man sporting it set him back on his heels for a moment, long enough for the new arrival to come to a halt next to Lord Exford, his brow lifted expectantly.

"In the middle of another scrape I see, Alex. It has been a long time since last I looked upon you, old friend, but coming upon you bound and awaiting judgment like this brings back many memories of our time together."

By the Holy Rood, this just kept getting better and better.

Alex pulled himself together to offer what would pass as a sardonic nod of acknowledgment. "Luc. I seem to recall that you sported chains as well during our last meeting."

"So I did." Luc's dark eyes hardened to granite. "Thanks to you." But without warning his expression shifted again, and the glint came into his gaze once more. "Of course, I suppose I should be grateful for your part in my liberation from the Brotherhood. I didn't know it then, but now . . ."

His voice trailed off, and Alex watched his former comrade's mouth curve into a tight smile. He wouldn't call him friend. Nay, Sir Lucas de Compton had never been that. A cohort in crime, perhaps. Aye, and a damned fine warrior. They'd both been members of the Brotherhood's inner circle of knights, along with several others, including Damien, John, and Richard. But as impossible as it seemed, Luc had been even less suited for the holy vows of the Templars than Alex had been.

Both of them had chafed at the restraints imposed upon all who were part of the Order, relishing the fighting aspects of being a Templar while resenting the other rules they were charged to abide by. The Templars were the most elite and feared warriors in the world, it was true; they served under authority of the pope alone in the effort to defend Christianity, not only in the Holy Land before it had been lost to the Saracens at Acre, but also in every other part of the known world as well. Yet the key to that power, many believed, came in the willingness of those accepted into the Brotherhood to cast off the temptations of the flesh. To join the Order one was compelled to take the same vows, in essence, as those of a priest: poverty, obedience . . . and chastity. Eventually, Alex and Luc had both rebelled against that last requirement, aiding each other by keeping quiet their secret dalliances with women, mostly lowborn, who were only too happy to steal a few moments of pleasure with such famed knights.

It had gone on for a goodly time, for no matter where they traveled, willing women were always plentiful, drawn as they were to powerful warriors, be they sworn to celibacy or nay. But when Luc had crossed the line to taking his pleasure with a female who was *unwilling*, it had all stopped for Alex; he'd barely been able to keep himself from exacting a permanent vengeance when he'd stumbled upon the scene—though he'd enjoyed throttling Luc to within an inch of his life.

However, the scandal of it all had exposed their

sins to the world. They'd been thrown into chains for their transgressions against the Brotherhood. Luc had been punished and expelled from the Order a mere two weeks before the details of Alex's own crimes and their suitable punishments were finalized. John, Damien, and Richard had been ordered to bring Alex in custody from Cyprus into France, to face questioning and sentencing by the Grand Master of the Templars himself, Jacques de Molay.

And that is exactly what would have happened, had not the mass arrests in France intervened and the whole world descended, it seemed, into madness, with the call for the dissolution of the entire Brotherhood.

"What, then—are you so different from me in your feelings about our service in the Order?" Luc asked lightly in the face of Alex's continued silence. His tone of gentle mockery sounded, as it always had, somehow refined coming from his lips. "After all you experienced as a Templar, I would think—"

"I *am* different from you, Luc," Alex interjected sharply. "A truth for which I am profoundly grateful."

Without another word, Luc lunged forward to grip Alex's throat, while at the same time lifting his other fist with clear intent to answer the insult with violence, regardless of the fact that Alex was bound and could not retaliate. But Lord Exford yanked him back.

"Peace, man. If his face is marred further it will do my cause no good."

Luc let go. "*What* cause?"

Coughing to restore the flow of his breath, Alex

watched Luc scowl, his eyes still sparking with anger. But he pulled his gaze away from Alex to look at Lord Exford. "I thought you wished only to know before the hanging how the man your patrol apprehended had come into possession of Templar treasure. That has been answered. What has not been answered, however, is the account between Ashby and me, and I—"

"You forget your place, sir! This prisoner is mine, to do with as I see fit," Lord Exford ground out, his entire body thrumming with annoyance. "I need him untouched for what I have planned for him. Is that understood?"

Luc snapped to attention with a mumbled apology.

Alex shook his head, clucking his tongue. "I am surprised. Taking orders was never one of your strong points, Luc."

"Rest assured that I will be quick in obeying the command to hoist you by the neck come dawn," Luc muttered, still at attention.

Ignoring that comment, a decision he knew would only madden his former comrade further, Alex swung his gaze to Lord Exford again, continuing, "However, I also must confess that patience has never been one of mine. So to pick up on Luc's question . . . what the devil *are* you talking about?"

Exford arched his brow. "I am talking about the fact that your hanging on the morrow is not a foregone conclusion, Ashby. I am prepared to offer you a choice."

"*What?*"

The question was uttered simultaneously by both

men; their gazes snapped to Lord Exford, incredulity tingeing Alex's exclamation, and angry disbelief filling Luc's.

"What I propose will sound unorthodox, I do not deny, but I can do no less now that I have seen you."

Luc looked as confused as Alex felt, an emotion that swelled tenfold when Lord Exford continued.

"Stephen alerted me of it when he reported your arrest. You bear an uncanny resemblance in face and form to one of my most prized prisoners from the Scottish wars. Had my own eyes not confirmed it, I might never have believed, but it is irrefutable—and the key to your salvation, should you be bold enough to accept my offer."

Alex shook his head, still frowning. He'd never been the most gifted of intellects, but he wasn't stupid either; yet this man might as well have been speaking a foreign tongue for all he was following him.

Exford must have read his expression, for he finished his statement slowly, as if to be sure Alex caught every word. "Implausible as it may seem, Ashby, you appear the veritable twin of Robert Kincaid, the disgraced Earl of Marston . . . lord of the formerly English-held Dunleavy Castle in the Scottish Lowlands."

From the corner of his eye, Alex saw Luc start and felt the tension ripple from him.

But neither Luc nor Lord Exford said more, and though Alex felt foolish, his survivor's nature would not allow this or any other potential bid for freedom go by without knowing what the hell it might mean for him. Raising his brows to Lord Exford, he asked, "And my unfortunate likeness with this Lord Marston involves me how, exactly?"

"Marston is dead," Luc finally supplied in a tight voice. "He died in English captivity after several years of questioning authorized by King Edward and undertaken by Lord Exford's best interrogators."

Alex felt a tingle of unease. This was not sounding good. Nay, not at all. A man had died under torture instigated by the English Crown, and he shared an apparent likeness with him. Regardless of aught else, it boded ill for his future travels in the realm . . . if indeed he had any future at all.

"Marston was not supposed to die," Lord Exford continued. "It was a miscalculation, for he was very near to giving us the information we needed to successfully retake Dunleavy."

"How unfortunate for you, then."

Alex had recovered his wits somewhat, and his softly delivered sarcasm earned him a glare from both Luc and Exford.

"His death may serve you well, Ashby. I would not mock it were I you," Exford grated.

"I do not mock the man's death, but rather your—" Alex shook his head and scowled, trying to dispel the bitter taste this was all leaving in his mouth. "Never mind," he muttered before looking up to meet the earl's gaze again, deliberately provoking. "What is more pressing at the moment is that I do not understand, still, what part you think I play in any of this. Kindly spit it out and get on with it."

Whatever Exford planned was important, Alex decided, for even after such impudence, the earl did not abandon the conversation, but actually did as he was bid. "We are under direct command from King Edward himself to see Dunleavy brought to heel,"

Exford continued. "Several times I've attempted traditional means of gaining access to the stronghold, leading sieges and assaults, but all our efforts to overwhelm the castle's defenses have failed."

Alex said nothing, but Luc's jaw looked clenched tight enough to crack his teeth.

"I feel compelled now to consider a more . . . unorthodox route to victory, since the opportunity has been placed before me."

"You cannot be in earnest, my lord," Luc ground out at last, his burning gaze glancing from Exford to Alex, and then back again. "This man is little more than a cutpurse. A tarnished former Templar Knight who felt no qualm about stealing from his own brother-in-arms. He cannot be trusted, or—"

"He is an exquisite swordsman," Lord Exford broke in, "more skilled perhaps than Marston himself, not to mention that his arrest and questioning in France has left him with the kind of lasting marks that will make his identity less questionable, once he miraculously reappears to his people, alive and well." As he spoke the last, Exford nodded to the scars that were the parting gifts of his torture by the Inquisition, visible here and there through Alex's torn shirt.

Alex frowned, the tingle of unease rising like a choking tide with every word out of the earl's mouth.

"Of course there are the other irrefutable points," Exford continued. "You never saw Kincaid in the flesh, Luc, but none who did could deny the resemblance. I was damned startled, I can tell you that. Ashby stands as tall and shares an astonishing likeness in coloring and form. It has been five years since any at Dunleavy have seen Rob Kincaid." He shook his head, letting his gaze drift over to Alex again, satisfaction evident in his eyes as he added, "The man's own wife will not be able to tell them apart, once we have given Ashby the proper instruction in his mannerisms and habits."

And with that, Exford's entire plan came crashing down on Alex, undeniable. *By all the fires of hell . . .*

"I trust this is some kind of depraved jest," Alex growled. "For if it is not, then I am not amused."

"Oh, it is no jest," Exford said smoothly. "And the choice for you is simple. If you desire to avoid the hangman's noose come dawn tomorrow, you will agree to impersonate Robert Kincaid, the Earl of Marston, and reclaim Dunleavy Castle as its rightful owner."

"You've lost your mind."

"And you'll lose your life, unless you comply," Exford retorted with quiet and deadly conviction. "We need to infiltrate that castle. We must learn firsthand about her garrison, the inner fortress, and its weaknesses. We need men behind her walls to glean that information. Only then can I risk leading my forces again in another strike for King Edward."

Alex went silent, every muscle screaming for the release of punching something—or someone. Even if the entire idea wasn't asinine, it stuck in his craw, choking him with bitterness. The thought of being used again by powerful men for their own greedy purposes sickened him. He had been down that path before, most recently when the French Inquisitors had forced him to become their battle champion—compelling him even to fight against his own best friend in a death duel—by using his brother Damien's torture at their hands as his incentive not to disobey their commands. After that experience, he'd sworn never to yield to anyone's authority so again.

And yet he had no wish to die either.

He gritted his teeth. It meant he'd likely have to at least consider the possibility of what Exford proposed. But he'd be damned if he'd sit passively by and accept the deal as if it were manna from heaven.

"So?" Exford demanded none too patiently. "What is your answer?"

Quirking his brow with even more insolence than he'd managed to muster thus far, Alex straightened against his bonds. "That depends."

"On what?" Exford asked, incredulous.

"On whether or not you're willing to offer additional compensation for my trouble."

This time there was no mistaking the earl's shock. His mouth actually gaped, and even Luc couldn't hide an appreciative smirk at Alex's daring. But Alex was in no mood to acknowledge any of it, nay, he was feeling more reckless than ever, and he cared not what anyone thought of him.

"I'm offering you your life, man!" Exford finally managed to sputter. "Isn't that enough?"

"Nay." Alex kept his gaze cold and even, feeling a surge of dark satisfaction as the earl recoiled even further in response to the danger he apparently read there. "I think it only fair to demand something more, for let us be honest here. My participation in your scheme is apt to do naught but postpone my execution. I will be hanged regardless, swung from the nearest battlement once the people of Dunleavy realize they've been played a farce."

"That rests upon you and how well you assume

your role," Lord Exford said after another moment's silence, his imperious tone restored, along with his apparent calm.

"Even so, I will have terms, or I will not comply."

The earl looked as if he'd like nothing better than to throw Alex's demands back in his face, but he clearly wanted his plot to go forward, and he couldn't do so without complete cooperation.

"What are they, then?" he snapped.

"For a start, return of the leather sack taken from me by your soldiers when they brought me into custody. The remaining contents have sentimental meaning to me."

"Are there other Templar riches in the bag?" Exford demanded, shifting his glare to Sir Stephen, who had by now rejoined them.

"A few small parchments rolled and tied. Naught like the golden bowl's worth in coin."

Alex forced himself to remain as impassive as he could while he waited for Lord Exford to make up his mind. He felt Luc's steady gaze upon him, but he gave naught away. Luc might remember the bowl from their time in the Brotherhood, thanks to the worth of it in coin, but Alex knew he'd never seen the parchments. They were in truth priceless, part of the famed Templar treasure from the Holy Land that, unbeknownst to Alex when he'd stolen the sack from John's keeping, had been tucked into a pocket beneath the golden vessel he had thought was the limit of what he'd lifted from his old friend.

At last Exford scowled. "Very well. Let us finish with this business, then, and begin preparations. Release him, Sir Stephen, and—"

"Return of the parchments and sack is not all," Alex broke in, feeling that old, familiar rush that always came from deliberately placing himself on the edge of the blade. "In the unlikely event that I am successful in this plot you're arranging for me, I'll need some means of sustaining myself when it is over and you have what you seek at Dunleavy."

"You wish to be *paid* for the privilege of avoiding the noose?"

Alex allowed a half smile. "In coin. Before your men apprehended me, I had intended to use the funds gained from the goldsmith in Carlisle to seek a life of seclusion in some remoter part of Scotland. But with that option gone, now . . ." He let his voice drift off and raised his brow.

Lord Exford's tone was flat. "How much?"

"Five hundred pounds." Alex paused for but an instant after announcing that outrageous sum, adding, "And I want half of it paid up front."

As he had expected, silence greeted him. But to his surprise, Lord Exford seemed to be actually considering his demand, by God.

Still, Alex knew the man couldn't help but bear in mind all the reasons that allowing this would be more than unwise. After all, what would there be to stop Alex from taking the two hundred and fifty pounds once he was freed, and escaping off to the north of Scotland, leaving Dunleavy entirely out of his plans?

Unless, of course, Exford believed he could extract some kind of heartfelt oath from him, to bind him to this ridiculous plot.

And if he was counting on that, then he was a bigger fool by far.

Lord Exford turned on his heel and moved out of earshot to speak with Luc, likely to get his reaction to Alex's audacious proposal. The intervening silence gave Alex time to think further on the unflattering truth he'd just been compelled to acknowledge about himself . . . that unfortunate quirk of nature that had plagued him for as long as he could remember.

For the sad fact was that he wasn't like his brother Damien, or even his friends Richard or John when it came to matters of honor. A long time ago he'd realized that flaw in his character. It had begun when he'd been a year or two past twenty and a new knight at court; he'd foolishly allowed himself to fall in love with a highborn woman and daughter of an earl—the beautiful and gentle Lady Margaret Newcomb. When she'd discovered herself with child, her furious sire had given Alex the choice of remaining by her side and suffering the kind of dishonor and pain a blooded earl could bring down on the head of a common knight who had wronged him, or joining the Templar Brotherhood and leaving England for good.

Though not easy, his choice had seemed clear. Oh, he'd convinced himself that it was the best for everyone involved, including Margaret. But in his heart, he'd known it was the coward's way. That inner awareness was what had spurred him to excel as a knight for the Brotherhood, his lack of sincere dedication to the holiness of the Order notwithstanding. He had had one thing to offer, at least: He was gifted on the field of battle. He might not be the truest of the Templars, but he could fight and kill with a level of excellence that had earned him a place within the ranks of the Brotherhood's inner circle. Damien had joined him there shortly after, and he'd forged his friendships with John and Richard then as well.

But that was where his similarities with them had ended. His brother and his friends lived, breathed, and slept decency and integrity. That he fervently *wished* he possessed a similar sense of conviction had not mattered. Over the course of the past six years, he'd discovered that he was rarely capable of living up to his word, regardless of how important the matter or how good his intentions.

The only time he'd managed to follow through on a noble deed for someone else's sake had been a year and a half ago, with Richard, when they'd faced the wrath of the French Inquisition together in their ordeal by battle. But that moment of self-sacrifice had been a single oddity in the long list of ignoble actions that had comprised the miserable life he'd led both before and since. And he had paid dearly for it, rewarded with agonizing torture at the hands of men more skilled in the infliction of human pain than any other beings on earth.

It had been worth it for what Richard had gained in the process, he supposed. And that Richard had met and fallen in love with Margaret in the time since Alex had left England had seemed fitting, even. He had been happy for them. But he could not deny that a part of him had hoped his friend would return the favor he'd done him by finding a way to free him from his hellish imprisonment with the Inquisition. Fair payback, a perverse voice deep inside Alex had asserted at the time.

It had appalled him to realize that his internal self sought such petty recompense for having done a good deed, but he could not refute it. It was who he was: not the honor-bound man his brother and his brothers-in-arms were, but rather a mere shadow of that . . . a man bound by his own instincts of self-preservation above all else.

That realization was the main reason he'd stolen the bowl and headed for the north—he'd wanted to sell it and use the funds gained to disappear somewhere up in the Highlands. To get away from all the reminders of his faults and his moral weaknesses.

Aye, unless the life of someone close to him was quite literally hanging in the balance, Alex couldn't be trusted in matters of friendship, loyalty, or love, and he knew it.

He just hoped Lord Exford didn't.

There was no time to think further on the matter. Exford had turned back to Alex, while Luc strode without a backward glance, off in the direction from which he'd come. Stephen was left standing guard as the earl spoke once more.

"I have considered your terms, Ashby—and I accept."

The impossibility of the earl's answer rocked through Alex, though he managed to keep his expression schooled. Either this man and Luc were both suffering from brain fever, or there was going to be more to this little bargain than he could see at the moment. Since neither looked particularly ill, and since he knew Luc, at least, was no imbecile, he would have to bide his time to find out what the catch was going to be.

"Well—have you nothing to say, then?" Exford asked smoothly.

"How about 'Untie me,'" Alex drawled.

Smirking, Exford nodded to Stephen, and the guard reluctantly stepped behind the tree to release Alex's bonds. When his arms were free, Alex spent a few moments stretching and shaking the numbness from his limbs, all the while glaring at Stephen, before complying with Lord Exford's murmured command to follow him back to the small encampment where approximately two dozen of the regiment's soldiers had gathered.

"The initial coin you have requested will take some time to procure, as will arrangements to bring into our company the men who knew Marston best, to school you in his history and habits," Exford said, as they reached the circle of fires. He paused then, stopping near one of the cook fires and fixing a critical gaze on Alex. "And there is something else as well. This is likely pointless to ask considering that you're of the knightly class, but are you schooled in reading and letters?"

Alex did not answer, unwilling to admit the truth of his ignorance aloud, even though few men of his status ever had reason or opportunity to learn such skills. The sight of his tightened jaw, though, prompted Lord Exford to nod and glance away, continuing, "I thought as much. That will need to be addressed as well, in the limited time we have. Marston was an earl of the realm, after all, and he was educated as such."

Alex remained silent as he waited to see what else he needed to learn about the deal he'd struck with this powerful English lord.

He knew he was about to find out, when Luc came

striding back toward them, from a place beyond the edge of trees in the clearing. He gave Lord Exford a short nod, and the earl acknowledged it before turning his attention to Alex and murmuring, "And now we have one final bit of business to conclude, before our terms of agreement are complete. Come with me. There is something I want you to see."

The prickling sensation Alex had experienced up the back of his neck from the moment he'd first sensed the direction of this ridiculous scheme returned full force—magnified when he caught sight of Luc's expression, both grim and self-satisfied at once. Luc and Stephen fell into place beside them as they approached the edge of the clearing, and though it was dramatically dimmer within the cover of the trees, thanks to the thick leaves, Alex's eyes adjusted quickly enough to make out an area twenty paces or so in, where the ground growth seemed tamped down. There was a man lying in the center of it, and there were two English guards posted nearby.

A shock lanced through Alex, and he squinted to see better, almost at the same time as the identity of the figure burst upon him, and he lunged forward.

"John!" he called, jerked back in his progress by strong hands gripping his arms. He looked wildly around, noting that Lord Exford watched, unaffected, as Luc and Stephen kept him from going to his friend. John did not react except to moan slightly, his head rolling to the side and his brow furrowing with pain.

"Christ, what did you do to him?" Alex rasped, ceasing his struggles as he shifted a burning gaze to Luc.

"Nothing he wasn't commanded to do."

That implacable answer had come from Lord Exford, who continued to watch Alex closely. "A friend of yours, I take it?"

Alex didn't answer, his mouth twisting with bitterness. Clearly, Luc had provided him already with all the pertinent details about John and their history together. He glowered at Luc, mentally reviewing the ways he'd enjoy getting even for this latest act of treachery against yet another comrade to whom they'd both once sworn allegiance until death.

"Sir John de Clifton was apprehended shortly after you yourself were subdued," Exford continued, undeterred by Alex's silence. "A loyal ally to you, by all accounts, for he leaped from hiding and into the fray when it appeared you might be bested by my men. The only way he could be made to surrender his sword and submit to arrest was under threat of your immediate demise." Exford made a clicking sound of false commiseration, and it was all Alex could do not to yank free from Luc's grasp and plant his fist in the earl's face.

Instead, Alex shifted his gaze to Luc and said through gritted teeth, "If he has suffered mortal injury at your hands, I promise you will pay for his death."

"I am terrified by the threat, Ashby," Luc clipped back, "but you needn't fear. John has a few bruises, and his head will undoubtedly beat like a drum when he awakens. But he will recover in time. This was but a warning of what could be, that is all."

Even before Lord Exford finished what Luc had begun to explain, Alex closed his eyes, feeling the sickening drop of awareness about what was going on here—knowing it was going to be the one cursed thing they could have chosen that would bind him to this godforsaken plot and force him to see it through to the end. Resignation swept through him in pounding, waves as he heard Lord Exford voice the words that proclaimed his doom and cast away in a single swoop any bid for freedom he might have hoped to make.

"You see, Ashby, Sir John de Clifton is going to be my personal pledge of your full cooperation. Several of my men, including Luc, will be accompanying you to Dunleavy Castle and reporting back to me regularly on your activities there. Deviate from our plan, fail to be successful in the ruse you have agreed to play, and I assure you, your friend will suffer greatly for it . . . and then he will die."

Chapter 2

Two months later
Dunleavy Castle

The sun was dipping toward earth, casting a rich golden sheen over the land, as Elizabeth peered out from the battlements just above the outer gate. Her gaze tracked a dark speck on the horizon. With every moment that passed, the speck got bigger, close enough now to make out the number of riders. There were three. Fingers clenching against the cool stone of the castle wall, she watched dust sift up in a kind of cloud around them as they approached Dunleavy's main gate. The message she'd received but a few hours ago had said that one of those men would be Rob.

She reminded herself to breathe, as she'd had to so often, it seemed, since she'd opened that unexpected parchment.

Rob was coming home.

After all this time of needing to be strong, of having to lead this castle alone and protect those within it, she would know the blessed relief of sharing the burden of it with the man who had brought her here as his bride more than five years ago. The man who had been captured by the English only a few short months after that. She'd no longer be alone fighting battles that exhausted her as much as they enraged her for the needless suffering they caused.

Rob was a gentle, peace-loving man, aye, but he would want to defend the home that had been passed down to him by his sire. He could do naught else and still be true to himself. For this and other reasons, she knew she had been more than fortunate in her own sire's choice of him as her husband. Rob had been attentive and thoughtful throughout their brief courtship and even briefer union, calm, reserved, and kind in all his dealings with her.

She had missed him. Aye, she had . . . in many ways. Glancing down for a moment, she felt a flush warm her cheeks in the wake of her wanton thoughts.

But she could not deny it; along with all the rest, she'd missed the intimacies her husband had shown her—the physical aspect of their union as man and wife. The act of joining with him had not been at all what she'd been led to fear by her elder sister, wed these seven years to Laird Ian MacGavin of Inverness. Siusan had warned Elizabeth of the pain that must be tolerated as one's wifely duty.

But to Elizabeth's surprise, her coupling with Rob hadn't been painful or unpleasant, except for the first time. Nay, it had been more than tolerable. Sometimes even enjoyable. In truth, she had begun to look forward to those intimate moments with him before he'd been taken from her.

Elizabeth bit the inside of her cheeks, glancing quickly to see that none of the others who stood with her awaiting the return of their lord had surmised the wayward direction of her musings. None seemed to be paying her any mind, however, and so she shifted her gaze forward again, fixing it as well on the now discernible riders who had slowed a bit in their approach as they came within clear sight of Dunleavy.

Just then, a stiff breeze gusted through the battlements, whipping into her face a few strands of her hair, which was unbound and adorned with naught but a circlet for the first time in longer than she could remember. Impatiently, she brushed them away with her fingertips.

But for an instant, that movement caused her attention to stray from the riders to the roughened area on the back of her hand; her constant toiling around the castle had done little for the state of her skin, it was clear. Pausing, she examined both hands with a critical eye. With a frown she rubbed at the dryness, reaching up next to test her cheeks for any similar quality. *Hmmm* . . . not as bad, but not altogether pleasing either.

It was not a surprise, really; her precious giltencircled mirror had told her of the tiny lines encroaching around her mouth and eyes. But they hadn't mattered much until now. Not until she considered that Rob would see them and perhaps be disappointed in her appearance since last he looked upon her . . .

"You have naught to fear, my lady," Annabel murmured next to her.

Elizabeth glanced at her lady's maid in surprise.

Annabel was unsuccessful at stifling her knowing smile as she gestured toward Elizabeth. "You are still more than lovely, Lady Elizabeth. Lord Marston will be hard-pressed to keep from gazing upon your beauty, I warrant, once he's safely at home again."

Elizabeth offered a nervous laugh. "My husband was never one to spend idle time just gazing at anything—or anyone—for very long," she mused, swinging her stare back to the men who had come close enough now for her to discern that the middle one looked most like Rob. "He would need to be a very changed man to undertake such now. Either that or else he will be studying the disappointing results time has wrought on my outer form."

"Time has been kind to you, my lady," Annabel countered, leaning her forearms onto the lower portion of the jutting sawtooth shapes that composed the battlement where they stood. "And as for Lord Marston seeming changed, it is very like he will be, in some ways. Five years of harsh imprisonment is bound to have an effect on any man."

"We shall see," Elizabeth murmured. The men were within thirty lengths of the gate now, and she realized there was no more time to dawdle, watching their approach. She needed to retreat to the top of the steps that led to the great hall and ready herself to give her long-absent husband the proper welcome he deserved. "Come," she said, nodding to Annabel. "Call to the servants and villagers to arrange themselves into columns on either side of the inner yard, while I await my lord's entrance at the portal of the great hall."

With a nod, Annabel slipped off to do as she was bid, and Elizabeth was left to make her way to the spot where she would greet her husband again for the first time in five years—the place where he would perhaps allow her to offer him an embrace or a chaste kiss, for she knew he favored propriety almost above all else.

The rest she would save until they shared some private time immediately after the feast she'd ordered prepared in celebration of his return.

Biting back a secret smile at the thought, Elizabeth pressed her palms to her stomach to calm its fluttering and strode into the cool, darkened corridor that led down from the battlements to the castle yard below.

As Alex rode closer and closer to the stately, imposing castle that would serve as both his home and his prison in the coming weeks, he reminded himself to remain outwardly at ease. To avoid letting his face or the way he held his body reveal the seething resentment that had invaded and spread through him these past two months spent under Exford's control. He could not afford to slip, lest John pay the price for his failure.

He'd been reminded of that bitter truth often enough recently. Aye, for as long as he'd made sufficient effort to learn his new role as the returning Earl of Marston, John was kept relatively comfortable. However, the few times he'd let his temper fly, especially in his dealings with Luc, John had suffered accordingly. It made his jaw ache even now in remembering it.

Of course he'd not been allowed to actually speak with John, and he'd only rarely seen him, and then from a distance. But the connection between his actions and his old friend's condition had been made more than clear. And so to ease John's sufferings as much as he was able, he'd done his best to cooperate, though he'd made a silent vow that if he ever had the opportunity to exact vengeance for all this on Luc, Lord Exford, or anyone else involved, he would do so, and with great pleasure.

"We're here."

Casting Luc a sardonic glance for pointing out that quite obvious fact, Alex looked forward again and continued riding.

"You'd be wise to put a more pleasant expression on your face," Luc said, "else the game will be up before it begins."

Though Alex wasn't looking at Stephen, who rode to his left, he sensed the man's frown at this latest flare-up of continuously simmering animosity between him and Luc. Still, it wasn't enough to keep Alex from making answer and perhaps providing himself with a bit of satisfaction in the process.

"Never fear, Luc, I'm well aware of what is at stake here." Alex glanced to his nemesis again. "However, I will remind you in turn that, so far as you are concerned, I am an earl now—a nobleman who was generous enough to bring you with me out of our captivity in England. Rather than schooling *me* further, you would be wise to follow your own advice and practice the fawning expression I'll expect you to wear around me from now on."

Luc choked back his laugh but could say nothing further, for they'd reached the first opened gate of Dunleavy Castle. They guided their mounts through the entrance. Except for a few sentries, this outer yard of Dunleavy was empty, and as Alex acknowledged the guards' salute and walked his gelding toward the second gate, he could not help but notice the arched patch of scorched grass and earth that curved out toward the outer wall.

"Interesting," he murmured. "What do you make of that?"

Stephen kept silent, but that didn't surprise Alex. The man never spoke much. Yet Luc also did not make answer, riding onward as unmoving as one of the statues in St. Jasper's garden back in Cyprus, with his gaze fixed on something ahead of them. Alex glanced to see what had him so distracted.

And it was then that he saw her. The woman who had so captivated Luc's attention. She stood at the far end of the second, inner courtyard, at the top of the main steps, looking every inch the lady of the castle. It took only that one glance, and he knew he was going to be in trouble. Enormous trouble.

Lady Elizabeth of Selkirk was of average height, perhaps, but the delicate lines of her form seemed at odds with the impression of steely resolve she exuded. The late-day sun accentuated the rich, golden color of her hair, and as she gazed at Alex with the edge of a smile softening her expression, he thought he caught a glimmer of something hopeful in her eyes. That shadow of emotion set off an unaccountable twisting sensation inside him. A kind of guilty twinge he was not used to feeling.

Luc made a soft whistling sound before murmuring, "She's a beauty." His gaze, when he shifted it from her, moved past Alex and on to Stephen, still on Alex's other side. "You weren't jesting when you claimed rumor painted her so."

"I never jest," Stephen replied, his voice low.

"Perhaps not. But you might have been more forthcoming," Alex said quietly. "I'd have been better able to prepare myself."

Luc made a scoffing sound in his throat. "You've never had trouble knowing exactly how to handle any woman in all the time I've known you. I don't suspect you'll be stricken with an attack of ignorance now."

"Enough," Stephen warned. "Listen."

Even had Stephen not uttered the softly spoken command, Alex would have had no choice but to hear the resounding shout that went up as his steed crossed the threshold to the inner yard. People lined the walls here so thickly, nary a stone was visible between them, and they picked up the chorus of cries that spread from the gate back toward the keep, welcoming him—welcoming Robert Kincaid, the Earl of Marston—home from English captivity.

He lifted his arm in salute, his gaze taking in the throng, reminding himself to smile. To look as natural as he could in this feigned role. Ever so slowly, he allowed his stare to sift through the folk, old and young, drifting, drifting through the yard and up the steps. To the golden-haired sylph dressed in a gown of deep emerald who stood in wait for him.

Their stares locked . . . and he allowed his smile to deepen.

Such an expression had never been difficult for him to muster when looking upon an attractive woman. But that truth did naught to explain the sudden tightening in his chest at the welcoming expression that lit her face.

So this was Elizabeth of Selkirk. Beth, her husband had called her, according to men Lord Exford had brought in to tutor him about assuming Robert Kincaid's identity. Along with Stephen, his instructors had commented in passing on her appearance. She was rumored to be fair enough, they'd said, blessed with hair the color of harvested wheat, though her complexion was not the milk-and-cream sort prized by English ladies. It was the fault of her Scottish blood, they'd muttered, since many of the women hailing from this primitive and rough-shod land seemed to possess robust constitutions, favoring outdoor pursuits and even the occasional bout of swordplay.

Alex hadn't responded to their descriptions then, though he'd been secretly intrigued. Aye, he'd hoped that she would be as they'd said, for an unpretentious, attractive wench might provide a bit of pleasant distraction, since he'd be forced to spend several months in her company and in her bed.

Seeing her now, he realized he'd had no idea.

But the time for ruminating on that or any other detail vanished as his gelding reached its destination. The cheers ebbed as he dismounted and made his way alone up the steps, feeling strangely distanced from himself, as if he was watching his own motions from afar.

At last he attained the top step and reached for Elizabeth's outstretched hand, keeping his gaze fixed to hers. The seconds slowed as if they'd spun into the unhurried cadence of some dream. He heard the even, deep rush of his own breathing, and felt the steady thump of his heartbeat . . . watching a myriad of emotions flicker in her eyes—pretty gray eyes, he noticed now that he stood so close. It was uncommon to see eyes of that shade in combination with fair hair, but the effect was striking.

Before another thought could take full form he touched her, his fingers sweeping across her palm before he clasped it. He bent to brush a kiss over the back of that hand, straightening again as the courtyard fell silent.

"Welcome home, my lord," Elizabeth murmured at last. Her voice was mellow, making him think of sweet amber wine. "Will you come inside? I have ordered a feast prepared in your honor this night."

"Aye, lady," he said in reply, offering her a gentle smile. "And I thank you for your greeting."

Though she nodded in response, her answering smile wobbled; in the next instant, she took a quick, almost panting breath and stiffened, her fingers clasping at his as if she teetered on the edge of a swoon.

Instinctively, he lunged forward, grasping both of her elbows in his palms and pulling her close to him for stability. A collective gasp rose from the crowd at his action, and he froze, recalling the care his tutors had taken to explain Robert Kincaid's highly developed sense of reserve, self-control, and propriety.

This wasn't good. Nay, not at all.

And yet . . .

A low rumble of stamping—the sound of rising approval—began to swell from the crowd again. The cheers bloomed to a crescendo, and with the sound came a tiny burst of relief that spread through Alex. It felt suspiciously like the ripples of warmth he used to feel when undertaking a new flirtation . . .

aye, the old heat of the chase bubbling up inside him, damn it.

He gazed down at Elizabeth of Selkirk, still held in his steadying embrace. Her lips were slightly parted, her intriguing eyes holding an expression that was at once serious, and surprised, and, damn it all . . . somehow *yearning*. Almost against his will, it seemed, he felt his lips cock into that half smile he'd used with devastating affect on countless numbers of females in the past. And he knew then that he was going to take advantage of the ebullient atmosphere surrounding them to do what he had intended to save for later, when he was in private with this woman who was supposed to be his wife.

Leaning in, he placed his mouth at the soft waves of hair between her temple and her ear, murmuring only loud enough so that she might hear him, "Are you quite well, now, lady—enough that I may release my grip upon your arms without fear of your stumbling?"

The cheers echoed around them so that he could not hear any reply, but he felt her nod.

"I am glad to know it," he said. "For it frees me, then, to do this . . ."

Pulling back just a bit, he slid an arm around her waist, using the other hand to gently tip her chin up as he brushed his lips across hers in a tender kiss. Her mouth remained slack beneath his for only a moment before she returned the caress, her own mouth warm and searching. The unexpected pleasure of it sent a shock of desire shooting through him, and he realized two distinct yet vital truths in that blinding instant: First, that he had quite obviously been without a woman for far too long, to react to this kiss as he was, and second, that these next months might not prove to be as trying as he'd feared if the woman was this responsive to simple delights.

But his enjoyment was mitigated in the next instant by another sensation that caught him by surprise. It was a feeling he'd experienced only on rare occasions in the past—a shadow of the same having come upon him just a few moments ago, as he'd ridden into Dunleavy proper—and so he was unprepared for the stabbing flood of it now. By God, it was *guilt*, plain and unadorned. Aye, the very truth was that he was leading Elizabeth of Selkirk down a path of deception by pretending to be her husband, and that knowledge cast a pall over the moment, leading him to ease back from their kiss.

He was still trying to make sense of it when she finally pulled away. He stood still and silent next to her, watching those expressive, lovely eyes snap with heat.

They held that frozen tableau for the space of several heartbeats, before her expression shifted to something more guarded and she took another step back, placing some further distance between them. Then her brow rose and she said more loudly, so that he might hear her over the still-cheering crowd, "Well, my lord, you are clearly famished. Come inside, I pray, for the feast cannot begin without you."

Something was very wrong.

Elizabeth knew it in her bones, though her eyes—and yes, curse it, her own desperate longings—asserted otherwise.

But she could not ignore the prick of instinct that told her the man sitting next to her at the feasting table of honor, upon the dais, was *not* Robert Kincaid, the Earl of Marston.

He was not her husband. She was almost certain of it.

He seemed to exude a kind of leashed power that her composed and even-tempered lord had never displayed. And yet she could not deny that his appearance was uncannily similar. He was tall and powerfully built, with the same rich, dark hair and blue eyes. Yet these eyes held a hint of playfulness, of deviltry and masculine confidence, that she could not remember ever seeing in Rob. And his smile . . . ah, but it was pure seduction. When he'd kissed her, the play of his mouth over hers had been a tender torment that had set her blood to racing. Aye, he'd stolen her breath with that caress in a way she could never remember Rob having done.

And perhaps that was part of the problem. She could not remember much at all that might help her sort through this unexpected dilemma. She and Rob had been wed for so short a time before he was captured that many of the details about him, his quirks and his ways, had faded with the passing of these five years. She had never made any great effort to recall particulars during that time—had not thought it necessary or even wise, considering how much more deeply she felt his absence when she dwelled on the memories of their time together. She'd simply waited for word or, praise God, for his return.

Never in her worst imaginings had she expected that she would react as she had this day, with doubt seething through her like a wily serpent to invade all the hopeful places in her heart.

And yet here she sat, partaking of the feast next to a man she could not help but feel was a complete stranger to her.

At that moment, one of the soldiers of Dunleavy's garrison lifted his cup from across the hall, standing and calling out, "To your health, my lord, and a curse upon the English dogs who kept you from us!"

Shouts of "Huzzah!" and other calls of drunken encouragement rang forth, though she noticed that with the toast a few of the garrison cast pointed stares at the table where sat the two men Rob had brought with him from England into Scotland. Elizabeth shifted her gaze to meet that of Dunleavy's steward, Edwin Tamberlain, noting that his expression looked troubled as well. He sat at the end of the head table, close enough to be heard, should he decide to speak, and as soon as Rob had acknowledged the cheer and drunk from his own cup, Edwin called out, "My lord Marston?"

"Aye, Edwin?" the man who claimed to be Rob answered, twisting to face him.

"Mayhap it would not be amiss to address the assembly regarding the Englishmen with whom you rode through Dunleavy's gates."

It was a bold comment for any steward to make to his master, yet all the others seated nearby—the esteemed castle reeve, several religious men, including her own beloved confessor, Father Paul, and Dunleavy's captain of the guard—remained silent, their expressions measured, watching, and waiting. All turned their eyes to the man seated next to her, to see how *he* would react and what he might say.

He did not answer for a goodly moment, his face revealing little. However, Elizabeth saw a glint of something hard in his eyes, just visible over the rim of his cup as he took another deep drink before setting it down. A kind of tightness twisted the smile he directed to the steward, as he replied, "I will overlook the audacity of your comment, Edwin, in light of the unusual circumstances of my return and my gratitude for your efforts to assist my lady in my absence. However, I will remind you that it is not your place to question your lord in matters about which you have no knowledge. Ever."

Edwin paled before flushing with anger, looking as if he would like to say something by way of retort to the chiding he'd just received. But several of the others around them murmured with seeming approval at the master's assertion of the proper order of things. Elizabeth chose to keep mute, simply watching.

After a strained pause, Edwin inclined his head stiffly. "My apologies. I only thought to diffuse the tension that seems to be arising amongst some of the men in regard to your . . . companions."

"I know what you thought, and I assure you I had decided an action on the matter *before* you felt need to speak on it." An uncomfortable silence settled over the table, but then, with a nod in Edwin's direction, Rob stood up from his position next to her. Close as she was to him, she could not help but be reminded again of the power contained in every tall, muscular inch of him. Lifting his cup, he waited for the attention of the assembly, and the silence that would necessarily follow.

It descended swiftly over the gathering of four

score villagers, soldiers, clergymen, and servants, and when all eyes were upon him, he spoke. His voice was rich and deep, and it echoed through the chamber, large as it was.

"Good people of Dunleavy, I am fortunate to have returned to you in health and strength from my imprisonment in England. Yet I would not be standing here at all, I can assure you, were it not for those who entered Dunleavy with me: Sir Stephen of Cheltenham and Sir Lucas of Dover. I trust you will welcome them to Dunleavy as honored friends."

Over the new rounds of "Aye!" and "We will, my lord!" that erupted at the end of his speech, Rob directed his attention to Dunleavy's captain of the guard, Sir Gareth de Payton, instructing him to find berth for the two men in the garrison with the other soldiers, for as long as they wished to stay.

Elizabeth frowned. She watched the renewed raising of cups and cheers of welcome to the two men Rob had introduced, and she couldn't help but feel uneasy. If these knights he had brought into their midst were not what they appeared to be, then . . .

She shuddered to think of the possibility. The English strangers were being given full entry into the garrison . . . mingling with Dunleavy's best soldiers, training with them, learning all the details of life here among the very men most integral to the castle's protection. The thoughts whirled through her mind, settling a fist of nausea into her belly.

It was too much to consider all at once. But she *could* address one aspect of it. She need not—nay, she could not—sit here longer and be eaten alive by her suspicions. Aye, she could test the waters of it right now, and praise be to God, it would free her from the need to remain in the great hall, feeling the overwhelming confusion that the powerful, attractive man who sat beside her had inspired.

"My lord?"

At first, she was afraid that he had not heard her softly spoken question. But then he turned his gaze to her, nearly stealing her breath anew at the intensity of his stare upon her.

"Aye, lady?"

"It grows late, my lord. I—I wish to retire to our chamber." Here she paused for a moment, swallowing hard and keeping her gaze steady upon him, trying to appear unaffected. "Should I expect you to join me there later?"

He looked startled for a moment, and she could not avert the fleeting thought that he had not previously considered the detail of where he would be sleeping. He paused, seeming to select his words carefully before he spoke, though a kind of warmth and teasing lit his eyes when he finally gave voice to his thoughts.

"Do you wish me to join you?"

Now it was her turn to be surprised, by the question itself, not to mention the intimacy inherent in it, and by the heated images that shot through her mind's eye, unbidden, in accompaniment with a tingling flush of warmth. Damn him, be he her true husband or nay, for making her feel so unsteady after all this time. Annoyance followed fast upon that thought, giving her courage to raise her brow slightly and retort with a sense of control she did not feel, "My feelings concerning that matter not. *You* are master of this holding. You may choose to sleep when and where you desire . . . my lord."

There was no mistaking the glint of humor and heat in his gaze then. He smiled at her, and she had to remind herself that the melting sensation it set off inside her likely had more to do with the cups of wine she had drunk than any true reaction to him.

"You seem to have forgotten something very important about me, wife," he answered quietly at last, as he glanced down and reached out to take her hand in his. She tried not to let the soft gasp that came from her throat slip past. But she was unsuccessful, and his mesmerizing blue gaze slid up to hers again, keeping her still like a rabbit before the wolf, as he stroked his finger in a lazy, seductive pattern over her palm.

Resisting the urge to lick her lips and glance down at the sensual mischief he was playing upon her with his touch, she settled for a husky "And what is that, pray tell?"

"That there has never been a time when your feelings have *not* mattered to me. Especially in regards to what might occur during our private time together." His sensual mouth quirked again, and he leaned in closer, to murmur for her ears alone, "I shall consider your forgetfulness a challenge and do my best to remind you of that truth between us more properly in the future."

Her breath caught in her throat, then. She made a slight choking sound, but thankfully, the need to reach for her cup and take a drink of her wine allowed her to disengage her hand from his without seeming overtly discourteous.

For a few, agonizing moments of silence that

spread out between them, she thought he intended to wait for her to speak again . . . and she had no clear idea of what she should say next. But then he seemed to take pity on her, and he shifted that intense gaze from her face, murmuring, "However, in the meantime, if you wish to retire, lady, then by all means, do so. There are several others here I have yet to greet, and I intend to bathe the dust of my travels away as well before I retire to bed this night. I will join you ere long."

He flicked a glance to her again, as she pushed back abruptly from the table and stood. She twisted away from the heat of his stare, somehow maintaining her composure even as she felt his gaze still hot upon her while she gestured to her lady's maids to accompany her from the chamber.

But in the instant before she went, she could not keep from glancing back over her shoulder at him one last time. He took the opportunity to mouth something more to her, with that smile still playing in his eyes. Five words that sent the blood rushing through her anew . . . that sent her hurrying through the door and into the corridor beyond the great hall with his words pursuing her in relentless waves.

"Be ready for me, lady."

Chapter 3

By the time Alex approached the door to the chamber he was to share with his counterfeit wife, it had been dark for several hours and most of the castle was asleep. He'd gone with Luc and Stephen to the guardhouse under the pretext of honoring his rescuers by escorting them in person, but in truth he had wanted to get a first look at the garrison, since none of those who had tutored him had been able to provide much detail about it.

Once he saw it, he realized just why the castle had not fallen under siege—and why King Edward wanted it under English rule. The defenses accrued in manpower and supported by structure and weaponry made Dunleavy a veritable fortress, the likes of which he'd rarely seen, aside from the Brotherhood's Temple in Cyprus, perhaps. The repeated assaults against the castle had created some areas of weakness, there was no doubt, and it would be Stephen and Luc's primary effort to make note of those so they might be exploited later, when Lord Exford made his next attack. But the depth of the garrison here remained surprising for a castle of its size. By rough count, he had seen perhaps two score full knights and a hundred common men-at-arms, as well as a dozen engineers. And that didn't include the archers.

From one of them he'd heard the story of the burned trench that curved toward the wall of the outer yard; it had been used against their most recent attacker, a Scottish earl to the north, after he had been enticed through the gates along with a group of his highest-ranking men. The ruse had been successful to a point. The enemy had been lured in, the trench had been lit, and an attempt made to lower the outer gate, to trap them. But the earl's men had managed to overcome the gate's guards and escape before the portcullis could be brought down. Still, the earl himself had been forced to retreat, wounded, with his army. It had been only a partial victory, but it had freed Dunleavy from attack for the time being.

Alex slowed his steps as he neared the door to the bedchamber he had learned was the one he would share with Elizabeth. But he didn't go inside. Not yet. Leaning back against the wall, he took a deep breath, wanting to collect his thoughts before he entered and completed this day's reunion the way he knew he must, as would any long-absent husband returning home to his young wife.

It was not that the act itself would be difficult to complete, for he'd been too long already without the kind of comfort only a woman could provide. And it wasn't that he feared he could not perform properly, for though he bore many scars from injuries inflicted by his Inquisitors, his body had healed and grown strong again.

A rueful smile pulled at his lips. Nay, all his parts seemed to be in fine working order. Add to that truth the fact that Elizabeth herself was pleasing to the eye, and he could think of no logical reason for his hesitation right now.

But something else nagged at the back of his mind, making him pause. It was a kind of awareness that all was not as it seemed with her. The thought was ironic, considering the ruse he himself was playing here. But there it was. She had reacted as if she wasn't entirely certain about him, and his own instincts, along with what he had learned from the guard in the garrison, made it clear that what he faced this night might not be as simple as just walking into the chamber and expecting a warm welcome into her bed.

She had been the one to come up with the plan for trapping Lord Lennox behind the burning trench, the guard had told him. The entire plot, from her choice of an enticing gown and seeming capitulation, to the heated pitch, raised portcullis, and archers bearing bolts ablaze, had been her idea. A plot worthy of a shrewd military adversary, if ever he saw one.

Aye, it seemed that Elizabeth of Selkirk was as intelligent as she was lovely . . . and he sensed a kind of stubbornness in her as well. A fire that boded well for one who helped it to flare in passion, but poorly for any who thwarted her iron-centered strength.

It was time to see which she harbored, in regard to him.

Pushing open the door to the bedchamber, he slipped inside, not surprised to see only one taper burning on the mantel. It was late, after all. However, a tingle of warning slipped up his back as he realized the hearth was lit with a blazing fire. In August. The flames danced and flickered, creating wild shadows and masking the true contours of the room. Almost simultaneously, he heard a faint rustling sound to his right, near what appeared to be an enormous tapestry that hung from ceiling to floor.

And then his instincts, finely honed from his years as a Templar Knight, clicked into place with deadly precision. A blade flashed in the muted light, its sheen visible for but an instant along the lethal edge of steel. He spun, lifting his arm up and out, even as he grasped his assailant, slamming them both into the wall and sending the tapestry tumbling down on their heads. He couldn't see anything now, but he held on tightly and pressed the entire weight of his body against his attacker, struggling to grip the man's arms and prevent that dagger from slipping up and into his belly.

He became aware of several things in the confusion of that moment. Steel clattered as the dagger dropped to the floor. He caught the scent of roses, mingled with the thick, woolen smell of the tapestry, and he heard a low cry. It might have been of pain, but it was tinged far more with anger than with hurt.

And by God, he felt curves. Soft, feminine curves, of breast, belly, and thigh, pressed along the length of him.

"*Elizabeth?*"

He rasped her name, his breath coming harder than usual after their scuffle and the sudden rush he'd felt in response to danger. But she did not answer, only continued to struggle against his grip. Irritated, Alex kept her arms pinned at the wrists and shrugged off the tapestry, dragging her with him away from its confining folds and into the relatively lighter area of the bedchamber.

It was her, all right.

That long, honey-gold hair was tousled from their fray under the tapestry, but there was no mistaking the biting-hot expression in the slits of eyes peering out at him through the tangled strands. He was surprised, but not enough to loosen his grip, and so she yanked against him, trying to pull free.

"Damn it, woman—cease!" he growled, tugging her back into position in front of him. To his relief, she went still, no doubt readying herself for her next foray against him.

"Let me go."

"Nay. I prefer to keep my liver *inside* my body, thank you."

She jerked her head to move her hair from her eyes as much as she could without use of her hands, casting a look at the dagger where it had come to rest after she'd dropped it, glittering in the firelight ten paces away. When she brought her glare back to his face, he cocked his brow, daring her to refute that such had been her intent.

She remained silent. For the moment.

But she was a woman, Alex reminded himself, and as such it was more than likely that she would react with a woman's standard wiles, pretending to have made an error . . . blaming someone or something else for the action she had taken. A nightmare, perhaps, or an instinctive reaction to what she thought was an intruder after having so long been without a husband to protect her. Aye, she would offer him a convenient lie now, to try to remove herself from responsibility in the deed against him . . . a deed that, were it made known, could at the least see her punished by his hand, and at worst, cause her to be brought before a council of justice and tried for an attempt against his life.

And so he felt a grudging sense of admiration when she did nothing of the sort. Instead, she tipped her head up further to meet his gaze full-on, her expression of strength and . . . *honor*, by God, intensifying her beauty more than he would have thought possible. Something inside him responded to that look in a way that he never would have to pretty words, apologies, or coy glances, and he scowled down at her, none too happy with the realization.

Beth swallowed—hard—but she did not give ground. "I was not trying to kill you. I only wanted to force some answers from you."

"And the fire?" The oppressive heat undulating from it into the already warm chamber made any further explanation of why he was questioning her about it unnecessary.

"A distraction," she admitted, still keeping her gaze fixed to him. "However, I give you my word now that I will not attempt to retrieve the dagger or harm you in any way if you release your hold upon me."

"Your word has become suspect in our years apart, lady, for you also gave it when you took me as your husband, and yet you have just wielded a blade against me."

"You are not my husband."

She said it quietly, and he heard the catch in her voice as she spoke. But she'd spoken the words, there was no denying.

Again something pulled and twisted inside him as he forced himself to smile, to seem incredulous with disbelief. "That is ridiculous. Of course I am." He bullied through, thinking he far preferred intimidating her to enduring her quiet, unbending conviction. "You are fortunate right now that I have not called the guards to have you removed from this chamber and held under lock and key until I decide what to do with you for your action against me."

"Why do you not, then?" she asked. Challenging him, by all that was holy.

He kept his gaze hard upon her. "Because I am not a tyrant. My return was sudden and has clearly left you feeling confused."

"Your arrival, not your return. It was *too* sudden, after five years with little word. And there is too much about you that is not right . . ."

She was beginning to waver now, whether under the force of doubt, grief, or frustration, he could not tell. She blinked twice, but he saw that she did not cry. Yet her voice sounded husky as she finished, "You may look like Robert Kincaid, but you are not him."

"I am your husband, Beth."

"Prove it."

He resisted the urge to let loose the half groan, half laugh of exasperation that had lodged in his throat. This wasn't going as he'd intended. By now he should have had her naked and moaning beneath him in their bed, but that clearly wasn't going to happen any time soon. He would need to take a different tack with this woman, for she was like no other he had ever before encountered in his life.

What to do, though . . .

Put the control—some of it, anyway—back into her hands.

The idea asserted itself in his mind, and, helpless, he obeyed, having naught else to go on in this damnable situation in which he'd found himself tonight. Giving her a bemused look, he released his hold on her and took a step back, watching as she too backed up and rubbed her wrists where he had gripped her, all the while keeping her gaze fixed upon him.

"There. I have conceded to your request, Beth. Do you stand by your word and affirm that you will not seek to harm me further?"

Wordlessly, she nodded.

"Good. Then why don't we—"

"Nay, I am not satisfied. My questions have not yet been answered."

"Saints, woman, but you test my patience. I have released you against my own better judgment. What more do you want?"

"Tell me of the weather on the day we wed."

"*What?*" Alex stared at her aghast before making a sound of annoyance. "You cannot expect me to recall such things. I am a man, not some swooning maiden."

She simply raised her brows at him, clearly waiting for him to answer, and he scowled. His tutors told him naught about the weather on Kincaid's wedding day or any other. However, the union had taken place in October, he recalled, at the conclusion of the harvest. And if it happened in Scotland, at that time of year . . .

He would just have to chance it and hope for the best.

"It rained."

He tried not to show his relief when she continued without comment, "The place of my mother's birth?"

"North Yorkshire."

"My favorite pastimes?"

He cocked his brow again. "Naught to do with a dagger, I hope."

She did not react to his jest. Sighing, he responded with the information his instructors had provided him, regarding the woman who had been Robert Kincaid's new bride. "We were not together long, lady, before my capture, but if I recall correctly, you rather enjoyed playing *merels*. You also were fond of dancing and riding and favored taking a mount out daily, weather willing."

Elizabeth paused in her flurry of questions, her face expressionless in the heat and flickering shadows of the chamber. Yet he felt those eyes of hers on him, studying him, trying to read his very soul, it seemed.

Well, she could try all she liked; she would see naught. Aye, he had become adept at keeping his thoughts and emotions to himself, not only during his difficult tenure as a Templar Knight—several years he tried his best not to think on—but also under the hell of his questioning by the Inquisition. There had been no other option; revealing anything of your true self accomplished naught but to give your enemies another weapon to use against you.

"Tell me then," she continued at last, "what you said by way of convincing my sire to accept your troth to me."

This was almost too easy. His tutors had known of this as well, not only through Kincaid's interrogations, but also through their questioning of his close comrades, captured along with him at the border.

Alex clenched his jaw, forcing himself to utter the words as if he had lived them himself. "I said that my blood may be English, but my heart was with Scotland and her fight for freedom. And I reminded him that your mother was the same, which is why she chose the path she did in becoming his wife."

Beth went silent again, and Alex almost frowned, worried that perhaps he had gotten something wrong. But in the next moment her arms slipped up to cross over her chest as she shivered. She gazed at him with eyes wide and luminous as if she was coming to believe something she did not want to believe. Something she was afraid to believe.

And with a strangely sinking feeling, he knew he was winning.

"Anything else?" he asked quietly.

"Aye. One more thing," she murmured.

He waited, watching those beautiful eyes staring at him in bewilderment, noticing the way her hands kept rubbing at the tops of her arms as if she'd never get warm again, even in this oppressive heat. And he found himself wishing to God that he was anywhere else right now. That he was anyone else other than the liar and cheat he'd become, filling this unsuspecting woman's heart with false hopes that would be naught but empty air when all was said and done.

"I want to see the mark on your back that has been with you from the day of your birth. The darkened spot shaped like my thumb that rests just below your right shoulder."

That came like a shock of icy water, her request

unleashing a swell of bitterness. His mouth tightened, though he tried to quell his reaction, knowing as he did that meeting this test would be easiest of all. Aye, it would be, though not by reason of tutoring or any help he'd received from Kincaid's interrogators. It would be accomplished, if he could not sway her from pursuing it, courtesy of the hell spawn who had tortured him in France.

"You do not wish to see it, lady, believe me," he ground out at last.

"I do," she answered in a voice low but firm. "And I will, else I will go no further in this with you."

His jaw clenched, and he stared at her for a long moment, trying to read the depth of her resolve. He was hoping to find some chink, some opening that would allow him to avoid this, for it cut too close to the bone of his own memories and nightmares.

What Kincaid had endured in English captivity was hardly the same as what Alex had known under the hellish questioning of the French Inquisition. Lord Exford had said as much, after seeing the extent of the scars on Alex's body, admitting that Kincaid had died of an illness brought on by exposure to the damp and foul conditions of his captivity. But no one at Dunleavy would know that. If Alex had ever had a birthmark on his back, it would no longer be visible, and so in this, at least, he might blend some truth into the lie he was building. But it would be wrenching nevertheless.

Beth did not waver. She simply waited.

So be it.

Standing rigid, Alex reached up to unfasten his over-tunic, removing it and tossing it to the side. Her gaze, wide and glittering with all the thoughts she kept guarded, remained locked with his as he next began to work at the laces of his shirt, untying them before pulling the ends of the garment free from his breeches.

And then he just stood there unmoving, his hands hanging loosely at his sides. He breathed in, slowly, deeply, not turning around yet . . . being careful before he did to shield all the raw, wounded places that still festered inside him. Aye, he had to, lest he reveal too much of the true darkness at work there. She would be the first woman to see the damage his Inquisitors had done to him, and he needed to prepare himself for it.

A heartbeat passed, and another. At last he pulled the shirt over his head, letting it slip to the floor as he turned to reveal his back to her.

And when she gasped in response to what she saw, he closed his eyes, willing the pain that rocked through him—of memory, of shame, and of impotent anger—to recede to a place of nothingness. To stay hidden in the black chamber of his innermost heart, where it could hurt him no more.

He would not react.

He would not remember.

And when she had looked her fill and turned away in disgust, he would—

He heard the whisper of her skirts at nearly the same instant that he felt her feather-light touch upon his shoulder. Sucking in his breath, he stood there stricken, frozen in disbelief, knowing that the sensation was not painful in any literal sense, but still feeling as if a blaze of fire shot from each of her fingertips into his body's core.

"My God, what did they do to you?"

He turned his head stiffly in answer to that softly uttered question, his gaze falling first on the gentle hand still resting on his shoulder before glancing down to meet her gaze. He could not speak for a moment, unable to say anything at all for the thickness that had suddenly invaded his throat. Swallowing against it, he breathed in and then exhaled, trying to steady himself until the feeling receded enough that he was able to form words again. "I trust you do not wish me to provide you with the details of it, lady."

She shook her head, those lovely eyes glistening and her own breathing sounding shallow and hitched. In silence, she simply stroked her palm down the length of his arm. Tingles sparked along the path she took, until she reached his hand and clasped it in her own, wrapping her fingers over his in a clumsy offer of refuge and strength. It caught him by surprise, sending waves of unexpected feeling pounding into him, unleashed by that simple gesture of compassion.

Sweet Jesu, Joseph, and the Holy Virgin.

It wasn't supposed to be like this. *He* was supposed to be in control. *He* was the one whose skill and prowess should have swept her off her feet, making her forget her doubts under the force of passion and need he incited in her. But she had turned this around on him with her soulful eyes. With her noble strength and gentle touch.

By heaven, he had to reclaim his rightful position in this now, before what was happening inside him spiraled any further out of control.

Twisting toward her in one smooth movement, he

swept his fingers along the side of her face and took her mouth in a searing kiss. If she was shocked at his action, she did not reveal it. Nay, her eyes closed and she kissed him back, alternately tasting and giving, her mouth warm and responsive under his.

Made bold by her compliance, Alex eased the tip of his tongue past her lips, gently exploring. When she met him in kind, hers testing, moving with inexpert but delightful eagerness against his, it sent sharp jolts of need surging into his groin, making him swell and harden. One of her hands was still linked with his, but the other slipped up to rest on his waist as they kissed, and that innocent yet somehow intimate touch made his breath catch and his heart seem to pound deeper and harder.

He wanted her. The need rose up to overwhelm him, the desire to feel her, to touch and taste and sink into the sweetness of her flesh. With a low, growling sound, he lifted their intertwined hands and brought them up behind her back. Holding her seductively captive in that position, he dragged her against him, deepening their kiss and reveling in the way her soft curves pressed along the length of his body. A moan came from the back of her throat, and he felt her arch into him for an instant, as if she too craved the delicious melding their closeness suggested.

But in the next she stiffened and pulled her mouth from his, gasping.

"Wait, I cannot. It is just—wait, Rob, please."

The sound of that false name ripped through him, stabbing deep in a way he wouldn't have thought possible. Releasing his hold on her, he backed up, and Beth shook her head, her eyes opened now, blinking, her expression startled, as if she'd just awoken from some tantalizing dream.

"I—I am sorry. It is just . . . that is, it has been so long, and I—"

Alex shook his head, indicating that she need not explain. He jabbed his hand into his hair, looking up to the ceiling and letting out his breath, trying to force himself physically and mentally back into control. But for the first time in as long as he could remember, he was having difficulty tempering his responses to the dictates of his will. He had always scoffed at such things; now he could not refute the danger he sensed in his desire for this woman or the risk he would be taking if he allowed himself to make love to her right now.

What the hell was wrong with him? He'd spent most of his adult life enjoying uncomplicated pleasure, keeping free of any deeper entanglement that might muddy the waters. But somehow he was reacting differently now, of all times, when he could least afford to slip.

It made no sense. It went against everything he had thought true about himself—everything he'd decided was not only useful but also necessary in reinforcing his position at Dunleavy as the returned earl. But he couldn't make love to her right now, much as his body wanted to. Nay, not if he wanted to maintain his self-control. It was all going to be distinctly awkward considering that he was trying to convince her that he was her husband.

Beth had wrapped her arms around her waist again. She too had backed up several steps, but she was staring straight at him with uncertain, muted need, and something akin to agony clear on her expressive face. *Sweet Jesu.* He needed some time. Time to think, to reevaluate, to try to insulate himself from the strange reaction he kept having to this woman who was turning his life upside down.

He cleared his throat. "Perhaps it would be best, lady, considering how long I have been gone—" He broke off for a moment, knowing he had to find the right way to make this make sense to her. "Much has changed, Beth. *I* have changed, and not only because of this," he said, gesturing to the scars visible on his body. "There is no denying that I am not the same man you married. With all that has happened, it would be impossible for me to be."

"I understand," she said quietly.

"In fact, we are like two strangers," Alex continued, grateful that for once he was speaking the truth. "Because of that, I would not be averse to taking a slower pace with our reunion. To give us time to learn of each other again."

He stopped and watched her, trying to gauge her reaction, to see if he was pounding the nails into the coffin of his efforts by taking this tack with her. To his good fortune, she seemed relieved rather than suspicious. After only a slight hesitation, she nodded and answered, "I would be grateful for such accommodation, my lord."

He nodded in return, the moment awkward following the flare of passion they'd just experienced. But it was settled, and that was all that mattered. They need not make love for the time being . . . or perhaps even for the entire duration of his stay at Dunleavy, if he handled it properly.

Yet even as the rational part of him heaved a sigh of relief with that knowledge, the darker, more rebellious part of him clamored in dissension. *If you give up too easily*, that persuasive voice prodded, *you'll be as suspect as if you'd demanded conjugal rights against her will. You need to find a middle ground or risk exposure of your part in Lord Exford's plot.*

That he sensed something very attractive about Elizabeth of Selkirk far beyond her beautiful face or lovely figure didn't help either. Her reactions to his kisses had made it clear that she was the kind of woman not one in ten thousand might be . . . a fiery siren wrapped in a cloak of respectability, promising untold bliss to the man skilled enough to set her passions free.

And God forgive him but he was highly skilled, his aptitude honed by years of delectable practice.

So it was that, as if from some disastrous distance, Alex heard himself adding, "We are agreed, then. I am a patient man, and as long as we are making progress, I am willing to bide my time until I am confident that you are ready to resume full marital relations."

Her eyes widened slightly. "How, pray tell, will you determine that?"

"You will inform me." Alex met her gaze with the heat of his own. "I may be changed in many ways, Beth, but not in this. I want you willing—preferably eager—or not at all."

She blushed, but to her credit she did not look away from him. "And what if I do not feel ready for years . . . or ever, even?" she asked, clearly daring him.

Alex gave her a slow smile. "I am not overly concerned about that, lady."

The rosy hue in her cheeks deepened, but she said naught more.

Breaking his gaze with her at last, he glanced over to the table near the hearth and the sand glass resting there, before walking over to take it up. "This, however, should help us in the task." He looked back at her again. "It is an hour glass, is it not?"

"Nay. That one is but a half hour."

He shook his head, making a clicking sound with his tongue as he put it back. "Not nearly long enough. Is there an hour glass in the castle?"

"In the kitchen," she answered with a half-bemused and half-shocked expression.

He gave her a wicked smile. "Much better. I will trade this glass for that one, so as not to disrupt Cook overmuch. Beginning one sennight from today, you and I will meet daily in private for the hour it takes to empty the glass. That should help us to become more familiar with each other."

"One sennight?" she repeated with a frown, and it was clear she wondered at his seemingly arbitrary decision of time.

He did his best to explain. "I need to accustom myself to the duties and rhythm of life at Dunleavy once more. You need time to accustom yourself to my presence again. A week should be sufficient to do so before we begin concerted, daily efforts to regain our . . . intimacies."

He saw her fingers clench in her skirts. "Very well. But I want to clarify—even so, that until I tell you I wish it, we will not . . . that is, we won't actually—"

"Consummate our reunion?" He relished the abashed expression his bluntness called forth on her beautiful face, finding some kind of perverse pleasure in being outspoken about the act he wanted to enjoy with her desperately right now, but that he had decided to resist for both their sakes. By all the saints in heaven, he must be mad.

But then she surprised him again by echoing, "Aye. *Consummate* our reunion." She lifted her brow, her hesitancy seeming to dissipate in favor of that other, more defiant air of hers. That almost insolent look that attracted him like nothing else he'd ever known. "You give your oath that you will wait and not attempt to resume our relations fully, no matter how great the temptation, until I bid you take the liberty?"

He felt the right corner of his mouth quirk as it always did when he was thrown a challenge, even as the blood began to beat hotter in his veins. "Aye, lady; that is my offer and my oath. But I think it only fair to warn you about something."

"What is it?"

"You will have one week of grace—but after that it is not *I* who will have the most difficult part of this bargain."

Again she did not answer, though he caught the glint of an expression in her gaze that inflamed him in the most delicious of ways. Yet when she finally did speak, it was to issue a command of sorts, uttered with all the confidence of a woman who had been responsible for an entire demesne for five years.

"Let us retire to bed now, my lord, for I find that I am very tired. I will trust you at your word to leave me at peace."

"And I will trust you at yours," Alex rejoined, "to

keep all blades sheathed in their scabbards and not in my flesh."

Beth shot him another look of exasperation, shaded perhaps with a touch of embarrassment. But in the next moment she seemed to dismiss him without another word, walking over to pick up the dagger and place it in full view on the mantel. Then, standing before the now lower-burning fire, she unfastened her jeweled girdle and set it aside. Following that, she began to unlace the front ties of her elegant, embroidered over-tunic, at last slipping it off, which left her in naught but her smock.

Alex held his breath, waiting to see what she would do next—knowing that the night was warm, not to mention how hot it was inside the chamber because of the blaze she'd stoked in the hearth.

But she paused in what she'd been doing to attend to her hair. Reaching up, she unfastened the circlet, a task that took longer than usual, he'd warrant, thanks to the way those long tresses had become tangled with the delicate metal during their scuffle under the tapestry. The ornament removed, she took up a comb and began to work it through.

And when at last she was done, he found himself swallowing against a dry throat at the sight of her standing there before the hearth with that luxuriant honey-gold hair, now silky smooth and hanging to her hips. Even more tantalizing was the way the flickering light seeped through the thin fabric of her smock, revealing her contours in a way that teased and tormented him.

He was grateful that he stood with the lower half of his body partly obscured in the shadows cast by the table. Full light would have revealed his embarrassing physical reaction to her, otherwise.

He could not move. Nay, he stood there, mesmerized, rooted to the floor.

She deigned to favor him with a swift glance that was at once challenging and assessing, noting his boots and breeches but, praise be, nothing more. "What, my lord—do you intend to sleep fully clothed this night?"

"I haven't decided yet," he managed to say, though his voice sounded as hoarse as if he hadn't spoken for a week.

However, as he voiced the words, latent memory surged to the fore, sending shock spilling through him. His time in the Templar Brotherhood and then his torment with the Inquisition had pushed the patterns of normal life into dim recollection for him. Now he could not forget that it was a common custom for lords and ladies to sleep naked within the confines of their curtained beds, especially in the hot summer months.

He swallowed again. Hard.

Shrugging, Beth turned slightly away from him to start unfastening the ties of her smock at the wrists, and he felt his breath catch again, though he couldn't seem to make himself look away. From the way she stood in profile, he could see the outline of her luscious breasts, tipped by nipples that poked out in delightful stiffness from beneath the cloth. The vision sent a renewed rush of full and heavy heat to his already uncomfortable erection, and he was forced to bite back a groan and shift his stance to prevent her from seeing the full evidence of his desire, shadows or not.

But then all was lost when, finished at last with untying all the various laces, Beth calmly bent to reach for the hem of her smock and pulled the entire garment up over her head in one smooth motion, leaving her completely naked before his unwavering gaze.

Alex felt something seize up in his chest, and he gripped the edge of the table hard enough that he thought he felt the texture of the wood's grain imprinted upon his palm.

Good God.

His gaze drank in the sight of her before him as avidly as a thirsty man might gulp a cool goblet of water. Elizabeth of Selkirk possessed an angel's form, slender in all the right places and well curved in all the rest, her breasts plump and round and tipped in a delicate coral hue. In fact, unclothed, she was all peach and honeyed cream, except for the golden bounty of hair spilling down her back—and crowning the apex of her thighs. Dark gold curls nestled there, looking soft against the smoothness of her skin, and drawing his gaze as inexorably as a siren luring her victim toward the rocks.

Seemingly unaware of his rapt attention, Beth twisted with a scowl to reach for an urn near the wardrobe, mumbling something about the oppressive heat. She turned back to throw the water from it onto the fire, extinguishing the flames to hissing ash and dropping the room into another level of shadow. All that kept the dark at bay was the single taper burning on the mantel.

After she set down the empty vessel, she picked up a poker and began jabbing at smoking wood. She broke it into smaller pieces . . . all while bent over the hearth in a position that seemed to welcome the dancing caress of candlelight, while at the same time sending the most sinful thoughts hurtling directly from Alex's brain into the part of him that throbbed mercilessly with every pounding pulse of his heart.

He stopped breathing as she shifted her stance again, her legs parting wider and her hips seeming to lift up a bit as she leaned forward to stab at some embers near the back of the hearth. He choked then, his vision clouding . . . and it had nothing to do with the faint haze of smoke now drifting through the chamber. Closing his eyes wouldn't help. The image was burned into his mind in erotic, blazing detail.

Forcing himself to turn away, he walked stiffly toward the window, his physical state making any other kind of movement impossible. Once there he yanked open the shutter to let in some fresh air, coughing to try to clear his lungs, his head—to clear *something*— and at the sound she twisted away from her task, straightening to face him and setting aside the poker to rest her hands on her hips.

Then she just stood there, completely naked and forthright in her demeanor, her gaze slipping down to that part of him that strained mightily against his breeches, in clear display now thanks to where he stood. Her gaze swept back up to his face and she frowned, as if she was questioning whether he would hold true to his word about not bedding her until she agreed to it.

She was supposed to be his wife, damn it. Even though years had come between, she would assume that he had seen her unclothed many times during their months of marriage. He had to stop acting like some besotted fool, gazing for his first time at a woman.

A lovely, seductive, very naked vixen of a woman.

He had to say something.

"Good night, lady."

He wanted to punch himself the moment the words left his mouth. Of all the stupid, inane things he could have chosen . . .

Beth frowned more deeply, before giving him a short nod and murmuring an answer in kind and walking over to their bed. Without another word, she climbed in between the deep crimson draperies surrounding it and disappeared from sight.

"Douse the candle before you come in, will you?" she called suddenly from within those scarlet depths. Matter-of-factly. As calmly as you please, while he felt as if he was going to explode from the need she had sent hammering through him this night.

He possessed a great deal of will and had always been able to trust himself to maintain control when thrust into uncomfortable proximity with an attractive woman, but this was ridiculous. And he realized with a sudden, dropping sensation that unless he relished the idea of a long night of torment, he would have no choice but to do something about it—which in the severity of this case would mean getting a bucket of icy water from the deepest well in the castle yard and soaking himself with it . . . paying special attention to the area between his waist and his knees.

Of course he knew there were other methods he could employ to ease his discomfort. He wasn't so ignorant that he did not realize castle lords wielded power enough to sate their unmet desires on any castle wench, willing or unwilling; however, he was no real castle lord, thank God. And even if he was, the idea of taking a woman under those circumstances left him cold.

A second alternative would be to resolve the need himself. The Church, however, considered self-pleasure a greater sin than fornication, and as ignoble as he was in many ways, he hadn't sunk so low that he was willing to undertake that option either.

Nay, the cold water would have to do. It was warm enough out of doors that he might even find the experience refreshing. And he wouldn't get as many strange looks as he would have if he'd had to avail himself of the remedy in midwinter.

Shaking his head at his folly, Alex stalked over to the lone candle and snuffed it out before he pried off his boots. Then, raking his fingers through his hair, he breathed in deeply and exhaled in the dark, before turning around and making his way to the door. He'd made his decision about something else as well, he realized, as he left the bedchamber and headed down to the yard.

He was definitely going to be sleeping in his breeches this night—and perhaps every other night he was forced to spend next to the Lady Elizabeth of Selkirk without making love to her.

There was no question of it.

Beth pretended to be asleep already, lying on her side and facing away from Rob's part of the bed when he finally returned to the chamber, padded over, and climbed in. She felt the mattress give under his weight as he turned—and felt several drops of cold water hit her as well. Twisting half on her back to look at him, she frowned. Though it was dark, she could tell that he was facing away from her, and that his hair, at least, was soaking wet.

By all the angels and saints, had he gone *bathing*, then?

Suddenly, the memory of what he'd looked like standing near the window a few moments ago, clearly aroused and uncomfortable, filled her mind, making her cheeks heat and prompting her to roll back to her side again.

He'd eased his discomfort with a dousing from the well, then. She felt almost ashamed to have driven him to such extremes. They were a married pair, and in the eyes of the world, it was her duty as his wife to provide him with certain . . . relief. But it couldn't be helped. Besides, he was the one who had suggested that they should wait longer to resume marital relations.

Her thoughts were troubled, which didn't surprise her, considering that they only kept pace with the confusion brewing in her heart. Everything had been turned topsy-turvy in the space of one day. There was no denying that some of her doubts had been assuaged tonight: The man lying so still next to her had known the answers to her questions about her favored pastimes, her mother's birthplace, and the argument he'd used to convince her father that their union would be a sound one.

However, other things still did not seem right, and those incongruities pestered her, some overt and demanding immediate attention, while others niggled at the back of her mind like annoying flies buzzing around a dish of sweet cream. She dared to twist halfway on her back again to look at the object of her musings.

It was too dark to see the scars he'd shown her, spread in awful array over the entire top half of his body. But she remembered what she'd seen. What his tormenters had done to him had obliterated the birthmark she'd hoped to find in proof of his identity. In truth, witnessing for the first time the evidence of the torture he'd endured had shocked her so that she'd forgotten everything but the desire to offer him solace and strength.

And then he'd kissed her again . . .

Beth closed her eyes, remembering that darkly intimate caress and the brazen way she'd responded to it. His kiss had been sensual and intimate and astonishing, filling her with a throbbing sense of need for something she couldn't even name. She had wanted him then—had wanted to take and give and make love to him with an intensity that had stolen her breath and caused her to arch against his body without shame.

It had been *nothing* like any of the pleasant kisses she'd shared with the man she'd known as her husband so long ago.

This Rob was a wholly different man. And to a point she could accept the possibility of that. He would have to have been changed by the ordeal he'd endured; he'd avowed it to her himself. Even her maidservant, Annabel, had warned her of the likelihood. But could imprisonment and torture alter the way a man kissed his wife? Did it transform his very nature, filling him with a sense of teasing playfulness . . . with an underlying masculine swagger and dallying smile, all topped with the glint of sensual promise that had never before shone in his eyes?

She supposed it was possible. She'd seen often enough how many of the soldiers at Dunleavy reacted after having faced death, whether in battle or from illness, with a renewed vigor for living when the crisis was past. And yet she could not imagine Rob responding in a likewise way. Nay, he'd always been so calm and even-tempered. So . . . *solid.* There had been nothing frivolous about Robert Kincaid. Naught that could be described as even overtly sensual in his disposition.

But she could not deny that the man who had walked into her life today had suffered experiences far worse than anything she could have ever imagined. And there would be no way he could have known the answers to the questions she'd asked him if he wasn't Rob himself.

He had to be her husband, then.

Only he was a peculiar new incarnation of that man—a virtual stranger whom she would need to learn of all over again.

That prospect was tantalizing, it was true, but she intended to make him work for every step they gained together. The mischievous churl had even dallied with her when arranging the bargain of private hours between them, and she could still see the sparkle in his eyes when she'd corrected him on the size of the sand glass. Of course she'd never admit how much she anticipated those moments to come, dedicated to naught but the two of them undertaking what would almost be a courtship again. But she could contemplate it in secret all she wanted.

Almost smiling with the idea, Beth closed her eyes and sighed, resolving to find some rest if she could manage it, now that this extraordinary night was finally drawing to a close. Yet as she drifted off to sleep, the nagging thought that had been pestering her wiggled to the surface, casting clouds over the beginnings of the happy dreams forming in her mind.

It had to do with their wedding day, she realized. Aye, a distinct memory from that day had popped, full-formed, into her mind's eye, as the fog of sleep closed over her. It was of the moment that she and Rob had stepped out of the castle to make their way to the village square, to confess their vows before the people of the demesne.

For at that instant, she'd looked up . . .

And seen the brilliance of the sun, backed by a cloudless, robin's-egg-blue sky.

·

Chapter 4

"**B**less me, Father, for I have sinned. It has been a week since my last confession, and I cannot deny that I . . . that—"

Beth stopped, her voice catching, and Father Paul glanced to her, his gaze reflecting concern. "Continue my child," he murmured, nodding.

But she could not. All she was feeling—all she had been feeling since setting eyes on Rob again six days ago—seemed to clamp down on her throat to silence her. After a moment, she pushed herself up from the chair next to her respected confessor. The elderly priest was a friend to her as well as a spiritual counselor, and she knew he would be patient.

She paced the small room in Dunleavy's western wing where she was wont to speak her confession, trying to form her thoughts into words. She'd awoken this morn as she had every morn since Rob's arrival home, with her heart and head in turmoil. Another restless night's sleep, the sixth, to be precise, filled with twisting dreams, had done little to assuage the doubts that kept assaulting her. The sun had not yet risen when those worries had jolted her awake.

And then she'd looked at the man lying next to her, asleep in their bed . . .

"Lady Elizabeth, you must unburden your heart if I am to help you."

Beth frowned, her gaze settling on the ornate candle plate perched on the mantel in this chamber. Father Paul did not favor use of newfangled sand glasses, preferring the old tried-and-true methods of keeping time. The plate on his hearth held a pristine taper marked with lines, each indicating the passage of an hour in burning time. Nay, it was no sand glass, but it nevertheless served as a reminder of the agreement she'd made with Rob.

An agreement they were to undertake on the morrow, exactly one sennight since his return home.

The sight of that candle sent an unsettling twinge through her, and to quell it she twisted to face Father Paul again, wrapping her arms around her middle.

"I am having doubts about my husband," she finally admitted.

Father Paul hesitated before asking, "What kind of doubts?"

"He is not the man I once knew." She squeezed her arms tighter around herself, trying to calm the anxious fluttering inside. "The man who rode through Dunleavy's gates is like a stranger to me, Father. I do not know how to quiet my fears about him or accept him again as my husband."

Father Paul nodded in silence for a moment before meeting her gaze, his searching. "I must ask you a delicate question, lady. Is it your . . . *private* reunion with him that has prompted these worries?"

For what seemed the hundredth time during the

past week, Beth felt her cheeks glow warm, but she answered in a husky murmur, "Nay. We have not yet recommenced our marriage in that way." After a moment, she added, "Though even if we had, it would change naught about my doubts, I think."

Father Paul looked startled at her admission, but his expression resumed its normal, calm lines before he spoke again. "Did your husband make this decision about the way of it between you, or was the choice yours?"

"He proposed it." She looked away, not wanting to admit her part in it or the less-than-convivial greeting she had given Rob upon his arrival in their bedchamber. To cover up her awkwardness, she glanced back to the priest and added, "He noticed my uneasiness with him on the night of his return and said he thought it better to wait until we learned of each other again first."

Father Paul made a low sound of surprise. "It is unusual for a man so long absent from home to willingly deny himself the comforts of his wife, I'll grant you that."

"And yet that is only one of the matters fueling my doubt. The Robert Kincaid I knew was a predictable man. A man who took the straightforward path in all matters, governed by propriety and what was expected of him as the lord of this demesne. Yet since his homecoming I never seem to know what to expect of him."

Father Paul looked thoughtful again, and he nodded sagely as she spoke, as if he mulled over something of great importance. Finally, he raised his gaze to her again. "There may yet be a logical explanation for his actions—or lack of them. Have you considered the possibility that your husband's hesitation in resuming the fullness of your marriage might be tied to his imprisonment? Perhaps his English tormentors left him unable to perform his husbandly duties."

"It is not that, I am almost certain," Beth answered, shaking her head, embarrassed and yet at the same time feeling ripples of something she was appalled to think the older man might see in her expression, as she recalled their first night together and the view she'd been granted of Rob, standing near the window after all but the candle on the mantel had been extinguished. She cleared her throat, struggling to sound normal. "From all appearances, he seems quite capable of performing his part."

"Then perhaps he feels ill at ease about exposing evidence of his imprisonment and torture to your sight."

She shook her head. "He revealed his scars to me willingly on the night of his return home, removing his tunic and shirt when I challenged him to show me the mark on his back, with him since his birth."

The priest looked aghast. "You demanded *proof* of him as your husband?"

"I could do no less." Beth fixed her confessor with a sharp gaze. "I thought him an impostor, Father. Accepting him without question not only would have been foolish for the safety of this castle but also sinful as well."

Father Paul nodded, but she could see that he was not finished. Quietly, he continued, "And yet you are still not satisfied in his identity."

"Nay . . . aye—it is just that so much seems different about him. I accept that what he endured at the hands of our enemies may be part of that. Such suffering is bound to change a man. It destroyed any vestige of the mark I sought near his shoulder, that is certain . . . and yet I cannot deny that he remembered details of our past that only he would know." She cradled her face with her hands, breathing deep in an effort to calm her confusion and frustration, shaking her head. "I just cannot make sense of it. It is all a muddle with no clear resolution."

"Ah, lady, it is difficult to be sure." Father Paul sighed, and Beth looked up, swallowing back the aching sensation that sprang up in her throat as the gentle priest took her hand between his own and patted it encouragingly.

Huskily, she said, "Father, I do not know how—or if—I can relinquish the control and safety of this castle to a man who seems a stranger to me in so many ways." She glanced away briefly, and added more quietly, "I do not know if I can relinquish *myself* to him."

"And yet it is far better for the people of Dunleavy to have their lord home again. The attacks from the north, at least, will perforce cease. Lord Lennox can no longer pursue an alliance with you, a woman whose husband still clearly lives. That will be a blessing, to be sure."

"Aye."

"Then it seems your wifely duty is clear."

"But why do I continue to doubt?"

"It is no surprise that you are confused, child," Father Paul murmured, leaving off patting her hand to sit back in his chair. "Much has happened quickly.

You were married only a short time before your husband was taken, and now he has returned, seeming vastly different from the man you recall in your golden-tinted dreams." He sighed, shaking his head. "Do not forget that time tends to smooth over the harsher lines of reality, lady; when we are confronted with the truth again, it can appear far different from the hazy sweetness of memory. The doubts you are feeling now likely arise more from that than aught else."

"You would not be the first to suggest so," she mumbled.

He nodded again, the movement decisive. "Faith cannot be seen with the naked eye, Elizabeth. We must accept the path given us by God and pray for the strength to follow it well."

"So you are saying I should ignore my doubts and accept this man fully as my husband?"

"I am saying that you should give yourself time to accustom yourself to him again. He seems willing to take that path with you. Learn his habits anew. Spend time together. All will sort itself out in the end."

At that moment they both heard a sound in the outer chamber beyond the secluded alcove where they sat. The noise was muffled, as if someone had bumped into a chair or tried to close a door quietly. Stiffening, Beth twisted toward the arched entry into the main room. "Were you expecting someone else this morn, Father?"

"Nay," the priest answered, looking ahead as he crossed into the alcove and then disappeared from her sight when he passed into the larger room.

Beth heard him walking about and recognized a

sound that indicated he was pulling open the heavy wooden door connecting to the corridor before shutting it again. His voice echoed into the alcove, though she still couldn't see him. "There are none here." He reappeared in the archway to the alcove. "A trick of the wind, perhaps."

Beth nodded, too miserable to worry about this as well. She sighed, pushing herself to a standing position and accepting Father Paul's brief embrace.

"It is nearly time for prayers at terce. Go now, my child, and pray to St. Monica for clarity of thought and heart in your marriage. She will intercede for you, helping you to follow the path God intends."

"Yes, Father," Beth murmured, seemingly compliant, though her thoughts and emotions were still awhirl.

As she left the priest's chamber, she pursed her lips, unable to completely suppress the renegade and likely sacrilegious thought that she was going to need far more than the intercession of one blessed saint to guide her through the maze of her emotions concerning this man who had returned as both her husband and lord of Dunleavy.

They'd been sparring for most of the morning, and a hot blanket of sunlight rippled over the assembled men in the yard, glinting off shield, blade, and helm. Alex had called for a training session first thing every morn for the past six days, thinking it wise to assert without delay his presence as Dunleavy's lord with the men now under his command—as well as to help integrate Stephen and Luc into the garrison. The sooner they all gained the trust of the fighting men of

Dunleavy, the sooner they'd obtain the information they needed and he'd be free of this godforsaken plot he'd been forced to undertake.

Winded and sweaty with the exertion of the sword sequence he'd just completed, Alex moved away from the group toward one of the troughs of water at the edge of the yard. Using his helmet as a vessel, he dipped it in and lifted to let the cool water cascade over his head. He was still wiping the wetness from his eyes when he sensed the approach of someone else. When he turned and saw that it was Luc, he felt a surge of animosity that only intensified when his former comrade spoke.

"You seem to have retained most of your fighting skill in the years since we battled side by side in the Brotherhood," Luc said low enough that only Alex could hear him. The empty smile he wore for the benefit of any who might be watching them did naught to dispel the challenge in his voice. "Not all, perhaps, but most."

"Enough, still, to outdo you." Alex fixed him with his gaze, adding in the same muted voice, "Just as I did in Cyprus, right before your arrest."

"*Our* arrest." Luc's expression tightened, though his false smile remained pasted in place until he cupped his hands and splashed water on his face. Anyone who looked on them would think they were exchanging the kinds of pleasantries or jests shared by men who had suffered and survived together. After a quick swipe of his sleeve to dry off, Luc finished, "And I think it bears stating again that my surrender was the result of fortunate timing on your part, naught else."

"So you say," Alex retorted. "I, on the other hand, hold a different view of my success over you that day."

Luc's expression shifted a bit and a leering shadow filled his eyes. "Speaking of successes, how goes it with that luscious-looking wench Exford's plan tossed into your lap? Has she proved an eager field to plow, or did you needs employ a bit of satisfying force to breach her defenses? Do tell."

"Why don't you try not to be such a bastard?" Alex ground out.

"And why don't you dispense with your tiresome habit of championing undeserving women?" Luc countered in a deceptively light tone, though Alex felt the same tension he knew rippled through his adversary as they squared off to face each other. "But before you loose that self-righteous anger on me again, I have only one word for you by way of reminder. *John.*"

Alex's hand clenched on the hilt of his sword, the desire to whip it out and smash it into Luc's smug face nearly overwhelming him.

"Just remember that he will suffer for every misstep you take, whether with me, the woman, or this assignment."

"That is the only thing standing between you and oblivion right now, Luc, I assure you. And yet there will come a time when even that protection will be gone."

The splash of another helm hitting the water caused both Alex and Luc to shift their attention away from each other long enough to see Stephen, who had undertaken the action to distract them. As he approached, he scowled at them and muttered, "Leave off now or risk the loss of everything at stake here, including our lives." He jerked his chin back toward the yard just before he spilled a helmet-full of water over his own head, adding, "All four groups have called a break in the training."

In another few moments, they were surrounded by two score of Dunleavy's sweaty, tired garrison. Several of the men tossed off ribald jests as they took advantage of the brief respite to drink from skins or cool off as Alex and Stephen had done. Because of it, Luc was not able to get in the parting shot Alex knew he'd so dearly have loved to make, but their gazes locked for another instant just before the captain of the guard pulled Alex aside to consult with him on a particular practice sequence.

The cold glare in his rival's eyes might have made another man at least consider the warning he'd been given . . . however, Alex wasn't like most men. Even as he listened to the captain of the guard, offering the man further explanation on their training moves, in another compartment of his thoughts he was aware of something stirring inside him in response to Luc's needling.

The burning sensation that settled in his gut was far more familiar to him than he liked to admit, and he realized that his reaction to Luc's attempt at intimidation was the same as it always was whenever anyone tried to bend him to a will other than his own; it unleashed whatever was pent up inside, propelling him into taking some sort of action, foolhardy or extreme though it might be. He couldn't seem to stop himself, though. The response was as instinctive to him as breathing.

And when that happened, the result always ended up one of two ways. Either he landed in immense trouble or he was catapulted from it by the force of his own audacity.

All that remained was to see which way it was going to turn out this time.

Beth was in an upper chamber—a sewing chamber by all appearances—when Alex found her an hour later, surrounded by several of her ladies. They were working at embroidery, intent enough on what they were doing that none saw him. He'd paused at the edge of the doorway, pulling himself up short from the headlong strides he'd undertaken in his search for her.

Inching back from the edge of the portal so that he could see into the chamber without being seen himself, he just watched her as she stitched a meticulous, scarlet pattern along the edge of some creamy fabric. The women were all occupied in working individual pieces rather than on one large piece together as he had sometime seen done in sewing circles, and when they spoke to one another it was in low murmurs. They glanced up now and again, smiling and even occasionally laughing, but he was too far from them to make out the details of their conversation.

His attention fixed on Beth, who was seated almost sideways to him, off a bit to the right of the group. Her lush blue gown stood out in startling contrast to the dark brown walls and jewel-toned tapestry hanging behind her in the chamber, the deep hue complementing the color of her hair and skin. *By God was a beauty*. For the first time in nearly a he allowed himself to truly study her . . . noting the way she worried her lower lip with her teeth as she concentrated, watching her push the needle into the fabric and then draw the silk thread through in one smooth motion before looping it over and pushing it in again.

She worked steadily, confidently, her movements graceful and almost sensual in their rhythmic cadence. The wide, bell-shaped end of her sleeve waved gently with her efforts, and he noticed as she squinted, tilting her head to look more closely at a stitch she'd just made, that a tendril of her hair slipped forward on her cheek. It was only a single curl, for she'd pulled the glorious silken mass back and fastened it into a thick braid behind her neck.

He preferred it freed from all constraints, spilling loose to her hips as it had been the first day he'd seen her. Aye, he liked the look of that golden bounty spread over her shoulders and down her back, and he would tell her so this eve. He might even go so far as to insist that she wear it unbound whenever they were together.

A husband had the right to demand such things, after all. As the noble lord he was playing, he had rights in many areas, and he needed to begin taking them, he realized. It could be denied no longer. Every galling interaction he faced with Luc made that truth more clear.

He had to begin his seduction of Lady Elizabeth of ~lkirk in earnest *now*, with all the finesse and skill ~ossessed.

~e just had to set his mind to it. Aye, he would her, charm her, persuade her over the course of the next few days. By the time he was finished, she would be so lost in her need for him that she would forget to question aught about him any longer. God help him, but he had to do it. Everyone, including John, would be safer that way.

He'd never had any difficulty keeping his emotions separate from his actions with any other woman. Not since he'd lost his first love, Margaret Newcomb, so many years ago and been forced to join the Templars. In the time since, he had never been cruel to any woman with whom he dallied and he would never permit a female to be treated disrespectfully in his presence . . . but he knew better than to involve his deeper feelings.

It would be the same this time, he told himself. He would remain emotionally detached while accomplishing the task he'd been charged with here at Dunleavy. He had to. His first night at the castle had been an incongruity, nothing more. Beth had caught him unawares when she'd viewed his scars with empathy instead of the repulsion he'd expected, and he had wavered for an instant.

He wouldn't let that happen again. He couldn't.

And there was no time like the present to test the truth of his resolve.

Chapter 5

Beth first noticed a change in the atmosphere of the cozy sewing chamber she shared with her ladies-in-waiting when she glanced at Annabel and saw the maid's startled expression. Several of the other women went quiet at the same time, and Johanna moved so quickly that she upset her sewing basket, sending silks, needles, and scraps of cloth spilling over the stone floor.

Stifling a gasp when she saw Rob, Beth lurched to stand. He strode farther into the chamber, fixing her with a brilliant smile that made her breath catch an instant before he swept past her on his way to Johanna. There, he proceeded to crouch down and aid her in gathering up all her scattered sewing implements, murmuring to everyone as he did, "My apologies in having disrupted your pleasant gathering. I came in search of my wife."

He straightened once more to his full, magnificent height, turning to face Beth again, his gaze ⸱king her in as if she were the only person there, ⸱ his sinful mouth quirking into that smile that ⸱ her blood racing. "Now that I seem to have ⸱ her, I beg your indulgence. If you will excuse us, Lady Elizabeth and I have something to attend to."

Beth finally found her voice, though she'd been caught so by surprise that she stumbled a bit with her words. "Is—is aught amiss, my lord?"

"Nay, all is well."

"Then should my ladies continue sewing, or—well, how long will I be needed?"

"For about an hour . . . give or take a few grains of sand."

She could have sworn she saw a twinkle in his blue eyes as he answered, at the same time that the import of what he was saying swept through her in a tingling, knee-weakening wave. He'd come to fetch her for the first of their agreed-upon meetings. Meetings that were to take place in private.

Sweet heavens . . .

"I thought we were meeting on the morrow," she somehow managed to choke out.

"I could not wait longer." His gaze smoldered with something wicked, and she knew it wasn't her imagination to think so when she heard Annabel's swift intake of breath as well. "Will you come with me now, lady?" he murmured, holding out his hand to her as he spoke.

"Aye, my lord," she managed to say, feeling somewhat stiff as she stepped forward to take his hand. The brush of his palm over hers as they touched startled her, and she decided she must be far more befuddled, even, than she'd believed herself to be, for she imagined an actual charge of hot energy surging between them when her skin met his.

Rob's face betrayed little, but he too seemed

nerved in that instant. Yet there was no time to think on it further, as he tugged her forward, toward the door. She only had time to glance back at Annabel, nodding through the flush of hot and cold consuming her to murmur something about seeing her later at supper.

And then she was in the cool dark of the corridor following Rob, the usual damp chill she felt in any of the castle's interior hallways accentuating the warmth between their clasped hands.

"Where are we going?"

Her voice echoed with authority, she was pleased to realize, considering the ridiculous sense of nervousness she was feeling at the moment.

"To our chamber, of course."

"Oh."

Oh? That was the best she could muster?

Well done, the voice inside her mocked. Such a clever response. Now she sounded vacant, along with acting like a dolt.

"It is possible that we won't remain there the entire hour, but it will be a good place to begin," he added.

"You make it sound as if you have it all planned in full."

She uttered the comment unthinkingly, still somewhat dazed with this sudden turn of events, but she could have bitten off her tongue the moment the words left her mouth.

He only nodded, giving her a little smile, and that maddening flush swept over her again, making her feel breathless and light-headed. Blast it all, but this was not how she was accustomed to feeling *or* behaving. She was a mature woman. A lady who had successfully managed her husband's demesne for five years. Her emotions did not run rampant. Ever. She was calm and levelheaded, and—and steady, by heaven—not giddy, excitable, and—

Her thoughts screeched to a halt as, with what seemed one smooth movement, Rob lifted the latch to their chamber door with a murmured "We're here," before pulling her through the opening and swinging her gently up against the wall. In the next breath he'd shifted his stance to stand directly in front of her, though not touching her, his action causing several details to come crashing in on her at once.

The chamber's shutters were closed, making it dusky and cool inside the room, even in broad daylight.

The man standing before her was close enough that she could feel his tantalizing warmth radiating through their layers of clothing.

And he smelled good—wonderful, in fact. She breathed in as surreptitiously as she could, muting the sigh of pleasure that welled up in her in response. He smelled of clean, sensual male, mingled with just a hint of orris and clove, perhaps. Remarkably like the subtle blend she had concocted for use by Dunleavy's male guests in their baths.

The scent seemed to come from his clothing. Or perhaps it was his skin. She could not be certain, for although it took a great deal of will for her to remain unmoving when they stood in such proximity to each other, she did not dare lean in closer to test the theory. Instead she breathed in again, her fingers twitching with the desire to slip up his arms to his broad shoulders, to pull him closer for . . . for *something*. An embrace? A kiss? More than that?

Oh, yes, much more . . .

Embarrassment swept through her. Only a few hours ago, she had been lamenting her doubts to Father Paul. The reaction she was having now was ridiculous. And weak. She'd promised to make Rob work for every step they gained on the path to re-newed intimacy, and yet—

"I trust it meets with your approval."

His voice startled her, the warm, low rumble of it carrying an edge of amusement that matched the expression in his devastating eyes.

"What?"

"My scent." His mouth quirked up slightly. "You've seemed preoccupied with it since we entered this chamber."

"You—you must be mistaken, my lord," Beth choked, hoping her cheeks would not flush again and give away her falsehood. "I am not preoccupied with anything."

"A pity. I was thinking you very astute to have picked up on it. When my bath attendant offered the powder to me, he mentioned that you had combined the scents yourself." Rob kept his gaze steady on her, still half smiling. "It is a skillful blend, lady."

"I am glad you find it pleasing," she managed to say.

"I would consider it more so if you found it pleas-ing as well." His teeth flashed white. "On me, I mean."

She couldn't keep back the flush this time. "Oh . . . I, ah—yes, well, now that you mention it, I do think it suits you." She made a show of breathing in deeply, as if to test her response to it. "I like it very much."

By all the saints, she was acting more foolish with every passing second. She considered looking down, desperate to keep from staring into the eyes of this man whose very presence seemed to tie her tongue in knots, but then she realized that she couldn't tilt her head to accomplish it; they stood so close together that her brow would have nearly collided with his chest had she tried.

And it really was quite a delicious chest, broad and muscular . . . another spot she should try to avoid gazing upon if she wanted to keep her wits about her. She could try to stare over his shoulder, she supposed. But that part of him was delectable too. And then her gaze drifted up a bit, to the side of his face, glancing over the strong, firm line of his jaw . . . and that mouth, formed for sinful acts, she was sure, if he could arouse her as he had with naught more than a few smiles and kisses . . .

She coughed lightly, determined to make him do or say something that would necessitate their moving from this tantalizing and all too dangerous position against the wall. Bracing herself to look him in the eye, she took a deep breath and lifted her gaze to lock with his. It was a mistake. His expression sent a rush of sensation sweeping through her anew. It seemed to pool with an insistent, pleasurable throb between her legs, so that she could not keep from shifting her weight a little, her thighs brushing together, which sent the feeling pitching higher. *Oh, my . . .*

"Is something amiss?" he asked quietly, keeping the intensity of his gaze fixed on her.

"I was just wondering . . . do you intend that we should stand like this doing naught for the entirety of the hour?" she asked, somehow forcing her voice past the huskiness that seemed to have invaded her throat.

"Nay. I have something else in mind," he answered after the slightest pause, charging his words with enough erotic weight to make her reach behind to press her palms to the wall for support. "However, I have not begun to measure our time with the sand glass yet." He glanced over his shoulder to the table near the hearth where perched the object of his comment, recognizable to Beth as the hour glass from the kitchens. "I did not want to waste the minutes it would take to bring you here from wherever I found you."

"We have arrived safely now, it seems," she retorted, determined to hold her own against the onslaught of arousal he was unleashing in her.

"So we have." The twinkle still lit his eyes. "And I will turn it in a moment. First, however, I want to propose a small wager."

Beth felt a lurch of surprise, and unconsciously, she licked her lips, noting with amazement that Rob reacted to the gesture. His gaze dropped to her mouth, and his breath stilled.

Ah, what is this? It seems he is not as impervious to the charged atmosphere between us as he's been pretending to be . . .

"I do enjoy wagers and games of all kinds," she commented.

He cleared his throat. "I know."

She almost smiled to hear the slightly strangled sound to his voice and reveled in watching how he struggled to drag his gaze up from her mouth.

Aye, two could play at this game . . .

"And, pray tell"—she blinked at him innocently—"what will be the prize for the winner of your wager?"

The heat in his gaze seared her. "I thought you might be interested in that part. I know I certainly am."

Beth just raised her brow, waiting for his answer, though she faltered a bit when he seemed to recover from his momentary weakness in the face of her flirtation, directing the full force of his stare—hot, sensual, and commanding—at her.

"However, I won't detail the prize until after I have your consent to participate in the wager."

"That is a pity, for I won't consent until I kn what is to be gained if I win."

Rob shook his head, chuckling softly. "Al but you possess astonishing resolve."

Beth paused for a beat, keeping her gaz his when she finally answered, "That trai well, my lord, during the many sieges leavy while you were away."

His expression softened. Reachin his fingers gently to the place bene are correct, and grateful I am f been easy to take on the defer you did merits my appreciati

Beth resisted the urge to to kiss them. Instead she an instant before lettin her emotions as level ised herself to do. " same."

"Perhaps." He lowered his hand as well and tipped his head in respect. "And perhaps not. I think not many would have resisted as long—or with such resourcefulness." His expression shifted again, to that more playful look, insistent and sensual all at once. "However, back to the matter at hand. The time has come to see if you are also confident enough to accept my wager."

"As I mentioned earlier, I will consider it"—she flicked another dallying look at him—"provided you ᵗᵉll me the prize first."

ᵗⁱᵐᵉ he laughed aloud, merriment written on ⁻⁻⁻⁻ᵉ ᶜlear in his eyes. "Very well, my stubborn ⁻⁻⁻ᵈe to your greater resolve and tell ⁻⁻⁻⁻ I envision. Just a hint, though, ⁻⁻⁻⁻⁻⁻ The victor this day will ⁻⁻⁻ble attentions to-⁻⁻⁻by the one in her husband's company and this sensual banter they were sharing.

"All right, then," she said at last, drawing out her words elaborately, as if giving in on this point was almost painful for her, "I will agree to take part." She blinked, playing the moment straight. "However, my lord, I trust you to be sensitive to my abilities in the wager you choose for me to play with you."

"I would not challenge you to a joust, love, if that is what you fear. Talented you may be with a dagger," he teased, "but it would be unfair to test you so, for I am unmatched in matters of weaponry and defense."

"You are a veritable god of war, I am sure."

"Aye, something like that," he said with a laugh. "But my idea has naught to do with martial skills. Nay, I have taken your abilities into account—against myself, even. You see, I wish to challenge you to naught more strenuous than a game of *merels*."

She tried to hide her surprise. "Really?"

"If you're willing."

Oh, aye, she was more than willing. Rob hadn't agreed to play the game with her since the third week of their marriage, when she'd trounced him and hurt his masculine pride in the process.

"And what has prompted your sudden change of heart about a match of *merels* with me, my lord?" she asked liltingly, cocking her brow at him.

"Perhaps having spent too much time under lock and key, with hours to think and remember." One side of his devastating mouth tipped up slightly. "I remember that you were very good at the game . . . but I think I will be better."

Beth laughed. "Very well. I accept your challenge."

He nodded, stepping aside at last with a gallant flourish, and she brushed by him, willing her amorous thoughts to turn to the new bent of their wager. She could do this. *Merels* was her game, and she would win, with or without his distractions. In fact, concentrating on it might help her remain grounded where this maddening stranger who was her husband was concerned.

Walking to the hearth to retrieve the wooden game board and pieces, she called over her shoulder, "All right, then, my lord—shall we begin?"

It didn't take long for Beth to realize she'd been mistaken to think the game might distract her from the sinful thoughts she'd been having about Rob.

Of course the man himself wasn't much help either. In fact, it was clear that he was deliberately setting out to tempt and tease her as they played. As a start, he had refused to sit across from her at the little table in the usual positions for play. Instead, he pulled his chair up right next to her. Every now and again, his thigh would brush against hers, or he'd touch his fingers to her hair or her cheek . . . and several times when he'd leaned in to murmur a suggestion for her next move, she'd felt the brush of his lips over her cheek.

It was more than distracting. Worse yet, she could not deny that it was also very pleasant. Or perhaps *stimulating* was a better word. Aye, that was exactly how he was making her feel. It was as if every inch of her skin had been jolted to perfect, sensitized awareness. The situation had become so dire that she could sense the pattern of his breathing, for goodness' sake. Her only saving grace came in the knowledge that, for all his attempts to pull her attention away from the game, she was still besting him.

Although it wouldn't have seemed possible, he was playing with less skill, even, than he'd exhibited five years ago, missing key moves that would have allowed him to capture her pieces. Yet every time she thought she might have him, he would take a move— almost as if by accident—that forced her to wait it out a bit longer.

The end was in sight now, however. He had but three pieces left on the board. If she could lull him into losing just one more, she would win the game. She kept deliberately silent and expressionless, not wanting him to catch her looking at any particular spot. There were four directions he could move with his pieces, three of which would allow her to capture it on her turn. With those odds and his poor performance thus far at the game, it seemed the most likely outcome.

Success was as good as hers.

He sat, staring at the board, tapping his upper lip. After a few moments, he heaved a great sigh, shifting his gaze to her, and she quickly averted her own, lest he read something in it. Even so, the look he'd given her sent a tingle up the back of her nape. He was up to something, she was sure of it.

Of a sudden, he reached out and made his move; it was in the fourth direction, and even worse, it allowed him to capture one of her remaining five pieces in the process.

Her mouth dropped open for an instant before she could clap it shut, a sound of exasperation bursting from her. "You cannot possibly have chosen that direction on your own!"

"Do you see anyone here to aid me?" he asked innocently, gesturing around the empty chamber with his hand. "Naught but the sand glass watches our progress . . . or I should say we are watching *its* progress."

Beth glanced to it, noticing that it was nearly empty. In a few minutes more, their hour would be finished.

"You caught me looking at the spot on the board, then," she muttered, trying hard not to sulk and not succeeding at it very well.

"I chose it all on my own," Rob countered, clearly trying not to laugh at her. "I told you I'd improved in the game. Not by practice but by thought." He tapped the side of his head this time and wiggled his brows at her. "And yes, I did look at you, but it was not to determine my next move."

"I thought I had you," Beth mumbled, readying to take her turn. Now she had only four pieces remaining. If she wasn't careful, Rob would win. And that would be unthinkable. *Rob*, beating *her* at *merels*. The words didn't even belong in the same phrase.

But as she stretched out her arm to touch her chosen piece, Rob grabbed her hand, forestalling her. She glared at him in irritation.

"Wait just a moment . . ." he murmured. He wasn't meeting her gaze but was instead looking at her arm. Or perhaps it was the board; she couldn't tell which, since they were both in the same line of his sight.

"What is it?"

"First of all, you don't want to make that move."

Beth scowled, shifting her stare back to the board. Her stomach dropped. Curse it, he was right. If she'd gone ahead to push the piece forward as she'd intended, he would have been in position to take it on his next turn.

He *was* distracting her, the lout . . .

"And second of all, you seem to have something on your wrist here . . ."

Beth was still preoccupied with studying the board so that she only half heard what he said. But she felt what he did next, as he pushed the end of her wide, belled sleeve back to her elbow and brushed the tips of his first two fingers gently over the sensitive span of skin on the underside of her arm, leading up from her wrist.

He gaze snapped to him then—or actually to his hand and the delicious sensations he was causing by touching her like that.

"You seem to have suffered a small cut here, only recently healed," he said in a quiet voice, still examining her flesh. "How did it happen?" His fingers continued to softly stroke the spot, even as he at last shifted his stare, filled with heat and tenderness, to her face.

"I . . . ah . . . I—it happened when I was sewing," she managed to say.

"I see."

Mesmerized, Beth watched as if detached from herself as he tugged her hand, pulling her arm toward him . . . toward his mouth, oh . . .

And then he was kissing her there, the sensation

of his lips against her skin light, sensual, and shiver-inducing. It spread along the whole length of her arm, tingling up to the back of her neck and sweeping down to tighten her nipples and pool in a renewed surge of delectable warmth between her thighs.

Merciful heaven . . .

The kiss was a simple one, but it felt so *good*. And then he was kissing her entire forearm, brushing his lips in a feather-light touch over that sensitive expanse—and she felt helpless to do anything about it. Absolutely and completely helpless to move, even. She was fortunate she was remembering to breathe.

The only way she knew she was doing that, still, was the fact that to her everlasting mortification, she exhaled on a soft, almost moaning sigh . . . which of course caused her to stiffen and in turn made Rob look up guiltily and release his grip on her all at once.

"Sorry." He had the good grace to appear abashed, but Beth wasn't convinced. Still, he did a fine job of seeming embarrassed. "I got a bit carried away, it seems." He sat back in his chair and waved his hands toward the board. "Please, go ahead and take your move. I wouldn't want to disrupt your concentration."

He had to be jesting.

But she refused to lose this game with her pride at stake as it was.

She took her move and sat back.

Rob considered for a moment, glanced at her, and put his fingers to his piece. She cringed inwardly as he began to push it in the direction that would evade her capture—but at the last moment, he shifted again . . .

and moved his piece into direct line with her own.

A tingle of suspicion ignited in the back of Beth's mind, but she subdued it and took her final move, capturing his piece.

Rob threw up his hands. "You've won!" He shook his head, making a feigned sound of disgust in his throat. "That was foolish on my part—I should have noticed you were in position to take me."

"Aye, you should have." Beth kept her gaze even upon him, trying to determine how sincere he was being.

He only sighed and smiled, leaning back from the board with his hands linked behind his head. "Ah, well. Perhaps I simply need a bit more practice. What say you to letting me try again on the morrow, during our hour's time together?"

"I—well, yes, if it pleases you to do so."

"It does. However, I also think that—"

He stopped mid-sentence, glancing over to the sand glass still perched on the hearth, before looking back at her to say, "Sadly, lady, it seems that our time has run out." His cheery tone belied his somber words, however, and she frowned at him as he pushed away from the little table and stood, offering her a brief bow and a smile before turning on his heel and heading for the door.

"Wait just a moment, my lord," she called, her voice also belying her words, for though they were very polite, her tone was far sharper. "While I will not belabor the propriety of actually bidding someone *adieu* upon leaving them, I will insist that you tell me what you were going to say, when you stopped mid-thought."

He halted at the portal, twisting to look at her with that mischievous glint at full force again in his eyes. "My apologies, lady. I was only going to point out that I wish to play tomorrow's game for different stakes. And I think it fitting for *you* to determine the prize, as you are the winner of the game today."

What? By the Rood, she'd almost forgotten. Winning today meant that tonight she'd be the recipient of his—

"Remember to choose well, however," he called, just before he vanished through the door, so that his remaining words echoed from the corridor. "I intend to win on the morrow, and I want you to enjoy giving me my prize as much as I plan to enjoy rewarding you with yours this eve."

She heard his chuckle, though in the next instant his head appeared in the doorway once more, that sinful smile still curving his lips. "Oh, and farewell, love. Until tonight, that is."

Sweet angels and saints . . .

But before she could formulate any kind of further response, the knave winked at her . . . and then he was gone.

Chapter 6

Alex wondered whether Beth would appear at supper that night. Servants were already clearing away the stew trenchers, though they left behind the bread and cheese, but thus far she hadn't deigned to come into the great hall.

Since leaving her, he'd spent the intervening hours as he had every day since arriving at Dunleavy, occupied in various activities required of him as castle lord. It had been a busy afternoon, to be sure. For a start, he'd ridden through the western portion of the demesne and seen more than a dozen peasant tofts, as well as several of the plots that supplied the castle with grain, which was as usual cultivated in alternating strips of fallow and planted fields. The barley in particular had looked healthy and strong, and the oats nearly as much.

Back in the bailey, he'd been called to the chapel building, where he'd heard the complaints of the tile maker and the plasterer, each of whom was getting in the other's way as they attempted to repair a corner of the building damaged during Lord Lennox's last siege. And later in the afternoon the falconer had greeted him, giving him a walk through the mews, while the brewer had pulled him aside just afterward, enticing him to sample her first-run, strong ale spiced with ginger, toasted rosemary, and fennel.

Lastly, he'd met with Edwin, his steward, to have a brief walk with him through the castle gardens and to instruct him in preparations for the upcoming feast Dunleavy would be hosting in the near future—a far grander event than the one Beth had been able to pull together so quickly on the day of his arrival at Dunleavy, and one to which all the local nobility would be invited . . . including Lord Lennox.

Edwin had been quiet and attentive, but Alex sensed an undercurrent of resentment, or mayhap even mistrust, in the man. It did not bode well, for the steward was second in position of power only to the lord and lady of the castle. If Alex could not persuade Edwin to his side, the possibility of trouble brewing with this ruse Lord Exford had embroiled him in would increase by leaps and bounds.

He would needs work on the steward, Alex decided. But it could wait until tomorrow. Daylight was waning, and he was impatient for Beth to show herself. Alex decided to wait a bit longer, instead sitting back in his chair and studying the many people who partook of the bread, cheese, and spiced ale that would be their last food until breaking their fast after Mass in the morn. Several of those in attendance caught his gaze and lifted a cup or hand in salute, and he responded in kind.

His gaze glanced off Stephen and Luc, who seemed to be getting on well with the other men of the garrison. Stephen, as always, seemed reserved, talking only infrequently to the man sitting beside him at the long trestle table. Luc, however, was full into his cups. Well on the way to being drunk, even. Fortunately, Luc tended toward ribald humor rather than the spilling of secrets when he imbibed too heartily. With Stephen nearby, Alex trusted that Luc would be kept in check enough to keep quiet about anything incriminating.

Taking another deep drink from his cup, Alex lifted his gaze to the mullioned windows lining the walls. The sun was setting, and it seemed his time was up. If Beth would not join him, he would find her or at least discern why she had not made an appearance, so that her seduction, which he'd begun to look forward to a bit too heartily, perhaps, could continue in the way he intended it to.

Spotting her lady's maid, he called for a serving boy, telling the lad to bring her over. She arrived posthaste, her cheeks flushed. She was having trouble meeting his gaze, and to his shock he realized that she was feeling intimidated. The idea that she considered him—*him*, Alex de Ashby, notorious reprobate and carefree carouser—an imposing and perhaps even frightening lord of the castle nearly made him choke on the last swallow of ale he'd downed. But he controlled his amusement enough to speak with her in what he hoped was a normal voice.

"Greetings, Mistress . . . ?"

"Annabel," she relayed quietly, so that he had to lean in to hear her properly.

"Aye, Mistress Annabel," he echoed, attempting to catch her gaze and put her at ease with a smile. At last she lifted her face to meet his stare for an instant, before blushing more deeply as she dropped into a curtsy.

"How may I serve you this eve, my lord?" she asked, her gaze once again trained on the floor in deference.

"I wish to know where your lady is."

That made her glance up again, though this time she wore a startled look, like a wren catching sight of a falcon prepared to swoop down for the kill.

"My—my lady?" she stuttered.

"Aye. I was expecting her at supper, and I wish to know why she has not appeared here."

Still Annabel kept her gaze locked to the stones of the floor, and Alex sighed.

This was getting ridiculous. Dipping his upper body down to force the woman to meet his gaze, Alex finished, "Do you know if aught is amiss with her, or why she has chosen not to sup?"

Annabel straightened at that, relieving him, thank God, from having to crane his neck to see her face. But he swallowed his gratitude before he could voice it, reminding himself that castle lords did not thank those beneath them in rank for any consideration done to them. Nay, they expected such treatment as a matter of course. It was far more likely, were he a true castle lord, that he might have reprimanded her for her seeming reluctance in cooperating with his attempts to gain her attention or answer his query.

Annabel coughed before answering. "My lady confessed to a—a lack of appetite this eve, my lord."

"Did she now?" Alex asked. A likely excuse, he thought. A sudden attack of cowardice might be more accurate.

"I pray she is not unwell," he said, managing to muster a tone of sincere solicitation. "She should receive immediate attention, if she has fallen sick. Is it your opinion that I should summon the surgeon to examine her?"

That got her attention.

"Oh—nay, my lord! That is—I do not think she is . . . I mean, she was only a bit tired from all the excitement of your return home. She confided to having rested but little the past few nights—"

Annabel choked off the rest of what she intended to say, apparently realizing too late how she sounded and what her comment seemed to insinuate about what he and her mistress were doing with the time they'd spent together each night, when the rest of the castle was asleep. If the maid's cheeks had seemed flushed before, then they burned crimson now.

"Forgive me, my lord," she murmured. "I meant no disrespect."

"None taken, Annabel," Alex assured her, not wanting the poor girl to faint dead away from mortification. He cleared his throat, doing his best to maintain a serious and level demeanor, as befit a man in the position he played. "I will seek her in our chamber, then. Thank you, Annab—"

"Pardon, my lord, but I—that is, I do not think you will find her in your chamber."

That, in turn, got *his* attention.

"Why not?"

"Because she—ah . . . that is, I believe she took her mount out for a short ride this afternoon, to clear her head." Annabel looked particularly nervous. "Oh— and to invigorate her palate, I am sure."

"Indeed."

Ah, this was becoming more and more interesting by the second. Until today, Beth hadn't resumed the pleasure rides his tutors had instructed him to expect. It was quite convenient for her to do so tonight, however, considering what he'd promised to deliver to her as her prize. Pushing back his seat, Alex stood, which caused him to tower over Annabel, who stood as nervous and trembling as a hare. But she was a loyal servant to Beth, there was no doubt, and that truth should be rewarded in what way he could.

"You may go, mistress. I will seek my wife, then, in the stables before I venture to our chamber. Perhaps she has returned and desires some light sustenance, should the ride have . . . invigorated her appetite as she hoped."

Annabel nodded primly, her mouth tight, before she glanced up at him from beneath her lashes, as if taking his measure. She waited for the space of several full beats, but she must have seen something in him of which she approved, for of a sudden she added, "My lord, you might wish to try the pleasure garden as well. In the years you were away it has become Lady Elizabeth's habit to spend some time there after riding and her bath."

Alex was too surprised to voice an answer, instead simply nodding in response. And with that, Annabel bobbed a curtsy, a tiny smile curving her lips now as she scooted away from the high table.

Through his continued shock, Alex simply stared after her, only moving from his position when the serving boy approached and asked him if he required aught else. Shaking his head, he stepped down from the slightly raised dais of the high table and strode from the great hall. He chose the corridor that would take him to the kitchens first and then to the outer reaches of the bailey where he would continue on to the attractive, enclosed pleasure garden nearby; it was set close to the orchard, and though the kitchen garden boasted a wide array of pungent herbs and medicinal flowers, the pleasure garden was a sensual experience of a whole other kind.

It was a place of peacefulness and beauty, and he was not surprised to hear that Beth had chosen it as her refuge. More surprising to him by far was the way he had learned about it. It seemed he'd found an unexpected ally in Beth's lady's maid, and though such a boon had been unforeseen, he was grateful for it. As he strode toward his destination, he realized just how fortuitous this was. It would play well—very well—into the plans he had for Elizabeth this night.

Aye, Beth was about to receive the prize she had earned by besting him at *merels* today . . . for the only force greater than her desire to hide from him was his determination to find her.

A truth she would be discovering for herself very soon.

Beth leaned back against a fragrant turf seat that was hidden behind the arbor in the pleasure garden, exhaling a sigh of contentment and reveling in the delicious scent of the warmed earth, herbs, and flowers all around her. The turf seat itself was planted with soft, creeping thyme, with some thicker-growing chamomile nearer to the ground, and the fragrances wafted up anytime she shifted her position, as was intended.

The roses climbing all over the trellised arbor behind her lent a sweet fragrance to the air. A bit farther away, the spicy smell of the gillyflowers blended with the rich perfume of lilies and the cleaner scent of lavender, and she closed her eyes, letting it all fill her senses as she listened to the trickling waters of the garden's spring-fed fountain and a skylark's occasional song.

And she was utterly, blessedly alone.

It wasn't exactly a secret that she took her ease in this garden after riding and her bath; most of the castle servants knew of her habit. But she'd taken care to seclude herself behind the arbor tonight, knowing it would be more difficult to find her—and also knowing that none would reveal her place of privacy out of turn. Certainly no one would think to speak of it to her husband, unless he specifically asked about her . . . which she did not think he would do, even considering the "prize" he'd promised to bestow on her this night.

Nay, Rob could not be all that changed. He was a man easily distracted by work, and that was what he had gone to do after leaving her earlier today. It was far more likely that he had forgotten about all else except the many tasks awaiting him as returned lord of the castle. Because of the sparks that had seemed to ignite whenever they were near each other, they had shared an unspoken pact this past week to maintain a careful distance when constrained to be alone together. Often either she or he would retire a good deal earlier than the other, to avoid any further uncomfortable scenes as had happened the first night.

With continued luck, she was bound to find him snoring happily away tonight when she crept into their bedchamber after her brief respite here.

In the meantime, she could cherish her half hour in this cool, leafy retreat. Being freed from the weight of her many duties, for even a short time, was a relief. Of course, with Rob returned to Dunleavy, that should not matter as much, but it did. Despite what Father Paul had said, she was still having difficulty relinquishing the burden of responsibility she had borne alone here for so long. It wasn't that she did not wish to. Nay, she nearly ached with the desire to hand it off—but only if she could do so with a peaceful heart. It was those nagging doubts that kept her from truly letting go.

As a result, she'd found herself anticipating her ride outside the castle walls more keenly than usual, reveling in those even more indulgent moments afterward, when she need not be accompanied by any lady's maid or protective castle guard. She had hardly been able to wait until her tub had been emptied and removed after her bath, so that she could send her attendants away and be left to her own devices.

Closing her eyes and leaning fully back now, she once more breathed in the many fragrances surrounding her. There was only one thing that marred her perfect enjoyment, and that was—

A loud gurgling suddenly erupted, in conjunction with a twisting sensation in her belly, and she winced. Aye, that was it, and she could curse her own stupidity for it. Missing supper to avoid reminding Rob of their wager's outcome was one thing, but forgetting to pack herself at least a portion of bread and cheese was entirely another. Because of it, she would not be able to linger here as long as she might have otherwise. Staring down at her belly with a mutinous expression, Beth gave a long sigh and then tipped her head back, closing her eyes as she willed her stomach to cease its demands for just a bit longer so that she could enjoy a few moments more of peaceful solitude . . .

A sudden rustling sound erupted in the foliage behind her, and Beth stiffened, her eyes snapping open as she twisted around to look toward the center of the garden. She held her breath, seeking out the intruder. Dusk was beginning to settle, but there was enough light still, even through the arbor weavings, to make out the contours of the rectangular beds, turf seats, the fountain at the center, and the single stone bench that sat farther off, beneath the willow in the corner of the garden.

Squinting, she waited with bated breath. There was more movement, and then, suddenly, a furred brown and white head poked into view from beneath a thick cluster of mint plants next to the bench.

Beth's heartbeat skipped for an instant and then immediately slowed. *Of course.* One of the stable cats must have found an opening in the garden wall and come in, chasing a mouse or a bird. Now the graceful feline leaped up onto the seat, blinking at Beth with a sanguine expression on its face before settling in to lick its paw and wash itself.

Shaking her head and releasing her breath on a nervous laugh, Beth settled back into her former position and closed her eyes again. Several more blissful minutes passed with naught more to disturb her than her empty stomach and the rising chorus of chirping crickets. But then a new distraction arose, tempting her to get up again from her peaceful position. Yet because of what had happened with the cat, she kept her eyes closed, remained still, and tried to convince herself that it was her imagination, even though the sensation was persistent.

It felt like the touch of soft, fluttering wings brushing over her face. And after a few moments, she realized with a start that whatever it was smelled suspiciously of roses.

At almost the same time, a familiar voice rumbled close to her, in a tone containing just a hint of a smile, "This is a lovely place of escape, my lady . . . but you will have to do better if you wish to avoid me altogether."

Choking back a gasp, Beth lurched forward away from the turf bench, twisting to face Rob and spilling in the process the handful of rose petals he'd been sprinkling over her before he spoke.

"I—what are you doing here?" she croaked, experiencing that bewildering sensation that often follows an abrupt awakening from a daydream. He was grinning at her, even as he leaned back with nonchalance against the arbor trellis. His brow lifted.

"I came seeking you, to fulfill the terms of our wager, of course."

That set off an oddly pleasurable twisting sensation inside her. But before she could muster a response, he held out to her the remainder of the fragrant petals he'd apparently collected to sprinkle over her, asking, "Are these the same that you use in your perfumed oil, lady? The scent seems familiar."

Mutely, she nodded, and with her answer he pushed away from the trellis to walk toward her.

"Nay, stay where you are," he murmured when she made a move as if to stand. "I will sit with you here for a while, with your consent."

"Of course," she answered, though inside a struggle was raging between feeling flattered and experiencing jittery anxiety about what might come next. She gestured to the large, lidded basket he held as he approached. "What have you brought there?"

"Part of your prize." He again gave her that half smile that melted her insides to warmed honey.

She did not speak further, however, as he settled in beside her, having decided that silence was far better than the dim-witted questions and comments she seemed bound to make on a regular basis whenever she was in his presence. Instead, she sat back against the soft turf, knowing he would tell her what the basket contained in his own time.

"Aren't you a little curious, even?" he teased, having apparently noticed her self-restraint.

A mouthwatering scent drifted up from the basket, and Beth's stomach made another very unladylike gurgling sound, clenching to remind her once more that it had been hours since she'd eaten. It might have been days, for how hollow she was feeling.

Ah well, she would have to brave the possibility of further ridicule, she supposed. The demands of her appetite could not be denied.

"Perhaps I am a bit curious," she admitted. She looked at him hopefully. "Is there any food in there by chance?"

"I thought you'd never ask." He flipped open the

lid to reveal an absolute feast. Well, in her famished state it looked like a feast, anyway. A clean linen cloth was folded along the side, and Rob pulled it out, snapping it open to smooth out the creases, and spread it in front of her, before he began to bring out the victuals: a lovely pork and almond-milk pie baked in an open crust, wild cherries held in a knotted kerchief, a thick loaf of bread, as well as several slices of rich golden cheese. Lastly, he placed beside all a sack of red wine and some finger towels for wiping their hands afterward.

"My, this is . . . wonderful. I cannot imagine that you thought to bring all of—" She stopped herself, not wanting to be rude, even if it was the truth. She settled for asking something just as honest. "Do you not mind eating supper out of doors, then? Even in the dark?"

Rob shrugged. "I find the setting quite pleasant."

"Aye, well, it *is* a pleasure garden."

"You see?" He grinned when she laughed at him. "I find naught to keep us from enjoying it. However, if you'll be patient just a bit longer, I can remedy one inconvenience, perhaps . . ."

He got up and strode out of view behind the arbor, ostensibly disappearing through the walled gate for a few moments before he came back into the garden, this time bearing two lit lanterns. They cast elongated shadows as he approached her again, for the sun's rim had dipped below the horizon by now, leaving naught but rippling lines of deep orange and crimson in the sky to indicate its leaving.

"Here we are," he announced, sitting down next to her again and positioning the lanterns on either side of the linen cloth. He pulled out a knife and began to cut thick wedges from the pork pie. "It's much better if you can see what you're eating, I think."

Just then, a low, strumming sound lilted across the garden, brought on the breeze. The tune was a familiar one—a haunting song of love unrequited—but it was so unusual to hear such a sound here, out of doors, that in the moments after the first notes echoed forth, Beth looked at Rob in bewilderment.

"I bid the minstrel bring his lute; at my signal he was to play awhile for us, outside the garden gate." He glanced up from readying the food, a twinkle in his eyes. "Retrieving the lamps was the signal."

Her surprise could not have been greater if he had told her that the King of Scotland would be joining them to sup this night.

Rob caught her expression. "I only thought that the music might further your enjoyment of this place, lady."

"You appear to have considered everything," Beth said, glancing down, somewhat abashed.

"And I've only just begun."

The rich, seductive tone of those murmured words made her look at him again—which in turn made her flush when she met his playful gaze.

A sense of awkwardness invaded her suddenly, and she didn't know whether she felt like laughing or crying. The old Rob never would have thought to arrange something like this for himself or for her. That the new Rob had done so was both welcome and unsettling. But she *was* enjoying herself, and there was no harm in that. Father Paul had suggested that she try to relax and allow herself to learn anew of this enigmatic man who was her husband, and so that was what she would do, she decided.

In the meantime, her awkwardness prompted her to pick up the sack of wine; she saw that it was one of the better vintages Dunleavy possessed, purchased from traders of southern climes, who came to the marketplace twice a year.

"This is more suited for a celebration than a simple supper, isn't it?" she asked, mostly to have something to say, before she set it back down.

"This *is* a celebration, lady—of your victory over me this morn."

She smiled back at him. "Well, if feeding me is part of what you had in mind for a prize, then I must commend you for it. I'm famished."

"I'm relieved to hear that you've recovered."

Beth gazed at him blankly, having no idea what he was talking about.

His pointed look was full of amusement as he added in the face of her very pregnant pause, "Do you not recall—Mistress Annabel?"

"Annabel?" Beth asked, wishing he would get on with it so that she could begin eating. "What of her?"

"She is the one who explained to me the reason you did not come down to supper in the great hall. Your loss of appetite came on . . . rather suddenly, it seems." He gazed at her devilishly. "Or so she claimed."

Memory slid into place with horrifying precision. She coughed, mumbling something about her appetite indeed being renewed, and finishing up that assertion with what she hoped was a disarming smile. But as her stomach was growling insistently by now, she determined to forgo any further niceties and asked boldly, "Do you mind, then, if I begin?"

"By all means," he answered, gesturing to the food and drink he'd spread out before her. "Here, allow me to help you—"

He didn't have time to finish before she lifted up a slice of the succulent pie and took a bite. The flavors burst in her mouth, smooth, rich, and savory. The crust was tender, filled with well-seasoned minced pork and chopped egg yolk, accented by the creamy almond milk. With an audible sigh, she closed her eyes, chewing and swallowing as if he'd presented her with manna from the heavens. Only when she'd polished off the entire thick slice and picked up a second did she look up to meet his astonished expression.

"Aren't you going to have any?" she asked.

He laughed as he watched the avidity with which she dug into the second slice of the pie. "I will. I'm rather enjoying watching you at the moment."

"Mmmmmmm, it's delicious," was all Beth managed to say for some time, as she finished the second slice and went on to sample the cheese and a bit of bread as well, all washed down with the hearty red wine. When she finally leaned back again on the turf seat, it was with a groan.

"I don't think I can manage another bite."

"I'm not surprised," Rob answered, gracing her with an appreciative look. "The fresh air must have done wonders in sharpening your sickly appetite."

"Knave. You know I was never truly ailing."

"Of course. But it's much more enjoyable to keep teasing you about it."

She glanced over at him, noticing the way his eyes crinkled at the corners when he laughed. It was a small thing, perhaps, but she noticed. And somehow, that mundane detail unleashed a swell of gratitude inside her.

"Thank you," she murmured, "for being so chivalrous in your efforts to make me feel comfortable with you again."

A beat of raw silence passed between them. Afraid she might decline into maudlin sentiment and embarrass them both, she placed her hand on her chest dramatically and added half in jest, "You are a man of great honor, sir, to provide sustenance for your lady even considering her appalling absence from your supper table. It truly rises above and beyond the call of husbandly duty."

She was surprised to catch a glimpse of what appeared to be a slight wince before he returned her gentle mockery with an exaggerated nod and flourish. "It is naught, my sweet—nor are we finished yet, for you still have not sampled the cherries I was so solicitous to procure for your enjoyment. Still, the night is young, and your appetite will undoubtedly return again ere long . . ."

With a soft laugh, Beth threw a handful of grass from the base of the turf seat at him.

To her delighted surprise, he grinned and returned fire, leaving her to pick grass and a few errant chamomile leaves from her hair while he cleaned up the remnants of their supper. In a matter of moments, all the scraps and dirtied cloths were placed back in the basket. All except for the square of soft linen that had served as their tablecloth.

"Don't you wish to take that up as well?" she asked.

"Nay." At her look, he added, "I have use of it yet."

"For what?"

"A moment's repose, perhaps." As he spoke, he stood, unfolding his tall, strong body in all its breathtaking magnificence. Her breath caught as he held out his hand to her as smoothly as the most celebrated court gallant. "Would you care to join me there, lady? I warrant it will be almost as comfortable as reclining against the turf seat." He gave her a half smile. "Perhaps even more."

"Oh . . ."

By heaven, she needed to stop murmuring that inane word every time Rob did or said something that took her by surprise. But then her hand was in his, and he was leading her onto the cloth, helping her to sit on it with him, so that her back rested against his chest, and her hips were cradled between his outstretched legs. It was quite a shock, after spending the week with little more by way of touching each other than the occasional brush of their hands at mealtimes. As he wrapped his arms around her now, she felt swept into another place . . . warm and safe . . . and very, very aware of his masculine presence.

He was a physically powerful man, and being held against him like this, feeling every warm, hard ridge of muscle at play in his chest and arms whenever he moved, made that more apparent than it was upon just looking at him. But the tenderness in his touch belied the deadly skill he could wield and provided a stunning contrast as she sat cradled in his embrace.

And then he lifted one hand to push her hair

away from her neck, exposing her sensitive skin to the cooler night air and allowing the warmth of his breath to brush over her . . .

She closed her eyes, her head tipping slightly sideways as she waited for him to touch his lips to her there. But he didn't kiss her. Nay, not yet.

After a long silence filled only by the night sounds, the softly strumming lute in the distance, and their own breathing, Beth felt Rob stir behind her.

"What it is, my lord?" she asked quietly.

"I wish to speak something to you, Beth. Something you alone should hear"—his voice caught for an instant, and she sensed rather than saw his smile—"for I do not think any other at Dunleavy would understand such things, coming from me. It is a ballade."

She mastered her surprise long enough to give a short nod, but she was loath to move too much from her position, pleasurable as she found it. When he spoke at last, murmuring the words into her ear, the wonderful, shivery sensation increased tenfold, while the words themselves made her heart twist for their beauty.

"Her song fills my soul with painful joy," he said, his voice a quiet rumble, "and the memory of her lips I cannot escape. In the cold black of night her fire inflames me. Only her embrace will bring my heart ease."

He paused for a beat before continuing, "I am the parched earth, barren and cracked. Without her near, my sight dims. She is balm to my spirit. Her touch revives me. Only her embrace will bring my heart ease."

Beth turned her head enough to meet Rob's gaze,

all her senses alight, it seemed. "What is it called?" she murmured.

"I do not know. I learned it during my imprisonment, from a French courtier who used to recite it on nights when the moon shone full into our dungeon cell." He blinked, still gazing down at her, and the emotions flickering in the stormy blue of his eyes made Beth's heart skip a beat. She swallowed, barely breathing.

"The words remind me of you, lady," he said. Tipping his head slightly down, he pressed a kiss to her temple, following that with a gentle sweep of his lips across the shell of her ear. She closed her eyes, his caress letting loose a wave of sparkling, delicious sensation across her nape and down her spine, spreading around to the front of her and causing her nipples to tighten into aching buds. Her breath released on a sigh, and she felt the whisper of his breath again as he spoke once more.

"Would you like to hear the final verse?"

She nodded, feeling incapable of speech at the moment. She just leaned back against his broad chest as he continued to recite the ballade with quiet passion.

"Death will bring no end to my torment. My love is as boundless as the rising sea. I will battle any enemy for the sake of her kiss . . ."

He paused to do just that again, this time touching his lips to the tender spot beneath her earlobe. Swept up in the beauty of it all, Beth stroked her palms over the strong contours of his hands, and she felt the muscles in his arms contract around her in response. His voice dropped to a huskier note as he finally finished, "Only her embrace will bring my heart ease."

Then he fell silent again; all that could be heard was the tinkling of the fountain and the chirping of the night crickets. The minstrel had stopped playing, it seemed, though when, she had no idea, for she hadn't even noticed.

"That was lovely," she said finally, when she could trust her voice again.

"Not as lovely as you are, lady."

Shifting her in his arms so that she sat sideways in his lap, Rob cupped her cheek in his palm, tilting her face up to him to take her mouth sweetly, hungrily with his own. She opened to him, felt the warm, silky-smooth sensation as his lips slid across hers, nibbling, tasting, pulling away for half a breath before coming back for more.

His kisses were long and slow and wonderful, and as the seconds drifted by, her hand slipped up his arm, over his shoulder, and up to tangle in the soft dark waves at his nape. She pulled him closer to hungry for the taste and feel of him in a w went beyond aught she had known before.

After a few moments more of that e tion, he shifted his mouth slightly the line of her jaw. When he got he nipped the lobe between h murmured "You're delicious passionate kisses down t igniting the warmth alr and making her rise press herself aga pressed against

ing him more of the place he was kissing . . . exposing more of herself to his mouth.

Easing her down to the linen cloth, Rob leaned over her and brushed a stray tendril of hair from her cheek before smoothing that warm palm down the side of her throat and sliding it under the edge of her gown near her shoulder.

Tugging on the neckline, he exposed a bit more of her skin. Her clothing was too fitted to pull any farther unless he first slipped off her sleeveless surcoat and at least partway unlaced the gown beneath; in some strange way she felt relieved about that, lying here as they were in the garden. But in the next instant her more wanton nature came to the fore; her breasts strained against the confines of her bodice, and an image shot through her mind of Rob exposing her to his sight and touch. Her fingers clenched in his shirt in response, and her breath came in pants with devote any further attention to it, Rob was kissing her again, this time interspersing those caresses with light strokes of his tongue, teasing a path just beneath her collarbone. Through a kind of sensual fog, she felt his hands on her laces, felt him slip her surcoat off her arms, before gently tugging at the opening of her gown. Another moment longer and she experienced the brush of night air across her heated flesh, making her gasp with the sensual contrast.

"By all the saints but you are beautiful, Beth," Rob murmured, his voice hoarse with passion.

In the flickering lamplight, she watched his large, warm hands close over her naked breasts, cupping, squeezing gently, and she sucked in her breath at the incredible feeling of it. He caressed her, pausing to rub his lightly callused palms in a circular motion over her erect, sensitive nipples. It was pure pleasure, and she pressed upward into his touch, unable to stop herself.

"And this, Beth," he asked raggedly, "tell me, do you like this?" As he spoke he bent his head down, guiding the tip of one breast into the warm and delightfully wet, hot depths of his mouth.

The shock of it shot tendrils of need deep into her core, at last dragging a groaning cry from her.

"Ahhh, yes, yes," she cried softly, writhing and arching as he suckled gently at her nipples, first one, then the other. She was desperate to feel more, to be closer, somehow, to him. Oh, but she wanted to touch and taste and drive him to distraction as he was doing to her.

Emboldened, she allowed her hands to lift up and tangle in the wavy softness of his hair as he tasted of

her breasts, letting her palms travel farther down to
brush over his shoulders, feeling the rippling muscles
in his arms beneath his shirt as he balanced himself
over her. Her touch drifted down farther and farther,
past the smooth contours of his sides and across the
flat, hard expanse of his belly, covered by naught but
the thin barrier of cloth . . . until she reached the part
of him that was straining for her against his breeches
with as much yearning as the melting sensation she
was feeling inside her was driving her toward the
same magnificent conclusion.

She closed her hand over his erection . . .

And felt him go still abruptly, while she gasped.

He was so . . . large. More so than she remembered
him being. Confusion flooded her for a moment.
She felt the veil of worry and doubt closing over her
again, all her uncertainties rising to the surface—only
to have them submerged once more by the wash of
startling, delicious sensation that spilled through her
as he pressed another kiss to her throat, even as his
hand slipped beneath her skirt to connect with unbearable pleasure at the juncture of her thighs.

"And what of this, lady?" he asked raggedly, his
strong, elegant fingers sweeping up and stroking her
silken folds. "Should I continue doing this?"

She moaned and cried out simultaneously with the
bliss of it, sparks dancing across her vision, unable to
keep from bucking up against his hand and the devastating expertise of his touch on her.

"Yes—oh, yes," she managed to gasp, the words
murmured against his mouth, for he'd come back to
tenderly, thoroughly kiss her again. Still she had not
released the part of him that throbbed and burned

against her palm through the cloth of his breeches, and as she clenched her hand, squeezing gently, he groaned.

"Ah, lady, it is too good—you must stop, lest I can control myself no longer."

"I don't want to stop," she confessed, overcome by all the feelings coursing through her, both physical and emotional. Nothing made logical sense anymore. Naught was to be examined or explained about this reaction she was having to this man who was her husband yet so much a stranger to her.

Aye, she had found herself married to an exciting, passionate stranger who was making her feel more loved in his care than she had ever felt before. Who was making her *feel* in a way she had never known.

"I want you to make love to me, Rob," she whispered hoarsely against his lips. "There is no need to wait longer. Be with me now, and take me again as your true wife."

Somewhere in the far reaches of her mind, Beth felt a tingle of warning in the way his body tensed ever so slightly as she spoke. There was no denying that he hesitated for an instant. But with all that she was feeling, the twinge of it passed by in favor of the heat and need and passion that gripped her.

In the next instant, he had loosed his breeches, and she opened her thighs to guide him eagerly to her. With a murmured endearment, he thrust forward just a bit, carefully, for though she felt the tension in his body and knew he fought against the instinct to drive deep, he was holding himself back. Impatient and greedy for him, Beth tugged him closer, lifting her hips in a wordless plea for more.

Rob murmured in a voice strangled by passion, "I don't want to hurt you by going too quickly, love." But she shook her head, beyond words as she urged him on.

At last with a groan, he thrust a second time, smoothly and fully, impaling her with the thick, blunt length of him and causing her to cry out with the ecstasy of it. He remained still once he was buried inside her—stunned, almost, it seemed—filling her completely.

But then he withdrew partway, and with a kind of jerking spasm slid deep again. And again, and again.

It felt magnificent.

Stars clouded Beth's vision, and as if from a distance, she heard her own breath coming in sobbing gasps, even as she began to rock up into his thrusts, the rhythm they fell into driving and almost desperate.

It had been so long. And it felt so good. He felt so wonderfully, splendidly good.

The sweet tension seemed to wind tighter and tighter with every thrust of him against her, into her. Arching up into him, Beth cried out soft, unintelligible words, gripping his back and feeling the flex of his muscles beneath her fingers, aware that every muscle in her own body was going rigid, reaching, tightening, readying to release into something . . . something more . . .

With one final thrust, Beth felt herself shatter into unimaginable bliss, her body seeming to slip away like water to leave nothing behind but pure, sweet feeling. The force of it took over her senses, and she was swept along on the tide without control anymore, her body clenching and contracting against that hard flesh buried deep inside her. Overcome with the unexpected force of it, she cried out again, curling up toward him, grasping him close, and pressing her lips to his neck—feeling him shudder to his release at almost the same time.

Sweet angels and saints, she'd never known such pleasure in lovemaking with Rob before. Never, oh, God . . . never before.

Her breath was coming in gasps, and the man lying atop her was breathing just as swiftly, his chest heaving as he pushed himself off her slightly sideways. He lay still then as did she, both of them too exhausted by what they'd just shared to do aught else for several long, delicious moments.

"Beth," he murmured at last, his voice a husky rumble. "Beth, I—"

She opened her eyes just as he ceased in uttering the rest of what he had been going to say. He had lifted his head and was gazing down at her with an enigmatic expression, his look of satiation mingled with a touch of astonishment. He seemed almost surprised. It pleased her at the same time that it set off another tiny jangle inside her. But her uneasiness was more easily dismissed this time under the force of the repletion easing like warm oil through her veins.

"Sweet Jesu, lady," he said, reaching out to brush a tendril of hair from her brow, and Beth impulsively clasped his fingers, bringing them to her lips to press kisses upon them.

"I know," she whispered, nodding and smiling like a fool, she was certain. "I felt it too."

He swallowed hard, still staring at her. "I—I do

not know what to say, Beth, except that I—that is, you—"

"My lord! My lord Marston!"

Scrambling to sit up, Beth yanked at her gown, desperate to put it in order again as she twisted to see who was coming through the garden gate.

Rob fumbled with his breeches, lurching to stand as he bellowed, "Hold, sir, and reveal yourself by name!"

It was too dark beyond the circle of light cast by the lanterns to see much, but she knew the voice and the shadow of the man who came to an abrupt halt at his lord's command.

"It is Edwin, my lord," she murmured, at the same time that the steward called out, confirming his identity. Beth fumbled as she tried to lace her bodice again, mortified that anyone, especially Rob's very proper steward, might see her in this state of undress. Her surcoat lay crumpled on the ground, somewhere beyond the light, but it would simply have to wait.

"Are you covered decently?" Rob asked in a quiet enough voice that only she could hear him.

"Aye. Well enough."

She saw him turn back toward the gate and Edwin. "Approach and state your business."

"Pardon, my lord—my lady," Edwin mumbled, seeing Beth but clearly trying to avoid looking directly at her. "There is a disturbance in the village, my lord, that requires your immediate attention."

"I trust it involves someone's imminent demise," Rob said in a clipped voice, "for I do not relish such disruptions for matters that might wait until morn."

"It does, my lord," Edwin answered, all trace of

his former awkwardness replaced by the cool, calm demeanor Beth recognized so well. His tone, however, was tinged with a kind of smugness that sent a prickle up Beth's spine.

In the next heartbeat he finished his explanation, and as he spoke, her trepidations were confirmed.

"I am here to report that one of your comrades brought from England is in mortal danger. Even now a mob has gathered in the village square . . . and if I am not mistaken, they intend to hoist him from the nearest hanging tree."

Chapter 7

Alex grasped Beth's hand as they followed Edwin out of the garden, calling upon all his will to remain focused on the task at hand instead of thinking about what had just happened between them. Their lovemaking had shocked and humbled him, the intensity with which she had responded to him and he to her having taken him by surprise. He hadn't prepared himself for that, thinking only to do what had needed to be done to solidify his position at Dunleavy as lord and husband—hoping to give Beth some enjoyment in it, aye, and using all his skills toward that end. But never had he envisioned the depth of pleasure they'd ended up sharing together.

In the moments since, he'd struggled to come to terms with it and with the unexpected shadow of something far less pleasant as well. It was that blade of guilt again, as unfathomable as it was to believe. If he hadn't felt the sting of it himself, he would have denied the possibility, for time and again he'd proven to himself and everyone around him how blithely he could overlook what would make the conscience of most men twinge.

But this was no twinge; it was a full-blown ache.

It nagged at him, refusing to dissipate no matter how he willed it to recede into the nether regions of his thoughts.

It was absurd. He had done what was necessary for this mission, for John's continued safety, and for the fulfillment of Beth's desires as well. She had been ready; she had asked him to make love to her, damn it.

Then why was he letting it get to him like this? He couldn't allow a sudden attack of scruples or whatever it was to distract him right now, and so he forced himself to direct his thoughts once more toward matters more pressing at the moment. To consider every scenario and try to prepare himself for what he might find once they reached the village, where the people were preparing to hang either Stephen or Luc. He'd retrieved his sword and belted it on, and they'd procured torches before setting off down the path toward the main gate.

Once through, they'd headed to the village a scant quarter mile below.

As they strode swiftly forward Alex shifted his gaze to Edwin and asked, "Which one of my English comrades is it, and why do the people wish him harm?" He was careful not to allow his demeanor to change, even though the seriousness of what all this might mean in light of his assignment at Dunleavy sat like a rock in his gut.

"It is Sir Lucas, my lord."

Damn.

Based upon past experiences with Luc when they'd both served in the Templar Brotherhood, Alex had a horrible inkling about what the steward was going to say next, concerning the matter for which Luc had fallen into trouble.

"It seems that a hue and cry was raised in the village after he was discovered in a compromising position with the blacksmith's bonny lass, Jane, betrothed these six months to the weaver's son."

"Sir Lucas won her away from her intended in so short a time?" Beth asked in disbelief. "He has been at Dunleavy barely a sennight." She sounded a bit breathless from their swift pace—or perhaps still from what they'd been doing before Edwin's most inopportune interruption—but regardless, Alex shortened his stride and slowed down.

In the awkward silence that ensued, he glanced to his steward, demanding an answer by his expression.

Edwin cleared his throat. "I—that is, ah . . . it appears that Jane did not go willingly with Sir Lucas, my lady."

That brought Beth up short.

"Perhaps you had better wait in the castle, Beth," Alex said, pausing with her. "What we find may not be a sight for your eyes."

She made a scoffing sound. "Nay, my lord. I will go with you." Her expression tightened. "If Jane has been ruined, then more substantial aid may be required. But for now I wish to be present at least in support of her."

Alex gave her a short nod, and the three of them fell into silence as they strode the remainder of the way to the village.

The sight that greeted them when they arrived was chaotic at best. It was dark and difficult to see, but he could tell that a large group of people pushed and moved against one another like an angry sea as they approached. Coming closer, he heard the occasional shout of "Lord Marston will settle this!" and "Wait for Lord Marston!" It seemed to be all that was holding the two factions back from literally clashing with each other.

It was fortunate that the real Lord Marston had wielded such power and respect, Alex thought, for in the gleam of torchlights held high, he saw that a third of Dunleavy's well-trained garrison faced off against a score of farmers, villagers, and tradesmen wielding axes, rusty swords, and—in the blacksmith's case—hot irons. A group of women and children from the village were crying and huddled behind the village menfolk—Jane and her mother likely among them—but Alex saw that more than a few were brandishing makeshift weapons of their own and shouting for justice as well.

It would be carnage if the groups went at each other, besides which these people were all part of the same demesne and in the habit of protecting and supporting one another, not calling for one another's blood.

Right now the division between them took the form of a small building they flanked, with the garrison on one side and the villagers on the other; it was no more than a hovel, really—naught but four short walls, a badly thatched roof, and a door—likely the dwelling of one of the village's poorest cotters.

It did not take a scholar to deduce that Luc was holed up in the place.

"Part for Lord and Lady Marston. They are

here!" someone shouted from the crowd as they approached.

Alex murmured for Edwin to remain with Beth as she made her way behind the throng of villagers to give comfort to Jane and her family; before she went, she nodded her encouragement to him, her beautiful face tight with concern.

The sea of people began to quiet somewhat as more caught sight of him, ebbing farther apart into two distinct groups as he entered their midst. He paused midway to the hovel's door, and the noise faded, leaving an uneasy silence hovering over the area. He met the gazes of several men in the villagers' crowd, including that of Jane's father, William Lott, and he also shifted his glance to the men of his garrison. Unsurprisingly, Stephen stood toward the front of the garrison group, nearest to the door of the cot. He was frowning, his expression more severe than usual; however, Alex made sure not to single him out with a look, for fear of adding any fuel to this already blazing fire Luc had begun with his reprehensible actions this night.

When he had everyone's attention, he called out, "I have been told the circumstances of this riotous gathering, and will order the accused taken and confined to Dunleavy's dungeon until the morrow, when I will convene a group of men to hear evidence that I may pass judgment in a hallmoot." He let his gaze lock with William's as he added, "As your lord I vow to seek out the truth in this matter and dispense justice with an even hand, calling any who wish to add testimony to come to the great hall after morning Mass."

William, his eyes reddened and his face hard with the anguish of a father whose daughter has been defiled, paused for a long moment before he gave Alex a sharp nod, indicating his compliance. The garrison echoed with the low-keyed sounds of men concurring with his command and his promise.

Alex nodded, directing his gaze at last to the hovel, and saying only slightly less loudly as he strode toward its door, "And now since I bought the wretch in, it is only fitting that I be the one to take him out."

Beth watched, sick at heart over all that had transpired, as Rob delivered a clipped order to the guards who carried the almost insensible Sir Lucas into Dunleavy. She watched them obey the command, pulling the errant knight toward the door that led to the small dungeon chamber below the main keep. The room was the only one in the castle suited for the purpose, though it had seen little use as such in the past decade. It was windowless and had a portion sectioned off by a barred door—in all, not an especially comfortable place, being so dark and enclosed.

But it was far less horrid than the dungeon keep of her own father's castle, which was older by a hundred years and prone to slime and rodents.

Then she just stood still, watching Rob as the bustle of serving lads and maids swirled around them, caused by this unusual nighttime disruption. His back was to her as he spoke to Edwin, but she could see the tightness in his muscles and sense the brooding anxiety that pervaded him—not entirely unexpected, she supposed, bearing in mind that the events tonight involved a man he had deemed a worthy enough friend to be brought into his home after their escape from England.

Thank heavens for one small boon: They'd discovered that Jane hadn't been violated in the fullest and most base sense of the word. Sir Lucas had been drunk, and his shameful deed had been interrupted by the arrival of some village lads who had heard Jane's struggles. It was still a serious matter, to be sure, but the fact that no lasting harm had been done to the young woman might mean Rob could dispense a lighter sentence, should the testimony fall as it appeared it would.

And yet perhaps that was what weighed on her husband so heavily, she could not help but think. He'd *wanted* to mete out a more punishing justice to Sir Lucas, if the way he'd dragged him from the hovel was any indication.

Even now, Beth's heart rose up in her throat with the memory of it. First the trepidation at realizing Rob had gone in alone after a desperate man accused of a shameful crime . . . and then her greater surprise in the moments that followed. They'd all heard great crashing and brawling sounds from inside the decrepit cot. But before long, Rob had appeared in the doorway, his expression grim and his powerful body taut with rage, gripping Sir Lucas by the back of his shirt and throwing him bodily into the yard.

It had been a startling sight for her and apparently for many of the others in witness there, for they all gasped at seeing Rob so. It was as he must appear to his enemies in battle, she'd realized: a stunning, fearsome lord of war, capable of anything required of him, including the dealing out of pain and violent death.

She had been shaken by the vision, even aware as she always had been of his capabilities and the actual need for such skills in the difficult and oppressive battles that were part of life. Witnessing it firsthand had been another experience altogether, though.

"My lady," a gentle voice murmured close to her, "do you require aught?"

Beth pulled her gaze from Rob to look at Annabel. The maid's eyes were shadowed with concern, and it was clear the events of the evening had disturbed her as they had everyone else. Still, the young woman's duty was to her mistress, and she'd clearly put aside her own worries to tend to Beth's needs, should she have any.

Beth took Annabel's hand, giving it a gentle squeeze. "I am fine, Annabel. Dismayed at what transpired this night, perhaps, but naught that warrants your attentions. Go and seek your rest if you will."

"At least allow me to go with you to your chamber, my lady. I can turn down the bed and help you plait your hair."

Annabel bit her bottom lip as she finished speaking, and Beth realized that her maid was likely more troubled, even, than she herself was; she mentally berated herself for not having guessed that truth earlier. It made perfect sense, though, once she thought about it. A young, vulnerable woman had been attacked tonight in the normally peaceful village. Such events were infrequent, but they served as a harsh reminder of the violence waiting in the shadows—the darker side of life for those with less power.

Those like Annabel or any other servant, higher or lower in status, at Dunleavy or in the village.

"Of course I would welcome your company, Annabel," Beth murmured, linking her arm with her maid's and walking with her toward the stairs leading to the main sleeping quarters. She did not meet Rob's gaze as she went; he was still occupied in discussing the details of tomorrow's impromptu hallmoot. But she felt the protective, rather pleasant weight of his stare upon her for just a moment as she walked by. Even with all the upheaval of the past hour, it lit inside her the delicious memory of the moments they'd shared in the enclosed garden together.

Heat swept through her anew as she remembered her boldness—perhaps her weakness—in asking Rob to make love to her.

Earlier, she'd vowed to wait until she felt at peace with the changes wrought in this man who was so different from the husband of her memories. There had been no time to truly reconcile all that, and yet she'd capitulated anyway. *Fool*. The pestering voice inside that had quieted when she and Rob were making love rose up again, knelling its warning. She could not lie to herself about it. It was true—she'd ignored her own sense of caution . . . because what he'd been doing to her had made her feel wonderful and alive. Because she had wanted to share herself with him in that way more than anything she'd ever wanted before.

Where it left her now, she did not know, except it was clear that she would need to think on it more and determine how she should handle these new feelings.

She and Annabel arrived at her bedchamber and began the tasks they'd discussed, the next hour or more slipping away under the flow of her thoughts. Annabel finished her duties and retired. The candle on the mantel burned out, and the wan glow of the moon stretched milky fingers through the cracks in the window shutters.

But still Rob did not come to bed.

And so Beth drifted off at last, her mind heavy with weariness, into a deep and dreamless sleep.

Dawn was beginning to appear on the horizon in a wash of pearly gray when Alex roused Stephen on the pretext of questioning him about his knowledge of the past night's events. Alex had not slept much. Nay, he'd been thinking—and stewing with anger at Luc.

With a few words, he ordered Stephen from the garrison to accompany him to the dungeon chamber where Luc was being held. He dismissed the guards for a few moments, sending them to the kitchen to break their fast, and once the heavy door swung shut behind them, he stalked over to the small cell. The padlock on it was old and partially rusted, and it took a few moments to unclasp it. Once it was done, Alex jerked his head in Stephen's direction.

"You'd better go in and wake him," he grated. "If I get close enough to lay my hands on him, it will be at peril of his life."

Stephen gave a sharp nod and strode into the cell, putting the torch he'd carried into a metal sconce on the wall to provide some light, before shaking Luc to dispel the lingering fumes of his previous night's debauch; Luc finally snapped to awareness with a growling noise, swinging his fist at the person who was so persistently annoying him.

Pulling back his own arm, Stephen let fly a punch to Luc's jaw that threw him back on the damp stones, not hard enough to send him into oblivion again, but just enough to get his attention. Luc lay sprawled there, rubbing his face and scowling up through eyes swollen to slits from too much drink and not enough sleep.

"Pox-ridden son of a—"

"Get up," Stephen muttered.

"What the hell is wrong with you?"

"Get up, you sorry bastard," Alex bit off while stepping just inside the door of the cell, "or I'll ensure you never have the opportunity to again."

That seemed to work.

Luc leaned back on his elbows for a moment before pushing himself to his feet, glaring at them both. Alex felt a small surge of satisfaction in seeing the marks on his face. Luc's lip was swollen, and he had a nasty bruise near his temple, where Alex had punched him last night right before throwing him out of the cotter's dwelling in the village.

"What's this all about?" Luc asked finally, looking around him with a wary glance and rubbing the back of his neck. He winced, having apparently touched one of the sore places—whether from Stephen's blow, Alex's beating last night, or the effects of sleeping on a stone floor, Alex didn't know. And didn't particularly care.

"Christ Almighty," Luc mumbled, "I feel like I've landed face-first at the bottom of a cliff."

"You almost did, only with a rope still attached to the neck of your lifeless body." Stephen's expression was hard. "If Ashby hadn't intervened, you'd be dead right now."

It was the longest string of words Alex had ever heard Stephen speak at one time, and he spared the man a glance before directing the ice of his gaze back at his nemesis to comment, "A regrettable decision on my part. I see you still haven't subdued your penchant for attacking unwilling women."

Luc glared at him, making a scoffing sound in his throat. "The way you're both acting, you'd think I strangled the chit." He rubbed his jaw again, scowling. "And she wasn't unwilling. Christ, she was asking for—"

"Don't say another word about her," Alex cut in coldly, "or I'll not be responsible for what happens to you."

Luc looked as if he might challenge Alex's assertion, but at the last minute he backed off, laughing softly as he sauntered over to lean against the barred door. "Very well. It's all the same to me, so long as you get me out of here without delay." He glanced around in disgust.

"What, you have complaints about your accommodation?" Alex mocked. "There are far worse lodgings you could have, I assure you, with far less pleasant prospects than simply being held captive. There are no rats, no deprivation in any real sense." He gave him a pointed look. "No torture to face."

Luc met Alex's stare. "Ah, yes, I had almost forgot-

ten about your time with the Inquisition in France."
A kind of sneer tipped up one corner of his mouth.
"Comparatively, then, this is a paradise, but it is one
I nevertheless wish to leave. Immediately."

"You will leave when I can arrange it."

"You will arrange it *now*. I need not remind you
why it is best to do my bidding and with attentive
care."

Stephen walked over to flank the other side of
Luc, and Alex felt his jaw tighten. "It is not so simple
as that. Charges have been leveled and must be answered."

"Answer them, then," Luc said, choking back a
sarcastic laugh. "You're the almighty Earl of Marston, so far as these dolts are concerned. Arrange for
my release!"

"I have called a hallmoot for later this morn. That
is what I came here to tell you, so that you would be
aware of the sentence I will impose."

"*Sentence?*" Luc jerked forward, away from the
bars, but Stephen held him back.

"Be still and listen," Stephen muttered. "Though it
is far from ideal, your actions have left this the only
way open to us."

"There are several in the village willing to testify to
your assault of Jane Lott," Alex said.

"They were hardly more than boys," Luc argued.
"Their testimony means naught."

"Be that as it may, there are at least a half dozen of
them. However, you are fortunate in the fact that you
did not fully violate her; it is all that is keeping her
father from demanding amends in coin or in physical
punishment."

Luc made another mocking sound. "Ridiculous."
He shifted his glare to Alex again. "What, then, is
your plan for getting me out of here?"

"You will be banished from Dunleavy Castle before nightfall."

"What?" Luc looked from Alex to Stephen and
then back again. "You cannot be serious—"

"I am. Your position here is tenuous at best, now.
We will be risking all if you are allowed to stay," Alex
argued, wishing he could do as his instincts prompted
him and hand Luc over to Jane's father and other rel-
atives to mete out a more just form of punishment.
"We will all become suspect if I pretend that what
happened in the village last night means naught. I
will appear to have taken the side of an Englishman
against my own people."

Luc went silent. His expression shifted through
several stages, from shock, to anger, to deliberation,
and finally to disgruntled acceptance.

"You may have a point," he admitted grudgingly.

"I am relieved that you agree," Alex drawled softly,
wanting nothing so much right now as to drive his fist
with a satisfying crack into that smug face.

"It may work out well enough if I leave," Luc continued, clearly unmoved by Alex's animosity toward
him. "Getting word of our progress to Lord Exford
has proven awkward. With the army in place readying
for our eventual attack, he cannot approach closely
enough to make the sending of messages effective."

"I will continue to gather information about the
garrison for his use in determining the time of attack," Stephen said.

Luc nodded after another moment of consideration. "Upon leaving Dunleavy I will go to our base camp, retrieve a small group of men, and return here in a day or two, to the woodland south of the castle. There will be but a few of us, and we will remain undetected, so long as you steer any hunting parties clear of the area. We can arrange times of meeting for you to keep me apprised of what you learn here."

"Ashby, you will need to become more involved now in my part of the work here," Stephen added, frowning. "With this happened, I cannot ask too many questions beyond what might be deemed reasonable interest about the garrison."

Alex nodded, though he clenched his fists, feeling sicker with every instant that passed as they discussed the details of betraying the people of Dunleavy. Of betraying Beth. It had been bad enough when the plot was first proposed and these were nameless, faceless people. Now it was far worse. He hated himself for his part in it, and yet he could see no way out. Even if he could suppress his own unshakable instincts of self-protection, John's life still hung in the balance; he couldn't consign his friend to death simply because he was feelings twinges of rusty conscience.

Luc, as damnably perceptive as always, raised his brow, tossing off in challenge, "I see you are recalling the gravity of the situation, Alex. But do not fear; uphold your end of this bargain and John will suffer no ill effects." He gave a malicious grin. "As long as I don't become too bored, waiting for news. So pray, do not take too long either."

"You're a bastard, Luc."

"I believe you've told me that before."

"It bears repeating."

"I only do as circumstances require," Luc answered with a shrug before gesturing at his surroundings. "However, you would be wise to remember that regardless of what appearances might seem at the moment, I am the one in control of this assignment, whether inside the walls of Dunleavy or out of them."

"There is no need to remember; you remind me at every chance you get."

Luc laughed, striding closer to Alex, attempting to use his similar size and physical proximity in a subtle form of intimidation. It didn't work.

"Perhaps it also would be useful for you to remember that the role of earl—and lord husband—is only that . . . a role you play," Luc said in a smooth and deprecating tone. "Get the information we need as swiftly as possible, and we can be rid of each other for good." He paused, shifting his weight back and smiling with a look that set off warning bells in Alex even before he spoke again. "Would you like my advice on how to achieve that end most efficiently?"

"Nay," Alex managed to ground out between nearly clenched teeth. "And yet somehow I don't think that is going to stop you from giving it."

Luc leered. "It is for your own good, and it is this: I suggest that you call on all your notable skills in the bedroom. Get that unsuspecting, pretty wench you've been handed for a wife all hot and writhing beneath you in bed, and then spring it on—"

He didn't get to finish. Alex clamped his hand around Luc's throat and squeezed, digging his fingers into the sides of his windpipe and trying very hard to remember that he could not go as far as he wished and rip it out. He could, however, say what he pleased and the rest be damned.

"Regardless of what we are doing here, Luc, I will not allow you to speak of her as if she's naught but some common whore from the docks. *You* would be wise to remember *that*." Alex felt Stephen trying to pull him away, and he heard Luc make choking sounds and saw his face turning red.

He let go, shoving his former comrade away from him. He wanted to exact a harsher revenge, but he knew he would not be the one to pay the price if he did.

"Damn you, Ashby," Luc rasped when he finally could, bending over and coughing, his hand to his throat.

Stephen didn't speak, but Alex noted his frown, just before he swung his gaze back to Luc, who straightened up again, trying desperately to restore both his breathing and his cocky demeanor. "You will regret taking that action against me before we are finished with each other, Alex. I promise you that."

"As you said to me on the day you bound me to this scheme, Luc—I am terrified by the threat."

"You should be. And if you allow yourself to soften in favor of a traitorous bitch like Lady Elizabeth of Selkirk, then you're a bigger fool than I imagined." Luc's eyes were cold steel, and his hand still rubbed his throat. "I may be leaving Dunleavy temporarily, but I'll be back to take what is England's by right. If you know what's good for you, you'll cut your losses when the time comes, and leave the spoils to the victors."

Alex had turned his back and walked from the cell

while Luc was talking, murmuring to Stephen to lock the door behind him and meet him outside the dungeon chamber when he was through. But Luc continued on, knowing he could hear every word, and Alex had to clench both his jaw and his fists to keep himself from responding to the bastard's taunts . . .

Until the dungeon door shut and blessedly separated him from the man he wanted to kill more than any other he had ever known.

Before the sun had set Alex stood at the battlements with his captain of the guard, four sentries, and Beth, watching Luc being escorted from the castle by a half dozen of Dunleavy's soldiers; they would lead him to the limits of the demesne, where he would be abandoned to his own devices and left to manage his own protection.

He had been told already before the assembly of people from the castle and village that if he returned, it would be upon pain of death. Only Alex and Stephen knew how duplicitous that statement was. Of course Luc would return. And he would bring with him an army of Englishmen, prepared to storm Dunleavy's walls and exploit the weaknesses in its defenses that Alex and Stephen had found for him. The people here were dupes, being primed for the fall of an axe they had no idea was aimed at their necks.

It made Alex sick to think on it.

He had been wracking his brain trying to find of a way out of it—a way to alert Beth and her people of the doom aligning against them. But there was naught he could do. He could not tell her the truth. What he had done here already was heinous enough to warrant being executed by these people, and yet he could not forget that it was not his life alone that he risked. He was a man with no help, no friends to aid him in facing the English forces when they came. It was a trap with no escape.

He turned his head and met Beth's gaze where they stood at the battlements, realizing that the troubled look in her soft gray eyes mirrored his own. But were her fears connected to Luc's banishment, or were they the result of her suspicions, still, about him as her husband?

He could not take any chances. Aye, he had no choice but to continue his lies, falling deeper and deeper into the web of deception he was spinning with her every day, every hour, and every minute. Yet each time he closed his eyes and forced himself to think about how best to win her over, all he could see was her as she'd been with him in the garden last night, her skin gilded by the flickering light of the lanterns and the softer glow of the moon.

All he could feel was the need rocking through him, not only to make her his in every luscious, sinful way imaginable, but also to defend and protect her from any that might wish to harm her.

God help him for being a fool, but he could not shake the feeling, and there was no solution to any of this that he could see . . .

Alex felt the touch of Beth's hand on his arm, and it pulled him from his reverie into the here and now. She was ready to go inside. Nodding, he took her arm. His jaw was tight and his neck stiff as he escorted her from the battlements back to the great hall, pretending that all was well and the crisis was past.

Pretending.

It was what he was becoming best at, it seemed. Pretending, pretending, always pretending. Except when it came to the one thing he could not feign, no matter much he wished to or how hard he tried . . .

The strangely burgeoning feelings about Beth that he could not seem to control.

Chapter 8

Four weeks later

It was almost time.

Beth nodded to the lads who'd brought the heated water into the bedchamber, giving them permission to go back to their usual duties. They bowed quite officially, the gesture ruined only when they grinned, exchanging knowing glances with each other. Thomas, the elder of the two, jabbed an elbow into Henry, as Annabel rounded on them with another of the lady's maids who had come to help Beth with her preparations, shooing them from the chamber.

Imps.

Beth couldn't help but smile at their antics, even though she couldn't let anyone see it. The lads were having a bit of fun, that was all, knowing just enough of what was happening to make it worth jesting about with each other. Aye, there were two reasons the bath had been readied in the morn, rather than at the usual time she called for it in the evenings after her ride.

The first was the great feast they were hosting tonight in honor of Rob's homecoming—an event to which all their neighboring lords had been invited.

And the second was that Rob had won his first game of *merels* against her. Finally. The bath was to be part of his prize.

Annabel had been assisting the other lady's maids in bringing in piles of clean towels, as well as the pots of unguents and the mixture of bath herbs Beth had blended herself. But then she came closer, piling several of the towels alongside the steaming wooden tub near Beth, before straightening to look at her.

"May I ask something of you, my lady?"

Beth took from her a pot of primrose and violet salve, used especially to aid aching muscles, and dismissed the other two maids with a nod. "Of course. What is it?"

"I must know whether or not it's true." Annabel looked toward the door, presumably to ensure that the women had left, so that none would be privy to what she was about to ask. "Mariah and I disagreed about it this morn, for I said it could not be so. Yet she insists it is." Crossing her arms and raising her brow, she asked, "Did Lord Marston truly win against you at *merels* yestereve?"

Beth tried to bite back a smile, though she wasn't completely successful, and so she turned slightly, busying herself with some of the last-minute preparations for Rob's bath. "Aye, he did."

"And this?" Annabel asked, gesturing to the tub.

"Part of his prize," Beth answered, being careful not to give away any hint of what else she planned for when his bath was finished. "He has spent the morn hunting and will need to be refreshed before the feast this night. And of course he deserves to be rewarded, for he worked mightily to achieve victory over me in the game."

"Considering that he suffered resounding defeat day after day for nearly a month, his success was rather sudden, wouldn't you say?" Though she tried to mask it, Annabel's gaze was clearly suspicious.

But Beth pretended not to notice, nodding primly. "The twenty-sixth attempt was the charm for him, it seems."

Annabel made a sound in her throat, and Beth made the mistake of glancing at her again. The maid's expression made her laugh aloud, unable to contain her merriment longer.

"Very well, I admit that I may have helped him a just little."

"Only a little?"

"Well, perhaps quite a lot," Beth admitted, smoothing the top of the towels.

"I knew it!" Annabel's voice dropped a pitch and carried with it a note of accusation. "My lady, you *let* him win."

Still chuckling, Beth admitted, "Perhaps I did—though he is much better than he used to be."

"Much better at what?"

The masculine voice echoed from the doorway, and Beth looked over to meet Rob's warm gaze. He stood there, filling the portal with his tall, strong form, and Annabel dropped into a curtsy, murmuring, "My lord."

Beth could not help but smile back at him, even as a flush spread over her. The air was thick with the scent of the herbs she'd sprinkled into the steaming bathwater . . . and her husband was gazing at her with a penetrating, enigmatic look in his eyes.

She cleared her throat, wondering how much of her discussion with her lady's maid he had heard.

"I was just telling Annabel that you have become much better at coming upon me unawares—as happened in the garden last month . . . and as you did just now, in fact," Beth answered, not too quickly to be suspect, she hoped. Annabel looked guilty, however, and to keep him from questioning further, Beth stepped up to block her maid from his view, using her hand to surreptitiously gesture for Annabel to leave the chamber.

"Ah . . . if you will excuse me, my lord—my lady," Annabel said, still keeping her gaze trained to the floor as she grasped an empty bucket left behind by one of the boys. "I—ah—need to return this to the kitchen, lest Cook scold Henry for his carelessness in forgetting it."

Then she was gone, and Beth was left standing with Rob alone in their bedchamber, wondering how he would react to this brief respite she'd arranged for him. He had been out of sorts ever since Sir Lucas's banishment, and though they had allotted private time together each day during that interval—sharing meals, going berrying, hawking, playing at *merels*, riding to the far reaches of the demesne . . . making love—he had kept to himself so far as his thoughts or worries went. It was as if he was being held in sway by something that preyed upon his mind but that he would not discuss.

That in and of itself was no surprise, really. Rob had never been one to talk openly about much of what he felt—except for that night in the garden, with his recitation of the ballade and his sweet efforts to woo her. His actions that night had surprised her, but she'd shrugged it off as another example of the way his captivity had changed him.

When he'd gone back to being quiet and reserved, she hadn't fretted much about it; it had been naught but a reversion to form. It would have remained a point unremarkable to her these past weeks if she hadn't sensed a kind of sadness in him as well. It was that which had disturbed her and made her wonder—

"Beth?"

His voice broke the spell of her thoughts. "Aye, my lord?"

"Edwin delivered me a message saying you wished me to join you here posthaste," he finally murmured, still fixing her with his warm stare. "What is this all about?"

She offered him a hopeful smile. "It is your prize, of course."

Beth might have sworn she saw dismay shadow Rob's eyes for an instant before he mastered the expression, shifting to a look of polite interest.

She fought back a frown. Could he be displeased? By the Rood, it could not be the prospect of actually bathing that made him discomfited, for she knew he undertook the pleasure of a bath almost daily, if not in an actual tub, then in the river just south of the castle.

"What, my lord?" she asked, a bit put out by his continued silence. "Do these arrangements not meet with your satisfaction?"

"Nay—I mean, aye. It is only that I, ah . . ." He cleared his throat, glancing again to the curling steam before bringing his gaze back to her, this time with an air of determination. "Thank you for your foresight, Beth. I did indeed wish to bathe before the feasting of this night." He stepped brusquely forward, taking up a towel and a pot of soft soap before moving around her toward the tub. "And now, as I am sure you have many other tasks awaiting you before the arrival of our guests this night, please feel free to go and—"

"I will not," she murmured, unable to keep the faint tone of exasperation from her voice.

"Why?"

"Because *I* intend to bathe you, my lord," she said firmly, taking the linens and soap from him.

Alex's heart sank, even as another part of him threatened to rise in response to the promise in her words. *Good God.* He took a step back, desperate to maintain whatever distance he could between himself and the very *thought* of Beth's hands moving over his naked body in the bath. What they'd shared thus far had been difficult enough, with the intensity of pleasure he experienced every time they were intimate increasing, no matter how brief the encounter or how firmly he'd tried to school himself to look upon the act as a necessary duty and naught more. This would be too much to withstand.

His attraction to her was affecting him. Deeply. And the guilt . . . Christ, it swelled every time he met her trusting, beautiful gaze, worsening each day until the agony of it was near to breaking him in a way his Inquisitors had never come close to doing with all the torments of their hellish dungeons.

Just the image of those graceful hands, slippery with soap, all warm and wet, sliding over his naked body . . . Heaven help him, but it had the power to bring him to his knees.

He tried not to sound strangled as he forced a small laugh, moving farther away from her toward the wardrobe, and saying as he removed his stained over-tunic, "While I appreciate your offer, lady, there is no need for you to go to all this effort when I can surely bathe myself."

"Of course there is. Beyond the fact that it is to serve as a portion of your prize for besting me at *merels*, this bath was due you as lord of Dunleavy upon your return home." Her lips pursed, and she glanced away. "I was supposed to offer it as lady of the castle, yet it did not come to pass, if you recall, in the . . . the fervor of my greeting in this chamber on that first night."

"Ah, yes, your attack of me, you mean."

She gave him a look that made clear she was not willing to revisit that memory in any detail. But a definite glimmer of something mischievous lit her beautiful eyes, and her mouth edged up just slightly as she said instead, "I intend, therefore, to assist you now and resolve both my obligations"—she raised her brows—"perhaps all three of them, in one fell swoop."

"Three?" He could not seem to stop himself from echoing the number, even though he knew the moment he spoke that it was a mistake.

"Aye." She counted off on her fingers, "First, fulfillment of your prize, second, your rightful honor of the bath as lord of Dunleavy . . ."

Her voice trailed off before she stated the third reason, but by all that was holy, the glimmer in her eyes was an outright gleam now, and Alex felt something inside him curl into a tight, hard knot of desire as she finally finished, "And we shall have to see whether or not my third obligation to you comes to fruition when your bath is finished."

She gave him a brilliant smile.

The sensation that rocked through him in response sent him soaring at the same time that it plummeted him to the darkest depths. Somehow, he managed to give her a wan smile in return, knowing that if she intended to bed him today, there would be no possibility of resisting her. For as good as he seemed to have become at lying, even he could not deny how much he wanted her.

Need for her—sweet, searing, aching—lanced through him with every breath he took. He wanted to make hot, satisfying love to every luscious inch of her, more than he'd wanted anything else in his life. But he hated the thought that it could only happen within the shadow of this deceit he'd been compelled to create with her.

It was destroying him to know that every time they were together, she believed he was someone else.

And that was why after the incident with Luc, he'd held back as much as he could. And he'd redoubled his efforts to accomplish the requirements of his mission so that he could leave Dunleavy before the need to be near this woman whose company he enjoyed—and who he was coming to regard with a very real sense of admiration and *respect*, by God—overwhelmed his reason.

He could never have more with her than he did right now, and even that would be over with soon enough. It was that awareness which was slowly driving him mad and compelling him to keep whatever distance he could from her, both physically and emotionally.

To avoid revealing what he was struggling so hard to hide, Alex turned away and busied himself in disrobing, knowing there could be no escape from this without being blatantly rude.

"The water is just right, my lord," he heard her say behind him. "Hurry or it will cool overmuch."

He gave a kind of grunt in acknowledgment, even as he closed his eyes in a futile attempt to maintain his equilibrium. Damn, but this was going to test every ounce of his resolve—and in such matters, he had never had much to begin with.

The now familiar desire for her was pounding through him in rising waves, and it was all he could do not to turn around, stalk over to her, and strip her to nakedness so that he might pull her into the bath along with him. The memory of every one of the intimacies they'd already shared had been seared into his mind, the image of her sweet body, all gentle curves of cream and peach, lodging like an arrow in his brain, piercing his resolve. He had to stop . . . had to think of something else, preferably unpleasant, to keep his mind from veering onto those dangerous paths.

Sweat. Aching muscles. The pain of pushing his body to its limits in training each day.

The memory of just what he was doing at Dunleavy.

Stephen was even now making his way alone to

their usual meeting place with Luc, to bring back details about the impending English attack.

Aye, thinking of such things should help.

If only he could keep dwelling on all that instead of her, and the thought of her sweet, trusting eyes and her velvet hands . . .

He coughed and pulled his shirt off over his head—leaving him completely unclothed except for the thin linen braies he wore under his breeches. She was looking at him, by God, mayhap even studying him. He knew it without turning around, and he called to her as nonchalantly as he could, "I am ready, lady. Take care to move away from the tub lest your gown be marred by the splash of water when I get in."

"It is of no matter, my lord. The robe I am wearing is suited for such things. It is of a thin, soft weave and will not be harmed if it gets wet."

Alex wasn't going to risk looking at her to confirm it. Nay, he avoided her gaze and strode over to the vessel, intending to get in quickly, bathe even more swiftly, and escape from the chamber without any further interaction with her if he could. But before he could lift one foot into the water, she reached out and touched his arm, the contact with her making him choke and stilling him as effectively as if she'd flicked her wrist and magically thrown a wall up before him.

"Haven't you forgotten something, my lord? It is customary to remove *all* of your clothing before bathing."

Damn.

He'd hoped she wouldn't notice, though he should have known better. Over the course of the past few

weeks, he'd come to realize that Lady Elizabeth of
Selkirk was many things, perhaps, but unobservant
was not one of them.

He paused, pretending to have known exactly what
he was doing and choosing to make light of it.

"I only decided to forgo walking about in broad
daylight as God created me in an effort to spare your
sensibilities, lady."

He caught just the edge of her smile. "There is
naught you could reveal that would shock me, husband, for there is naught I have not seen of you oft
before—and with much pleasure, I might add." She
gestured toward him, the smile more visible now.
"Feel free, for I am eager to bestow your prize."

Trying very hard not to think about her gaze upon
him or the actions she seemed poised to take once
he had removed the final barrier of clothing, Alex
slipped off his braies and nearly jumped into the tub,
sitting down as quickly as he could.

It did little good.

He'd managed to fold his legs up enough to sink
down to his waist in the water, but with no soap
or powders mixed in, it was clear as glass, revealing nearly as much as if he was standing as still as a
statue before her gaze. And part of him was as hard
as a statue, of that there was little doubt.

"If you would pass the soap, Beth," he said, sounding choked, "I'd like to hurry"—he paused in what
he was saying for a beat—"so that the water will not
cool before I have bathed completely, of course."

"Of course," she repeated, her voice slightly
raspy—was it with laughter or something entirely different? he wondered.

But in the next instant all conscious thought fled as he felt the first stroke of her warm, wet, and soapy palm across his skin, followed by the rougher texture of the bathing cloth. She chose to wash his shoulders and back first, praise be, though her touch still sent unbearably pleasurable chills up his spine and around the front of him, shooting like lightning bolts to his cock and engorging it even further with heavy, throbbing heat.

"Good God," he breathed on a muted groan, hoping his exclamation might sound as if he responded so to the simple sensation of her hands rubbing sore muscles rather than the much more complex feeling burgeoning between his legs. He kept them pressed together as much as he could in the close confines of the tub, hoping she wouldn't see the result of her ministrations on him.

"Do you like that, my lord?" she asked quietly, and he realized with a tantalizing shock that she was echoing the very question he had asked her during their first magnificent coupling when he'd seduced her in the garden. Now she used the phrase against him, rubbing her elegant fingers in a kneading, circular motion across his shoulders, before she began working on his neck.

He managed to make some sort of wordless reply. Enough that he heard the smile in her voice as she told him they would continue with it in a moment, if first he would tip his head forward and close his eyes, to allow her to wet and then work lather into his hair.

"There," she said, once she was finished cleansing and rinsing. She guided him to sit up straight again, combing her fingers through the soaked strands, and the sensation was surprisingly pleasant. It might have been relaxing, even, had it not been for the jutting part of him that burned with need hot enough, it seemed, to keep the bathwater from cooling and his attention distracted from all but the call for finding satisfaction. He kept his eyes closed, determined to be strong through this and pretend oblivion to the raging demands of his nature.

"Back to what we were doing before, then," she murmured, almost to herself. From her position behind him, she eased him back against the wall of the tub again, and Alex might have barely noticed what she said, but the import sank in when she added a murmured "And what of this, my lord—do you like this as well?" at the same time that she reached around the front of him and smoothed her soapy hands and that thick, deliciously rough cloth, for several delightful moments over his chest.

And down.

Over his ribs, slipping across the flat of his belly, his muscles all clenching in spasmodic response to the delectable sensations she sent spilling through him as her hands stroked and rubbed, slipping lower, and still lower . . .

Sweet angels of mercy.

This time he could not mute the groan that came from him, as she grasped the thick, burning length of him in her soapy hand and began to stroke. It was fortunate he was pressed back against the tub wall, else he might have fallen over with the onslaught of exquisite feeling . . . intense jolts of tingling heat and almost painful, aching need. That traitorous part of him twitched and his hips tipped up toward her touch almost against his will. All of it was intensified by his sudden awareness of the way she was leaning into him from behind . . . of the way her sweet, soft breasts pressed into his back above the edge of the tub, moving against him with every shift of her arms as she reached around and worked her hand sweetly up and down his shaft.

It was too much.

Even the best of men could not have resisted such temptation—and he had never claimed to be even a good man.

Desperate with need, Alex twisted toward her and reached out, water splashing over the edge and onto Beth as he pulled her to him, taking her mouth with a searing kiss. She tasted so good—so good, by God. She released her hold on him with a slight gasp of surprise at his unexpected movement, the sound fading into a moan as she kissed him back, softly at first, and then with a passion that rivaled his own, taking and giving. Her hands threaded in his hair, pulling him closer. He wrapped his arms around her waist, still kissing and hungry for her, even as he prepared himself, waiting only until he shifted enough on his knees to maintain his balance.

"What are you doing?" she breathed, pulling back with an instant's bewilderment before he wiped the expression from her face with another kiss, pulling her near and holding her tighter . . .

With one concentrated movement, Alex lifted her in his arms, swinging her over the edge of the tub, water splashing everywhere, to plunk her down into it with him. Right on top of him.

The shock of it made her go very still so that only the water moved, slapping against the sides of the tub in ever-decreasing waves. He couldn't shift right or left, forward or backward, even had he wanted to, both because of his uncomfortable erection and because she was straddling his thighs in a way that made any kind of movement almost impossible.

The air that had been trapped beneath her skirts with the swiftness of her descent made the fabric balloon up before it was slowly dragged down, saturated by the water. Beth's hands rested on his shoulders. Her spine was stiff, and as Alex watched, a drop of water slipped down from where it had splashed up to her brow, perching for an instant at the delicate tip of her nose before dripping off into the now quiet bathwater with a slight plunking sound.

It was that water drop, finally, that set off her giggles. She started to tremble with holding them back, the sound welling up and then transforming into gasping laughter even as he murmured wryly, "Well, you said you didn't mind if your dress got wet, didn't you?"

"You are incorrigible, Robert Kincaid," she choked at last, the words still interspersed with a few hiccuping laughs. He was fortunate, he thought, that she was so merry. He'd become much better at hiding his reaction to the use of that false name in connection with him, but it had never been so difficult to bear, it seemed, as it was right now. God, but he wanted to forget the tangled mess of this and just love her. Just the two of them without name or identity or plan. Naught but one man and one woman joined by feelings that were real despite anything else outside.

Her laughter subsiding now, she leaned forward and gently pressed her lips to his again, and he closed his eyes, surprised at how overcome such a simple gesture could make him feel. The caress was tender— with just a hint of naughtiness beneath, to match the flashing look he saw in her gray eyes when he opened his again to meet her gaze.

"And you are also impatient," she continued. "We could have been quite comfortable on our bed, you know, once your bath was finished." She smiled. "This tub is cramped, and I am already clean."

"Ah, but I wanted to ensure that you were also . . . wet."

She uttered another slight gasp in response to both his words and touch, for he could not stop himself from slipping his hand up her leg beneath the warm water . . . smoothing a path under her skirts as he made his progress up the long, silken expanse of her thigh.

He couldn't help himself.

His fingers reached the apex. As was customary, she wore naught but a chemise and stockings beneath her gown, and so nothing impeded his hand from making immediate, direct contact with the delicate flesh it sought. He swept his fingers in one smooth, long stroke along those gentle folds, and her gasping cry made him close his eyes momentarily and swallow hard, just absorbing the delicious sensation of it.

Oh, she was wet all right. The slippery evidence of her arousal, combined with the heat emanating from her even in the warmth of the tub, nearly made him groan aloud once more.

Her hands clenched on his shoulders as he stroked

again and again along that silken path. He dipped the ends of two fingers into her at the end of each caress, and though she remained still at first, it was not long before she began to rock against his fingers, encouraging his pace.

"Come for me, Beth," he whispered as he worked his fingers over her, reveling in the eager need she showed him and the abandon with which she was throwing herself into this delightful yet unorthodox form of love play. "I want to feel you contract around my fingers and know that you're experiencing unbearable pleasure. Pleasure only I can give you." He met her gaze, the look on her face as he stroked her nearly sending him over the edge himself.

He had to slow down, or he would finish here and now, releasing into the bathwater instead of sheathed deep within her as he yearned to be. He could not seem to get enough of her, and he'd never known the strength of intensity he was feeling now for this woman, never in his entire life.

Breathe, he reminded himself. *Just breathe.*

Beth's breath was coming in shallow gasps as well, as she reached toward completion. He tipped his head forward, taking one of her nipples—erect and pushing in bas-relief against the saturated and therefore almost sheer fabric of her bodice—between his lips, nibbling and suckling at it. She was almost there, he knew. Almost . . .

A few moments later, she bucked against his hand with a soft cry, and he felt her thighs tense as the marvelous, pulsating waves of her climax began to sweep over her. Ah, but she was magnificent, with her head thrown back, that golden hair cascading down to the water, and her face contorted sweetly in the agony of her bliss—

"My lord! My lady!"

The muffled summons came from behind the door of their bedchamber, from someone outside in the corridor, and Alex stiffened along with Beth, his groan echoing hers as the glorious moment was cut short. Damn it to everlasting hell.

"What is it?" Alex managed to call out after a few moments passed, in a voice that sounded authoritative, if a bit strangled, as he shifted a little, trying to find a comfortable position considering his still raging erection.

"Apologies for interrupting your bath, my lord," the voice—was it Annabel's?—called back, "but the first of tonight's guests is approaching Dunleavy—"

This early? Alex's thought intruded, and a kind of bewilderment clouded his mind before the servant's voice finished the phrase and provided context for that unusual circumstance.

"—and it is Lord Lennox. I would ne'er have disturbed you otherwise."

Lennox. Alex didn't have to see Beth's face to know that the news was unwelcome. Her last interaction with the man had involved repelling him during his assault on the castle. He'd come face to face with the trench of burning oil that had left that blackened strip in the outer yard, greeted so after Beth had enticed him through the first gate with the promise of easy victory.

Their reunion was sure to be strained at best and perhaps even hostile.

"Comes he armed or in peace?" Alex called out to the herald.

"Leading a retinue of men, but none that appear outfitted for battle, my lord."

"We will make our appearance to greet him in the great hall anon," Beth called out, having finally found her voice, it seemed. "Ready the rest of the servants, Annabel, and bid Edwin see to Lord Lennox's comforts; offer him a cup to ease his thirst until we arrive."

The maid replied her affirmation and it was silent again. Alex caught Beth's gaze upon him, and he paused, breathing a deep, frustrated sigh, a half smile quirking his mouth. "So it begins, it seems," he murmured, watching the way her tongue flicked out to moisten her lips and feeling a twist of thwarted desire deep in his belly, even as he tried to will it to subside, having no outlet for now, at least.

"Aye." Beth glanced at him, questions full in her expressive eyes. "However, I—that is, you are still . . . unsatisfied, I gather." Her cheeks flushed, and she bit her bottom lip, making him smile despite his discomfort.

"You gather correctly, lady." He tried to play the moment straight, enjoying her blushes. But she looked so distressed that he could tease her no longer, and so he added, "Yet it is naught for you to worry over. Circumstances have clearly conspired against us this day."

"But there is still time, if we are quick about it."

Sweet Jesu, how I'd love that.

The thought pitched through his brain, and yet several reasons, not least of which involved his own increasingly conflicted feelings about her, held him back from accepting her delicious offer. He couldn't well tell her that truth, though, and so clearing his throat, he settled for something that might sound reasonable to her.

"Being quick is not what I had in mind, lady." He forced what he hoped was a warm smile that would make him look far more relaxed than he was truly feeling. "I intend to take our time when next we make love. You deserve no less, Beth, nor would I give less to you."

"Oh . . ."

For some reason, just after uttering that word, which she seemed to say rather often he'd noticed, Beth's cheeks pinkened even more. "Well then," she added somewhat breathily, in turn clearing her throat before she finished, "I suppose we shall have to wait until later . . . when we have more time, I mean . . ."

Her voice trailed off, and she glanced up at him from beneath her lashes, the look filled with gentle flirtation, humor, and *trust*, by God; it made something twist inside him again. Something that had naught to do with the hotly erotic feelings she never failed to inspire.

"That would be best," he murmured, stroking his fingers along her cheek and brushing back a stray tendril of her hair.

Nodding almost shyly, she made a move as if to stand, clearly intending to step from the tub. She would need change her garments, after all, to be in any fit form to greet a fellow lord of the realm.

But Alex placed his hand on her arm, forestalling her inevitable action for a little longer. With the interruption, cooler thoughts had intervened, and as frustrated as he felt in a physical sense, he still felt a

compelling need to ensure that she was ready to face
the evening and all it might hold.

"Are you worried, lady, about what is to come
with Lord Lennox?"

Her expression twisted with animosity at the mention of the earl's name, and Alex could not suppress
once more the renegade thought that if Beth had been
a man, she would have proved a formidable opponent on the field. "Nay," she said without hesitation.
"It might well be uncomfortable, considering the outcome of my last confrontation with him—but all the
better for reminding him of his folly in thinking to
coerce me to his will." She raised her brow. "I will
enjoy knowing that the sight of you standing by my
side will not only gall him, my lord, but make him
look a fool, for I still retain the parchment wherein he
claimed you were dead."

"Ah, yes," Alex murmured, trying to ignore the
shaft of dull pain that pierced him with her words.
Beth had shown him the parchment in the course of
his first week at Dunleavy. Somehow, it had been easier to pretend derision at the absurdity of that claim
then than it was proving to be now.

Unaware as she was of the bent of his thoughts,
Beth smiled, though the expression was cold. "Aye,
the arrogant Lord Lennox will likely spend the evening wondering if I will bring it out for the entertainment of the others who will arrive. 'Twill keep him on
his best behavior, I would think."

Alex's lips quirked up. "You have a calculating
streak to your nature, methinks, wife."

"Perhaps." This smile she gave him was far warmer
than the one she'd sported moments ago. "You would

do well to remember it, husband, lest I find reason to turn it against you."

"Heaven forbid."

Alex forced himself to grin back at her. He touched his hand to her cheek, rubbing the pad of his thumb across the plump, pink expanse of her lower lip, not only because he enjoyed doing it, but also to revel in her sweet reaction to his caress.

"Fear not, Beth. I could never forget anything about you," he murmured, reluctant, suddenly, to let her go.

"That is fortunate, my lord, for I am also stubborn—and your prize has not yet been fully bestowed." The sparkle in her eyes before she climbed from the tub stoked the fire inside him with bittersweet force, as she added, "It will be, however, when we are alone again. Before the night is through, I promise you, it will."

Chapter 9

The feast had begun less than three hours ago, but Beth couldn't wait for it to be over.

It wasn't that the company was unpleasant, the food tasteless, or the minstrels and other entertainers not amusing. Nay, except for the presence of Lord Lennox, the gathering was a most pleasant one, and one she likely would have enjoyed had it come at any other time. But as it stood, it had disrupted the lovemaking she had initiated with Rob, leaving her feeling on edge. They had been interrupted before she could ensure he had reached his bliss as well, and it was that which annoyed her most.

Rob was feeling the same, if her perception wasn't playing tricks on her. Part of her couldn't help but smile at the restrained energy that seemed to power every movement he made and every word he spoke, yet in another way, sensing that tension in him only served to heighten her own desires more sharply.

Every time their gazes met or his fingers brushed hers over their trencher, the truth of their attraction pulsed between them, sensitizing her to him in a way that was both incredibly erotic and unbearable maddening, considering that naught could come of it for at least a few more hours and the termination of this very necessary gathering.

A short time ago, Beth had moved away from the long head table to greet some of those who had come to the feast. She'd just spoken with one of the three dowager ladies in attendance—the other two had retired a half hour ago to the chambers they'd been given for the night. They'd been tired, it seemed, of the happy din of eating, drinking, and dancing that many were undertaking now that the final course of food was being cleared away.

The trestle tables in the center of the hall had been folded up and pushed to the walls as was customary whenever a meal was finished. Now two minstrels who had been hired to assist Dunleavy's own musician, Seamus Elliott, played along with him, providing the music for those who wished to take their turn at dancing a *carole* or *rondeau*.

"My lady," Annabel said, coming close enough to murmur in her ear. "Lord Lennox approaches you. Shall I alert Lord Marston? He speaks with Lord and Lady Clifton near the tumblers."

Nodding, Beth turned her attention to the tall man who was indeed walking up to her with a retinue of attendants behind him. Archibald Drummond, the third Earl of Lennox, was not an unattractive man. In truth he was a strong, barrel-chested warrior of perhaps some thirty-five years, with pale blue eyes and close-cut, fair hair. His wife, a delicate woman and heiress from Inverness, had died the winter before from a wasting illness that had prevented her successfully giving her husband a healthy son to carry on his name and titles. It was that, in part, which apparently had helped place Dunleavy—and Elizabeth—in his sights. He wanted a new wife and heirs, and if he could use his connection with Scotland's king Robert the Bruce to gain rights to a rich holding like Dunleavy in the process, so much the better.

Even so, the attack he had waged against them after hearing the false rumors of Rob's death in England could not be so easily excused. If not for the fact that he was their immediate neighbor to the north and a favorite of Robert the Bruce, Beth would never have invited him into their home again. But in the name of peace, she had forced herself to overlook her dislike of the Scottish earl's grasping nature, knowing it was far better to maintain his alliance than it was to cultivate divisive hatred when English armies were at the door.

"Lady Elizabeth." Lord Lennox took her hand once he reached her, bending over it, though she noticed he did not touch his lips to her skin.

"Lord Lennox." Beth was careful to keep her tone cordial but cool, and she removed her fingers from his clasp as swiftly as she could without being overtly rude. A few faint scars were visible along the side of one cheek from the burns he'd suffered when confronted by her fire trap. It was not enough to mar his appearance, but it would be sufficient as a reminder of that day, she imagined, every time he caught sight of his reflection in a looking glass or bit of water.

"This is a far friendlier welcome than the one I experienced my last time at Dunleavy," he murmured, pointedly, and Beth could not discern if he was in earnest or merely attempting to smooth over the awkwardness of their first private conversation since the siege he'd waged.

She owed him no quarter after the events of that time, and so she decided to respond as she would under most circumstances—with forthright honesty. "The tenor of one's welcome is oft tied to the method of one's approach, I have found."

He did not flinch and even smiled faintly, though his eyes maintained the same hard cast they'd shown from his first moments here. "Ah, but that depends upon the circumstances and persons involved." Giving her a slight bow, he continued, "I must say that your husband looks exceedingly well for a man reported to have died under the extremities of illness and torture." His smile had vanished and his tone sounded almost accusatory as he added, "I was most surprised to hear of his return to Dunleavy, hale and healthy."

"Our prayers were indeed answered," Beth settled on saying, determined not to rise to the challenge he seemed to be throwing at her.

"Almost an act of God, wouldn't you say?" he persisted, stepping closer, so that she had to suppress her instinct to move back from him—an act that would have been impossible anyway, thanks to the wall directly behind her.

"It could not have been more well timed," he continued. "A woman without protection is a woman in need of a man. I intended to remedy that during my last visit, but then just like that"—he snapped his fingers—"Robert Kincaid returned from the dead and the landscape was changed."

"Even without my husband's return, I am capable

of my own protection, Lord Lennox, as I have demonstrated quite effectively in the past."

Beth broke her gaze with him, wanting naught more than to be done with this conversation. She tried to edge sideways, hoping to move around him and escape into the gathering again, but he shifted along with her, almost in some kind of perverse reflection of the dance taking place at the center of the great hall.

"You are clever; that I'll grant you, lady," he said, "but you could not have remained hidden away forever. There is naught a man enjoys more than the spirited fight—and eventual submission—of an opponent, and you are a lovelier adversary than most." He stepped closer, adding in a seductive whisper that made her skin crawl, "I would have broken through your defenses eventually, sweeting, to get to the luscious prize within."

Lennox's proximity was making it difficult for Beth to breathe freely. He smelled strongly of onions, and his bulk was making it impossible to see around him to the rest of the chamber. She tried to stand as tall as she could in her determination not to cower. From the little she could see, his men were scattered around them, forming a kind of barrier to keep her from the rest of the assembly, and he seemed to be enjoying the sense of control he was wielding over her.

For the moment.

But she was a lady, not some bawd from the street, and it seemed this overweening lord had not learned that fact properly yet.

"If you do not step away from me this instant, my lord," Beth said lowly, as she met the earl's gaze again with the veritable ice of her own, "then I will be forced to find other means of securing that courtesy from you. And I promise that you will find it as unpleasant as you did the trench of flames in my outer yard but a few months past."

His mouth twisted in laughing derision. "I would like to see you try again. Just remember that before all is over between us, you will pay a dear recompense for every one of your retaliations against me. If not in my bed, then in other ways."

"Step away from me!"

"I shall think on it. At the moment I am enjoying your—"

"I believe my wife said to move. *Now.*"

Beth heard Rob's voice at the same moment that Lord Lennox was yanked away from her from behind, gripped by the back of his fine, embroidered tunic. The rage crackling from Rob's eyes would have been enough to make the most stalwart man quail, but the leashed fury in his powerful body was even more daunting. He shifted smoothly to her side, positioning himself to buffer her from aggression though he did not touch her or react in any way to the metallic sound of swords clearing their sheaths around them, keeping his steely gaze instead fixed on the earl.

"Is there a reason you were not complying with her wishes?"

Lennox looked like a fish flung up onto the bank of the river, his mouth agape and his hand on his sword hilt as well, though Beth noticed that he hadn't pulled it more than a few inches from its scabbard. He made no intelligible sound at first, then his mouth closed and he seemed to assess the man before him. In the next breath he glanced to his men in silent signal to put away their weapons.

"I—that is, it was naught but a misunderstanding, Marston."

"A fatal one, should it happen again. Consider yourself warned, my lord, for in matters pertaining to ensuring the happiness and security of my wife, I am not in the habit of thinking overmuch before acting."

Lennox nodded, eyeing him closely with his pale eyes narrowed in appraisal. Then he leaned back on one leg, effectively backing away another step. "I must say, Marston, as I mentioned to Lady Elizabeth prior to your arrival, you look remarkably well considering news we had heard concerning the . . . severity of your ordeal."

Rob's jaw looked rigid, even though Beth saw him force a tight smile. "Rumors cannot always be trusted."

"It was no rumor. I heard it straight from a man imprisoned at York with you."

"There were many of us held there, and more than a few died. It is not surprising that he mistook my death."

Beth noticed just a flicker of something in his eyes as he spoke, but it was gone before she could discern its meaning.

In the process of this exchange, Lord Lennox had regained his arrogant composure, and now he straightened to his full height—still a half head shorter than Rob—to nod in challenge. "Perhaps you would welcome a reunion with him at some future time, my lord?"

"Very like." Rob's gaze remained flat. "Know you where he is now?"

"Some of my men are in pursuit of that information as we speak." Even though the words were civil, the tone was insolent. "I will be sure to alert you when he is found."

Rob nodded, his eyes still cold through the pleasant and carefully blank expression he wore. Beth had come to recognize that as a dangerous look, boding ill for the recipient. "Thank you," he said. "And now if you will excuse us, I promised my wife a dance this evening. It is one of her favorite pastimes for entertainment . . . excepting a game of *merels*, perhaps."

And with that he shifted his gaze to her, the light in it wholly different from that which he had directed at Lennox. It took her breath, and she felt that damnable heat creep into her cheeks as he steered her around the earl and away from the cluster of his men and other guests, leading her toward the musicians and dancers.

Somehow she found her voice. "Please . . . my lord, I do not think I am ready to dance just yet. I am not feeling especially well, of a sudden. Perhaps if I could escape the heat of the hall, for just a few moments . . . ?"

Rob paused in their pace, still holding her hand but twisting to look at her with concern. "You must be feeling truly unwell to postpone a dance, lady." His expression was warm with affection and worry as he looked down upon her, and she felt her heart lurch in response as he nodded. "Allow me to escort you into a secluded corridor until you catch your breath."

"Thank you. Though I hope your offer to return

here and dance with me once I have done so still stands." Beth tried her best to smile brightly at him, but she sensed how wan it must have looked, for Rob only nodded and then redoubled his pace to get her from the room.

"Just a bit further now, lady . . ."

Grasping a cup of wine from the tray of one of the servants as they passed by, he led her toward the door to the right of the great hearth, pausing only long enough to remark to one of their steward's underlings that they would be absenting themselves from the festivities for but a few moments, and instructing him to come and retrieve them if aught was needed before they returned.

And then they stepped through the large, arched door and out of the hall. Cooler, dusky air enveloped her almost immediately, and she heard the large wooden panel swing shut with a thud at the portal behind them. But Rob was not content to remain so near the revelry. Nay, he brought her down two other connecting corridors, finally pausing in one that led to the bedchambers. At this time of evening, with the feast still going strong, it was the least likely place to encounter anyone else.

At last satisfied with their position, he came to a halt, pulling her gently toward him. Even in the dim light, illuminated only by a slow-burning torch down the corridor, Beth could see the glimmer of humor in his devastating blue eyes, as well as the flash of his teeth. He handed her the goblet of wine, bidding her to sip.

"There. This is better than the crowd, heat, and noise, is it not?"

"Aye," she replied, dutifully taking a drink, though in truth she was not so much overwarm and thirsty as she had been shaken by her encounter with Lord Lennox. Handing him the cup after a few more sips, she took a deep breath and leaned back against the wall.

Rob, adept as always at discerning the truth behind her façade, turned to face her with his shoulder to the wall, crossing one booted foot over the other. As if he could read her thoughts, he said, "Lennox is a scoundrel to have cornered you like that. You should not have had to speak with him without me there."

"It could not be helped." She glanced at him, that softer feeling invading her chest again. "Still, I am grateful that you appeared when you did. I could have handled him longer, if need be, and I doubt that he would have undertaken anything more serious here in my own home, with scores of people about. But it was unpleasant, regardless."

"I would have thought the Bruce quick to discipline Lennox after his attack on Dunleavy in June," Rob said, frowning. "Such might have helped the wretch remember his place here tonight."

"I warrant the Bruce does not know. He has been traveling amongst his barons in the north since the parliament held up in St. Andrews in March. Besides, he might not reprimand Lennox so easily, methinks. The earl is one of his staunchest supporters."

"A pity."

"Aye, and yet it does no good to dwell on it. I shall use this time away from the revelry to redirect my thoughts to more pleasant matters . . . such as the dancing that is to come." Beth cast a glance up at him that she was sure would be perceived as dallying, were it being given by a maiden to her swain, rather than by a wife to her husband. "And yet before that, however, I must admit that I have noticed something very important while we are out here in the corridor."

"What is it?"

"We are alone again—for the first time since this afternoon."

Rob paused for a long moment, and the dim light made it difficult to clearly read the expression on his face. She wondered if he would remember the promise she'd made him in their chamber today, just before she'd stepped from the tub where they'd almost made love.

In the next instant she had her answer. She felt the heat of his gaze on her, warm and intense. "We are alone indeed."

Beth moistened her lips, wanting many things right now, but knowing that she would likely have to settle for something a bit less than what she yearned for, unless they were to absent themselves from the feast for the remainder of the night. Regrettably, that was out of the question.

"While what I promised then might not be possible at this very moment, my lord," she murmured, blinking up at him, "I could content myself for now with a kiss, if you would care to give it me."

His sensual mouth quirked into that half smile that never failed to send waves of honeyed desire rippling through her. "A kiss might be arranged, lady." His voice rumbled with yearning and teasing affection, his brow lifting and his gaze never drifting from hers as he added, "For a price."

"Oh?" she asked.

"Aye. First you must grant me the liberty to take you in an embrace of my choosing. Do that, and a kiss is yours."

Beth felt her pulse quicken, but she hid the reaction behind a show of playfulness. "Fie, my lord, anyone might walk by and see us here in the corridor—and your imagination knows no bounds in such things. Do you expect me simply to accept your terms without knowing the details of what you envision?"

"Hmmm, let me see . . ." He made a show of considering what she'd asked, before looking back at h[er] with a devilish glint in his eyes. "Yes."

She grinned back at him. "You seem to have a [pen]chant for making outrageous bargains with [me,] lord."

"And you seem inclined to accept them." [He tilted] his head. "So what is your answer this tim[e?] Do we have an agreement?"

"I suppose I can tolerate an emb[race," she] answered, sighing with feigned exa[speration, though] she could not keep her lips from [twitching,] continuing to smile. "However, [do not make it] ing long. I am eager for that k[iss."]

"I will make it worth you[r while."]

The sweet promise in th[ose words washed over] her, making the already [heady] feeling swell to a head[y peak, rising] higher as he moved [closer. Before she knew what he] intended to claim, s[he] her . . . close enough to feel his warmth, but entirely without touching her. Yet.

"Is something amiss?" she whispered when he remained still for the space of several slow breaths. She could feel her own heart thudding in her chest, deep and swift, its rhythm keeping pace with her rising excitement.

"Nay."

"Then why do you not take your embrace?"

"I am merely trying to decide how I wish to proceed. In a way allowable in public, of course."

His eyes twinkled down at her, the expression in [th]em tender and bold and wicked all at once. Oh, but [he was] handsome. She wanted him badly, more so [than a]y that had passed since he had returned [...]e was a different man from the [...] first married, it was true. [...]one with whom she

[Partially obscured by folded page; visible fragments:]

pen- / me, my / He tipped / me, my lady? / brace first," she / speration, though / playing traitor and / do not keep me wait- / iss." / ose while." / ose words rippled through / (delightful tension she was / y, bubbling simmer. It surged / nto position for the embrace he / hifting to stand directly in front of

lligent / he / ior / and / calm / of plea- / aning in / er to press / ent veering / ith any part of her flesh. He breathed in deeply, fully, and then exhaled on a contented sigh.

"You smell delicious, lady."

She was trembling lightly with the rising force of her desire, and she wasn't certain at first that she would be able to form a response at all. His faint and intoxicating scent enveloped her as well; he stood so close that she could take it in with every delightful breath. He smelled of warmed leather and sunshine, along with a hint of the orris and clove bath powders she'd concocted.

"I might say the same of you," she managed to say quietly. Her body seemed to lean toward him, almost desperate to feel his touch upon her—to press herself against him and slip her hands up his arms and over his shoulders. But still he would not touch her. The relentless longing for it made her bold, and she glanced up at him from beneath the veil of her lashes, adding in a murmur, "Delicious enough to taste, even."

His breath caught for an instant, and she saw the flash of a smile. "In time, vixen. I wish to make this last, you see," he murmured, his lips close to but not touching hers. "And yet I cannot seem to restrain myself. You are too tempting."

"Good. You deserve as much for teasing me like this."

She heard his low chuckle and felt the warm caress of his breath against her cheek; it made her strain toward him, lifting her face with a sound of pure yearning, aching for him. "If you will not take your embrace, then what of my kiss?" she breathed, meeting the sparking heat of his gaze again.

"It is coming. Right . . ." He shifted forward

smoothly, so that every magnificent contour of his body pressed against her from chest to knees, making her gasp with the pleasure of it.

"After . . ." he continued, lifting his hands and sweeping them up along the path of her arms, lighting tingles of delicious sensation all the way up to where he threaded his fingers in her hair and cupped the back of her head.

"This," he finished at last, slipping one muscular thigh between her legs, pressing up and into that most delicate, lightly pulsing flesh at the apex.

Her gasp of surprise quickly shifted to a moan. She already yearned for him far more than she could have believed, and this sensation did naught but increase that desire. She found herself rocking lightly against the expanse of his muscular leg, unable to control her shameless movements, even as he used his superior height to press her back against the wall, increasing her pleasure a thousandfold with the action.

Any sounds she made were captured, however, as he murmured, "And now for that kiss," before taking her mouth with such passion that she might have crumpled to the floor with the thrilling sweetness of it. All that kept her upright was the fact that she was balanced by the wall at her back, held by his powerful arms at her sides—and propped against his thigh between hers, deliciously tormenting her.

He felt like bliss and tasted like heaven. The hard, cool wall behind her served as contrast to the hot, wet sensation of his mouth playing against hers. Emboldened by the raging needs he'd ignited in her, Beth tipped her head up and opened to his tender assault, taking and giving.

Her fingers dug into his shoulders, and she felt every ripple of sinew and muscle at play beneath his shirt—darkly dangerous and sensual—as he gently thrust himself and the heat of his erection against her . . . rocking in rhythm with her movements against his thigh.

Oh, but this had to be sinful. It felt too good not to be, even though they were husband and wife.

It felt wild and just a bit forbidden, the way he was holding her, pressing her up against the wall in this corridor in full view of anyone who might happen to pass by . . .

It felt exhilarating.

The kiss continued for several more delectable moments. Still Beth could not keep back her soft moan of disappointment when he pulled back, his own breath coming harshly, and his eyes glazed with passion so intense, she thought her skin might burst into flames everywhere his gaze traveled across her.

"I cannot continue longer without ravishing you right here in the corridor, lady—and I would never dishonor you in that way," he said. "Responsibilities still await us back in the great hall as well. We must go."

Unable to form a coherent word, she simply nodded her concurrence, letting her tongue dart out to lick her lips. They were swollen and tender from his kisses, and she felt his gaze upon her mouth as she did it . . . felt his erection twitch in response even through his clothing. His hips jerked lightly forward in conjunction with his low groan, so that she could not help but be aware of the thick, full length of him pressed to her belly.

"We will continue this anon, my lord, when the feast is concluded," she said, and the sound of the words was low and roughened from the force of her desire for him.

"God help me," he murmured, stepping away. He jabbed his hand through his hair, releasing his breath in a single, forceful exhalation. In his absence, her limbs felt weak, and she willed the sudden rush of cool air between them to restore some semblance of self-control. He had half turned from her, clearly struggling to regain some balance of his own.

Facing her again after sufficient progress apparently had been made, he cleared his throat, offering her his arm so that he might lead her back to the feasting in the great hall. But even so, the gaze he shot her as they walked burned deep, piercing garments, skin, and soul, it seemed, in one fell swoop and unleashing a new wave of longing through her so great that she feared she would find herself unable to continue with him down the corridor.

In a kind of retaliation for it, she murmured a husky echo of his earlier vow as they continued their seemingly sedate, calm pace back to the feasting in the great hall. "There is one last thing, however, that I must mention, my lord."

"What is it?" he asked.

"When the time comes for finishing this between us, I intend to make it worth your while . . . well worth it."

Chapter 10

Alex was tempting fate by continuing along his path of seduction with Beth, and he knew it. Leaning against the wall and watching the revelry of the feast going on around him, he was very aware that a war was being waged inside him, the outcome of which remained uncertain.

The part of himself that he recognized all too well from his decades spent in pursuit of self-preservation—the part that tended toward the easiest path and that preached a message of doing anything necessary so long as the ends were achieved—kept calling him to ignore all else and continue making love to Beth, hotly, passionately, and as often as possible. It argued that undertaking that act with her was in fact expected of him as the husband he was playing.

There was no lack of attraction between them, after all. She was an eager partner, and the Alex of old would have felt few if any qualms in bedding her. The old him would be milking every drop of pleasure he could from the circumstances he'd been handed, convincing himself in the process that he had no other choice in the matter.

But a new and unexpected voice had been asserting itself inside him ever since he'd set foot inside the walls of Dunleavy Castle, growing louder and more insistent with every intimacy he'd shared with Beth. It flooded him with guilty regret in the awareness that he was taking her under false pretenses. He was deceiving her, and he hated it. How such scruples had arisen in him—*him*, of all men, who was so much farther from noble instinct than his brother or any of their Templar brethren—and why those newfound principles had such power over him, he had no idea. He only knew that they were relentless.

They kept saying that what he had done by coming here in the guise of Beth's husband was wrong enough. But making love to her was truly wicked—the worst form of betrayal he could inflict on her, perhaps. It might be worse, even, than the treachery he was committing by feeding Dunleavy's secrets to the English, for in becoming intimate with Beth he had violated her in the most personal sense, regardless of the fact that he had come to care for her deeply over the course of their time together.

He was an impostor. A tarnished former Templar Knight and a convicted thief who had been mere hours away from feeling the bite of the noose round his neck. He was *not* the esteemed Robert Kincaid, fourth Earl of Marston, celebrated warrior in the battles for Scotland's freedom ... or Elizabeth of Selkirk's lawfully wedded husband.

There was no escaping that fact no matter how much he wished to or how hard he tried.

The part of him that recognized it decried what he was doing here with her ... it urged him to confess, come what may. So strong had its pull become that only two things had forestalled him in bringing the problem to its demanded conclusion: the knowledge that John did not deserve a fate in which he had no hand other than having been a loyal friend . . . and Alex's own innate weaknesses.

Aye, he could not refute that his much longer-standing instincts of survival were putting up a mighty fight at the prospect of surrendering himself on the altar of noble intention. He'd had a taste of what doing the right thing could bring when he'd sacrificed himself for his friend Richard de Cantor during the Wager of Battle they'd been made to fight before the Inquisitors from France. The suffering that had followed for him in the hell of the Inquisition's dungeons had been something he would not allow himself to think on—ever—if he could help it.

And it was this conflict of perspectives that formed the root of the battle at work inside him.

It only kept getting worse with every hour he passed in Beth's delightful company, and with every moment he spent yearning more and more fervently for something he did not deserve and could never truly have with her.

Taking a healthy swallow from his goblet, Alex pondered that painful thought, trying to come to terms with it and with this deceit he was playing. But as he did, he found himself watching Beth take part in a *rondeau* with a dozen others at the center of the great hall. She drew his gaze almost against his will. Ah, but she was beautiful in her enjoyment of the dance, her lovely mouth curved in laughter, her cheeks flushed, and that soft, honey-gold hair of hers swinging silkily, rhythmically from beneath her veil as she swayed with the movements, going round and round in a circle with the other dancers.

He shouldn't allow himself to be so distracted by her, he knew—he had no real right to watch her like this . . . not to mention how dangerous this kind of indulgence was to his ever-weakening sense of self-control where she was concerned. But his gaze was pulled to her as inexorably as a moth fluttering closer to a flame. The two hours since their interlude in the corridor had been sheer erotic torment for him, all of it spent in delicious proximity to her. Every glance they'd shared, every touch and every breath seemed in concert with each other and the rising need between them. It was slowly driving him mad.

Even worse, perhaps, was the knowledge that she felt the pull of attraction between them too, and desired him as strongly as he did her.

His touches and the occasional kisses he'd feathered over her temple or her lips had called that delightful color to her cheeks . . . sending higher the blazing, naughty sparkle in her gray eyes. During the dances they'd shared together, the torment had been more delicious still, for then the opportunity to touch her more boldly—a brush of his thigh to hers, the stroke of his fingers across her palm, or the chance to pull her closer to feel the gentle press of her breasts against his chest as they moved through the steps—had been enough to call up every sinful thought he'd ever had about her.

It was why he'd begged off this latest dance, using the excuse of needing a respite and some wine. The only real respite he'd sought, however, had been from the pounding desire that was consuming him.

It couldn't last much longer.

He couldn't last much longer.

Christ, he had to get his mind off her and them and what he wanted to do to her, before he truly lost control and dragged her from the chamber without a by-your-leave.

Gritting his teeth, he forced himself to turn away from the dancing. His first cup drained already, he took another from one of the servants standing at the ready with libations, determined to find something else to think about, even momentarily. Something to provide him with a little relief from the heat pounding through him. It shouldn't be so difficult, he reasoned. He was supposed to be the lord of the castle, after all. This feast was to celebrate his safe return from English captivity, and there should have been plenty of distractions to take his mind off his troubles.

But all the greetings had been accomplished already and all the niceties completed. Even his fellow conspirator, Stephen, had not returned yet from his meeting with Luc in the forest. At least if he'd been present, it would have allowed Alex the opportunity to speak to him and remind himself of the very real dangers he faced here.

There would be no help from that quarter. Everyone in the great hall seemed occupied in enjoying one of the many pursuits such gatherings provided. The juggling men near the windows had a nice crowd standing around them, the dancers were enjoying the minstrels' efforts, and a bard was entertaining another group at the far end of the chamber, likely with tales of lords and ladies of long ago. Of love tested and destroyed, of secret exchanges of passion and desire, the forbidden fruits tasted and then—

Good God, he was doing it again.

What the hell was wrong with him, that he could not keep his thoughts in control? He had to reclaim his senses, by heaven.

"Has no one ever told you, my lord husband, that standing all alone at your own celebratory feast is hardly a fitting way to spend an evening?"

The flare of simmering heat inside Alex roared up to a full conflagration again, touched off to flames by the mere sound of her voice behind him. He spun slowly on his heel to face the seductive temptress who was his counterfeit wife.

"There are better ways of spending an evening, I know," he murmured, aware that he should stop himself now, even as he heard himself proceed blithely along the road to delicious hell. He quirked his brow and his lip in unison, watching her response, as he added, "Ways considered by most to be far more pleasurable."

"Ah, yes. Perhaps they could be described as . . . exciting, even," she rejoined in a husky whisper, her gaze locked with his.

Sweet angels and saints.

Stop! that nobler voice inside him cautioned. *Resist. Deny. Repress your baser needs and the dallying that will lead to the inevitable fulfillment of them.*

But he could not. Not when every fiber of his being was responding to her, yearning for her in a way encouraged by the selfish habits of a lifetime.

Not when he knew she wanted it as much as he did.

It was as impossible for him to stop right now as it would be for a man lost in a desert, parched and burning, to refuse a cup of blessed water to drink.

"What do you suggest, Beth?" he murmured, never letting his gaze break with hers . . . feeling something that might have been his heart, twisting in the desperate throes of its own demise.

She smiled, the sweetness of that look seducing him down a path of no return. "I think we should retire to our chamber, my lord. The feast is nearly concluded"—she broke her gaze with him for an instant to glance round the chamber—"and many are seeking their rest for the night."

But then something changed subtly in her, her next actions and words devastating him as fully as if he was a green lad, untouched and naïve to a woman's powers.

Moistening her lips with the tip of her pink tongue in a way that sent burning, wanton thoughts hurtling through Alex's mind and straight to certain already inflamed parts of his body, Beth gazed up at him again, blinking. She raised herself on tiptoe and lifted her face to him, brushing those plump, soft lips across his, before she murmured, "I do not think *we* will be seeking rest, however, husband." Through the blanket of need enveloping him, Alex saw her pull back just enough to meet his gaze again, her expression rife with both allure and innocence as she asked, "Do you?"

He couldn't have answered her if the king himself had commanded it. Instead, he swallowed against the thick feeling in his throat, willing the waves of desire sweeping through him to ease enough for him to find his voice again. When he finally managed to form a sound, he said huskily, "I think what we will do or not do will be dependant upon you, lady."

"Is that so?"

That dangerous light was sparking her eyes from gentle gray to silver. Grasping his hand, she tugged it playfully and leaned into him with a wicked whisper. "Then come with me, my lord, for I have delights in store for you."

And so without another word he went with her, pulled along on the tide of her will and his own yearnings, unable to stop himself from accompanying her out of the great hall and down the maze of corridors that led to her apparent destination . . .

The dark and private haven that was their bedchamber.

Even before they got inside, Beth tugged Rob to a stop at the door itself. He had been very quiet all the way to their chamber, and she feared that something weighed on his mind. Ah, but she hated the thought that he was burdened by anything. Nay, she wanted him to know the happiness he gave her . . . wanted to give him the same wonderful feeling in return.

Gripping the front of his tunic, she tipped her face up to press a kiss to his lips. Delicately, she flicked the tip of her tongue in a teasing cadence before dipping into the warm recess of his mouth for an instant, reveling in the low groan that rumbled from him in response. He returned the caress as he reached behind himself while still kissing her, to lift the bar on the door that allowed it to open so they could go in.

"You are a temptress, lady," he murmured, his breath warm and sweet against her mouth. She smiled.

"If I am it is because you make one of me, my wicked lord."

Lifting her hands to thread her fingers together behind his neck, she forestalled their entrance into the room to tug him closer and kiss him again, emotion filling her to the bursting. She was the happiest, most blessed woman in the world, married to a man who loved and cherished her . . . who found her as irresistible as she found him. Heat stung the backs of her eyes, and, smiling, she pulled back, smoothing her hand along the side of Rob's handsome face and letting her fingertips ruffle his hair.

Looking deep into his eyes, she whispered, "I love you, you know."

At first she thought she'd offended him by openly speaking of her feelings like this—remembering too late that, different as he'd seemed since his return home from captivity, from the first days of their courtship, Rob had always favored keeping one's most intimate emotions to oneself. But his reaction to her tender confession stemmed from something different than that, she realized in the next instant, the agonized look on his face reflecting a feeling that went far deeper. He seemed to be carrying an almost unbearable weight as he answered in kind in a voice even more hoarse and broken than hers had been.

"God help me, Beth, but I love you too."

The words soothed her, even as the worry over what was bothering him remained. But she had no chance to pursue it, for without speaking again, he pushed the door open further and strode inside. She followed close behind, realizing how dark it was without the torchlight that had illuminated the corridor. It was also a bit chilly, for though it was September, no fire had been lit, the servants not usually bidden to keep a blaze burning at night until October at least. She shivered slightly, and Rob grabbed a blanket from their bed, throwing it over her shoulders before he walked toward the cold hearth.

In the dim light she could hear his efforts to start a warming blaze, though she couldn't see much in the dark. She moved off to the side, searching for the candle beside their bed. She spent a few minutes in her efforts to light it—long enough that she heard the blaze beginning to crackle in the hearth. Rob had been successful in his endeavor as well, then, she thought. Satisfied, she turned back to face him . . .

And stopped as abruptly as if someone had loosed an arrow into her heart.

Something was very, very wrong. He stood with his back to her, directly in front of the hearth. His palms were clenched into fists and pressed against the wall above the fireplace, his head tipped down and slumped between his shoulders. She could not see whether his eyes were closed, but she sensed they were and that he was looking at naught outside himself so much as at something happening within.

The shock of seeing him like that jolted through her, stabbing deep and rupturing the heady cocoon of desire that had wrapped around her these past hours. "Rob?" she breathed. "Are—are you unwell? Is aught amiss?"

Light flickered up from the fire burning in the hearth, seeming suddenly perverse now for its cheerfulness. It burnished his dark hair and the handsome angles of his face with a warm glow, but still he did not speak and hardly moved, only shaking his head slowly, looking bowed down by something so heavy, he could bear it no longer.

Without speaking again herself, Beth let the blanket fall and strode over to him, placing her hand on his shoulder. At the contact, he sucked in his breath sharply, finally straightening before he turned to face her, even as he took a step back. The expression in his eyes was heartrending, filled with a kind of agony she had never seen there before.

"Aye, lady," he rasped at last. "Everything is amiss. Only I do not know how to make it right."

The world seemed to go preternaturally still for her. She could not move. She could hardly breathe. But she refused to stand here any longer as if death waited in the corner, ready to cut them down.

"What is it?" she asked quietly, the calm, even tone of her voice masking her desperate fear. "Please, tell me."

"I pray John will forgive me, but I can pretend no longer," he murmured, almost as if he uttered a holy plea meant to be heard by none but himself and God.

He breathed in once before exhaling fully, and with that he seemed to stand even straighter, his commanding, solid presence returning. An expression of resolve swept over his handsome features, tightening his jaw, though the shadows remained in his eyes. "I am not the man you think I am, Beth. I am not Robert Kincaid, fourth Earl of Marston." The shadow flickered in his eyes again, filling them with anguish. "I am not your husband."

Disbelief washed through her, and she shook her head, as if that gesture would have the power to undo the hurt of every word he'd just uttered, unraveling them like stitches pulled from fabric. But he did not stop. He would not stop, she thought, recoiling from him a step, and then another, reaching out to grip the back of the chair perched near the little table where they'd played *merels* so many times in the weeks since he'd returned home. Sweet Jesu . . .

He swallowed, the words coming harshly as if he had to force them out. "I am an impostor," he continued, every syllable flaying her heart, "sent to Dunleavy by the order of an English commander to infiltrate, gather information, and pave the way for an assault that is to take place within the next sennight or fortnight—I do not know which yet."

"Oh my God," she breathed at last, her eyes widening and nausea swelling up to choke her. The shreds of her old suspicions began to weave themselves back together, their message, unheeded before, seeming so finite and awful now. She pressed her fingers to her mouth, certain she had been swept into some dark, terrible dream from which there was no escape. "I don't believe you," she gasped. "I can't . . . it's not possible . . ."

"I am telling you the truth, lady, for once in my contemptible life," he said firmly, his mouth twisted with bitterness, "and I am imploring you, for the sake of a man—my loyal friend—whose life hangs in the balance even now because of this sordid scheme, that you hear me out fully before you decide to call guards against me or do anything rash."

"Call guards . . . ?" She echoed his words softly, staring at him in bewilderment. She felt sick, her mind so sluggish with the trauma of absorbing all this that she hadn't truly allowed herself to think past each instant and the next unbearably painful beat of her heart. "Oh my God," she repeated again, taking another two steps back and reaching for anything that she might use as a weapon, the import of what he was saying finally sinking in.

Her vision blurred with a swell of wet heat, and she shook her head frantically again. Choking back sobs, she felt her face twist into a mask of stunned disbelief and grief as she stumbled back a few more steps and raised the heavy iron fire tongs in front of her when he approached.

"Beth, please," he murmured, holding out his hand to her. "I vow I would never hurt you. Oh, God, lady, I could never—"

His voice cracked then too, though he did not break. The sight of the struggle he waged for composure seemed to help her regain some of her own. She felt herself go very calm again. Glancing down, she saw that her hands were clenched so tightly around the metallic length of the tongs that her knuckles were white.

"Just stay back." Her voice was low and commanding, a fact for which she was supremely grateful, considering that her insides were still an aching, raw jumble of emotion. "I want to know who the devil you are, if you are not Robert Kincaid." She tipped her chin up, grating out the additional words, "If you are not my husband."

She was proud that her voice wavered for but an instant. Aside from that she remained strong, unbending.

His answer came back as levelly, his gaze burning with intensity, as if he was willing her to believe him, painful as it was for her to do it.

"My name is Sir Alexander de Ashby. I am English by birth, formerly a Templar Knight of the inner circle, arrested in France and questioned for the crime of heresy. I was freed from the Inquisition by my Templar comrades, including one Sir John de Clifton, who is in English custody even now, being used as bait to compel me to the will of England in this heinous plot against you and the people of Dunleavy."

Beth felt her breath leave her on a single, slow exhalation, as if she was captured in the throes of some nightmare. Blessed Mother Mary, he was a spy. It was true. And if he was one, then—

"The two men I brought with me, Sir Stephen of Cheltenham and Sir Lucas of Dover, are part of the conspiracy against you," he confirmed, as if he'd read her thoughts. "Stephen left the castle grounds this morn on pretext of hunting, but in truth he went to meet with Luc, who has been hiding since his banishment with a small group of soldiers in the wood to the south of the castle. Normally, I would needs accompany Stephen, but I was released of that duty thanks to the feast hosted here tonight."

He looked down for an instant. "Luc is also a former Templar who once served with me in Cyprus. We have a dark history together, lady, and he is very dangerous. It is he who plans to lead the attack against Dunleavy, backed by an English army. Be forewarned."

Even as that awful information sank in, another thought startled Beth, the shock of it stealing her breath and making her yearn to sink to the floor, her knees went so weak with it. "Then Robert Kincaid . . ." she breathed, the knot swelling in her throat and threatening to choke off her breath altogether. She swallowed and managed to finish. "The true Robert Kincaid—he is . . . dead?" She'd paused, adding the last word as a final resort, not wanting to utter it at all, as if speaking it aloud could give it some power it could not possess.

Alex paused before answering, "I did not know him to affirm it with my own eyes, but the English earl who captured me claimed it as the reason he needed me to commit the crime of deception against you."

She did sink down, then, into the chair at the little table, keeping the tongs brandished before her. Grief filled her, milder, though, than she might have expected. It was there, but she could not change that the sadness she felt in knowing Rob was truly gone was less painful to her than the wrenching misery she felt in knowing that the man standing before her had made her fall in love with him and then played her for a fool.

She had to bite back a rueful laugh. It was becoming the guiding principle of her life, it seemed: blind acceptance of the way things were, rather than fruitless wishing for the way she thought they should be.

Perhaps your grief is less because you acknowl-

edged the possibility of Rob's death long ago, having believed it inevitable after so long with no word of him.

The voice was feeble, but its suggestion was valid. Yet it was too much to think on right now, with all the thoughts swirling through her benumbed mind. Shaking her head as if to clear away some of the muddle of it, she fixed her stare again on the man who had betrayed her.

Rob—nay *Alexander*, she reminded herself—had the good grace to look shamed by all he had told her, but after what had happened she did not dare trust her instincts in the matter. He might well be a consummate performer in that as well.

Beth brandished the tongs at him, demanding, "Why are you telling me this now—and how do I know it isn't another of your deceptions, being played against me and my people?"

She saw him wince and was glad. But even so, a kind of ache accompanied that moment of dark rejoicing, settling deeper in her chest and worsening the hurt in her already wounded heart.

"I told you the truth about me because I could not live with myself any longer, deceiving you as I was." He swallowed, his gaze burning into her. "My feelings for you are real, Beth. I never lied about that."

She couldn't speak in answer to that, the hurt in hearing him say it too much for her to bear right now. So she just waited.

"And I am telling you the rest of it," he continued in a voice raw with pain, "in an effort to protect you from what is to come, if I can—as well as for the sake of my friend John." He gazed at her, as if pleading with her to understand. "Lady, I entreat you to confine Stephen to the castle upon his return tonight. He will not be expected to rendezvous with Luc again for another four days. However, my friend will pay the ultimate price for my failure if Stephen gets clear of Dunleavy in the meantime and reports my arrest to Luc."

"Why should I believe you—or care even if I did?" she asked after a moment, knowing the question was a cold one and that it would hurt him. Knowing even as she posed it that she *did* care, far more than she wanted to admit, even to herself.

A dark shadow swept through his eyes again, but aside from that he did not waver. "You shouldn't. I cannot say I would in your place, and yet I swear that what I've told you is the truth." The grief and frustration she felt emanating from him was almost palpable. "Beth, they promised to kill John if I was not successful in my mission with you and in gathering information for waging their assault on Dunleavy. I could not let him die for me. That is why I am asking you to do what you can in your handling of this hell I've caused, to keep it from coming back on him."

Alex's voice lowered a few notches, filled with self-loathing as he added, "He is innocent, and like you his only mistake came in caring for me."

That statement drove home with stinging force, and to mask her reaction to its power over her, she shook her head, offering a hollow, sharp laugh. "Ah, sir, you must think me an enormous fool to have fallen for your ruse so easily."

"Nay, Beth," he answered quietly, after a pause. "I think you are a brave and magnificent woman. I was never worthy of you, and I don't expect you to believe me after all I've done." He swallowed, and his voice sounded hoarse, as if he spoke past a lump in his throat. "But I wanted you to hear the truth from me. Whether you can believe it or nay, you deserve at least that."

Beth never had the chance to make any other response. The door rattled, and she heard a hissed "My lady—Lady Elizabeth, it is Edwin! Open, lest we be forced to create a disturbance and rouse the guests!"

Alex didn't move as she hurried over and lifted the latch. The door swung inward, and then Dunleavy's captain of the guard strode in, followed by a half dozen other of the castle's finest guardsmen, with Edwin at the rear.

"Secure him," the captain murmured, grim-faced as he directed the guards toward Alexander, whose gaze remained fixed on her in resignation as they formed a human wall around him, keeping him separated from her.

"Explain yourselves," Beth demanded.

"You are in great danger, my lady," Edwin murmured. "We all are, thanks to this man. He has constructed a great pretense, leading us all to believe that he is—"

"There is no need to repeat the details, Edwin," Beth broke in, waving her hand to silence him. "I have already learned the extent of the danger and the deception he played upon us," she said evenly, nodding toward Alex.

Her steward looked from her to Alex, and then back to her, clearly perplexed and perhaps appalled as well. But it could not be helped. As strong as she was pretending to be right now, she feared that if she had to hear the litany of Alex's lies again and relive the pain of it all, then she would crumble.

And she could not allow herself that luxury.

She was Lady Elizabeth of Selkirk, and she had responsibilities to her people and to the demesne of Dunleavy. Ridiculous, but she could almost feel the old, familiar burden of it settling over her shoulders again. Oh, but she'd longed to give it over. There was no denying that she had welcomed the chance to share it with this man she had thought loved her and whom she had loved in return. Her own weak yearnings had played a part in the ease of her deception, she knew.

But that was over and done with. She'd learned the truth, and that was what mattered now in deciding what would come next.

Standing straighter and tightening her jaw, lest any hint of the tumultuous emotions inside her might be revealed, she directed her gaze past Edwin, past the captain of the guard, and past his men too . . . letting it lock with Sir Alexander de Ashby's. His gaze was equally anguished, equally stoic, and the impact of that connection and of the awareness that still crackled between them—of the hurt and longing and raw emotion that lingered even now in the very air they breathed—resounded in her imagination, falling like shards of ice upon her already battered heart.

"Aye, this man has already confessed his true identity and the extent of the deceit he has played upon us," she repeated in a quiet voice, her spine ramrod stiff and every muscle rigid. She cocked her brow slightly, still looking at him. "All that remains is for me to determine what I'm going to do about it."

Chapter 11

It was the dead of night.

Alex lifted his gaze from where he sat on the floor, staring up at the wooden-slatted shutter and hearing more than seeing the thick rain that battered down on the castle from the sky above. The rhythm and intensity of the storm varied, interspersed with gusts of damp breeze, but the sound of it all was a welcome distraction from the thoughts that had been bedeviling him for hours.

At Beth's command, he had been confined here in this bedchamber they had shared. It should have been a boon, but for him it was a curse, every corner of this room seeming to carry another memory of her. Of them together. Each one ached, providing a kind of torment no barren dungeon could hope to match.

He'd been told a guard was being posted down the corridor in position to keep an eye on the chamber without attracting undue notice. Alex had agreed to cooperate with the arrangement, concurring with Beth's decision to be as inconspicuous as possible in the matter of his arrest. To move him down into the dungeon cell where he belonged would have been to foolishly trumpet to all the guests at Dunleavy—Lord

Lennox included—that trouble was afoot, and that the castle was vulnerable once more.

No one wanted to invite another attack from any quarter. Excuses could be made come morning for his absence. Illness, a pounding head from the previous night's reveling—anything to quell suspicion. And then once the guests had all left, Beth would make a final decision about what to do with him.

He did not hold out much hope.

He had heard naught from anyone since she, Edwin, the captain, and the guards had left him here. He did not know how Edwin had learned the truth about him, or whether Beth had done as he'd asked for John's sake and confined Stephen upon his reentry through Dunleavy's gates. He did not even know if Stephen had returned at all. Perhaps Luc had decided to betray him, already having procured the information he needed to strike. Stephen might even now be resting safely in the berth of his English comrades again.

It wouldn't have surprised him. Naught could surprise him any longer, after what had happened and what he'd realized about himself in the past few hours.

For among all the astonishing events of this night, one stood out as most astonishing of all for him. He'd discovered that he had told the absolute truth when he'd admitted to Beth that he loved her. Contrary to every inner caution and what seemed almost a lifetime of vigilance against anything of the sort, he'd allowed himself to fall in love, and with none other than the beautiful and resourceful Lady Elizabeth of Selkirk.

It boggled his mind, disrupting his notions about himself and the emotional boundaries he had never had trouble setting and abiding by before.

And as if that wasn't shocking enough, he'd also realized that without bribery or coercion of any kind, he would be willing to lay down his life freely for someone other than himself. *For her.*

It was staggering. It meant that somewhere inside the hollow, selfish shell of a man that he'd thought himself to be, he wasn't entirely bad. He could taste redemption without pronouncing it bitter. Nay, in telling her the truth at last, he had found the experience a sweeter draught than he had ever imagined it could be.

He only wished that he would be living long enough to undo some of the harm he had caused her with his lies.

Another cool breeze gusted through the shutter, bringing with it the scent of the rain. In just three or four more hours the birds would begin sounding the arrival of the new day, Alex realized. And it might well prove to be the last dawn he would ever know, for if all the guests left this day, it was likely he'd find himself hanging from the battlements before sundown.

Better not to think of that now, he reminded himself wryly. He'd become expert in the process of preparing for his own imminent demise over the past decade or so, first as a devil-may-care young warrior, then as a Templar Knight of the inner circle, and finally as the mercenary he had been when he was captured by the English forces outside Carlisle. Dwelling on the prospect of dying did naught to change it; he'd accepted that truth long ago.

Instead he stood, releasing himself from his cramped position and moving to sit in the larger, armed chair he used to occupy during his many games of *merels* with Beth. It was positioned on one side of their little table, near the now low-burning fire, and the sight of it sent a pang through him. Pausing only long enough to toss another log on the fire in hopes of warding off the dampness, he sank into the chair with a sigh, stretching his legs in front of him.

He supposed he should be thankful that she had decided to forgo binding him in his confinement here. It made the hours easier to handle, it was true, keeping at bay the other haunting memories that would not seem to leave him alone ... the ones that being chained in the darkness surely would have unleashed in him. Those old nightmares still wielded vicious power over him, if he allowed himself to think on them too long. And tonight, all he *could* do was think.

There were many dark memories buried in his mind, all of them terrible, but in the blackest hours in particular, certain shadows came out more readily to torment him. For it was at this time of night during his hellish imprisonment by the Inquisition that many of his Templar brethren—men who had refused to die on the rack, or the strappado, or the wheel—had most frequently seemed to give up the ghost, almost *willing* themselves to breathe their last. He had always wondered why so many seemed to have chosen that time to die, never coming to any answer that satisfied completely.

Perhaps they had given up because it was at an hour when night was inexorable and everything seemed most futile.

Perhaps it was a way to thwart their Inquisitors, cheating them of a victim just before the start of a new day of questioning.

And perhaps it was simply God's method of bestowing a final gift upon His faithful servants, removing those suffering souls in the peace of the night, where they could simply drift away into the dark instead of leaving with a scream of agony frozen in their throats.

Regardless, it was an hour with which Alex was all too familiar in a wrenching, personal way, having prayed in *his* fetid cell more times than he cared to remember, delirious with thirst and wracked by pain, for the sweet release of death. It had never been granted.

He'd thought himself too sinful to deserve it.

Now he questioned whether it might just have been that he'd still had too much to learn before dying—about himself and the beauty that could be had along with the bitterness of life . . . about the miracle of loving someone without limit or ending. He felt the force of that knowledge now, giving him purpose, and filling him with heady power.

Letting go a harsh laugh and shaking his head, he leaned forward, lacing his fingers together loosely, with his forearms on his knees. How predictable, he thought. Ah, yes, and just like him to finally figure out what was most important in life only when he was about to lose it forever.

A creaking sound echoed from near the door, startling him in the relative quiet of the room. Though he couldn't tell from his position, the shifting of shadows told him that someone had entered the chamber. How many there were he could not tell, and he shifted his gaze in that direction, unable to see around the bed to discern any details in the matter. His body tensed in preparation, though he did not move overtly. Nay, he simply readied himself for facing what this might be about and how bad, the endless months of torment he had spent in France having left an indelible, awful mark upon him and his instincts in such situations.

He heard footsteps. It was one person, alone. Not too bad, then. Unless it was a very strong, very large man with several weapons, it seemed unlikely that whoever had come here intended to haul him away and use painful persuasion to extract further details about his spying activities.

That left the obvious question. Why was he being visited here, and at this time of night? And by whom? Unless—

Beth.

His heart lurched as thought and vision came together. She stepped out from behind the bed, approaching to within four paces of him; then she just stood there without saying anything for a few moments. Rain continued to beat its muted song on the roof, but it was still quiet enough in the chamber that Alex thought he could hear the gentle sound of her breathing.

He wanted more than anything to touch her. He wanted to soak her into his very skin, so that he could remember every nuance of her scent, how she moved, and talked, and felt in his arms. He yearned to wash away all the pain he had caused her and that resonated in him still.

But he couldn't do anything yet. He didn't know

how she felt about him or even why she had come here tonight.

"I wondered if you would be awake," she said at last.

Her voice was low, and he tried but could not interpret aught from the way she spoke. So he settled for handling this the best way he knew how: with honesty and a touch of dark humor.

"I decided not to sleep." He shrugged, his lip curling up on one side in that way he couldn't seem to stop himself from doing, regardless of how much trouble it usually brought him. "It seemed a waste of time if this night was going to be my last."

He was surprised at the expression that swept over her delicate features. Then she frowned for a moment before tossing her head almost defiantly and meeting his gaze again. "You are not going to be executed, Alexander."

"Alex," he murmured, watching her and wondering what she was about, even as something inside him twisted with a desperate hope he could not allow himself to fully recognize. Not yet . . .

She flushed, her gaze dipping down. "Very well, then—Alex."

"I am glad to hear it."

"What?"

He sat back in the chair. "That you've decided to forgo executing me, considering that I likely deserve it." He released his breath on a slow sigh. "It is a welcome reprieve, lady, and I am grateful to hear of it."

She looked almost embarrassed, which struck him as incongruous considering just who had wronged whom. "It is what I came here to tell you," she said, glancing at him again, though the movement was hesitant. "I thought you might be wondering about it . . . considering the severity of what you confessed."

He nodded. She didn't want him dead; that was good. What she actually *did* intend to do with him could wait until she was ready to tell him of it, he decided. In the meantime, there was something else he needed to ask her, lest every guilt-laden act he had committed already proved to be for naught.

"What of Stephen?" he asked quietly. "Has he been secured as well?"

From the way she stiffened, he knew she remembered why he was asking. But when she answered, he realized that her reaction stemmed from something far different from what he had anticipated.

"Sir Stephen was captured even before Edwin came here with the guards to arrest you."

"What?"

She did not shift her gaze away from him, her demeanor calm and cool in the face of his surprise. "As did I, Edwin also suspected from the first that something was amiss when you appeared so suddenly at Dunleavy, right after rumor of your"—she broke off, looking discomfited "of my husband's death reached us. Unlike me, however, Edwin did not find his suspicions lessening with time. When Sir Stephen left Dunleavy alone yestermorn, Edwin saw to it that he was followed by three of our best guardsmen."

Beth paused. "I do not know how closely you had aligned yourself with the two men who accompanied you into Dunleavy, sir, and so I don't know how to proceed with the rest of what I wish to tell you."

"Any *alignment* as you call it, lady, came from necessity, not affection, I can assure you."

She nodded. "Then I will just out with it. There was a scuffle when the guards attempted to forestall Sir Stephen, and in the process of it, he was killed."

Alex uttered a low curse, shaken by the news. *Stephen was dead?* He had been the enemy, it was true; his death could not be truly mourned, yet Alex was fair enough to recognize that he had also been a man of conviction, reliable and even-tempered in his approach to most circumstances.

"Some documents related to the plot against Dunleavy were recovered from Sir Stephen. Before he died he admitted your involvement in them," Beth continued.

Ah, the news just kept getting better and better.

"That is what compelled Edwin to come here last night," he finished lowly. Everything made perfect sense now, disturbing as it all was.

He saw Beth nod, but he was too overwhelmed with what he'd learned to acknowledge it. None of it was unexpected, perhaps, but it was devastating in many ways, not least of which was what it probably meant for John.

"God's blood, I couldn't have made it any worse if I'd tried," Alex muttered, tipping his head up and jabbing his fingers through his hair. "Luc won't spare him now—hell, he might already be dead."

"If you are speaking about your friend Sir John, I do not believe aught will have changed for him. Sir Stephen was slain near to Dunleavy, in the wood beyond the gates, I am told. Unless someone followed him back to the castle, no one else would have any way of knowing that all did not go as planned."

Alex grasped at the possibility. "Are you sure?"

Beth nodded. "The struggle occurred far from the meeting place with Sir Lucas, according to the guards who were involved in it. The wretch has no reason to think aught amiss here, with Sir Stephen or with you."

As she spoke, a kind of warmth seemed to edge out some of the cold inside Alex, just a little. John might still be alive. And Beth cared that he knew about it . . . aye, she had gone out of her way to share with him details that might set his mind at ease.

She *cared*.

It was a heady thought, this realization that she might cherish feelings for him other than hate. He held on to it for dear life, letting the possibility seep into his very bones.

"Thank you for telling me." He spoke with sincerity, trying to imbue each word with the full emotion of gratitude she deserved. It was so difficult not to reach out to her, but he kept himself tightly controlled. "I am grateful for your candor, lady, more than you know."

"You're welcome."

Her poised demeanor seemed to slip a little again in the next moment, however, and she glanced away. "It is not concerning the same matter, perhaps, and yet while I am here, there is something else I feel compelled to"—she stopped for a moment, looking back to him. "What I mean is that there is something more I think you should know."

"Aye?"

"I wish to assure you that you need not fear that any overt . . . discomfort will be employed against you while you are confined at Dunleavy."

There was that embarrassed twitch again. She caught her bottom lip between her teeth, and the sight sent a spill of pleasure through Alex, even as he recognized the ominous truth of what she was sharing with him. It appeared that someone had suggested torturing him as a way to get any information he might have neglected to tell them already. She had refused. He would wager it was Edwin who had recommended that method of questioning, for the steward had never warmed to him. No matter, Alex had another reason to be grateful to Beth, by all appearances.

"I owe you my thanks again, it seems."

She gave a short nod, and though she said nothing to indicate it, he got the distinct impression that she was readying to leave. Desperate to keep her with him, even for a few moments longer, he asked, "Is there aught else you came here to tell me, Beth?"

As he uttered the question, he kept his gaze fixed on her. Willing her to look at him again.

She responded as he'd hoped she would, lifting her head to meet his gaze, her gray eyes soft and lovelier than ever. "Nay—well, aye . . . it is just that—"

She stopped, shook her head, and then flashed him a look that strangely enough flooded him with relief and happiness. It was that almost insolent expression that had so intrigued him from the very start. It was Beth, being . . . well, *Beth*, full of spirit and fire. Far preferable to the uncertain, pensive woman of these past hours, and he found it difficult not to grin, seeing it.

"What, sir—do you find me amusing?" She nearly prickled with annoyance, and though he was able to keep from laughing, he couldn't stop the swell of sweet emotion inside him.

"Nay, lady," he said with utmost earnestness. "In truth I find you unbearably beautiful."

That stopped her in her tracks again; whatever other saucy comment she'd been about to make froze in her throat. She snapped her mouth shut and swallowed, just looking at him. "What did you say?"

"I said I think you're beautiful, Beth—and noble, generous, intelligent, and just." He kept his gaze level. "Naturally, you possess many more fine qualities, but that should serve for a start."

"Indeed."

Was that the hint of a smile?

"To be fair," he added, deliberately trying to provoke her further, "I suppose I could add 'exquisite when angry' to that list, having experienced it for myself last night."

"If you did, it was well deserved," she groused. "However, it would no longer be correct, for I am not truly angry with you anymore."

That set him back on *his* heels—or rather on another part of him, considering that he was still sitting. He stared at her, wondering if he had nodded off at last and all this was some kind of unexpected, pleasant dream. "What did you say?" he asked, not realizing until it was too late that he was repeating the same phrase she had spoken a few moments ago.

"I said I'm not entirely angry with you anymore."

"What does 'not entirely' mean?"

She fixed him with her gaze. "I have had a chance to think about all you said when you made your confession to me—and I am willing to admit that perhaps I understand a little of why you chose the path you did."

"You do?" He tried not to sound too hopeful.

"Aye. A little."

"Then you've forgiven me?"

"Certainly not." She arched her brow. "In fact, I hope you've suffered mightily these past hours as you sat in solitude, contemplating your fate."

Although the hours here had been tolerable enough compared to some he had passed in his life, he nevertheless admitted, "It hasn't been pleasant."

"Good."

Again he had to hold back a laugh. By the saints, she was a delight. He could think of no other woman who would have been capable of this kind of bantering with him after all that had happened.

He kept his smile at bay as much as he could to counter, "Very well, lady . . . is it fair at least to say that you no longer consider me a bodily danger to you?" He let his gaze drift toward the fireplace; all implements had been removed when she and the others left last evening, and now he decided to chance a small jest. "No need to raise the tongs against me again?"

"I can forgo such defense, I believe," she said dryly, "though it would behoove you to remember that I am more than proficient with a dagger." She widened her eyes with exaggerated seriousness. "Be warned that I may have one tucked up my sleeve at this very moment."

"I will be on my guard, to be sure."

But then they fell into silence again, the lighter moment having passed and neither one of them seeming to know what to say in the face of this awkwardness that still stretched between them.

He gestured to the chair opposite him on the other side of the small gaming table, hoping to perhaps bridge that distance, even just a little. "As we seem to agree that I am harmless—"

She gave him a pointed look, and he amended, nodding in deference, "—that I am not an immediate *danger* to you, would you be so kind as to sit with me for a while?"

She hesitated, clearly uncertain, and he raised his hands in mock surrender, murmuring, "You can bind my arms behind me, if you like, to be assured of your safety."

"You would deserve it, knave that you are."

"Anything for your comfort, lady."

He offered the pledge quietly, only half in jest this time, forcing himself to be patient and to wait, when what he wanted to do was to leap up and pull her close, persuading her in a way that any words he could conceive never could.

She was so beautiful to him.

Ah, just looking at her fed his soul like naught else on earth. It was because her beauty came not only from the pleasing arrangement of her features, but also from something deep within. He saw all the nobility, honor, and goodness that had drawn him to her from the very beginning reflected in those expressive eyes, and his arms ached to hold her, even though he had no right to do it.

She would have to come to him first, he knew, if she would come to him at all, and he prayed he still had a chance.

At last she shook her head lightly. She had worn no veil or wimple when she came into their chamber, and that honey-gold hair picked up the fire glow that turned it to burnished silk, while her brow was furrowed with the doubts at work inside her. "I should go, sir. After all that has happened . . ." Her voice trailed off, and she shook her head again. "I should be doing everything in my power to separate myself from you. I should *not* allow myself to venture closer again . . ."

Alex felt every slow, heavy beat of his heart as if it might pound out of his chest. He was holding his breath, he realized, and as he met Beth's gaze, something inside him twisted to see a yearning there that echoed his own, by all the blessed angels and saints. It gave him the courage to span the silence with one word—an invitation, really—to cast away logic and embrace only the wonder of what could be felt still between them.

"But . . . ?" he murmured.

She took a swift, sharp breath, her eyes glistening with all she was trying to hold back and could not.

"But I cannot leave," she said, the whisper ragged, as if it was being wrenched from her. "Oh, God, I cannot stop myself from wanting to be near you."

Alex closed his eyes, what she had just said pounding into him, filling him with an intensity of joy the like of which he had never known in his life.

He stood, taking a tentative step toward her . . .

and then she was in his arms, and he was pulling her to him, holding her close, and cradling her to his chest—pressing endless kisses atop her head and across her brow and all along the salty wetness of her cheeks.

"Sweet Jesu, but I love you, Beth," he murmured hoarsely. "And I am sorry—so very sorry for the hurt I've caused you." He held her against him, knowing in that instant that he never wanted to let her go.

"Are you truly?"

The question sounded muffled and more than a little soggy, and he smiled as she leaned back in his embrace to gaze up into his eyes with a loud sniff. Her hair was mussed. A few tendrils of it clung wetly to her cheeks, accentuating those luminous eyes with the lashes clumped into darkened spikes. Her cheeks were blotchy, and her nose was reddened at the tip.

He thought her the most beautiful woman he had ever seen.

"Aye, I am." He brushed her hair back from her temple with his fingers, willing his hand not to shake with all that he was feeling. "I should have told you the truth long ago and trusted your generous heart, knowing you would do what you could to keep John from suffering for my misdeeds."

"Yes, you should have." She pressed her cheek into his palm, putting her hand over his and closing her eyes for an instant before she looked at him again. "I cannot remember ever being as angry or hurt in my life as I was when you told me of your deception. It was only later that I found myself imagining what you must have felt, facing what you had faced."

"You would have handled it far better, I am certain."

She shook her head slightly, gazing up at him again and lifting her hand to brush her thumb over his lips. "I do not know what choice I might have made were I thrust into the same circumstances that you were, Alex. All I know for certain is that what happened between us is real and true, regardless of what name I call you."

He smiled. "I am relieved to hear you say it—though I would not think it amiss should you decide to call me knave rather than Alex from now on, considering."

"It would suit," she agreed, that hint of something lighter showing once more in her expression.

She went very still in his arms, looking at him, seeming as if she wanted to see into his very soul. There was something at work in her, he could tell. What it was, though, he had no idea. She had welcomed his embrace again, it was true, but he could not deny that she'd remained silent in response to his declaration of love for her, returning no such words in kind. He didn't blame her for it, of course. Nay, he couldn't; not after what he'd done. But now he wondered if she was readying to push him away again. Uncertainty wound its way once more into the chambers of his heart, so recently filled with happiness at her seeming acceptance of him.

"What is it?" he managed to ask quietly.

Her gray eyes seemed more luminous than usual, but that look of utter seriousness she'd worn had indeed shifted gradually to something else before his gaze. Something arch and teasing and just a bit seductive. The uncertainties inside him altered in kind, changing to something very different. To a need that began to take root as she spoke, in a voice husky and sensual, carrying with it a note of challenge.

"Are you willing to do aught in the way of making amends to me for what I've suffered, Alex?"

"Of course," he replied, watching her and wondering if he could be mistaken about her mood and intent right now . . . and hoping that he was not.

She nodded, that pink tongue darting out to moisten her lips. The tiniest of smiles tipped up the corners of her mouth as she spoke again, and that expression along with the three words she uttered next sent any doubts about just what she meant hurtling into the abyss.

"Then prove it."

Chapter 12

Beth's command rocked through Alex, sending jolts of tingling, red-hot desire where not even a hint of the same had resided moments earlier. He stiffened—in two very distinct ways. At the same time, his breath caught, and he just looked down at her, never having imagined in his wildest dreams that he would veer in the course of one short hour from contemplating his own hanging to the glorious prospect of making love to the woman he had come to cherish more than anything or anyone else in the world.

"Ah, lady," he murmured, shaking his head in bemusement, "do you know what you are asking of me?"

"I believe I do," she rejoined, and her look gave credence to that claim, even as it pitched his fever higher.

He smiled and tipped his head, taking her mouth gently at first, then more fully, deeply, responding to the dangerous urges she'd lit inside him. She tasted wonderful, the sweetness of her mouth moving under his a bliss he'd thought he'd lost forever. After a few moments of that delicious torment he shifted to press a few more kisses to the soft skin beneath her ear, feathering his lips along the delicate curve of her jaw until he reached her mouth again. He ceased his kissing long enough to whisper, "Do you have any idea how much I want you right now, Beth?"

He felt her smile in return as she nodded, knew the delight of her touch when she reached up and brushed her fingers from his temple to his jaw. "I seem to recall that we have been interrupted in our amorous pursuits several times in the past few days." She pressed her lips to a spot beneath his chin, and her fingers threaded into the hair at the base of his head, lightly stroking. The exquisite sensation made the skin all over his body tingle, sending shuddering pleasure down the length of his spine.

Then she pressed herself full to him, so that he could feel every luscious hollow and curve, fitting against him in the way a woman's body was meant to mold to a man's. It drove him mad with desire for her—though what she said next made that yearning rise even higher.

"A woman suffers differently from a man in such things, I think," she said matter-of-factly. "You have been forced to stop so oft in the midst of our lovemaking that I hope it might add a certain . . . piquancy to the idea of undertaking the act again with me now, *without* stopping." She kissed him again, full on the mouth this time, ceasing only to murmur, "Until you are satisfied . . ." before renewing the kiss, flicking out her tongue over his lips once more and whispering, "completely."

It nearly brought him to his knees.

"Minx," he growled, "you must cease with your

tempting, lest what I wish to do with you is brought to its conclusion before I can truly begin."

"I pray you wait no longer to begin, then"—she flashed him an undeniably coy look—"for I would hate to miss a single moment of what you have planned."

A low chuckle rumbled from him, and he ran his hands down her back, kneading, rubbing, making her arch into him with soft sounds of her own need before he let his palms slip down to the curve of her buttocks. Then he tugged her flush to him so that she could not help but feel his jutting heat against her belly even through their clothing. She moaned so sweetly in response that he thought he would explode from the desire to make her his again.

Swinging her around, he pressed her up against the wall and kissed her hard, cupping her face and whispering hot, wanton descriptions of what she was doing to him with her dalliances . . . and of what he wanted to do to her as well. All the while her graceful hands worked at his breeches, unlacing and then loosening them so that she could grasp the heated, needy flesh beneath.

She bared his erection and took hold of it, and the contrast of her cool touch against his burning skin made him suck in his breath with a hissing sound. Oh, that was good. Her grip was firm—pure heaven as she pulled and stroked him—but he knew it was only a hint of the paradise awaiting them.

Unable to withstand the temptation any longer, Alex slid his hand up under her skirts and chemise, lifting them round her waist in a crumpled pool of wine-hued damask and white linen, and keeping them pinned there with his arm tucked beneath the luscious curve of her buttocks. At the same time, he slipped his other hand behind one of her knees, raising her leg up, opening her to accept him.

Her arms clung to his shoulders, her head flung back in the intensity of her desire as he lifted her from the floor, pulling her toward him and the part of him that ached to be buried deep inside her . . .

Beth stiffened for just an instant, touching the side of his face and murmuring, "Wait, Alex . . . look at me. Look at me now . . ."

Through the haze of his passion, Alex did as she asked, and as his gaze locked with hers, he saw the depth of her emotions shining clear in her eyes. She whispered, "I want you to know that it is *you* I give myself to, Sir Alexander de Ashby. Only you . . ." The words and the gentle sound of her voice filled his very soul, it seemed.

The beauty of what she was saying washed over him then, seeming to ease a lifetime of wounds, slights, and struggles with the balm of her sweet acceptance. His voice was ragged and his heart overflowed with the intensity of what he felt for her as he answered, "By all that is holy, Lady Elizabeth of Selkirk, I don't deserve you, but I swear that I will try to be worthy of this gift you have given me . . ." His words faded into a rasp, and he paused for another moment more, wanting this to be perfect more than he'd ever wanted anything before.

As if she was in some kind of silent, wonderful communion with him, Beth nodded, her eyes glistening as she murmured her encouragement for him to continue. He needed no second invitation. Still with his gaze fixed on her, Alex lifted her a bit more, her back pressed to the wall . . . and then with one smooth, firm thrust, he impaled her on his thick length.

The shock of pleasure was overwhelming, and they both went still. Alex's breath had been captured on a gasp along with hers as the extraordinary sensations spilled through him, rippling to the ends of his fingers and toes. It was magnificent. Almost too much to withstand . . .

He closed his eyes. Heat stung the backs of his lids with the love he felt for this woman—this wonderful, giving, honorable woman—and the knowledge of that truth flooded him with warmth and life.

Every muscle in his body tightened, and sparks swept over his vision. Then she rocked against him once, twice, and it felt so incredible that he was forced to let go of her knee, slamming his palm against the wall to brace himself and remain upright through the glorious onslaught of it.

But Beth had only begun his delicious torment. She kept shifting and squirming on him, and the feeling maddened him with desire until he could not help but begin to move in concert with her. With a low groan he surrendered to the allure of her sweet writhing on him and began to rock in and out of her welcoming, silky-wet warmth. The muscles in his arms and legs strained, flexing with the effort to go slowly. Trying to make it last for both of them.

Ah, but it felt so good . . . so good . . .

Alex buried his face against Beth's throat as he stroked into her, loving her completely, and using his mouth too now, to kiss and taste the salty warmth of her skin. She smelled of roses in a spring rain; her scent filled his senses, making him want her even more as she arched against him and murmured his name mingled with sighs and soft cries of passion and devotion to him.

God, but he loved her, Alex thought as he worshipped her body with his own, trying to show her with this as much as he had with the words he'd spoken to her earlier. He wanted her to feel how much he cherished her and absorb her into him until he could not tell where she began and he ceased to be.

They moved together as one flesh, their pace gradually increasing. Her body met his thrust for thrust as he slid almost free from her slick, tight embrace and then rocked in deeply, fully, again, and again, and again. He felt her begin to tense . . . felt the half moons of her nails biting into his shoulders through his shirt. He welcomed the sting of it as she strained against him, her body trembling, her breath coming in harsh, shallow rasps as she reached for that bliss he so longed to give her . . .

Alex shifted slightly, changing his angle so that each stroke slid down more firmly across that tender bud at the apex of her intimate flesh. She gasped with the pleasure of it. Another thrust . . . another . . . one more . . . and suddenly, she went rigid. Her body arched violently, and she cried out as she shattered around him, the force of her orgasm rippling through her and causing her to rhythmically clench and release inside, over and over in spasms that caressed him to the edge of perfect bliss.

But no further. He would not let himself tip into paradise. Not yet.

With a gentle oath, Alex caught her, pulling her close to his chest as she began to go limp once her climax passed. Swinging her over to the bed, he gently laid her down. Their bodies were still joined and he kept rocking, following her lead as she came down from the heaven of release. With Herculean determination, he kept himself in control, forcing his ardor to cool to manageable levels. For now, anyway.

"Ahhh, that was wonderful," Beth sighed, smiling as she stretched her arms up over her head before bringing her hands down. Those gentle fingers played over him, caressing his back and buttocks and tugging him deeper, more firmly into her. "And I am the most fortunate of ladies in knowing there will be more, since you have not yet finished," she said with a mischievous lilt to her voice.

"You are truly a vixen," he murmured, kissing her again. "Insatiable . . ."

In answer, she cradled his hips between her lifted knees, coaxing him to penetrate her more fully and sending shocks of delicious sensation through him that no amount of his will could lessen.

". . . and a wanton as well," he managed to add hoarsely, feeling the swell of need building, spiraling upward again.

"Mmmmm . . ." she replied, tipping her hips up to him while still smiling. "If I am, it is your fault, sir."

"Isn't everything?" he teased.

"You are beginning to accept that important truth, I see." She laughed softly, even as she tilted her head up against the mattress with a throaty groan, her eyes closing as an expression of ecstasy swept across her already beautiful face, making it even more lovely, impossible as that seemed.

"Careful, lady," he said, bending to kiss her throat

again at the same time that he captured both her wrists in his hands, pulling her arms up to pinion them in seductive captivity above her head. "I have ways to make you submit to my greater will." He dropped kisses toward her gown's neckline, using his other hand to tug the bodice open, and adding in a whisper filled with sensual promise, "Ways to make you beg for mercy . . ."

With that he freed her breasts from the constraints of cloth and lacing, delighting in her gasp as he kissed and suckled at each creamy, pink-tipped mound in turn, tickling her lightly with his fingers as well.

"I surrender," she cried out far too soon, arching up toward his mouth another instant before an impish light came into her eyes again, and she rolled away from him onto her belly. Her voice was husky as she looked over her shoulder, her words and expression a bold invitation. "As you have subdued me, sir, you may now have your way with me. I am yours for the taking."

It was a sight that would have set a eunuch afire.

Alex swallowed. Several times. His erection twitched, throbbing so hard he thought he could feel the beat of his heart in its pulsing. Beth had lifted herself up onto her knees, perching on the bed in front of him. The rich wine and pristine white of her skirts and chemise were still bunched up around her hips, framing the creamy curve of her buttocks, with the delicate, glistening pink folds of her sex displayed provocatively between.

Heaven have mercy . . .

She wiggled her backside, tossing her head so that her golden hair spilled down her back as she called playfully to him, "Am I not submissive enough for you, my lord?" She tilted her head to meet his gaze again. His throat went dry, and he was struck once more by his good fortune in being so in love with a woman who seemed to delight in sensual pleasure as much as he did . . . even a forbidden pleasure as wicked and tantalizing as this.

"Will you not give over your noble restraint at long last?" she murmured, the trust in her eyes as she gazed at him now undoing him in a way that went deeper than all the passion in the world could have done.

"Aye, nymph," he answered lowly, his voice a rasp of desire for her. "You have seduced me beyond hope."

As he finished speaking he placed his hands on her hips . . . and in the next breath he lunged smoothly forward, sinking into the soft, silken paradise of her with a groan of pure surrender.

It was indeed a paradise. And more.

Alex felt his reason leaving him, felt every logical thought fleeing, lost in the magnificent sensations that spilled through him, pounding him like a violent, heady storm. He felt the pressure of his release building at the base of his spine, driving him forward, making him dip deeper into her honeyed warmth, again and again and again . . .

Vaguely, he was aware that Beth cried out with another climax, her inner sheath clenching and fluttering around him. But then his own release was sweeping over him, stunning him with its force. He bit back a shout as he spilled into her, his hips jerking with the spasms, unable to control the incredible waves of sensation he felt as he emptied himself into her.

When it was over he collapsed, somehow managing to jerk sideways at the last moment so that he would not crush her with his weight.

He had never felt such intensity of lovemaking in his life, with any woman. It took several long minutes before his breathing resumed an even somewhat normal pace, and several more before he found the strength to open his eyes.

When he did he saw Beth lying there, replete, thoroughly beautiful . . . and staring directly at him. She wore an enigmatic expression that made something twist inside him, and struggling to gather his wits after the unbelievable power of what they'd just experienced together, he smiled.

"I am afraid you have depleted me, lady. Give me but three or four weeks and I might be capable of properly sitting up again . . . and breathing and thinking and seeing as well," he finished on a jesting note.

Beth smiled too, but her mouth was tremulous as she continued to gaze at him. Reaching out, she brushed her fingers through the hair at his brow, pushing the waves back. "There is not time enough for that, I fear," she said softly. "You have but a few hours at most until dawn."

Something went still in Alex. He felt more alert by necessity, suddenly, for it seemed he was about to learn the alternative to execution that she had planned for him.

"And why is that important, lady?" he asked.

She paused before answering, and he heard the

light catch in her breathing that warned him what she was about to tell him was difficult for her. Perhaps even painful.

Her eyes glistened, but she blinked the wetness back. The expression on her face was courageous and heartbreaking all at once as she finally answered, "Because you must leave Dunleavy by then, Alex. Before morning breaks, you must be as far from the castle grounds as you can get. I am afraid there is no other choice."

Chapter 13

Beth watched the array of emotions shift across Alex's handsome face in response to her request that he leave. He rolled to sit next to her on the bed, shoving back his hair with his hands, and her heart twisted in the knowledge that he was likely more than a little confused at her sudden turnabout from the passion they had shared just moments earlier. She was too, in her own way, though it had been at her urging that they'd made love. She hadn't been able to stop herself from seizing one final moment of joy with him, even knowing what would need to come afterward.

But now cold, harsh reality would be denied no longer.

"I wish there was another way," she said quietly.

"There is always another way," he countered. "The one you are suggesting is the one I've always taken in the past."

"It cannot be helped."

"Aye, it can." He went still for a long while after that, his expression filled with self-loathing. He met her gaze before he spoke again. "You recall what I told you last night of my brother, Damien—and my friends Richard and John, do you not?"

She nodded in silence, the details of what he had told them all during his questioning fresh in her mind's eye.

"They are good men, Beth. All three are warriors of noble heart who risked their lives to save me—and I repaid them by stealing the Templar treasure they'd vowed to protect. When I was captured near Carlisle and coerced into deceiving you, I was trying to sell a golden bowl so that I could break all ties with everyone and everything I knew. Leaving in the midst of trouble is how I have always handled difficulties in my life."

"This is different," Beth argued.

"Nay, lady." He shook his head, looking distraught. When at last he spoke again, his admission was bittersweet. "Unfortunately, I am very good at running away. For the first time, I wish to stay and do what is right. It is contrary to everything I thought I knew about myself, yet there it is."

"But I am not giving you the choice, Alexander. I am telling you to go."

She'd thought that her blunt command might hurt him or at least prompt him to react from his pride, but to her surprise, he appeared more determined than ever as he said, "I'd wager that only means you have not told me all there is to know about your decision to spare me execution."

By all the saints, how could he tell so easily?

Beth looked at him hard for a moment before shaking her head. "I wield a certain power as lady of Dunleavy, it is true—and yet that position was gained through marriage, not heredity. It is not unassailable. Especially now . . ."

She didn't finish that thought. *Especially now that I have shown myself capable of being duped by an impostor, who found means to work his way into my bed, my heart, and my trust as well.* Even without saying it aloud, Alex seemed to know well enough what she meant.

"And?" he asked.

"There are those who feel less certain of my ability to remain objective in this matter. They favor questioning you further." She stopped, feeling awkward. Her gaze was serious on him as she finished, "It is no secret that at least one also hopes that additional questioning will be followed by a swift trial and even swifter hanging."

Alex did not answer, only nodding.

"I have used my greater voice to defer pronouncing any immediate judgment," she continued, "but I cannot hold off indefinitely. There has been talk of sending word to King Robert the Bruce about what has transpired here. In order to forestall that, a decision must be made. Some of those clamoring for action are more persuasive than others about what it should be."

"Edwin."

Beth's silence spoke for her, but she tried not to show any weakness, forcing herself to continue, "Though I cannot completely overlook what you did here at Dunleavy, I do not wish to see you hanged for it—and yet if I do nothing, it will be difficult to maintain my authority as lady." She caught his stare. "That is why you must leave before dawn."

Alex just looked at her, his expression firm with resolve of his own as he thought about it for a moment. When he finally answered her, it was to utter something she wasn't expecting.

"Nay."

Nay? She choked out a disbelieving laugh. "Did you not hear me, Alex? You will be executed if you stay, and there will be naught I can do to stop it."

His jaw—masculine, elegant, and chiseled to perfection—tightened, and the muscle in his temple twitched. "I will not leave you here unprotected."

"Unprotected from what?" she clipped, more annoyed with him than she cared to admit . . . which was fortunate, as it helped her to hide the wrenching loss she felt at the idea of sending him away, necessary as she knew it was. "I survived here well enough before you came, and I will do so again once you leave, never fear."

He shook his head. "I paved the way for the coming battle with the English. Because of me they know of Dunleavy's weaknesses. I will not leave you here to face that alone."

"You will be dead long before then if you stay."

"The battle will begin in a sennight, give or take a few days. Aside from that," he continued maddeningly, as if she'd spoken naught of import, "even if I could see fit to do your bidding in this, you would be blamed for setting me free. I will not leave you to face the consequences of that action for me either, Beth. I refuse to do it."

Ah, but he was obstinate! Beth's lips pressed tightly together and she looked away, her annoyance with him supreme. Clearly, he was not going to bend in anything that demanded he think of his own self-protection, and yet she had to make him see reason.

She could do naught else, for she hadn't exaggerated when she'd told him what would come to pass if he stayed.

There had to be another way . . .

Beth called his gaze to her again. "You spoke of the Inquisition when you told me of your true identity last night, Alex. You said that you were a Templar Knight of the inner circle, taken into custody during the arrests in France, did you not?"

For the second time in less than a quarter hour, he looked startled in a less than pleasant way. After a brief silence, he answered, "Aye."

The way he uttered that single word, along with the expression that had swept across his face, made Beth wish she'd never had to invoke the name of that most notorious and feared arm of the Church's justice. But she'd decided to use whatever weapons she could find in this battle for his survival.

"And your wounds"—she nodded in sober reference to the marks of burns, lashes, and other horrible injuries he'd suffered over much of his body—"they are not the result of any captivity suffered in England, then, but from your imprisonment and questioning by the French Inquisition?"

Again, Alex did not answer immediately. Her questions apparently had uncovered memories he found difficult to face, and as he looked down to his hands, loosely clasped between his knees where he sat, she silently cursed herself for having forced him to think on them at all. He'd gone very still, as if every nerve and sinew in his body was strung tight with the effort not to let whatever was locked in the recesses of his mind overwhelm him. The only movement she saw came in the rise and fall of his chest with his breathing.

At last he looked at her again, fixing her with his gaze—cautioning her, perhaps, to leave off this subject once his answer was given—before he uttered a second confirmation, in a far huskier voice, "Aye, lady, they are."

Beth's heart twisted anew with the thought of the pain he must have endured to have carried with him such horrible evidence of it ever since. She remembered having wondered, when first she saw the signs of the torments that had been applied to him, how he had survived them—and what he could possibly have known that the English had been so desperate to make him confess.

Now the truth of his involvement with the Templars and the enormous scandal that was even now affecting the Brotherhood through the Holy Mother Church made the severity of what he had suffered more comprehensible. Still horrible to think on, but comprehensible. Yet she could not desist in this. Not if she was to convince him that her argument was sound.

"Then the truth, Alex," she continued, "is that you were an elite Templar Knight, rescued from your torment under the Inquisition by other Templar Knights." He winced, and she knew that he realized, suddenly, why she had broached this painful subject with him. "One of whom still languishes in English captivity, threatened with death if you failed to infiltrate this castle successfully."

Alex cursed under his breath, looking away before he stood and strode over to the hearth.

Beth allowed him a few moments to let the fullness of that which she'd reminded him sink in, before she added more gently, "The friend that you mentioned in connection to this—Sir John—may still be alive. None of the English know yet that their plot against us has been uncovered. Sir Lucas will learn of it, though, and quickly, if news of a traitor's hanging at Dunleavy reaches him. And it will if you stay, for there are those who would see you dead, Robert the Bruce among them, should he learn of it, for your role in this betrayal of Robert Kincaid's memory, coerced though it may have been."

Still Alex said nothing in response, only staring into the flames with an expression that seemed to rival their anguished twisting. She decided it was time to dispel once and for all his hesitation in leaving her, for though he would surely be risking his life in trying to rescue his friend, it was far preferable to the certain death he faced by remaining at Dunleavy.

"You have but a short time to help Sir John if you hope to have the benefit of surprise on your side. Otherwise, you consign him to death along with you. I will have his blood on my hands as well then, and all the suffering that you caused here ... that you caused *me* will have been for naught."

Again, Alex shook his head, the movement slow as if he could not believe he was hearing what he did. Finally, he turned away from the hearth, meeting her gaze, and she felt the shock of warmth, and love, and near desperation from clear across the chamber.

"By God, lady, but you have a way of transforming the most clear and unbending argument into naught but bits of air and sound." He looked resigned. "I cannot deny what you have said about John and what I owe him—and you—in this, any more than I can deny the need I feel to stay here and fight to my last breath to keep you safe from those who wish you harm. You have placed me in the untenable position of needing to find a way to accomplish both of these goals at once—though perhaps not in the way I had intended."

Beth held steady, reminding herself that this was what she had argued so vehemently for. This was what needed to happen, as awful as it might feel right now. "Then you will agree to leave before dawn?" she asked quietly.

He looked as if what he said and how he felt were opposite each other, but he finally nodded and said, "Aye. I will leave, for the chance to rescue John from his imprisonment—and then I will return to help you. His rescue must come first because of time and the circumstances aligned against us, reluctant as I am to agree with that."

She winced slightly but decided to ignore the part about his coming back. For now. "I am relieved that you understand."

"That does not mean I like it."

"It is necessary."

Alex lifted his brow. "It will be moot if I cannot find means to get clear of Dunleavy first. Regardless of all else, I will only go if you agree not to involve yourself in my escape, for I refuse to participate in anything that will bring you retribution because of me."

"There is naught to fear in that respect," Beth assured him. "I entered this chamber an hour ago unseen by the guard through the same method you will leave it."

Again, he looked surprised, but she only motioned for him to follow her, and, carrying the candle with her, she led him back toward the main chamber door and the large tapestry that hung on the wall next to it. Once there, she lifted the edge of heavy fabric and pointed to a rectangle of wooden panels that upon close study looked slightly different from the others that formed the wall.

"It is one of several entries into passages hidden deep within the heart of Dunleavy, leading to an exit in the wood beyond the outer wall. They are used regularly during sieges and assaults, as a secret means of egress—for runners to obtain food, ammunition, or aid . . . or for the lord and lady to escape should the situation become truly desperate." She let the edge of tapestry fall back into place. "It is one of the reasons Dunleavy has been so difficult to vanquish, through all the sieges against her."

"But the enemy must know of these secret passages. This castle was an English holding originally, was it not?"

"Aye—and nay," she answered. "It is true that King Henry of England ordered the castle built and presented to the first Earl of Marston more than a half century ago, as a boon for the earl's support against Simon de Montfort at the beginning of the second barons' rebellion. But Scottish craftsmen and laborers constructed it stone by stone, under the eye of Marston's nephew and heir—my late husband's grandsire. It was he who ordered the secret corridors in the initial construction. When Rob's sire inherited the castle upon his father's death, the secret passed to him—and he entrusted it to only a few loyal servants before passing it on to his son."

"So the Earls of Marston have always been Scottish loyalists after a fashion?"

"Aye, though Rob was the first to openly fight on the side of Scotland. England has been trying ever since to reclaim the castle as a base for their wars to achieve domination here."

Alex still looked concerned. "What of Edwin? As castle steward he must know of the passages. He will blame you for telling me of them when I escape."

"Aye, Edwin does know of them. But he will not know I have been here tonight, and I will feign surprise as much as anyone when it is discovered that you found the one leading from this chamber," Beth lied, walking back toward the center of the chamber so that Alex would not be able to read it in her expression.

The truth was that she intended to tell Edwin and the others everything once Alex was safely away and free of their plans to destroy him. They could be damned then, all of them. *She* was lady of Dunleavy, and it was time for them to accept that truth now—along with the reassertion that these were *her* decisions to make, and no one else's. The subtle threat to involve the king might have compelled her to use this subterfuge, but once Alex was clear of Dunleavy, she would reassert her authority with ruthless deliberation.

Alex remained quiet. When at last he nodded once, in acquiescence, Beth's heart lurched in a kind of anguished relief. She nodded back, glad that he had seen the wisdom in her argument at last, even as she felt something inside her breaking.

But there was another promise to wrest from him if she could do it, else he risked losing all with what was aligned against him.

"Alex?" she called out to him, and he rejoined her near the hearth. Reaching for her hand, he lifted her fingers to his lips and kissed them.

"Aye, lady?" he asked quietly.

"You must agree to one more thing if I am to be at peace with this."

"Your happiness is vital to me; there is no doubt. Yet I must hear what you wish of me first, to know whether or not I can give you my vow," he answered, giving her just a hint of that devastating smile of his.

"You must promise not to return to Dunleavy. Ever. Do it for my sake, if not for your own. There is naught but death for you here, and I—"

She had to stop for a moment, her voice catching. Swallowing hard, she gazed into his eyes, wanting him to see how serious she was about this, though she could not deny that it was nearly destroying her to ask it of him. "Just promise me," she whispered.

"Nay, Beth," Alex murmured in reply, the emotion he conveyed in the speaking of her name sending wonderful, pain-filled shivers of love and loss through her. "Lady, I cannot—"

"Promise to consider it at least," she broke in, desperate to have something to cling to that would allow her to go forward with what she knew she must.

He looked torn, his expression revealing love, denial, regret . . . and at last a kind of bittersweet acceptance. "Very well, lady. I promise to consider it for your sake."

The back of her throat ached, and so she nodded and tried to smile. She allowed herself to be swept again into his embrace, hoping, as she rested her head against the firm, warm expanse of his chest, that he understood her well enough, even in the silence.

Aye, she hoped for that—as she hoped that when the time came he would do as she had bid him and go as far as was possible from her, Dunleavy, and the death aligned against him here.

It was the only way, she thought, holding herself still through the waves of grief consuming her, soaking in the feel of Alex's strong arms around her so that the memory of it might sustain her through the long, bitter time to come.

Pray God, but he had to see that it was the only real way open to them both.

"You let him *go*?" Edwin asked her, incredulous.

Beth stood, spine stiff, in the middle of Dunleavy's bright and spacious solar several hours later. Morning sun streamed through the opened shutters as she faced Edwin, along with the captain of the guard and Father Paul, who also stood nearby. Thus far only they and a few of the captain's best men from the upper garrison had been told of Alex's true identity. It was necessary for now, at least, until they could determine how best to keep potential attackers like Lord Lennox at bay.

Beth intended it would remain so.

"Aye," she responded icily, when at last she did. "Though you were clearly not listening yestereve when all of this came about, I will remind you that *I* am lady here."

Edwin looked ready to say something more, glancing to the captain for backing. Beth watched, her gaze hard on them both, and was pleased to see that the captain remembered his place, only bowing his head in acquiescence to her wishes as he avoided meeting Edwin's gaze. Father Paul seemed troubled, but he remained silent as he had for the most part since Alex's deception had first come to light.

"Have you aught else to say, Edwin?" she demanded, her tone still cold.

"Nay," he answered at last, enunciating that word as he bowed sharply—making clear the fact that while he might be compelled to cooperate in practice, he continued to disagree with her actions.

"Then you may go. Both of you." She nodded to the captain and steward, adding, "However, I would ask that you remain for a few more moments, Father Paul."

The elderly priest nodded, still silent, and moved toward the window to gaze out of it.

The other two prepared to do as they had been bid, heading to the door. But before he left, Sir Gareth turned to her, his gaze still partially lowered in deference to ask, "Pardon, Lady Elizabeth, but I must needs ask, as it involves defending the castle against the coming English attack . . ."

His voice faded as if he was uncertain how to phrase what he wished to say. Clearing his throat, he apparently decided to try again. "My lady, I need to know how you wish me to instruct my men to proceed, should Sir Alexander de Ashby make his appearance again at Dunleavy." He glanced up to her, his expression tense. "In our dealings with him, should he be considered friend or foe?"

Beth stiffened, the question calling to mind an event she was forced to pray would never come to pass.

"I should hope that the answer to Sir Gareth's question would depend upon which side the impostor turns up in the fighting, if he turns up at all," Edwin drawled quietly from where he stood near the door, clearly unaffected by her pointed reminder of her position as lady of Dunleavy.

"Of course," Beth countered, her tone of sarcasm just as thick as Edwin's had been. Curse it, but if she didn't owe the steward so much from his years of unwavering assistance, she would dismiss him now, without hesitation.

"However, I see no immediate reason to consider him a foe, Captain," she said. "The English coerced him to his betrayal of Dunleavy, and he went to great lengths to reveal on his own, without any undue persuasion"—she flashed a dark look at Edwin—"all of the secrets regarding Dunleavy's security that he had supplied to Lord Exford. It was for no selfish benefit, but rather to aid us in preparing for the most likely prongs of the English attack."

"Very good, my lady," Sir Gareth murmured.

Edwin remained silent.

"In any event, it is unlikely he will make his appearance here again, so there will be naught to concern you," she continued lightly, speaking as if what she was saying meant naught to her, when in truth she had to wrench each word from the depths of her wounded heart.

"Why do you think that, lady?" Father Paul at last interjected. She looked at him, seeing his frown, and her heart twisted another painful notch.

She fixed her gaze on her confessor, her fingers clenched so tightly together that they began to ache. "I think it, Father, because I myself asked Sir Alexander to stay away. It would serve no purpose for him to return here, considering all that has come to light."

Edwin made a scoffing sound. "Your asking and the wretch obeying are two separate issues, Lady Elizabeth. I would have thought you'd have realized that truth by now, after all you were made to suffer because of him."

"I am at peace with it, Edwin," Beth countered. "I discussed with Sir Alexander what needed to be resolved before he left. That is enough for me as your lady, and therefore it should be enough for you as well."

"So it seems."

Edwin's answer was just respectful enough to avoid a dressing-down for impudence. But without another word, he bowed again, turned, and strode through the door out of sight.

Sir Gareth followed his lead, and in the next breath, she and the old priest were left alone. Father Paul remained ill at ease. His eyes seemed troubled, and he shook his head, sighing, as he walked over to her, taking her cold hand between his two warm and wrinkled ones.

That simple gesture of kindness wielded far more power over her than any amount of opposition or argument could have, undermining the strength of the wall she had built around her innermost thoughts and feelings. For the first time in the entirety of the morning's interview, she felt the sting of tears welling behind her eyes.

"Ah, my child . . ." Father Paul murmured, shaking his head again upon sight of them. "Though I hesitate to mention such things in front of your steward or the captain, I need to ask you now . . . what of the tenderness you claimed you felt for Sir Alexander—and he for you—when you spoke to me yestereve?"

"What of it, Father?" Beth echoed, her voice hoarse. "It has no bearing on what must be now."

"But if you share feelings for each other despite this wretched situation, then do you think it likely that he would stay away, once he has resolved whatever he is able to regarding his friend?"

"Aye—nay . . . I do not know," she whispered, her throat closing up again with the feelings roiling inside her. "I pray that he will not return. For what have we between us, really? We are not married. God help me, he is *not* my husband, regardless of aught else—"

Her voice did crack, then, and Father Paul patted her back gently as she struggled to regain her composure. In a few moments, she had managed it well enough, the old mantle of responsibility fitting far too well to allow her to forget the lessons she had taught herself over the course of five long years managing Dunleavy alone.

Father Paul had gone quiet again, and glancing to him, she saw his troubled look had grown more so.

At the question in her eyes, he cast his gaze down in embarrassment, murmuring, "I am sorry to bring this up to you, lady, indelicate as it is, and yet as your confessor, I must needs broach it for the sake of your immortal soul . . ."

Beth waited for Father Paul to resume speaking, unable, still, to say anything more at the moment. He seemed to forcibly take command of himself, meeting her gaze directly to ask, "Lady, is it possible that you are with child? You and Sir Alexander may not have been wed in truth, but you lived as if you were, for many weeks—"

"I do not believe I am with child, Father," Beth broke in hoarsely, unable to bear hearing another word, as even the thinking on what he suggested caused such a burst of bittersweet agony, she feared it might undo her. "I—I cannot deny that there is a possibility of it, based upon recent—upon . . ." Her voice trailed off and she could not go on, only squeezing her eyes shut and shaking her head.

Father Paul waited in sympathetic silence, and when she could speak again, she looked at him once more, clearing her throat. "I cannot consider that possibility right now, Father. Should it come to pass, I will confront it then and deal with what may come of it."

"But will not Sir Alexander wonder the same, and would that not also compel him to return?"

Beth wrapped her arms round her middle. "I do not think it. Even were I with child, Sir Alexander would have little to gain in coming back here, and much to lose. Too many know the truth for him to continue posing as my husband, and he cannot assume his own identity without facing charges of treason against Scotland."

Hopeless acceptance had wound cold fingers round her heart in the past few hours, and now it seemed to squeeze tighter, reminding her of the futility of what she was feeling . . . of what she could not help but feel for Alex even now, burning deep and strong inside her. She loved him. Aye, she did, regardless of all that had come to pass. Only she hadn't allowed herself to admit it. She had made love to him with her body, it was true, enduing the act with all the feelings inside her. But she had deliberately withheld those words from him, perhaps out of a desire to protect herself— and perhaps to wound him just a bit in return, she could not deny.

Now she would never have the chance to speak those words to him again, and the knowledge gnawed at her, adding a new layer of hurt to what already weighed down her soul. She swallowed against the lump that refused to leave her throat.

"You were present when Sir Alexander confessed that his desire, prior to his capture, had been to travel to the north and lead a life unconnected to anyone or anything, were you not?" she asked Father Paul.

"Aye, I heard him say it," the priest admitted.

Beth straightened, forcing herself to push all weak thoughts and feelings to the back of her mind where they belonged. There was no room for any of them now. The past was over and the future held a dangerous and looming battle with an enemy who would try to strike at the heart of Dunleavy.

"I must believe, then, that he will do what his instincts and logic prompt him. He will not come back. I must go forward from this point with no other expectation or desire."

Father Paul nodded slowly, sagely, taking her arm and walking her to the door. On the outside, she held herself stiff and tall, trying to exhibit an air of strength, while inside she felt naught but grief. The rawness of it all was only intensified by the knowledge of her complicity in this; she was as much at fault as any, for having allowed herself to believe. For having allowed herself to fall in love with a man she'd known deep down was not her husband.

She tried to concentrate on breathing in and out. *In and out.* There was naught to be done about any of this except to make an effort to carry on, as she had so blithely said she would. Heaven help her, but trying to forget about Sir Alexander de Ashby was proving the most difficult thing she had ever attempted in her life.

"If you do not mind, Father Paul, I would welcome the chance to confess my sins now," she murmured, trying to ignore the grinding, wrenching sensation that had taken up residence in her chest. "They are many, I fear, and I pray to find some absolution in offering them up."

She closed her eyes, images of the man she'd loved and lost hammering through her memory, tender, sweet, and aching to the point of pain. "God willing," she whispered, forcing herself to look forward again, "perhaps I might find some peace as well."

Chapter 14

Alex paused as he neared the place of Luc's encampment, in the woods south of Dunleavy Castle. He'd traveled the path to it often enough these past few weeks with Stephen to find it with relative ease. Though he didn't expect John to be there himself, he thought he might be able to listen in long enough without detection to learn the exact location of Lord Exford and the main army . . . and therefore the place John was being held captive, as well.

It was worth a try, at the least.

He had but four days to find his friend. Three now, really, for this day was nearing its end. He had to make his move or lose the advantage of surprise.

Crouching down, Alex made his way closer, heading toward a clump of rowan trees he deemed good as protection from being seen. The copse was thick, and it was clear that it was going to take a while to reach the clearing's edge this way, but it was the best option he could see. Leaves and branches scratched his face as he moved slowly forward, making his way under protection of the foliage. He dropped to his belly at last and pulled himself along the forest floor beneath the trees, making nary a sound; his years of Templar training and the survival instincts they had honed overtook his actions, and for that he was grateful.

His relationship with the Brotherhood had not always been a pleasant one, but it had sometimes served him in good stead. Like right now. It was regrettable that he had never felt the pull of connection and unity that many of the other brethren, including his own brother, Damien, as well as Richard and John, his two best friends, had seemed to feel.

What he wouldn't give for their backing now.

But he was alone in this as usual . . . trying to repair his own mess himself, the best way he knew how. Anything else was impossible, for even had he known the bond the others seemed to feel, he had cut so many ties with everyone close to him that none would want to help him, he warranted, even if they could.

He couldn't deny that when he'd committed his last crime against Damien, Richard, and John, he had done so purposefully, choosing something heinous enough that he'd thought it likely they would never forgive him for it. But something inside him had pushed him to do it. To break with those he loved and who had loved him in return. Perhaps it had been the shame that had consumed him after his bout with the Inquisition. Combined with his feelings of unworthiness as a man compared to his brother and his friends, it had been difficult to accept. But he'd faced the truth of it during those long weeks of recovery: He could offer naught of worth to anyone except the promise of his skill on the field. Fight he could, and he did it well. Yet inside he had felt empty and aching with all that he wasn't.

When he had been able to bear it no longer, he

had resolved to disappear for good into the farthest reaches of the Highlands. Unfortunately, he had needed money to do that. A great deal of money. And what he had done to get it had been a double—nay, even a triple—insult to his brother and friends, for they had gone to dangerous lengths to rescue him from the clutches of the Inquisition, imperiling themselves to bring him into safety and hiding in England, and then risking all to tend to his broken body and soul to restore him to physical health.

Wretch that he was, he had repaid them by stealing some of the treasure they'd all hazarded their lives to protect . . . the sacks of priceless Templar goods handed them in desperation by the Grand Master Jacques de Molay near Paris on the night of the mass arrests almost two years ago. The four of them had suffered miserably to bring those bags out of France that night, and it had set off a chain of events and torment beyond belief.

Damien had been caught that same night and spent the next half year being tortured by the Inquisition; Alex too had been captured and threatened with torture as well. But his commitment to the Templars had been naught like Damien's; nay, even then he had known he was less noble, less honorable. When faced with torture, he had cracked easily and agreed to serve as the cursed organization's battle champion to avoid the rack and to try to wrest from them a promise to spare Damien further torment.

In his first assignment, he had been forced to fight a Wager of Battle against Richard in England. A fight to the death. When he could not bring himself to do it, reneging on his agreement with his Inquisitors, he had felt their wrath, for they had not been amused at their champion's reversal. His torture had commenced then, with their application of pain against him more dedicated than he could ever have imagined.

And so it had gone.

Caught between a rock and a hard place.

It seemed to be a way of life for him that he could not shake, and the mistakes he continued to make only added to that outcome.

His own latent surge of nobility in sacrificing himself for Richard's sake in the Wager of Battle had done little to assuage the other sins he'd committed against the three people of any on earth who had mattered most to him.

Until Beth.

Though he had tried to discipline himself to keep his mind empty of all but the details of what he needed to accomplish right now in rescuing John, thoughts of Beth twisted through him again with a vengeance, aching with sweet misery. He could not allow himself to do this, damn it. He could not dwell on the danger she faced, awaiting the English army that was even now aligning itself against Dunleavy with information *he* had provided them for doing it most effectively.

He had to find John first and save him if he could. *Then* he could return to Dunleavy and fight to his last breath to keep Luc and anyone following him from breaching the castle's defenses and harming those inside. From harming Beth. Against his will, panic shot through him, clear, cold, and agonizing. Sweet Jesu, he only prayed he could do it all in time—that he could do it at all, with no help. Alone as always, thanks to the terrible choices he had made and the people he had hurt.

Gritting his teeth at that splendid thought, Alex at last reached the edge of the rowan copse, peered through the bottom branches into the clearing beyond, and saw . . .

Nothing.

What? He blinked to be sure his vision was clear.

It was as sharp as it had ever been. There was naught before him but some trampled grass, an old pit from where the cook fire had burned, and broken branches from the repairs Luc had been making to some arrow shafts that had been cracked.

He was too late, curse it to everlasting hell.

Was the assault against Dunleavy going to be waged sooner than he'd been led to believe, then, based on his last meeting with Luc? Perhaps Stephen had been returning with news of it when he'd been intercepted and killed by the castle guards.

Or had Luc somehow learned of Stephen's death? If he knew the English plot had been discovered, he might even now be back at their base camp, taking the action he would deem necessary with John.

Cursing again under his breath, Alex crawled out from the rowans, brushing away the twigs and leaves that still clung to him as he made his way to the pit to see if he could discern how recently the fire had been lit. He squatted next to it, brushing his fingers into the ashes along the edge of it.

They were cold.

Luc had been gone for more than a day, then. And that likely meant—

"Looking for something, big brother?"

Alex froze, his spine stiffening with disbelief.

It could not be who he thought it was. There was no reasonable way it could be, and yet he recognized that voice. Turning slowly to face its owner, Alex felt a shock of something far stronger than surprise jolt through him, blended with relief, caution, denial . . . and a sense of unabashed happiness that overwhelmed all else.

"*Damien?*" Alex asked in disbelief.

"It hasn't been that long that you fail to recognize me, do you, Alex?"

"Nay . . ." Alex swallowed. "Nay, it is just—"

Alex's throat tightened with the emotions washing over him. He fixed his gaze on what he might have thought was no more than the spiritual embodiment of his younger brother, had not the beams of sun piercing the trees in the glen gilded Damien's dark blond hair with gold and caused his powerful warrior's form to cast tall shadows. Standing there as he was, Damien looked every inch the "Archangel" of his tourney-given moniker. Then he smiled, and the impression increased tenfold.

"Perhaps you will not be disagreeable to greeting me as brothers should?" Damien offered, with only a slight hesitation in his voice as he held out his hand. In an instant, Alex had come forward to clasp him, forearm to forearm—and in another they were in each other's fierce embrace, the hug rife with all the bittersweet feeling that was between them—holding on in a way that made it clear neither had thought to have the chance to do it again.

When it was over, they both backed up a step, and Alex cleared his throat, looking around the clearing for any other signs of movement and life. "How in hell did you find me out here, Damien?" he asked, gesturing around the now-empty glen.

"We'll get to that in a moment," Damien said evenly. "First just let me know the pleasure of seeing you again in the flesh." He assessed his brother from head to foot, relief clear in his handsome features. "I have been seeking you these many months, Alex, and I must say that I am relieved to see you looking better than you did the last time I saw you at Richard's holding. You were in need of a few good meals then, at the least." A kind of shadow passed over his blue eyes, so like Alex's own. "Praise God you seem to have recovered fully from what they did to you in France."

"What they did to *us*, Damien." Neither needed to talk further on it to know they were speaking of their questioning by the Inquisition. "I am recovered as fully as is possible," Alex continued, adding with false humor in his voice that hid the blackness roiling beneath the surface, "Though like you, I bear several reminders in body and soul that refuse to wash away."

"We are brothers in that sense as well, it seems," Damien said lightly in return, and Alex realized they'd both managed to adopt an outward air of nonchalance in regard to the horrors of that time—a necessity, he knew, for the extent of what they had both survived was unbearable to think on and almost impossible to comprehend for its cruelty.

"No matter, it is good to see you again, Alex," his brother added at last, his voice quiet. "I was beginning to wonder whether I would have the opportunity again, after all I had heard from John."

Alex looked at him sharply. "Heard how recently?"

"Within the past sennight."

Alex did not try to hide his reaction. "Thanks be to God—he is alive, then."

Damien nodded. "And doing well. At least as well as can be expected after being kept captive by the English for nearly four months."

"But how did he get free of them? And how did *you* find him—and me?" Alex's head spun with all the strangeness of this. "By the Rood, it boggles my mind to think on it."

Damien laughed. "What is it the bards always sing about—that what happens in life oft proves more extraordinary than aught they can weave with their words."

"It would have to be in this," Alex admitted. "But I am eager to hear the details of it anyway, as well as share with you some of what I must needs do still, based upon what has happened to me."

Damien nodded. "For a start, we found John after weeks of searching, when we had no word of him. He had gone after you, you know, once you left with the sack of treasure."

Alex winced. "Aye. I intended to take only the bowl, I swear. I did not know the scrolls were secreted there as well."

"I thought as much. John told us he had hidden them in the bottom of the sack." Damien fixed him with a pointed look. "It was you he was after, though, most of all. He feared you might fall into some kind of trouble, considering the state of mind you were in when you left."

"He was right." Alex shook his head. "But he should not have risked himself for me. It was how he was taken."

"So he said, once we found and liberated him. It took us until last week to locate him in the English encampment."

"And you freed him from there yourselves?" Alex asked, surprised. "It must have taken some doing, for the English position was well fortified when last I saw it."

"We had some help," Damien admitted, throwing his arm around Alex's shoulders and leading him off to the side of the clearing. "But before we get into all of that, let me ask—have you been traveling long this day?"

"Since dawn—and without sleeping at all the night before."

At Damien's questioning look, Alex added, "It is a long story. I'll share it with you later, I promise."

Damien nodded. "I look forward to it. First, though—brought you a sack of ale or some victuals with you?"

Alex replied in the affirmative, and Damien indicated he should follow him to a large log lying just into the brush at the end of the glade.

"Sit, rest, and refresh yourself for a while, and I will tell you what I can to begin at least. We have much to discuss. Much you will be interested to hear, I think."

Alex nodded, grateful for the respite, brief though he would ensure it would be. Offering his brother a drink while he pulled from his bag a half loaf of bread and some dried venison, he asked, "Is John nearby, then? Is he in good health, or did the bastards mistreat him against their vows to the contrary?"

"One question at a time," Damien chided gently, chuckling before he took a healthy swallow from Alex's ale sack. "John is within two hours of here—as are Richard and the others."

"Others?"

"Aye. In the past year we have found two score or so other Templars, many of them knights, who sought refuge in Scotland from the arrests and the madness that has overtaken the Church in regards to the Brotherhood. None but we four are of the inner circle, however."

"There is one more in this country who once served in the inner circle, though he fights on the side of the English and is no friend of ours longer," Alex said grimly.

"Luc," Damien said, sparing Alex the need to speak their former comrade's name. His brother nodded, jaw tight. "John told us about his involvement in the English scheme you were compelled to accept."

Alex looked at him in question, wondering how John could have known any of the details of the foul bargain Alex had been forced to undertake—unless Luc had told him of it for some reason.

As if he'd read Alex's mind, Damien added, "It seems Luc couldn't resist boasting to John about his success in managing the mission at Dunleavy. He considered John secure enough in Lord Exford's control to risk the bragging—which was delivered along with some useful details." Damien nodded. "It was thanks to Luc's loose tongue that John was able to tell me of your meeting place in this clearing. I was planning to make my way into Dunleavy to find you, but I'd decided to stop for a day here first, to monitor any activity that might come about." He flashed a grin. "I am certain that Luc would choke to think he had a hand in me finding you again."

"If he did not recover from it, it would be justice," Alex grated. "Luc is more a bastard than he was when he was in the Brotherhood, and not only for what he did in regards to the English plots." He spat off to the side, wiping at his mouth with the back of his hand.

Damien nodded. "I never liked the man."

"You were correct in your instincts."

"Aye, well, we have aligned ourselves with the other escaped Templars, who all seem to be good men, loyal and true to the Brotherhood. We meet periodically at the holding of a knight named Sir Gilbert Sinclair. His family has the backing of Robert the Bruce, and they are supporters of the Order as well. Sinclair himself served a term with the Brotherhood in a way similar to Richard, having a wife living when he joined. He was no longer active when the arrests began, but he feels the connection as strongly as if he still wore the crimson cross."

"Aye. The crimson cross . . ." Alex echoed, taking a bite of bread and washing it down with a gulp of ale. His former lack of commitment to the Brotherhood had been an irrefutable truth and point of heated, angry contention between himself and Damien for as long as they'd served as Templars together, and he hated to think their reunion would be marred now by a renewal of that friction.

However, Damien seemed to recognize Alex's conflicted feelings, surprising him when he added more quietly, "The past is over, Alex. You may not have become a Templar with a committed heart, but you more than made up for it when you sacrificed yourself for Richard in the Wager of Battle you were made to fight against him as the Inquisition's champion."

"I did not realize you knew of that," Alex said, scowling. Though he and Damien had seen each other twice during the long period of Alex's recovery from his torture, they had never discussed the particulars of anything related to the Order or what had happened to them both in the intervening time after the mass arrests.

Damien nodded. "Richard told me of it, after he found me last year fighting in a tournament at Odiham Castle."

"You were *tourneying* last year?" Alex asked. "But I thought you had been rescued out of France and your captivity with the Inquisition by a widow who fancied you for herself. What in hell were you doing fighting in a tournament?"

"Another long story. Suffice it to say everything worked out well in the end." Damien glanced away, his face taking on a softer expression that Alex had only ever remembered seeing there years ago, when his brother had first been in love. It had ended badly and had been the reason Damien had joined the Templars in the first place, for the woman in question had cast him off publicly, before hundreds of tournament spectators . . . aye, she had been a lovely, virtuous maiden, far above him in social standing at court, named—

"Alissende and I found each other again last year, Alex," Damien continued, the invocation of the name that was even now ringing in Alex's memory making him choke on his bite of bread. Unaware of his brother's reaction, Damien went on, "She was the widow who arranged my rescue from the Inquisition. We married late last fall and have a child together now—a daughter named Margery. I was going to tell you when last I traveled into England to visit you at Hawksley Manor this spring, but you had already fled with the treasure by the time I arrived."

By this point, Alex was choking so visibly that Damien finally gave off conveying any further impossible news to thump him on the back and help him breathe again.

"What in God's name are you talking about?" Alex rasped, when he could finally talk again. "You married *Alissende de Montague* and have a *child* together? Christ's blood, man, how can that be? Why— and where did you—"

"I told you, there was much to catch up on between us," Damien broke in.

"You were not jesting, I see," Alex commented dryly, polishing off the remainder of the ale. He nodded, thoughts of Beth never far from the surface for him either, adding, "I too have some news to tell that you might find . . . unexpected."

"Is that so?" Damien glanced sideways at him.

"Aye." Alex stood. "But for now, we had best continue traveling to reach John and Richard."

Damien looked skyward. "You're right. It will be dark in another few hours; we should go if we are to reach them before nightfall. Come." He gestured toward a barely discernible path leading south of the glen, indicating that Alex should follow him. "We can continue our discussion while we travel to the Sinclair holding."

Alex nodded, turning to go back to the clearing's edge to retrieve the bags he had brought with him from Dunleavy. But before he could take more than a step, Damien gripped his arm, forestalling him in the motion and calling his attention back to him.

"I just want you to know how glad I am to see you again, brother. Truly, I am."

"As I am to see you, Damien," Alex answered in complete sincerity. "More than you know."

Slapping each other on the back, they both grinned, before Damien walked over with Alex to pick up one of his sacks, slinging it on his back . . .

And then they began the trek south to Richard, John, and the other Templars together.

Chapter 15

Three days later

"**E**dwin has gone, my lady."

Beth looked up at Annabel from the parchment on which she was tallying the stores of munitions left at Dunleavy, according to the latest accounts given her this morn. She was in the solar, with all the records spread out around her. She had been holed up there for most of the afternoon—both because she wanted to meet with her captain of the guard before nightfall and to keep her mind occupied, to aid her in keeping thoughts of Alex from tormenting her as they had since he had been gone.

"Edwin . . . ?" she echoed, feeling slightly disoriented. Shaking her head, she rubbed her fingers over her brow. "Gone—where? And why is it of concern to me?"

"My lady, he has left Dunleavy." Annabel looked down, her face tight with dread. "One of the laundry maids claimed she'd heard he traveled to the north."

Beth still looked at Annabel in bewilderment, not grasping what her lady's maid was trying to tell her.

"He is going to seek Lord Lennox, Lady Elizabeth," Annabel said with finality, dropping her gaze as she finished speaking. "He intends to bring him back to take Dunleavy from your control."

"*What?*" Beth demanded, lurching to her feet. Parchments and quill pens spilled to the floor with a rustling clatter, but she paid them no heed. "Why would he do that?"

Annabel was near tears as she bent to scoop up the parchments, but Beth came around the table, reaching down to grip her hands, raising her up with a silent nod to leave the things where they lay. Beth's throat felt dry as she gripped Annabel's fingers in her own, asking again, "I need to know who told you this, Annabel, as well as what else was said."

"Oh, my lady, it is horrible," Annabel answered raggedly, her voice thick with tears. "It was Eleanor, one of the laundry maids, who told Isabel, who carries the milk from the castle dairy each day. And it was she who told me."

When Beth showed no sign of understanding the connection, Annabel continued, "Eleanor's sweetheart is Gerard, the stable lad . . . he readied the mount for Edwin this afternoon and overheard him speaking to one of the soldiers of the upper garrison about where he was going and why." Annabel squeezed Beth's hands a little tighter. "Lady Elizabeth, he plans to tell Lord Lennox what happened with Lord Marst—"

She stopped, her face reddening, before she continued, "With Sir Alexander. Edwin believes you unfit in judgment to manage this demesne any longer alone."

Beth uttered several less than ladylike curses, letting go of Annabel's hands and walking over to the window, pushing it open to gaze down at the practice yard below.

All looked as it usually did. The autumn sun shone down on bare patches of earth, thick sawdust, and grasses trampled and brown from the garrison's daily practice with sword and shield. A few pigs rutted near the back garden, and chickens scratched in the dirt near the kitchens, the movements of various soldiers, servants, tradespeople, and villagers unremarkable for this time of day. There was naught to indicate that beneath their very noses the seeds of betrayal were being sown.

Two great deceptions brought to light in twice as many days.

It was almost beyond comprehension, and yet if naught else, she should have learned by now that such was to be expected. At the least, it gave her a sense of steely strength now that banished the remaining fog that seemed to have surrounded her since Alex's departure.

She was Lady Elizabeth of Selkirk. *She* was in command of this castle. And she was in command of it alone. Alex was gone and he wasn't coming back. That was not going to change, no matter how much she wished otherwise.

Turning to look at Annabel, Beth asked, "Was the man to whom Edwin spoke in the stables our captain of the guard?"

"Nay, my lady. I think 'twas one of his lieutenants—Sir Reginald."

Beth clenched her fist against the edge of the window opening. "Very well. Send message to the captain that I wish to see him. Now."

With a swift curtsy, Annabel left to fetch Sir Gareth . . . and Beth was left to gather up the remainder of her papers and begin making preparations for an attack it seemed would now take place from two different directions, perhaps all at once. Both opposing forces would be seeking dominance of Dunleavy—and one would try to gain her in the bargain.

Beth's mouth tightened grimly, and she rustled through the parchments, looking for those that would aid her in making battle plans with Sir Gareth . . . for only one thing was certain in this mass of deception and betrayal that had begun to billow in a dark cloud all around her.

Neither of her attackers was going to succeed if she had anything to say about it.

Alex sat before a cozy, crackling fire in Gilbert Sinclair's solar, looking at his brother, who sat beside him, as well as at two of the best friends he had ever known, one standing opposite him at the fire, with the other in the chair nearest the blaze for warmth, as he was recovering from his imprisonment with the English. Gilbert had retired to bed, bidding the four of them to stay up and reacquaint themselves with one another for as long as they wished.

Alex was warm, dry, and for the first time in almost half a year, not in imminent danger of losing his life.

He should have been happy with his lot, or content at least. Instead, he was more miserable than he could ever remember being.

It was because of Beth . . . because he wanted to be with her, near her, comforting her and protecting her from the dangers to come. *Now*. Not on the morrow, when Richard, Damien, John, and the other Templars here had vowed to join him in returning to Dunleavy to help in her defense against the coming English attack.

Now.

"From what you have described, Lady Elizabeth is a strong woman," Richard said, trying to sound encouraging as he glanced at Alex in commiseration from his position near the hearth. "And after that tale of her response to the assault of the Scottish lord who tried to overwhelm Dunleavy before your arrival, I'd say she is resourceful as well, nay?"

"Aye, she is that," Alex murmured, looking into his cup of ale and remembering doing the same thing, countless times, it seemed, during the feast several nights ago, when he'd been struggling to come to terms with his feelings about her.

"She must be good-hearted as well, if she was willing to treat you with fairness even after you revealed your true identity to her," John added, leaning over to toss another log on the blaze and wincing when he pulled the wrong way against a rib that still wasn't fully healed from a beating he'd suffered during his imprisonment.

Richard made a sound of irritation, taking the fire tongs from John, and muttering about him allowing the rest of them do these things for him lest all their efforts to bandage him properly came to naught.

"You might want to rethink coming with us to Dunleavy, friend," Alex said to John, after they'd settled him comfortably in his chair again. "You've had enough to manage these past weeks without throwing yourself onto a battlefield again, and for my sake, no less."

John made a scoffing sound. "Do not think for a moment that I'd let you fight this one without me." Though his smile was tired, John's eyes shone with a familiar light. "We are still Templars—some of us more in spirit than by vow any longer, I will admit," he amended, glancing to the others, all of whom had taken wives, or, in Alex's case, a lover, which precluded them from service with the Order as full brethren. "Yet we still fight together for justice and the glory of God. That you found the cause for us to defend this time makes it no less important."

"It is generous of you to say that, considering my past with the Brotherhood," Alex said with a laugh of self-deprecation. He took a deep swallow from his cup before adding, "It bears remembering that you were all in the process of escorting me in chains from Cyprus to Paris to face sentencing by the Grand Master when we were divided during the mass arrests. My history as a Templar Knight has been less than laudable."

"It is of no matter now," Richard interjected quietly. "Your sins against the Order are naught compared to those committed by the very ones for whom the Brotherhood fought and died. Whether or not you stumbled in your holy vows, you were always loyal to the Order on the battlefield, Alex—and a trusted friend to all of us."

Alex shook his head, feeling twinges of something he hadn't known he could feel, so caught up had he been in his own misery and sense of isolation. These men were good in heart and soul, and so he had never considered placing himself on their level, even in his own mind. The contrast between them and the darkness he'd always recognized in himself had seemed too great to bear.

Now he realized that he might not be as worthless as he'd always thought himself . . . and that his brother and friends had never held his failings against him as strongly as he'd held them against himself. They accepted him for who he was, flaws and all, without judgment.

"By God, I don't deserve your friendship, any of you. And yet—"

He stopped, his throat tight. Clearing it after a moment, he finished, "And yet I am grateful for it. More than I can tell you."

It was Damien who finally broke the poignant silence that had spread over them in response to Alex's heartfelt declaration.

"You are aware, of course, that none of us would be offering you anything, wretch that you are, had you not brought back the Templar treasure you lifted along with the golden bowl." Damien tossed out the comment in jest, clearly trying to lighten the mood in the chamber as he raised his brow in that way that was so similar to Alex. "You'd be on your own if you'd actually sold the scroll or left it behind when you made your bargain with Lord Exford."

That prompted a round of laughter and exaggerated cheers of agreement directed toward Alex, making him laugh too in the process.

"I would have deserved it, had I been so thoughtless," Alex agreed, still smiling, "even more than I do now."

"Aye, well, just remember, brother—we stick together, all of us," Damien said, more serious now, though the look of affection he directed at Alex remained firmly in place. "Come what may," he added more quietly, raising his cup to him as he uttered the Templar maxim, spoken by every Templar Knight before each battle fought together to the death for justice, honor, and truth, in God's name.

Richard and John joined in—as did Alex after only a moment's hesitation, the feeling of connection and belonging surging up of a sudden; real, vibrant, and demanding recognition. The truth of it spread through him, reassuring and strong. These gifted warriors and loyal friends ... these awe-inspiring Templar Knights would ride back with him to aid the woman he loved. They would help him in defending her against the enemy.

He nodded, too filled with emotion to say anything aloud—and so John obliged him by speaking the statement all were thinking.

"Tomorrow then, lads," he called out loudly before taking a deep draught from his cup and then lifting it up again. "Come dawn, we will ride together once more under the beauséant banner, with the crimson cross upon our chests."

Beth was at the far end of the bailey conferring with Sir Gareth regarding the location of their recently repaired trebuchet, when a lad from the village came running through Dunleavy's inner gate. She noticed only because of the minor commotion the boy caused when the guard grabbed his arm, forestalling him. He could not have been more than five or six years old, and he looked distraught from the way his hands were waving as he almost jumped from foot to foot in his urgency.

She motioned for Gareth to look, knowing that her captain of the guard should be apprised of anything that seemed out of the ordinary as they prepared for the English assault . . . just as she had apprised him of Edwin's perfidy in going to Lord Lennox, who was also surely in the process of aligning against them again right now.

Gareth shifted his gaze toward the gate, at the same time that the guard there nodded to the boy to let him through, directing him to speak to another of the senior garrison over by the blacksmith's forge in the bailey. A moment more, and the soldier had brought the boy toward her and the captain.

"What is it?" Sir Gareth asked, turning slightly toward them.

"This lad is the farrier's son. His sire was called to a village five miles off at the request of a stranger whose horse had thrown a shoe on the journey north." The soldier's expression looked grim. "The man was a mounted archer traveling with an army from England. This boy felt compelled to tell of the incident, but he fears his sire will face retribution for abetting the enemy before he knew who it was."

Beth felt her stomach drop. Lord Exford had approached to within five miles of Dunleavy, then. The assault would be waged within the next day or two at most.

The boy stood next to the soldier, trembling violently, his breath still coming in deep gasps. Stepping away from Sir Gareth, Beth approached the lad, lay-ing her hand on his shoulder in a gesture of comfort. "What is your name, sirrah?"

His eyes widened, and he looked amazed that the lady of the castle had deigned to touch one as lowly as he.

"I am—I am C-C—" He stumbled over what he wished to say, his voice broken from the after-effects of running and nervousness.

"Slow down and catch your breath . . . there is naught to fear, I promise you," she said gently, trying to put him at ease.

"My—my lady," he answered, and she could not free herself of the image that came to mind when she looked at him, of a lean, brown rabbit readying to dart away at the first sign of danger. He took in a deep breath, and then another, the movements exaggerated in the way of the very young. After another few seconds, he threw back his thin shoulders and said, "Me mum calls me Camden, lady. Cam for short."

"Cam, then," Beth said, doing her best to smile at him, though she too felt the weight of the doom that was aligning against them. "You did well in coming here to tell of the army nearing from yonder village. Your sire will face no reprisal from me."

Cam's eyes suddenly welled with tears, relief overcoming him, apparently, but he dropped his chin to his chest, shamed to have shown such emotion before these men and a fine lady to boot.

Beth simply squeezed his shoulder, going against every instinct that made her instead want to drop to her knee and pull him into an encouraging embrace. Nay, she could not do that, for such action on her part would do naught, surely, but mortify him further. Instead, she added with quiet conviction, "Very like, the soldier your sire aided would be dismayed as well to learn he has taken service from a man so loyal and true to Dunleavy—for now we have been warned of the English army's approach."

Cam nodded, wide-eyed, managing to blink back the tears that had threatened, and she smiled down at him. "In fact, far from wishing him ill, I owe your sire a great debt for alerting me to the approaching danger, and I shall be sure to see he receives due recompense for his allegiance to me."

"Gramercy, lady," Cam whispered, gazing up at her as if she was a celestial queen, rather than a simple lady preparing for yet another deadly siege against her castle.

She kept the smile pasted to her lips as she turned to the soldier who had brought Cam to her, murmuring instructions for sending a token of her appreciation to Cam's father. At the same time, she bid the soldier send out runners to confirm the location of the English forces. Once that was done, others of the garrison would be sent to the castle village and the farther reaches of the demesne, to alert everyone of the impending assault, so that measures could be taken for the safety of men, women, children, and livestock dwelling outside the castle walls.

By nightfall, the drawbridge would be raised for the last time. Dunleavy was as fortified against attack as it would ever be; they could do no more than hunker down to await sight of the enemy on the hill beyond the southern woodland.

Cam pulled his forelock, bowing several times, even as he kept his adoring gaze fixed on Beth while he backed away toward the gate again.

Emptiness thrummed through her in the wake of his leaving, more poignant than ever in face of the now imminent danger he'd conveyed to them. It echoed painfully through the place that, for a little while at least, had been filled with the comforting warmth of Alex's strength and love.

She could think of that no more, curse her feeble heart. Nay, she needed to carry on without Alex for the sake of everyone here. For the sake of people who depended upon her to defend them and keep them safe.

"So it begins again, my lady," Sir Gareth said lowly, calling her gaze back to him. She straightened and faced him, the tension that radiated from her captain but a shadow of the feelings she herself contended with right now.

They were in trouble, she knew. Not enough time had passed since the last brutal siege, and they were down in both manpower and weaponry, not to mention their inability to correct all the weaknesses that Alex had told them Sir Stephen and he had found and reported back to the English.

But in the end it mattered naught. She had to do this and be strong in her leadership. Aye, she had done it before and she would do so again, regardless of who was aligned against her.

Raising her brow, Beth forced another smile, this one more brittle than the one she had conjured for Cam. Then she murmured the reply she dreaded to speak, knowing that this moment spelled the beginning of their very real and inescapable troubles . . .

"Aye, Sir Gareth, so it begins again. God help us, for I fear we will need His divine intervention to survive it this time."

Chapter 16

At any moment, Beth expected to hear the crack of stone against masonry as Lord Exford's catapult launched the strike that would begin the siege of Dunleavy. As much as she dreaded it, she almost wished for it to come, having felt perched on the edge of a great precipice for the past two days . . .

Waiting.

Watching.

Knowing the English earl was gathering his scores of men, weapons, and munitions just beyond the clearing.

There had been no sign of Edwin or Lord Lennox yet, and for that she supposed she should be grateful. Contending with one enemy at a time was enough. And yet she could not help but wonder how Lord Lennox would respond if he arrived in the midst of the English assault.

Would he stand by and wait for the enemy to do its damage and perhaps tire, before he launched a counterattack to drive them off and take the castle himself? Or would he join in the fray, doing all he could to push back the English, expecting her to capitulate when it was over in gratitude for his aid?

She did not much care either way. If she had aught to say about it, Lord Lennox would receive the same welcome into Dunleavy as the English did, and nothing more.

A grinding sound echoed from beyond the outer curtain wall, reverberating through the tense silence that had settled around the castle yard. It was followed by a loud whirring, as of a thousand wings beating at once . . . then she heard the shouts of several of the guard, positioned on the crenellations, trying to alert everyone below of where the missile would land.

Crack!

The boulder smashed into the south tower, just above the top of the curtain wall. Debris and pieces of stone, mostly skull-sized or larger, rained down on those unfortunate enough to be standing nearby. There was a cacophony of noise. Of screams, the clatter of falling stone, cries of despair and pain.

And then silence.

Dust billowed up and settled to earth again, even as people rushed forward to pull away the injured or dead from the area. Too soon, another boulder hurtled over the wall, hitting a different spot, but with the same terrible results.

Yet the tower held.

"Return fire!" Beth shouted to the captain over the building noise, waving her hand to indicate he should loose their trebuchet on the enemy.

Sir Gareth gave the command, and it was followed by the retaliatory launch. The castle archers positioned themselves on top of the battlements in long rows, pots of burning tar nearby with which to light their bolts before letting them fly at the command.

But before that second order could be given, another stone careened toward them, smashing into the wall where the archers stood and sending a score of them hurtling to their deaths into the moat below, some still clutching their longbows. Before the men could regroup, a volley of burning arrows—hundreds of them, it seemed—arched through the air overhead, loosed on them by the English forces.

With sickening and indifferent accuracy, the flaming bolts plunged into the thatched roofs of buildings in the yard and human bodies alike, bringing fire, destruction, and death. The sounds, and sights, and smells of the aftermath were horrific.

The devastation was mind-numbing.

It was like every siege that had come before.

And it made Beth furious. Too furious to remain in the relative protection of the stone enclosed area on the far side of the yard.

Annabel followed her out into the yard, pulling on her sleeve, begging her to come back as Beth made her way through the smoke, shouting men, bleeding bodies, and raining debris toward the curtain wall and the battlements above, where she could get a clearer view of the opposing army. She leaned down and grabbed a handful of rags bundled near the carts that would carry the wounded into the makeshift infirmary they always made of the great hall during times such as these.

She shook out the largest of the cloths, her gaze fixed ahead of her, seeing in her mind's eye what she planned to do, once she reached the summit of the battlements. She had chosen a crimson gown this day, and it would serve her well. For when she reached the top of the battlements, she would stand straight and tall, gazing down at the array of stunning force gathered below her castle walls. Bedecked in the fiery hue, she would certainly be seen. The pompous Lord Exford would fire again. And when he did, she would use the cloth she'd brought with her to show him how little he intimidated her.

Aye, let the cursed dogs see her dusting off the stones after each launch of their damned catapult or volley of flaming bolts. Let them see that she was unafraid of them, scoundrels and tyrants all.

But before she made it halfway up the steps leading to the crenellations, she noticed something strange happening with the men still posted on the walls above—and also in regard to the barrage of fire from English weaponry.

Everything had gone still.

Her men seemed stiff-frozen where they stood, gazing out at something that left them with their mouths gaping open. Even Sir Gareth looked stunned, standing in position on the wall next to the trumpeter, whose music gave the captain's orders to the soldiers.

Scrambling the rest of the way up the stairs, Beth hurried over to him, unmindful of the soot and ash wafting through the air around them. But for the black fluttering of it, everything was still, with no movement on either Dunleavy's or the English side. She'd never seen the like in any of the battles she'd witnessed before.

"What is it?" she demanded of the trumpeter when she came close enough to be heard.

Wordlessly, the man pointed to the hill off to the right of the English position. Beth's gaze followed to the point indicated . . . and her heart leaped into her throat.

Sweet Jesu in heaven, it couldn't be . . .

It couldn't.

"The damned fool has come back," Sir Gareth murmured in a tone rife with disbelief and admiration. "And he's brought company."

She stared at the impossible sight before her, joy, fear, and incredulity all battling for precedence in her. It was Alex. He sat atop a magnificent war steed, and he was bedecked in full Templar regalia—with some two score or more other mounted Templar Knights gathering behind him.

"Dear God," she murmured, unable to tear her gaze from him.

She would have known him anywhere, even had he not been leading the group of Templars. His bearing was so commanding, so filled with authority, courage, and power.

Two of the knights behind him held aloft the black and white beauséant banner that the Holy Order always carried into battle. It flapped in the stiff breeze, and the silence, as the English and the defenders of Dunleavy continued to do naught but stare, allowed the sound of it to carry to where she stood. All the Templars wore dazzling white surcoats, emblazoned with the distinctive crimson cross that was their symbol and the emblem under which they lived and died . . . the same sign that had sent fear through the hearts of their enemies for centuries upon the mere sight of it.

"I cannot believe it is him," she managed to utter, her chest aching with the force of love she felt for him. Desperately, she looked away from Alex to assess the enemy forces, noticing that several pockets of them appeared to be moving at last, dissolving into chaos, with some of the men abandoning their posts and fleeing at the sight of the legendary military force aligning itself against them . . . a group of the most skilled and formidable warriors the world had ever known.

It was no secret that Templar Knights never gave up the field; they would fight until every one of them was dead rather than surrender. Even off the battlefield they were a daunting presence, showing determination in the face of terrible persecution—which was one reason France's King Philip the Fair had found the process of obtaining papal dissolution of the Order to be far more lengthy and difficult than he had anticipated.

Every person within Dunleavy and every man fighting on the side of the English knew the reputation Templar Knights had earned in their two hundred years of waging skirmishes, battles, and full-blown wars fought for the sake of the Brotherhood's justice. Battles fought without mercy or quarter given to those who opposed them. And for a moment, it seemed that that alone would be enough to send the enemy from the field.

But then a rider burst forth from the ranks of the English. He was impressive in his own right, wearing armor that flashed in the sunlight and carrying a shield bearing the king's device in one hand while brandishing his sword in the other. He wore a helm, but his visor was up as he spurred his steed to the middle of the field . . . and then on a direct line with the Templar force amassed on the hill.

"It is Sir Lucas," the captain murmured. His gaze, like hers, was fixed on the scene playing out so unbelievably before them. "By God, he would need to be a former Templar to find courage enough to ride alone against an array of combatants such as that," he added under his breath, shaking his head.

Oh, nay . . . blessed angels, nay . . .

The prayer swept through Beth's mind, though she knew it was futile to think it. Sir Lucas had thrown down a challenge by riding out in this fashion—and one of the Templars was going to have to answer it. She did not need to be a scholar to know which one it would be.

In the next heartbeat, a lone knight had broken ranks from the warriors at the top of the hill to ride down toward Luc on a collision course, with both of them charging forward at full tilt. Beth's heart was lodged in her throat still, love spilling through her, pierced now by a lance of fear sharper than any she'd ever known . . .

It was Alex.

Chapter 17

Alex thundered down the field toward Luc, the pounding of his steed's hooves naught but an echo of the thirst for vengeance pulsing through his veins. Sun glinted off Luc's shield, and Alex's vision narrowed down to a pinprick, the magnificent agony of bloodlust he always felt in those last moments before he physically clashed with his enemy as alive as ever inside him. But it had a deeper edge to it now.

This time, the battle was more personal than any he had fought as a Templar Knight.

This time he fought for Beth.

Sliding his sword free of its hilt with a metallic hiss, muted under the sound of air whistling past his helm, Alex steadied himself, his body tensed, and he moved as one with his mount, leaning forward in the saddle, readying to collide with Luc. Readying to have the chance at last to make the bastard pay for every wretched action he had taken against Alex and the people he loved.

Just a few more strides . . .

With bone-cracking force, Alex's sword clanged against Luc's, jerking his shoulder back so hard, it might have been wrenched from the socket, had he not been a warrior trained through the exertion of a hundred conflicts fought before. Their steeds also slammed together, however, the shearing blow sending both mounts careening. Alex heard a shrieking whinny, and then the sky and ground seemed to tumble together in a dizzying whirl as his gelding toppled over.

Alex crashed to earth, the impact knocking the air from his lungs and his helm from his head. He lay still for but an instant, disoriented, doing his best to bid his wits sharpen against the pain . . . rolling to retrieve his sword and stand, even as he blinked the sweat from his eyes and looked wildly around, trying to gain a fix on Luc. Surely his nemesis had been thrown from his mount as well. Yet Alex knew if he had, he'd likely righted himself just as quickly, his own Templar training having taught him the value of speed in recovery from such setbacks.

Alex realized how fortunate it was that he had learned that lesson so well himself, for in the next instant and without any other warning, he sensed movement behind him and half turned to see Luc's sword come slashing down toward his head.

On sheer instinct, he lifted his blade to deflect the blow, spinning around the rest of the way to lash out with a retaliatory stroke. It rang out against Luc's shield, driving him back. With the advantage of surprise he'd hoped to gain lost now, Luc stumbled a few more steps, his helm also missing, eyeing Alex and then taking a battle stance Alex recognized from their training in Cyprus . . . centering himself for the remainder of the fight.

Through the side of his vision, Alex saw that a

portion of the English army had advanced on the field, and that the rest of the Templars—Damien, Richard, and John included—had ridden out and were even now clashing with them nearer to the hill. Soldiers poured out of Dunleavy to join the side of the Brotherhood, and the all too familiar sounds of battle echoed over the area, filling Alex's senses like the pulsing flow of hot, thick blood.

But he could not concern himself with any of it. Not yet. First he had to defeat Luc.

Alex's jaw tightened, his mind going to a place of intense concentration, with no drop of energy wasted upon feeling the pain that throbbed through his body. With no thoughts of anything except the enemy before him.

Luc uttered a low growl and Alex lifted his weapon, both of them lunging forward to engage again. Blade clashed on blade, sending up sparks. Alex knew naught but the desire to vanquish his opponent; it gave him strength to continue. Helped him to push forward against this warrior with whom he was so evenly matched in skill and power.

It would not be an easy victory, of that he was certain.

Luc possessed the same deadly training as Alex. His body had been honed to an instrument of war, just as Alex's had. There was but one real difference between them, Alex realized, and he prayed it was that which would tip the scale to determine who walked from this field and who was carried from it, a stiffening corpse: Luc fought for the sake of pride and status in the eyes of the English lord he served. Alex fought for the woman he loved.

"You could not stay away, Alex, could you?" Luc grated, using his body to batter Alex back, even as he swung out again with his blade, catching his shield. "You were free to go north, and yet you were stupid enough to come back."

"I will run no more, Luc," Alex answered, breathing heavily as he swung his sword to the side and feinted right, nearly managing to slice Luc's upper arm. The miss was only the result of Luc shifting his weight at the last moment. "It is time you paid for your crimes."

"You'd have been wise to keep running," Luc muttered, his breath coming hard as well as he struck again, catching Alex's thigh with the very edge of his blade and sending a streak of fiery pain down the limb. "It is what you were always best at, wasn't it?" he taunted.

Trying to ignore the hurt, Alex stumbled back a step, knowing that he could not risk checking it, lest Luc use the chance to strike. Predictably, his opponent moved in without delay and attempted another blow, clearly hoping Alex would be distracted by the pain of his wound.

Alex had trained too long and too hard to let that happen.

Deflecting the blade, he twisted around to inflict his own cut to Luc's forearm, underneath, where his armor plate did not protect—and this time it was Luc who jerked back, his breath hissing in sharply.

"Well done," Luc admitted through gritted teeth. They swung and their blades clashed again, both of them gasping with exertion. "I will remember the sting of that wound when I am battering down th bedchamber door"—he grunted with the energy it took to deflect another of Alex's blows, before finishing—"to take my turn with that spirited wench you've been fucking these past weeks." He could barely utter his perverse claim for the intensity with which they fought, but still he managed to leer as he choked out the words.

For an instant, black hatred rose up inside Alex, threatening to cloud his intent with distracting emotion—a lethal mistake in the midst of battle, he knew. For Beth's sake he would not allow his mind to be swayed from the moment at hand.

Maintaining the same calm and deadly center he had called upon from the very beginning of this confrontation, Alex muttered, "While I live, I will never let you take what is not yours, Luc." His breath burned in his lungs, but he met his former comrade's gaze, his own steely, he knew, with conviction born of the love he felt. "Not Dunleavy—and not Beth."

"Then you will die, Alex, for I intend to have both."

Their blades locked at that moment, and the momentum of their fighting slammed them together, chest-to-chest. Alex could see directly into Luc's eyes in this position, and the darkness emanating from that flat gaze might have made another man recoil in aversion or even fear. But Alex had his own fury to contend with, along with the stronger and far deeper emotion that urged him on, giving him courage.

Love for Beth.

He had to protect her . . . had to keep her safe from Luc and Lord Exford, and the price they would extract for her resistance to the English king's will.

Too much weighed in the balance for him to falter now.

Lifting his shoulder, he managed to unhook the edge of his hilt from Luc's, using the impetus of the movement to sweep his arm up and around, smashing his armored elbow into the side of Luc's head.

It was a brutal strike, knocking Luc nearly senseless and throwing him off balance . . . and Alex wasn't going to wait for another opportunity like this to come again. Lunging forward, he struck at Luc with his blade—coming at him from all possible angles—above, sidelong, directly to the middle. Raining blows down on him, hard and steady. Relentless.

At first Luc managed to repel the assault, falling back and taking the strikes on either his blade or his shield or both at once. But he could not sustain that kind of defense for long. Alex swung again. And again. His arm felt heavy, aching with the strain of pushing himself to the limit. Luc fell back another step before Alex was forced to pause, still holding a fighting stance, but gasping with breath. Luc planted his feet shoulder-width apart, his own powerful form trembling with exertion.

Complete silence seemed to wrap around them of a sudden, enveloping them as if they stood suspended in time. What happened next unraveled in the sloweddown motions of a dream. Uttering a battle roar, Luc raised his sword with both hands, high over his head, and Alex swung his blade up one last time to counter. They lunged forward . . . only Alex brought his weapon down more swiftly, in an arc born of endle practice—sweeping down and sideways, to end i killing strike.

His blade bit deep into Luc's unprotected right side, slicing through the vulnerable, exposed flesh under the edge of armor plates at his lowest rib, before he yanked back and slid the blade free of its human sheath.

Luc had jerked once beneath the deadly impact, hunching forward and making a choking sound. His sword fell to the earth, and then he went completely still, his face rigid with shock even as blood spilled down his side. Grasping the front of Alex's surcoat, he held himself up long enough to turn his head stiffly, the gaze that burned into Alex already darkening with death. Those eyes blazed with hatred, and his mouth twisted in a look of evil mockery.

"I—I can't believe it . . . you . . . bastard"—Luc breathed, falling to his knees. But the grip of his hand, still twisted in the crimson cross, pulled Alex down with him.

"It's over, Luc," Alex said grimly, leaning back and trying to disengage from that death grip. "Go and face God, knowing I will pray for His mercy on your immortal soul."

Luc barked a laugh choked with blood, teetering there and clutching relentlessly at the fabric on Alex's chest as he yanked him closer, rasping, "Pray for your own soul, Alex . . . for you're going to hell with me."

And with that, Alex felt more than saw Luc's other arm jerk up . . . felt the cool, deadly blade of Luc's dagger punch into the mail high up on his chest, just below his shoulder. Luc smiled again through blood-ned lips, meeting Alex's stunned gaze for but an nt. In the next breath those eyes went dark. As

Luc fell back dead, the dagger pulled free with stinging force, before rolling from Luc's hand as his body hit the ground.

Alex looked down at his chest, seeing it as if from a distance. Vaguely, he realized that it was his own blood soaking a bright red bloom into the white of his surcoat, its scent metallic and faintly sweet. He watched it seeping down to drip onto the cuisse plates that protected his thighs. He swayed on his knees and heard a buzzing in his ears that matched the increasing onslaught of dark spots converging on his vision.

Just before he lost his senses, Alex managed to tilt his head up toward Dunleavy's battlements; he saw a flash of crimson, and his mind latched on to one final, aching thought. It was Beth standing there . . . and he'd failed her. *Oh, God, he'd failed her* . . .

Then he toppled over into blackness.

Beth's hands trembled so that she nearly dropped the basket of needles and thread she kept for stitching wounds, as four of Dunleavy's soldiers carried Alex toward the small chapel, which was the nearest chamber inside the walls past the gatehouse.

Commotion swirled around them, intensified near the gate, now that the battle was finished. It was over, as impossible as that seemed. The English had called a retreat only a few moments ago, having no other recourse once Lord Exford fell in the battle just after Luc's defeat. Dunleavy's wounded, along with any Templars who had sustained injury, were dragging themselves or being carried through the gates into the castle for treatment, while the enemy pulled back beyond the wood, taking their dead and wounded with them.

It had been a rout. Dunleavy had been saved through the magnificent defense that had been led by Alex and his Templar brethren, fulfilled through their efforts combined with those of Dunleavy's garrison.

But at what cost?

Oh, God, the cost would be far too great if Alex died.

Sweet Jesu, don't let him die, she repeated over and over like a prayer, in the benumbed silence of her mind as she hurried alongside his still and blood-stained form.

"Lay him down there," she commanded hoarsely when they finally entered the chapel, pointing to a soft pallet she'd ordered prepared for him from the moment he'd fallen on the field. From that awful moment when she had seen the blood soaking his surcoat, visible even from her position atop the gatehouse tower battlements.

"Carefully!" she cried, when one of the men stumbled in carrying him. She rushed to Alex's side as soon as the soldiers set him down, using a wad of clean rags to apply pressure to the bloody puncture wound below his shoulder. Panic swelled up to choke her, nearly undoing her, but she forced herself to remain as calm as she could until the warmed wine, hot iron, poultice, and clean bandages she'd sent Annabel to gather arrived.

"Alexander," she whispered, leaning over him, brushing a kiss over the cool clamminess of his brow. He was so pale. If not for the shallow movement of his chest, she might have feared him dead.

Holy Mother Mary, where are they with the things I need?

"Hurry, I pray you!" she cried out to the servants near the door, who waited for those bringing the items she needed. "Tell Annabel I must have the things I ordered brought for him without delay!"

She tried to loosen Alex's surcoat, stained so red with his blood that it was difficult to discern the cross stitched onto its front any longer. Tears stung her eyes when he groaned in response to her attempt to move his arm so that she might loosen the ties. Oh, God, she could not do this alone. She needed help. She needed—

"My lady—Lady Elizabeth?"

Dazed, her eyes blurred with the emotions she was struggling to keep back, Beth looked up from where she knelt at Alex's side. Up into the face of a golden-haired warrior so angelic in appearance that he might have been mistaken for one of God's holy seraphim. He was a Templar Knight by the surcoat he wore, and he was frowning down at her with an expression of worry on his chiseled features, the shadow of it apparent in his eyes as well, which were the same startling blue as Alexander's.

Then it struck her . . .

Eyes the same blue as Alexander's . . .

"Sir Damien?" she whispered.

"Aye," he murmured, dropping down beside Alex, assessing his wounds with a practiced, careful touch.

"How is he?" Another Templar warrior appeared behind Damien, as tall and powerful in build, on¹ slightly older and darker in coloring—and ther third with reddish-gold hair.

"I cannot tell yet," Damien said, taking over the loosening of Alex's surcoat and moving on to the hauberk and tunic beneath as well, with Beth's aid and the help of a servant he'd gestured over to aid in the task. "I will know in a moment."

All the men bore their own cuts and bruises from the battle they'd just fought, but none seemed to heed those injuries, concerned only about Alex and his condition.

"I am Sir Richard, lady," the darker-haired warrior said quietly, crouching down beside her. "And this is Sir John." As he spoke, he indicated the reddish-haired Templar who had come in with them; the man acknowledged the introduction with a short bow, and Beth suddenly realized that this was the friend Alex had spoken of, who had been captured by the English and for whom he had agreed to go from Dunleavy, when she'd coerced him to leave for his own safety.

She nodded, feeling a small sense of comfort in their presence as they assessed Alex's injuries. She gripped Alex's hand, her worry increasing with every passing second. Her chest felt tight and her breath caught in her throat as she watched, waiting and praying.

When the items she had requested arrived at last, the commotion around them increased, with various servants bringing forward the warmed wine, poultices, and bandages.

"Perhaps it would be best if you allowed us to work on him, lady," Sir Richard suggested. "We are well versed in treating battle wounds, and it will help Alex if we can do that without delay."

"I will not leave him," Beth answered raggedly. She

glanced to Damien, who was still tending his brother with such care, adding, "Yet I will be glad to do what is necessary for you to work more effectively." As she spoke she shifted her position, taking a place near Alex's head and stroking her fingers over his brow and cheeks in a soothing rhythm as she spoke soft words of encouragement.

His clothing had been removed to his waist and some of the smeared blood cleansed away from the area of the dagger wound. Damien kept the heel of his hand pressed against the wad of bandages he'd used to help stem the bleeding, but each time he let up on the pressure, the flow began anew.

"It needs burning," Damien muttered at last. "It will not stop otherwise. I do not think the lung has been pierced—his chain mail and the bone seem to have deflected the worst of the blow—but the wound bleeds heavily and is in danger of putrefying if we cannot cleanse it properly." He turned to Richard, murmuring a request for some specific herbs to be added to the poultice that would be applied later, and Richard left to gather what was necessary.

"A hot iron stands at the ready," Beth said, gesturing for one of the servants to bring it forth. "I ordered it prepared, so that no wait would be necessary if it was needed."

Damien fixed her with an assessing gaze, and she felt a flush of bittersweet feeling to see a shadow of Alex in that look. "Your foresight in this is mo welcome, Lady Elizabeth," Damien said, his vc somber. "Pray God it will aid in my brother's recovery."

She nodded, but before aught else could

John drew her gaze, murmuring, "You may not wish to witness this, my lady. It is quick but very painful."

Anguish in the knowledge of that already burned in her heart; she'd seen wounds cauterized before and knew it would be difficult to bear watching Alex suffer under the iron. But there was no real choice.

"I will not leave him, Sir John," she asserted again, steeling herself. "Do what must be done."

Richard had returned by this point with the herbs, mixed into a poultice, and after a few murmured instructions among the men, they positioned themselves around Alex. Beth moved around to his side again just for this portion of what needed to take place; Damien had asked for her aid in pouring the cleansing wine over the wound before he burned it, and she'd agreed, relieved to have something she could do to help.

Richard took the position at Alex's head, gripping his shoulders, John knelt to restrain his legs, and Damien readied himself at his side, holding the iron by some rags wrapped around the cooler end of it.

"At my command," he said quietly, still pressing down on the puncture wound. "Steady yourselves."

Everyone settled into his position.

"Ready . . ." Damien murmured.

The men tightened their grips and Beth tensed, sending up a litany of prayers and keeping her gaze fixed in anguished love on Alex, even as she clutched the ewer of warmed wine so tightly her knuckles had gone white.

"Now . . ."

Damien swung the ewer directly over Alex's chest,

knowing that time would be of the essence once Damien released his pressure on the wound.

"Now."

As he spoke the final word, Damien lifted the heel of his hand along with the wad of rags, and Beth poured the wine over the spot. Tears blurred her vision as Alex jerked upward in painful response, awakening at last. Then she stumbled back as the burning iron was jabbed into the wound immediately afterward, dragging a roar of agony from Alex's throat as he cursed and thrashed against their grip on him.

Once the moment of burning was past, she rushed back to his side, cradling his head in her lap and stroking his face, which had gone ashen, while Damien applied poultice to the burn, holding it in place with a firm wrapping of linen strips at an angle around his chest. She rested her other hand soothingly on Alex's uninjured shoulder, while his chest heaved with the gasping breaths he sucked in after the agony he'd just endured.

Then it was done, and Damien leaned back on his heels.

In another moment, it was clear to everyone in the chamber that Alex had gone senseless again; his breathing had shifted to short, shallow inhalations once more.

Giving each other glances that revealed the seriousness of what Alex was contending with through this injury, John and Richard walked without speaking further to the front of the chapel; Damien joined them there a moment later, after he had checked Alex's breathing one more time and taken care of bloodied rags and other implements they'd used in the procedure. Then all three men knelt, bowed their heads, and together began to pray.

Beth could not join them. Nay, she could not bear to be away from Alex, and so she remained by his side, holding his hand and sitting where she was to offer up her own appeals to God, praying harder than she ever had before.

It was all she could for him now, she knew. Pray . . . and wait.

Chapter 18

New morning sun streamed into the chapel through narrow, peaked windows of stained glass, spilling onto the stone floor in a wash of color, when Beth first noticed a movement from Alex that indicated he might be awakening. Subduing the thrill of hope that swept through her, she nudged Annabel, rousing her and sending her out for a fresh cup of wine mixed with the healing powders she been giving Alex in drops throughout the night. Then she called out a low summons to Damien, John, and Richard, who had also slept in the tiny chapel that had been converted into Alex's sickroom.

They got up quickly from the pews where they'd rested and hurried to gather round, while she eased herself to a sitting position. Ignoring the shrieking protest of her joints and muscles, stiff from hours spent curled on the cold stone floor, she took Alex's hand in hers. He made restless movements and frowned, tipping his head to the side as he struggled to pull himself from the grip of his wound-induced sleep.

A few moments of tense silence passed as they waited. And then he opened his eyes a crack, look to see who tended him.

"Beth?" he croaked.

"Aye, love, I am here," she whispered, tears welling in her eyes as she pressed a kiss to his cheek.

He blinked, and after another few seconds, that sensuous mouth of his tipped up at the corner just slightly, the sight of it sending a wash of relief and love through her, so great that if she had not been kneeling next to him, she would have sunk to the floor. "When I awoke in the presence of an angel, I thought myself dead," he murmured.

A happy sob bubbled up in her throat, but she choked it back. "Hush, knave—and pray do not ever set me to worrying so over you again," she said to him, her voice catching. "I will save the scolding for your stubbornness in returning to Dunleavy at all for another time."

"I await the moment with bated breath," he rasped, offering her a weak smile.

She smiled back at him, tears of joy still clouding her vision. "You may not be so eager to hear it once you are well enough. Thanks be to God, though, the worst seems to be past now."

"Thanks be to God indeed," Damien offered, placing his hand on Alex's arm in a gesture of affection and solidarity. "You gave us a few uneasy moments, though, I do confess it."

"You'll not be rid of me that easily, little brother," Alex said, his voice still tight with pain.

"Do you remember aught of what happened?" Richard asked.

"Most of it." Alex winced, his body tensing. "I re-thinking that it hurt like hell—and that I could have without the scorching you gave me at the end."

"Here," Beth said firmly, holding the fresh goblet of medicinal drink Annabel had brought back and pressed into her hand. "Can you tip your head up enough to swallow?"

At his nod, she helped him to a few sips. Then a few more. He grimaced, but at least the color was coming back into his face.

"What in God's name is that?" he asked, scowling as he let his head fall back. "It tastes awful."

"Strong wine fortified with crushed marjoram, fennel, and some nettle juice," she answered matter-of-factly, her relief in his ability to complain making it difficult for her not to grin. "You've been getting as much of it as I could get into you, all night. It will aid in the pain and speed your healing too."

"Curse me if the cure isn't worse than the injury," he groused.

"Listen to the lady, Alex, and do as you're told," John called out, a smile in his voice as well. "'Tis obvious she cares more for your sorry hide than you do yourself."

Alex made a disgruntled sound. Clearly uncomfortable being the center of so much attention, he tried to push himself up onto his forearms, wincing again.

"Hold there, man," Richard called out, reaching out to grasp a large, rolled-up blanket from one of the pews. "Use this," he added, coming forward to prop it behind Alex. They helped shift him back a little, toward the wall, so he could use its solid expanse as well with the blanket in between.

"I am better now," he muttered once he was s tled, waving his hand and looking irritated. "You all go back to what you were doing, damn it—"

He stopped still as if remembering something of a sudden.

"Ah, damn it," he breathed, shaking his head, "There is still a siege to counter. How long have I been out?" He tried to curl forward to sit up more, but the movement made him grimace with a new wave of pain. "Come, lads, and help me—"

Beth rushed over to him along with Damien, who'd moved in quickly on his other side; together they pressed him back to rest against the wadded blanket. "Lie down," Beth ordered him firmly. "You're going nowhere for a good while."

"The siege is over, brother," Damien added. "It ended yesterday, just before you were brought inside these walls. Lord Exford fell in battle, and the English army was forced to retreat."

"What?" Alex looked bewildered. "How did that happen so quickly?"

"It was our stunning masculine prowess, of course," Richard drawled, smiling as he sat in one of the pews again and stretched his legs.

"And our flawless skill as brothers-in-arms," John added, grinning as he too joined in the jest.

"It was all of that, and all of you as well," Beth said more seriously, moved beyond words, almost, to think that these men and their Templar brethren had been willing to sacrifice themselves for Dunleavy. For her castle, her people . . . for her. Looking at each one in turn, she murmured, "I owe you all a debt of thanks I shall never find means to repay, I fear."

They looked both abashed and pleased, though shook his head in denial of any obligation on part.

"It was justice, pure and simple," Damien said.

"We are always ready to lend our aid for a cause such as yours, Lady Elizabeth," John concurred.

"Defending Dunleavy Castle provided us our first opportunity to fight side-by-side again since the night of the mass arrests in France," Richard reminded them all quietly. "And while I cannot say I enjoy what we must do when we take the field in battle, there are no men I would rather have standing by me than the ones with me in this chapel right now."

Damien and John concurred in low tones that conveyed a far more serious bent of mind than they'd shown before.

And then Alex decided to offer his opinion.

"You are all very noble to be sure," he murmured, clearly feeling more like himself again from the mischievous tenor of his voice. "Yet you seem to forget that it was I who nearly passed on to the next life yesterday. *I* am the one owed the largest debt of gratitude." He swung his gaze to where Beth knelt beside him, his blue eyes tired, but nonetheless filled with something teasing, dangerous, and oh-so-wonderful as he added pointedly, "Wouldn't you agree, Lady Elizabeth?"

She flushed as of old under the force of that look. It maddened her, for she knew her red cheeks would betray the wayward path of her thoughts to the others far too readily. John coughed and pulled a grinning Damien aside to join Richard where he sat in th pew—and in the next moment she was left to spe with Alex alone, for all intents and purposes.

Raising his hand to touch just below her chin. encouraged her to meet his gaze, adding softly

I know just the way you could show your appreciation to me, lady . . ."

Bending over him on pretext of adjusting his bol-
ster, she whispered, "Enough of that, sir. You are in
no condition to do aught but try to recover from your
injuries." Flashing him a look she hoped would soften
her scolding, she added, "To suggest anything else is
unruly and indecent."

"I did not realize they were such undesirable qualities."

She could not keep back her smile, then, or the soft
laugh that followed it.

"Knave," she repeated, shaking her head and lifting a cloth from a bowl of warm, scented water Annabel had brought with her along with the fortified
wine. After wringing it out, she began to cleanse the
remaining stains of dirt and blood from his upper
body, glad to be able to do so more thoroughly now
that he was awake and on the mend. She was careful
not to brush against the bandage holding the poultice
to his wound, but still, when she pulled the damp-
ened cloth over the muscular expanse of his chest,
he gripped her hand, forestalling her, and her gaze
snapped to his.

"I may be a knave, lady, but I know one thing," he
murmured, his stare intent upon her.

"Oh?" she said, trying not to show how much she
relished the feeling of his hand atop hers again . . . or
the steady, deep rhythm of his heart thumping against
palm below it. "And what is that?"

He smiled, his thumb stroking tenderly across
back of her hand. "I know that I would die a
nd deaths, if it meant keeping you safe. And

that more than anyone or anything in this world, you—"

The door to the chapel was yanked open of a sudden, and morning sunlight spilled in for an instant before it was blocked out by the imposing, anxious form of Dunleavy's captain of the guard, Sir Gareth. Richard, Damien, and John had lurched to their feet, their hands on their hilts, and Beth felt Alex tense beneath her hand as he turned to look at the doorway.

"Pardon, my lady—sirs," he said, indicating the men with a glance before his gaze settled on Beth again. "I come bearing tidings of an approaching army."

"What?" Beth's heart dropped. "The English have regrouped, then, and are readying to launch a new assault?"

"Nay, lady. There are two banners held aloft before an armed force some two hundred strong, complete with archers, foot soldiers, and mounted knights. One banner bears Lord Lennox's coat of arms."

Sir Gareth paused then, his mouth tightening and his spine held more stiffly than before, if that was possible. When he brought himself to finish, each word fell like a death knell on the chamber.

"The other, however, bears the device of the king himself. Robert the Bruce has come to Dunleavy, Lady Elizabeth, and he is about to gain entrance at the gates."

Chapter 19

Alex waited in a small chamber off the great hall, alone except for three of the king's men who guarded him. His entire body ached, the wound near his shoulder burned, and his head pounded, but he felt strangely alert as he readied himself to face the crisis to come.

A hasty trial had been called by the Bruce himself, to investigate claims by Lord Lennox and Beth's steward, Edwin, of treason committed against the Scottish Crown; Alex had been named as chief offender.

To avoid more bloodshed and the possibility of Beth being harmed through any skirmish within the castle walls, Alex had allowed himself to be taken without struggle when the king's guards had come to the chapel to collect him. Damien, Richard, John, and the other Templars had been willing to close ranks and raise arms against the Bruce and his entire army if such was necessary to keep him from being questioned and taken to trial, but Alex had convinced them to stand down for now and let this play out as would.

 stice would prevail, he'd said.

even as he'd spoken, he'd known his chances of

walking out of Dunleavy a free—or even breathing—man were slim. It was something they knew as well, but they had felt bound to respect the path he had chosen to take in the matter.

He had realized, as he'd been led away, that for the third time in the space of a week, the path he was choosing was one of honor and truth. He'd almost smiled to think it might have become a habit with him, stronger, even, than the self-serving choices he'd lived by for most of his life.

It was a comforting thought, though the facts lodged against him were irrefutable; he was in enormous trouble this time. He was a common knight who had impersonated a nobleman loyal to Scotland. He had spied for England, gathering Dunleavy's secrets to be used against her in a siege. That his reasons for undertaking those heinous crimes had some larger merit would not matter much, he knew, when it came to countering the charge of treason against him.

Nay, not to Robert the Bruce, the volatile young earl who had declared himself King of Scotland only three years past. France had not recognized him as the sole ruler of this land until this very year, after he'd waged a brutal and successful campaign against his political rivals, the Comyns. He was a hardened warrior-king as comfortable hiding on the moors, a hunted outlaw, as he was in placing a golden diadem on his head during lavish court ceremonies.

Robert the Bruce was not a man to be trifled with—and he would not be amused by anything that even hinted of treachery against him or the country he h been fighting so strenuously to free from Engla incursion.

Alex knew this and accepted it. It had been a risk he'd deemed worth taking when he'd come back to fight for Beth. When he'd left Dunleavy to seek John, he had not known of Edwin's defection to Lord Lennox, or that Lennox would bring the Bruce into the mix. But he also realized it would not have mattered. He would have come back anyway, willing to undertake anything to try to keep Beth safe from harm.

There was but one spot of hope in this whole, horrible mess. The fact that he had taken the side of Dunleavy during the siege might show favorably to the Bruce and mitigate some of the evidence compiled against him. But he wasn't willing to wager the cost of the rope they would use to hang him with on it turning out that way.

It was better than nothing, though, and so he concentrated on the possibility of it . . . and on the knowledge that Beth was safe from English aggression for the time being; she would be under the Bruce's protection now that the truth of her husband's death had come to light.

Aye, she would be as safe as she could be in these volatile times, and that made all the difference for him as he readied to face yet another powerful nobleman bent on destroying him. It was a more deadly conundrum, perhaps, than he'd ever known before, in that this time he would be dealing with the wrath of a king. But if all hope proved lost and a traitor's death was imminent, he would have the knowledge that Beth was safe to cling to—that and knowing that a splendid, intelligent, noble-hearted woman such as had found something in him to love.

Pray God it would keep him strong and courageous to the end.

"It is time, sir. We have been bid to enter the great hall."

Alex turned his head toward the guard who had spoken and nodded his answer, slowly easing himself to stand. He ignored the pains of his body and willed himself to go into this with his bearing proud and his back straight.

He would not falter.

He was Sir Alexander de Ashby, eldest son of an impoverished family, who had made a name for himself as a skilled warrior and a Knight of the Temple's innermost circle. He had known the affection of a devoted brother and loyal friends, and the love of a magnificent woman. He could take his place alongside those he had admired his whole life and feel no fear . . . for at long last, he had learned to be a good man.

As he prepared to take that first step into the chamber where he would face his fate, he knew that he was grateful for all of it.

And that it was enough.

Beth tried to see around the mass of people and soldiers that stood between her and the door at the back of the chamber, feeling something inside her clenching tight. She felt ill in body and soul. Though the were so many in this great chamber, the atmosph was hushed, the mood tense as everyone waite Alex to be brought in to face the royal tribur wrapped her arms around her middle, tryin the trembling and churning sickness there.

It was agony, her heart twisting to know that such horrible danger loomed for Alex, and there was naught she could do to stop it. For a brief moment, she shifted her gaze to the front of the hall where a dais had been set up; she saw the hard, accusing stares of those positioned there—powerful warriors, noblemen, the king himself—all seemingly aligned in readiness to condemn the man she loved.

King Robert the Bruce, a powerfully built noble with a commanding presence and penetrating eyes, had taken the place of authority at the center, flanked on one side by Lord Lennox and Edwin, who were Alex's primary accusers, and on the other by his senior officers. She stood opposite the sovereign, across a makeshift aisle from the table to which Alex would be led for questioning. Sir Gareth stood just behind her, as did most of the castle garrison, and the entire Templar contingent to the side of that, fronted by Sir Damien, Sir Richard, and Sir John. Glancing to them, she caught Damien's gaze, and the troubled look in his eyes only added to her growing sense of dread.

She had not wanted Alex to give himself up for trial. She had wanted him to flee—to use the intricate series of hidden passages to escape from Dunleavy altogether, before the king's men could reach him.

But he had refused, and no matter what she'd said or how she'd begged him to reconsider, he had been adamant. He had lived as an outlaw in one way or other for too many years, he had said—in Cyprus, e, and England—and he could not undertake again. He would run no more. Nay, he would was right by facing his accusers, and rely on revail.

But she knew better than most how fickle the winds of justice could blow. He was taking his life into his hands with this, and she could not talk him from it. *Cursed honor!* she'd wanted to scream. What good was it now, if it brought only death and suffering? Yet to her everlasting misery, his brother and his friends had reluctantly supported him in his decision, and so she had been forced to concede, having little opportunity in the end to do aught but press a desperate kiss to his lips and clasp him close for a moment before the king's men were at the door.

Now she waited.

A creaking groan at the back of the great hall echoed through the stillness, and the crowd reacted with a low hum as the four men who had been inside the chamber beyond walked out into the room.

It was Alex, surrounded by three of the king's heavily armed guards.

He strode forward without hesitation, so handsome, so strong, and so noble in bearing. Had she not seen the dagger wound herself and helped in the treating of it, she would never have known that he'd suffered any physical injury. He would show no weakness before these men who wished to destroy him, and that knowledge made her chest seize up, her eyes clouding with tears she refused to shed as he came closer through the crowd that was parted by the guard in front of him.

"Stand aside—make way," the guard repeated every few paces, as they made their way to the front of the chamber.

Alex reached the front of the crowd . . . and as he passed within two paces of her, his gaze lifted to lock with hers. A swell of unbearable emotion swept through her at the solemn, resigned expression on his face and the look of concern for her that shone in his eyes. Here he was, facing trial and death as a traitor, and he was still worried about *her*.

"Be strong."

He murmured the words to her just before they led him to a halt at the table across the aisle, continuing to caress her with his stare, trying to give her courage. She understood, and desperate to do what she could for him, she nodded before stiffening her spine and swallowing back her tears. She would try, for his sake. Sweet Jesu, she would try . . .

"This trial shall begin!" the king's top official declared.

And then the Bruce himself stepped forward, walking a few steps down off the dais to come closer to Alex, still as visibly startled as he had been from the moment Alex had come close enough for his face to be seen. The Bruce swung his gaze back to the two accusers, Lord Lennox and Edwin, his scowl making clear his doubts of their sanity. But turning back to Alex and the crowd behind, he spoke. "We had intended to begin the telling questions of this trial for treason framed in different words, but the sight before Us begs a more direct approach," the Bruce called out.

Backing up a step, the king continued with his gaze locked on Alex, "Speak before this gathering, then, and confirm or deny your identity as Robert Kincaid, fourth Earl of Marston—for Our eyes have rarely deceived Us so boldly if you are not he. Speak then further and answer whether you did indeed consort with the English enemy in providing them with the secrets of Dunleavy Castle, for the sole purpose of abetting them in an assault they planned, to bring her under their unlawful domination once more. Do this now, We command you."

The great hall rang out with silence following those portentous words, for everyone present knew the seriousness of the moment and the terrible fate awaiting a man foolhardy enough to have betrayed a king—especially one as volatile and warlike as Robert the Bruce.

Beth tore her gaze from the leader of her country, to whom she had sworn fealty and had done all in her power to uphold as the rightful ruler of Scotland, and settled it on the man she loved. She shook her head slightly as she met his gaze a second time in this chamber, seeing that naught had changed . . . that he was ready to place his neck in the noose for the sake of speaking the truth and protecting her from any stain in this miserable circumstance.

Her heart sank as Alex tipped his chin down and took a deep breath, before lifting his face again and calling out loudly, strongly, "Sire, I do deny that I am Robert Kincaid, fourth Earl of Marston. My true name is Sir Alexander de Ashby. I am a knight of England and a former Templar of the inner circle who sought refuge in Scotland from the persecution of the Brotherhood." He paused for just an instant, the second part of what he was admitting to more difficult for him, clearly. "And under the force of foul coercion, I confirm that I did submit to and serve as an agent of England in her efforts to bring Dunleavy Castle back into English control."

Sounds of surprise began to rumble throughout the hall, but Alex wasn't finished yet. His voice sounded quieter, humbled, it seemed, by the feeling behind the words he spoke, as he continued, "In pursuing my treacherous deeds, my heart was lost to the valiant and innocent lady of this demesne, Lady Elizabeth of Selkirk." He would not, or perhaps *could* not look at her as he spoke, and she was glad of it, for she did not know if she could have borne it. "Through her, I found strength at long last to do what was right and rise up against the will of my oppressors. The damage of my perfidy had already been done, however, and the English siege was inevitable."

When he finished, a full hum erupted in the chamber, of shock from those who had never had an inkling of this possibility, and despair from those who knew Alex and had known that the action he'd taken against the king had been unwilling—just as they knew it likely would not matter in the end.

Only Edwin and Lord Lennox looked smugly pleased. The king himself appeared as if he had been struck, so surprising must the admission have sounded to him, for he had known Robert Kincaid and clearly saw in the man before him a nearly identical likeness.

After the first moment's shock had passed, King Robert seemed to gather himself again, turning on his heel to give Alex his back and striding up onto the dais.

Oh, God, Beth prayed, *please let him be merciful. Let him hear the truth behind the crimes committed and allow his renowned respect for the Templars to sway him to see this in a better light than it seemed by unforgiving fact alone.*

Having reclaimed his place on the dais, the Bruce spun to face the assembly again. His jaw was tight with what seemed a combination of anger and disappointment as he proclaimed, "Having confessed to your ignoble deceit before the eyes of all these witnesses, sir, you are urged to share with Us now the names of any others involved in your seditious actions."

The Bruce paused, a shadow passing over his gaze as he added in a voice that rang with ominous import, "Think carefully before you speak, man, for such an admission has the power to mitigate some of the pain that is to come for you. Yet hold back the names of your accomplices, and we assure you that you will suffer every indignity of a traitor's death to the fullest, by Our command."

After a brief pause, Alex shook his head, his voice low with resignation as he answered, "I can give you no names, sire, for none who bore complicity in it still live. The burden is mine alone to carry."

The king gazed at him, his look hard, though perhaps tinged with a glimmer of respect as well. But in the next instant his features tightened in preparation of carrying out the dark promise he had made, and it was clear that by his refusal to implicate anyone else, Alex had condemned himself to the full and terrible course of a traitor's death.

"So be it," the king said flatly at last, waving his hand in dismissal. "May God have mercy on your immortal soul."

Looking down to the table and the parchments

there, the king prepared to read Alex's crimes in formal and hand down the sentence those acts had earned . . .

In but a few more moments, his fate would be sealed.

Beth thought she was going to be sick. This could not be happening.

An idea that had been slowly gathering impetus in her thoughts as the proceedings had gone on suddenly bloomed forth, and she knew now was the time to take action on it, before it was too late. She was not powerless. Alex had once told her there was always another choice in every situation, and she saw the truth of that now.

He could not go to his death like this.

She wouldn't let him.

"Sire, I beg permission to speak!" she called out, and the hum in the chamber rose to gasps and murmurs.

No one confronted a king like this, speaking without being spoken to first—especially a king like Robert the Bruce, who was known for his long memory and oft brutal responses to any insult. Yet to her great fortune, he seemed not angered by her interruption but rather understanding as he cast his noble gaze upon her.

"Permission is granted, Lady Elizabeth, for though perhaps improper in form, it is recognized that you have suffered much in this affair. What have you to say?"

Beth had been trembling since the moment Alex had been taken from her, but now the shaky feeling receded to a sense of peaceful calm. Taking a step forward, she looked at the king and at the other members of his council on the dais, carefully avoiding the gazes of Lord Lennox and Edwin. Nor could she bring herself to look at Alexander yet. Not yet . . .

"Great king," she called out in a voice clear and strong with the force of love for Alex at work inside her, "I wish to refute the claims of the man standing before you today. He has spoken so in an effort to shield me from your righteous justice."

She paused for just an instant, glancing down and praying Alex would understand, before she lifted her gaze to the king once more and finished firmly, "For I avow that he is indeed my true husband . . . and it is not he but *I* who am guilty of treason against you and Scotland."

Chapter 20

The chamber exploded in an uproar in the wake of Beth's announcement, and Alex swung his gaze to her in stupefied shock. Terror and sickness filled him at the thought of the danger she had just thrust herself into because of him. Guards stepped forward at the command of the king's chief security officer to surround Beth with their weapons drawn, and Alex lurched forward, nearly breaking free of his guards in his effort to go to her. He wanted to grab her, protect her . . . try to shake some sense into her. But the soldiers surrounding him gripped him tightly, yanking him back, and he grimaced with the pain of it, even as his gaze locked with hers.

Tears welled in her eyes, but her strength, magnificent and noble as always, held firm, and they did not spill over. She only shook her head at him, a wordless plea that he not struggle against his bonds, before she mouthed the words, "I love you." And then she turned resolutely away from him, cutting him deliberately from her vision to face the tribunal of men and her sovereign, all of whom seemed as disconcerted by her pronouncement as the people in the chamber, held back in their surging masses only by the efforts of the king's guards, with spears pointed.

"Lady Elizabeth," the king said sharply, his voice cutting through the tumult and bringing the chamber to relative quiet again. "These are serious claims, and We remind you that they carry with them a heavy punishment if they are proven true. None are spared in matters of treason, lady. Not even members of the gentler sex."

"I understand, sire," she said in a voice that still rang clear and true with conviction, damn her. "Yet I know also how much my husband has borne already for the sake of king and country. I will not allow him to throw away his life atop all that." She stood straighter, it seemed, and Alex was made speechless by the regal effect of it as she added, "You will remember, sire, that my mother was of England. I do confess to having wearied of defending this castle alone against the superior forces of my own countrymen from that land. My allegiance shifted against my husband's knowledge, and when he returned from captivity, it was too late to go back."

Oh, God, but she was stubborn, and foolish, and so very beautiful in her efforts to save him. Alex's heart lurched with love and fear for her as he jerked forward against his bonds, mindless of the pain it caused him. "Nay, sire, it isn't true, I swear it! I am the one who betrayed you, not she."

The crowd reacted again, and the king looked more distraught than ever, rubbing his temples and closing his eyes, as he seemed to mutter to himself, before lowering his hands to shout, "Enough!"

Dead silence wavered over the chamber at last, and it was clear that the king's ire had finally reached a boiling point. Tight-jawed and appearing as if he would like to wring the life from someone—anyone—with his bare hands, the Bruce clipped without turning to look at him, "Lord Lennox—what have you to say to these claims? It was you who first alerted Us to the treason brewing here, and now this"—he flicked his hand in the general direction of Alex and Beth both—"is the result. We want the truth in this and the mess of it dealt with without delay. Speak to these additional claims—now!"

Lord Lennox cleared his throat, his complexion pale. "Sire—I—I do not believe Lady Elizabeth speaks true."

"If you do not think me a traitor against Scotland, then why did you wage an unlawful siege against Dunleavy, one Scot against another, within this half year?" Beth called out in challenge.

"You laid siege to Dunleavy without Our permission, Lennox?" the king asked, his voice dangerously quiet, and his uttering of the earl's name ending in a clipped, lilting sound that boded ill for the bearer of it. The sovereign had stiffened as he spoke, still facing the assembly with his fingers laced behind his back. But he would not turn round to look at the errant earl, and Alex decided it was just as well, for the rage crackling from the Bruce might well have caused Lennox to burst into flames, were the sovereign to direct that fiery stare on him directly.

Lennox gaped and closed his mouth, reminding Alex of the man's similar reaction when they'd had their confrontation during the feast at Dunleavy.

"Answer!" the king demanded suddenly, and Lennox managed to choke out a reply.

"I—ah—I did lay siege to Dunleavy, sire, but 'twas only from desire to help guide Lady Elizabeth after hearing rumor of her husband's death while captive of the English. I can avow that when her steward, Edwin, came to me with his concerns of treason, he spoke naught of his lady excepting her lack of judgment in taking to her bosom a man who was so clearly an impostor."

"The man in question appears very like Marston to Us, Lennox," the king retorted sharply. "Do you impugn our judgment as well, then?"

"N-nay, sire! I only meant to make clear that the call of treason stemmed from the arrest of Sir Alexander here at Dunleavy, upon discovery of his perfidy. It did not involve any claims concerning Lady Elizabeth."

"It is true, my lord," Edwin added. "I witnessed Sir Alexander's confession with my own eyes. It is he who is guilty and not—"

"Have We bid you speak, sirrah?" the king snapped, breaking into Edwin's explanation, though he still did not deign to turn around and grace either of them with his direct sight. "Be still!"

Alex saw Edwin go pale; the steward dropped back in his seat as if his legs would no longer support him. It was small satisfaction, but it was something.

"We will address the matter of your unlawful siege at a later date, Lennox. For now this must take precedence." Steely-eyed, the king let his gaze drift over the assembly. "Are there any others present who can speak for or against the claims that Lady Elizabeth has made? We bid you step forward now, without delay, lest We be compelled to order both of our errant subjects put to a traitor's death, having no other recourse or proof."

The hum rose again, but Alex held firm, knowing that the threat would be enough to bring forward those who would speak the truth about his identity and Beth's innocence; even those who loved him could not stand by and let a blameless woman be hanged along with him.

He did not need to wait long.

"I can answer to the charges, sire," rang a voice from behind them. Looking over his shoulder, Alex could see it was Sir Gareth.

Beth's captain of the guard stepped into view of the dais, coming into line with Alex and Beth. Beth looked distraught by this turn of events, and Alex wanted nothing more than to pull her into his arms and comfort her. He clenched his jaw, welcoming the burn of it as he fisted his hands at his sides and compelled himself to be still . . . knowing that a further outburst would accomplish nothing for her.

After glancing at his lady apologetically, the captain stood with perfect military bearing and addressed the king and his council. "I affirm that I was present at the confession of one Sir Alexander de Ashby, the man standing here before the council. He does bear a likeness to my former lord, the Earl of Marston, but he did claim the truth of his identity when confronted with undeniable evidence, in the form of parchments detailing the assault planned against Dunleavy that were retrieved from the body of another spy, killed in a scuffle outside the castle gates."

"Nay," Beth cried softly, shaking her head. "Please, Sir Gareth, retract what you have said. Do not do this."

"Forgive me, my lady," Sir Gareth continued quietly, clearly distressed to be the cause of grief to her. "I cannot allow you to go to your death when I know you are innocent in this."

The king paused, looking round the chamber. "There are no others, then? We must make this judgment based upon the testimony of naught but a disloyal steward"—he finally flashed a glare at Edwin before turning a more respectful gaze upon Sir Gareth—"and an admittedly far more steadfast captain of the guard?"

Oh, God, it still wasn't enough. The king was not convinced. Panic surged up in Alex, the fear that Beth would be dragged into this more than he could bear. Much to the chagrin of his guards, who pulled painfully on him to make him comply, he twisted around to face the assembly, seeking Damien, John, and Richard, who were backed by the other Templars who had survived the fighting. They all looked grim, but Damien's face bore a heavier burden than the others, his features pulled tight with grief and anger.

"Speak, Damien," Alex called lowly. His voice shook with the importance of what hung in the balance here. Their gazes locked, the telltale sheen in Damien's eyes mirroring his own, he knew. "Tell them who I am."

"Do not ask it of me," Damien said hoarsely. "By God, I will not see you consigned to the noose by my testimony."

"I am begging you, Damien, do what is right. I

cannot go to my death with courage if I know that Beth is not safe. Do it for me."

The muscle in Damien's jaw twitched and he closed his eyes. When he opened them again, Alex knew by the look he saw there that Damien would do as he had asked, even if it was the most difficult thing he had ever done. He would tell the truth so that Alex might die with honor.

"It is true, sire," Damien uttered at last, sounding as though each word was being wrenched from his throat. "I can attest that I know the man standing before you and have for my whole lifetime. He is a dedicated warrior, unmatched on the field." His eyes glittered, but he stayed firm. "He is a Templar Knight of the inner circle beside whom I would fight any battle or enter any fray, knowing he would always take my back, and I his. He is a *good* man, honorable and true." His voice cracked then, and he had to stop. He looked at Alex, and the feelings and memories of a lifetime together were in his eyes as he finished on a rasp, "And God forgive me, as I avow on my soul that he is the brother of my blood, christened Alexander de Ashby a year and a half before my birth."

The assembly could not help but react to the offering of this heartfelt yet irrefutable evidence of Alex's identity. As the commotion engendered by that response swirled around them, Alex nodded to Damien in gratitude, knowing that even if he could have been heard above the crowd, he would have found no words to match what was in his heart. He looked to Beth after, but she would not meet his gaze; nay, she stood still and silent, her chin tipped to her chest and her eyes closed.

After a few more moments, the hubbub began to die down again, and the king spoke once more. "The matter of Sir Alexander's identity appears to be settled, then." He paused, and Alex could not help but notice that where before he had appeared determined in his ire to root out treachery, now he seemed somehow uncertain. Even troubled, perhaps. Glancing from Alex to Beth, the sovereign intoned, "All that remains is to determine your part in this, lady."

Alex looked at Beth again, willing her to meet his gaze. He needed to make her recant. He had to make her see that her death would accomplish naught in this. And since he was a dead man anyway, he decided it would be worth the risk to speak out of turn again in making that effort.

"Sire," he called out, shifting his gaze for the moment to the king. "I know I have no right to ask aught of you, but I beg your permission to speak once more, directly to the Lady Elizabeth." He hoped the Bruce would be able to read the sincerity in his eyes as he added, "Pray God I will find means to obtain the answer to that remaining question for you, Highness."

The Bruce paused for only an instant, startled perhaps by what he saw in Alex's gaze, for he was known to be a perceptive man, capable of assessing character the way some men judged a fine weapon or a war steed for swiftness. But eventually he nodded, and Alex turned to Beth once more, moving as close to her as the limit his captors would allow, so that he was but two paces from her . . . almost but not quite close enough to touch.

"Lady, look at me," he said quietly.

For a moment, she did nothing. But then slowly, as

if the action was being compelled beyond her will, she complied. When their gazes met, Alex felt the power of it rock through him, exquisite and life-giving at the same time that it set him to aching with the bitter-sweet knowledge of what must be. He studied every graceful line and shadow of her face, every nuance of her as she fought to hold back the emotion over-whelming her as much as it was him.

"I love you, Lady Elizabeth of Selkirk, and I cher-ish the love you give me," he murmured, speaking to her as if no one else stood in the chamber with them, aware that he was humbling himself before everyone by discussing his feelings for her openly like this. Yet he didn't care. Not if it meant saving her from sacrificing herself for him. "I know now what it is to feel love for another beyond all mean-ing, even that of my own life," he continued, gently persistent. "You too are willing to lay down yours for me, for the same beautiful reason—but it would be profane, lady."

He swallowed, never breaking his gaze with her. She had pressed her fingers to her lips, as if she could somehow hold back the gentle sobs that were even now wracking her form. God, but he wanted to touch her, wanted to hold her. But he couldn't. He could only give her this, and he would do it properly, he decided, so that she could carry it with her always and remember him well.

"You must tell them the truth, lady. Do not cor-rupt what we have shared with the baseness of more lies. Tell them, Beth. Please."

"But I do not want to live without you, Alexan-der," she whispered on a ragged breath, and when she blinked, those glistening eyes of hers spilled over in a silent path down her cheeks.

He could not speak for a moment, his throat tightening as well with all he was feeling for her. "You must, lady," he said huskily at last. "You must be strong and carry on."

"I can't—"

"Aye, you can. You must live to keep me safe and warm in the memory of your heart."

Beth's heart did lurch then with the emotion she saw filling Alex's eyes—and she knew that she had lost. She could not demean his goodness, his nobility of soul by continuing this any further. "I love you, Alex," she choked softly. Then closing her eyes, she sucked in her breath and pressed her lips together, willing herself to be strong.

When she opened them again, she faced the king and admitted, "Sire, I have done a great disservice this day to you, this court, my loyal captain"—her voice caught slightly—"and to the man I love. I am not a traitor to Scotland, nor do I live under the confused belief that this man is my late husband, Robert Kincaid, Lord Marston."

"You recant, then, lady?" the king asked.

"Aye, sire, in that—though not in my assertion that Alexander de Ashby is undeserving of a traitor's death."

"That is for Us to decide, lady," the king reminded none too gently. However, he was not offended so much that he was willing to deny her the opportunity to expound on her statement, adding, "Yet you have leave to explain to us how a man who has confessed to impersonating a Scottish nobleman for the purpose of spying for the English should be spared execution."

It was all the opening Beth needed.

She stood taller, and her voice felt stronger as she asserted, "The deeds this man committed were coerced through loyalty to his friend and fellow Templar, Sir John de Clifton, who was also being held by the English and threatened with death if Alexander did not comply. Further, he confessed of his perfidy freely to me, assuring that I knew what secrets regarding Dunleavy's security had been given to the enemy."

The king appeared to be considering what she said, and so she was encouraged to continue. "Later, he was given opportunity to escape and be free of any connection to the crimes he had committed here. Yet he refused, returning to this castle—and not alone, but with a force of two score Templar Knights alongside him—to rout the English from their intended siege in less than a day, resulting in grave injury to himself, but far less loss of life for our people than would have happened had the siege continued as would have been expected."

The king scowled, the last bit having clearly pricked his interest, pertaining as it did to warfare and driving back the enemy English. "Can you confirm this?" he asked of Sir Gareth.

The captain seemed only too happy to be able to say something that would aid in this difficult situation. Nodding, he affirmed, "Aye, sire. I witnessed Sir Alexander ride in lead of a group of valiant Templars and watched him personally slay the English captain before falling from his wounds."

Gareth glanced to Alex, and Beth saw the surprise on Alex's face as her captain cleared his throat and continued, albeit sounding a bit more nervous, "I would consider him a hero of the siege, Highness, and would go further to give my testimony that, like Lady Elizabeth, I would not think justice served were he to be put to death, for he has shown on many occasions throughout the weeks I have known him a support and love of Dunleavy and her people—and Scotland through that. Even at expense to himself."

The king seemed almost stunned at the captain's admission . . . but then one by one, various members of Dunleavy's garrison began to step forward, each asserting the same claim. And with that the Bruce went very still. The look of shock and pride on Alex's face as he heard all these statements, given in support of him by the men he'd led these past weeks, sent a thrill of happiness through her, but when Damien stepped forward with the rest of the Templars, it turned into sparks of joy.

"Your Highness," Damien called, standing at the head of the impressive group of warriors, "we wish to proclaim our allegiance to you as our king. We offer our swords in the fight for Scotland's freedom and throw ourselves on your great mercy in asking that you reconsider a charge of treason against my brother, Sir Alexander de Ashby. He will swear his fealty to you, Your Highness, and serve you as we will—as he did in the fight against Lord Exford's forces yestermorn. I give you my word of honor and stake my own life on his loyalty."

Lord Lennox had clearly been overwhelmed by the sudden turnabout he was witnessing, and he was none too happy with it. He strode forward from the dais, saying, "Set him *free*? You wish the great Bruce to simply release a man confessed of treasonous activity against him? You must be—"

"There may be room on the gibbet for a disobedient and meddlesome earl, Lennox," the king broke in, his tone brooking no argument, "We will remind you that this is *Our* decision to make, and none other's."

"Of course, sire," Lennox muttered, bowing and backing up a few steps. He looked desperate, however, as if he could feel the moment slipping through his grasp, and with it all his other nefarious plans. "But—but what of Dunleavy, Highness?" he could not seem to resist asking. "With Marston gone, I am the nearest neighbor, and I would bid for your permission to marry the Lady Elizabeth and join our forces to present a better and stronger front against any further English incursions."

"I am no breed cow to be bid upon, Lord Lennox," Beth sputtered.

"Nor can she be married to anyone else," Father Paul chimed in from somewhere in the crowd. Twisting around, Beth craned her neck to catch sight of him as he made his way forward through the people who parted for him.

At last he reached her side, standing just between her and Alex, and opening his hands in a gesture to connect each of them through the symbol he represented as the Holy Mother Church. "These two have shared the marriage bed. Though it was under false purposes, the union is binding in the eyes of the Church unless one or both of them cries foul in the matter."

He looked at Alex. "Sir, have you aught to say about it?"

"Naught but that I love her," Alex replied, the first smile Beth had seen him give since their few private moments in the chapel tilting up the corner of his mouth.

Father Paul shifted his gaze to Beth. "And you, lady? Have you anything to add?"

"Nay, Father," she said huskily, all the feeling in her coming through the words. "Other than that I do love Alexander de Ashby as well, with my whole heart and soul."

The priest faced the king again. "There you have it, sire. What God has joined together, let no man put asunder."

"Aye, Father—and heaven forbid We should attempt that. We are already in conflict enough with the Holy Mother Church and suffering under excommunication. We need no more distress on that score."

"I am more than willing to lend my voice to the many other clergy in Scotland, sire, who intend to band together to appeal to the pope in that matter."

"We appreciate any aid We can acquire, of that there is no doubt," the Bruce said, his mood clearly lighter as he tipped his head at the prelate. "And now, it seems We need to make judgment in this matter, difficult though it has proved to be."

He looked for a long moment at Beth, and then shifted an even harder stare to Alex, holding it without speaking for a goodly while. When he did utter something, it was to make comment on a subject she was not expecting.

"You love each other, that much is clear," the Bruce

said somberly. "But while love can be splendid, it can be dangerous as well, as you both have discovered these past months, we would warrant."

The king's eyes darkened then, a cloud of sorts seeming to pass over him, as he added, "We too know what it is to fight for a loved one, knowing it is not always possible to keep the beloved from danger."

The realization of whom and what he was speaking crept up on Beth, sobering her, for he spoke of his own queen, Elizabeth, held under house arrest in England these many years after being captured by English forces on the hunt for the Bruce himself.

"As king We are given, sometimes, the chance to right a wrong or make a path easier for the ones forced to tread it—and when that opportunity comes, We like to think Ourselves wise enough to recognize what is good and what is dangerous to Our well-being and the safety of Our kingdom."

The Bruce took a step forward, sliding his sword from his sheath with a metallic hiss and advancing on Alex. For a moment, Beth stiffened to think he intended to do Alex violence then and there, but Alex stood firm and tall as the king approached him and asked, "Do you, Sir Alexander de Ashby, swear fealty to Us as your sovereign lord and king, vowing to uphold Our kingdom with your whole honor, serving no other but Us and God?"

"I do so swear it, sire," Alex murmured, crossing a fist over his chest and bowing his head. Nodding, the Bruce held out his blade, and Alex knelt on one knee and pressed a kiss of fealty to the blade.

"We accept your homage, Sir Alexander," their sovereign said quietly after it was done, "and offer you Our royal pardon, recognizing you as a loyal subject of Scotland—and as Lady Elizabeth of Selkirk's lawful husband. You are charged to keep Dunleavy safe from all incursions of the enemy, at the cost of your own life, if need be."

"I give you my word of honor, sire. It shall be done," Alex answered hoarsely, wearing an expression of humility, awe, and gratitude, all wrapped in one.

"We shall stay long enough at this pleasant berth to share a night of feasting with you, for We have much We would like to discuss with you and your former Templar brethren regarding strategies of battle." The king raised his brow, enjoying himself more now that the conflict was passed and all resolved in a way suited to his sense of fairness and justice. "Can such be arranged?"

"Of course, sire," Alex said. "We would be honored."

"Good." The Bruce smiled, and Beth realized what a handsome man he was, when he wasn't forced to maintain a warlike visage. "Then We suggest you give your wife the embrace she deserves, for she has proved very patient, loyal, and true to you during the course of these difficult proceedings."

So saying, the king nodded to Alex's guards, who released him at the same time that the soldiers surrounding Beth stepped aside . . . and with two short steps, she found herself wrapped in the warmth and security of Alex's embrace. Breathing in deeply, she relished the sensation of his arms around her, her heart lighter than she could ever remember it be

He pressed a kiss to the top of her head, murmuring his love to her, and she lifted her face to him at long last. His mouth descended on hers with sweet intensity, and the kiss was so good that she was loath to have it end.

But when it did, she remained in the curve of Alex's arm, and the world came into her vision again. People milled around, and she saw that, scrambling perhaps to find means of maintaining some modicum of favor, Lord Lennox was quickly exiting the great hall to follow the king, with Edwin in tow, while the garrison and the rest of the crowd were dispersing to their other duties.

Then Damien, Richard, John, and several of the other Templars made their way to them, and Beth stepped back for a moment to allow them to offer their congratulations and relief. She felt happy tears threaten again when she watched Alex pause an extra moment with Damien, gripping his hand before being dragged into an embrace that would have been rib-cracking except for the fact that Damien held back in honor of Alex's recent wounds.

And then they moved off as well, and Alex was left alone with her.

She simply looked at him, brimming to the top with a feeling that defied description. He was alive, the king had pardoned him, and naught could separate them again. She did not think she could be happier. But then he smiled at her, the corner of his sensual mouth quirking up in the way that never failed to send a spill of heat to her very core, and she knew she was wrong.

"You managed to do it again, lady."

"What?" she murmured, gazing up at him with a smile of her own.

"Transform the most convincing argument into naught but bits of air and sound." He smiled more deeply, leaning down to brush a tender kiss over her lips, before he pulled back and looked into her eyes once more. "Of course, that you turned your power on the King of Scotland this time and not on me is a welcome change."

"Knave," she said, the word rife with affection and all the feelings she could not put into words, as she reached up and brushed an unruly lock of dark hair from his eyes.

"You saved me, Beth. If it was not for your persistence . . ." His voice trailed off, and she knew the weight of what he'd faced was heavy enough that, with the crisis now past, he could not speak of it easily, no matter how strong he'd seemed during the moment itself.

"It was naught, Alex. You have saved me as well, in so many ways—"

"Ways too great to repay properly?" he murmured, with that devilish glint in his eyes that made her pulse beat faster.

"I did not say that."

She slid her hands up to rest gently around his neck, being careful not to hurt the area of the wound he'd received. But when she let her fingers ruffle through the hair at his nape, she reveled in the low sound of pleasure he made. And when she lifted herself up on tiptoe to kiss him again, filling that caress with the promise, passion, and love still to come between them, he gave a low growl that set her to sp anew. He kept nibbling over her lips, her cheeks, her brow, along the sensitive length of her neck . . . anywhere he could reach.

"I am glad to hear you are not averse to discussing it," he said at last, making her laugh after he'd finished kissing her thoroughly. "For I still have the suggestions I'd planned to make to you in the chapel before we were interrupted."

"I have a few suggestions of my own, husband."

"You do?"

"Mmm-hmm," she murmured, nodding her head. "To start, I might offer to play endless games of *merels* with you."

"That could be interesting, wife," he murmured back, nuzzling another kiss into her neck and sending tingles of pleasure up her spine, along with the happiness she felt bubbling up inside her. "What else?"

"Another meal out in the pleasure garden, perhaps, or a warm, scented bath . . ."

He paused and pulled back to look at her, all shade of teasing gone as he asked quietly, with sincerity shining in the depth of his eyes. "How about agreeing to love me forever, flawed as I am?"

Her heart twisted with the love she felt for him, flaws and all . . . but she did not tell him that at first, only answering, "Perhaps—on one condition."

He raised his brow in question.

"That you love me as much in return."

He smiled again, and the joy she saw in his expression sent her soul soaring. "That is easy, Beth," he
 d, "for I will love you with all that I am for the rest
    y days. You have my word on it."

        he gazed down at her she knew that she might

never be happier than she was at this very moment—but she had the remainder of her life with this wonderful man to enjoy trying.

"I do believe that is the best bargain we have ever made, Alexander de Ashby," she said, smiling back at him. "And I would be honored to take it."

Epilogue

October 1315
Strathness Manor, Kinross-shire

It was a fine day for a celebration.

Beth turned her attention away from the door to watch the progress of a group of servants as they wove through groups of guests to deliver several platters of victuals for the table. The final preparations for the feast were under way here in the main chamber of Richard and Meg's new home—only neither Meg nor Richard was anywhere in sight.

Meg had stepped out earlier to check on their newborn daughter, Anne, in whose honor these festivities had been called; likewise, Beth knew that Richard had been gone all morning with Alex, John, and Damien, completing the long-awaited moment when they would rejoin the pieces of Templar treasure that had been separated by necessity as they'd fled France almost eight years ago. But she hoped, as she glanced around at the clusters of these two score guests, that ~~t~~hey would hurry in their return, else the celebration ~~w~~ould end up beginning without them.

~~J~~ust then, Beth saw Damien's wife, Alissende, approaching. She was a truly beautiful woman, dark-haired and still slender though she'd given birth to her second child only a few months ago. Beth might have been envious if she hadn't loved her so much. Alissende smiled and waved as she headed in Beth's direction, and Beth returned the gesture, watching as her friend made her way through the throng toward her.

"I'm happy to report that the children are content under the watchful eye of the nurse," Alissende said when she came close enough for Beth to hear her over the hubbub of the guests and musicians. "Your two are engaged in a game of hoodman blind with Gregory and Margery. The baby is fast asleep, thank heavens, though I suspect he'll awaken and demand I feed him again before the feast is fully under way."

"Undoubtedly," Beth answered with a smile. "I do hope my boys aren't being too rough with your daughter. She may be the elder, but they aren't always as careful as they should be when they get full into their play."

Alissende murmured something reassuring, and Beth nodded. However, she'd shifted her gaze away from the woman who had become one of her closest friends these past years, her attention drawn, suddenly, to two lads who approached the table, carrying a platter thickly laden with succulent roasted pheasant. The heavy charger looked ready to topple at any moment, tipping and swaying with each step they took. Reaching out, she helped to steady it as they slid it onto the hard, welcome surface of the table. They both offered shy smiles and bows of gratitude as they retreated to the kitchen again.

"You caught that just in time," Alissende said, laughing and offering Beth a small hand towel to wipe away some of the rich juices that had splashed onto her as she'd reached out to help. "And a good thing too, else Meg would have had another worry to contend with this day."

"I fear I could not take on more right now, I do confess it."

Beth and Alissende both turned to face Meg, who was approaching them from the door that led to the family's private solar, her slightly anxious smile shifting into one far more jovial as she gripped both their hands in turn and pressed quick kisses to their cheeks.

"So," Meg asked, not looking very hopeful, "I take it the men haven't returned yet?"

"I'm afraid not." Beth tried to sound encouraging. "They should be here at any moment, though."

Meg sighed. "It would be just like my husband to delay the festivities. He seems to have a penchant for such things. He nearly missed Anne's birth six weeks ago, though he'd promised not to be late after having missed Gregory's arrival seven years past. And now this . . ."

"There is still time," Alissende said laughing and giving Meg's hand a squeeze. "Besides, you may recall that your husband's tardiness to Gregory's birth was *my* husband's fault. It could easily be Damien who is responsible again this time."

"Or Alex," Beth chimed in, nodding and raising her brow. "He has been known to turn up at the last possible instant, long after anyone full in their wits would have given up on him."

"We must all be short on wits, I think, considering

that we allowed ourselves to be swept away by the lot of them," Meg said, offering a gentle laugh at last as she linked her arm with Beth's.

"It is true that our lives have never failed to be interesting in the years we've known them—and each other." Beth patted Meg's hand, grateful all over again for the friendship she'd known with these two women, thanks to her marriage to Alex.

As if their conversation had some mystical power to summon those they'd been thinking of from thin air, at that moment the main chamber door swung inward and Richard stepped through, looking wind-blown but still strong and handsome, even with a bit of gray at his temples; he caught Meg's glance from across the room and grinned, raising his brow at her in a way that made it impossible for her not to blush and smile back at him, perturbed though she had been just moments ago. With a few murmured words to Beth and Alissende, she headed across the chamber to meet him, taking his hands and lifting her face for a kiss once they'd reached each other.

John had come into the chamber by that time as well. Ordained into the priesthood just last year, he wore the dark cassock of his calling as if he'd been born to it, his grin as he shared some happy conversation with Richard and Meg wide and genuine. Damien entered just behind John. His cheeks were ruddy from the chill outdoors, and he jabbed a hand through his unruly golden hair as he strode in, grinning as he twisted to say something to the person just behind him in the corridor before he glanced forward and saw Alissende, who had begun to walk toward him.

And then Alex strode into the chamber.

Alex . . .

Beth felt a little catch in her breathing at the sight of him, even after all these years still not immune to the effect he had on her. From the side of her vision she saw Meg and Richard stepping forward to formally welcome all their guests, and she was aware that the feast was now officially under way. But her gaze remained fixed on Alex. He caught her stare, the twinkle in his deep blue eyes making her heart skip a beat. Then the corner of his lip quirked up, and she felt a spill of heat through her so potent that she was afraid she might need to find a chair to support her, her legs being of little use any longer.

It proved unnecessary. In another few breaths he'd reached her and she was in his arms, held close in the comforting strength of his embrace. She snuggled her cheek to his chest for a moment, breathing in the fresh outdoor smell, mixed with the fainter scent of her herb concoction that he still favored using in his bath.

"You look even more ravishing than you did this morn when I left you," he murmured against the top of her head before his lips nibbled along her temple down to her ear, nipping the lobe for an instant before he pulled back a little to meet her gaze again. Beth laughed as she took a step back in awareness of the crowd of people surrounding them, loath as she was to pull away from his touch. As if he felt the same, he linked his fingers with hers, keeping her hand, at least, clasped close to him.

"I find your flattery difficult to believe, sir," she ided gently, "considering that I had not yet left our bed when you departed. My hair was uncombed, sleep bleared my eyes, and I was wearing no proper clothing to speak of—"

"What you were wearing was more than enough for me," he broke in with another grin. "I thought you looked most fetching. Would that you could always go about our castle thus." Then he sighed, though he could not seem to keep a straight face. "However, if you did, I doubt I would manage to accomplish anything at all during the day."

She shook her head, her own lips twitching traitorously. "Always a knave, Alexander de Ashby. I don't think you will ever change."

"Yet always truthful with you, my lady, for"—he paused and glanced up as if counting before meeting her gaze again, still with that twinkle in his eyes— "six years now, almost to the day."

"It is one of your many charms, to be sure." On impulse, she rose up on tiptoe and pressed a gentle kiss to his cheek.

"What was that for?" he asked, his voice a rumble of jovial good nature and sensual promise, all in one. As he spoke, he began to steer them away from crowd that had been gathering around the table where they'd been standing, bringing her closer to the hearth so that they could continue to speak with a little more privacy.

"For no other reason than because I wished it."

"Ah . . . it is fitting, then, for your wish has ever been my command."

"Truly?"

"Aye," he murmured, cocking his head to look at her. Knowing her well enough by now, she realized, to know that the seemingly innocuous phrase she'd uttered was only the prelude to something else.

"I wish you to tell me of this morn, then, and how the ceremony went," she finished, blinking up at him. "If you are at liberty to speak of it, that is."

He paused for just an instant before he nodded and lifted his hand to brush a thumb across her lower lip. "I cannot think why not. The Brotherhood and its secrets are of the past, now—though I would ask that you keep what I tell you close and not speak of it to others for now."

At her nod, he continued. "Our task, begun eight years ago, is done at last. The scroll we retrieved from France two months since has been placed with the others and secreted until such a time that the world is ready to know them."

"When will that be?"

Alex shrugged. "The pope has dissolved the Brotherhood. Those who gave us charge of the treasure have been put to death by those whose greed for it overstepped the bounds of decency and truth. But the scrolls have been kept secret for more than thirteen hundred years already, and so we have decided it would be best to wait a little longer."

Beth nodded again, silent as she contemplated what Alex had told her—distracted from her thoughts only when he grabbed her hand and called her attention again, saying, "And now I have a question for you, my lady."

"Aye?"

"Have our two small ruffians driven their nurse screeching from the manor yet?"

Beth laughed, her mood shifting again to one more

suited for the festive atmosphere of this feast, "In fact, they are behaving themselves quite well, according to Alissende. When she checked on them last, they were playing hoodman blind with Margery and Gregory above stairs."

"I shall have to go look in on them myself, shortly, if only to partake in the fun for a little while," Alex said, anticipation clear in his expression. "It must be near riotous up there, with all those children and babes in one chamber together. Six in all, between ours, my brother's, and Richard's."

"Just the kind of atmosphere I know you prefer," she murmured, glancing sideways at him as they continued to walk toward the feasting table. Trying to gauge whether it was the right time to tell him what she had been keeping to herself since his return home from France.

"I am fond of a good revel," he admitted, smiling. "Though in my younger days I never would have believed that the joy I have with our children would surpass anything else the world has to offer." He glanced at her with a wink. "Well, almost anything."

She smiled back at him, knowing it was time.

"If you but wait another half year, my lord, you will likely have a third innocent to influence with your wild ways."

"A third?" Alex echoed blankly. Then, as the realization of what she was saying sank in, he stiffened and his eyes widened. Swinging around to face her, he took both her hands into the warmth of his, the happiness bubbling up in his gaze a reflection of her own. "Beth, are you saying that—"

"Mmm-hmm," she answered, grinning and nodding at the same time like a fool. But she couldn't help it; her emotions filled her to bursting. She'd held off telling Meg and Alissende out of a desire to tell Alex first. Now she had, and she felt herself being swooped up into his arms before he swung her in a giant, laughing circle, attracting the attention of many of the guests and especially Meg, Richard, Alissende, Damien, and John.

Beth faced them along with Alex, finding it difficult not to blush when in answer to Richard's smile and questioning expression, Alex called out, "My beautiful wife has just told me there is another de Ashby in the making!"

The announcement was greeted with a chorus of "Huzzahs!" from the assembly of guests, along with raised glasses and grins from Richard, Damien, and John.

Meg and Alissende were smiling too as they rushed toward them, eager, Beth knew, to offer hugs and congratulations. But before they could reach them, Alex tugged Beth around to face him again, taking her mouth in a tender kiss that set her pulse to pounding and her heart to singing.

"I love you, Beth," he whispered against her lips. He kept his palms cupped to her cheeks as he pulled back enough to look into her eyes. "Do you know how much?"

Happy tears stung the backs of her eyes, for she did know. She knew because it was the same glorious feeling that was sweeping through her now, filling her insides with joyous, sparkling bubbles. But it wouldn't be as much fun, she decided, if she came right out and told him that.

"I love you as well, my lord. However, in answer to your question, I must admit that nay, I do not know the full extent of your feelings for me," she teased. "I think I will need you to tell me—and show me—as often as possible for the rest of our lives, lest I fail to accept the truth of it properly."

Alex's gaze was fixed warm upon her as she spoke. But just before the others reached them, he tipped his brow to rest against hers and murmured, "I will take your words to heart, my love. Yet I would not feel I was being honorable if I failed to remind you of just one thing first."

"And what is that, my wicked lord?" she asked, smiling now too and breathless with all that she was feeling for him.

His lip cocked up, the expression so dear to her that she threw her arms around his neck and pulled him closer . . . close enough that she could feel the warmth of his breath tickling her as he whispered into her ear.

"I have ever enjoyed a good challenge, lady. Especially one that involves the prospect of loving you."

Author's Note

History plays an important part in any historical romance, and while several of the historical details included within the pages of Alex and Beth's story stem from actual happenings, with others I have taken a bit of fictional license. One of these elements is in my representation of Alex, Damien, Richard, John, and the other Templars wearing the crimson cross during the battle at Dunleavy. In fact, no Templar was allowed to wear the Brotherhood's insignia after leaving (or being removed from) the Order. Also, the likelihood of Templars wearing the cross and so boldly drawing attention to themselves in the years after the mass arrests, even in Scotland, seems slim.

Connected to this bit of information—in the course of the final scenes of this book I alluded to an urban legend that exists about the Templars in Scotland (which was indeed one of the only Christian countries to openly welcome them after the papal bull was issued, providing sanctuary to any Templar who managed to cross her borders). According to legend, one of the possible reasons for the surprising Scottish victory at Bannockburn was the sudden rush onto the field of a group of Templars in full regalia. The story goes that the mere sight of these famed warriors ready to engage in the fighting, with the beauséant banner flying above them, was so terrifying to the English forces that they fled the field rather than stay and fight. Of course, whether or not the Templars played a part in it, it is commonly accepted that the battle at Bannockburn was indeed the turning point in the Scottish war for independence from England.

The final bit of history I adapted concerning the Templar Brotherhood has to do with the actual fact that after the fall of Acre in 1291, Templar Knights lost much if not all of their purpose as an Order. Their entire reason for being was to protect Christians on pilgrimage to the Holy Land. Once the Holy Land was lost, there was no true need for the Brotherhood any longer. They retreated to Cyprus, as is mentioned in all three of my Templar books; however, they engaged only in training from that point onward, and few if any actual battles. Many historians cite this as one of the more compelling rationales behind the eventual fall of what had been such a powerful and wealthy Order. The other was greed in regard to the Brotherhood's immense wealth, amassed over their two hundred years of service as protectors and trusted guardians of treasures and secrets.

Another historical tidbit I found interesting and managed to work into my story involves Scotland's King Robert the Bruce. It is indeed true that in 1309, the Bruce was a new, self-proclaimed king. As mentioned in the final scene of the main story, the Bruce's family had been captured and was being held under guard in abbeys (or, depending on who they were, in small cages to be exposed to public ridicule) at the order of England's King Edward II. One of the stories attached to all this has to do with one "Black Agnes": Lady Agnes Randolph.

As a very young woman, Black Agnes did indeed fight for the Bruce in his struggle to secure Scotland's independence, but the more colorful story I borrowed comes from a little later in her life. In 1334, Black Agnes successfully held her castle at Dunbar against the besieging forces of England's Earl of Salisbury. After each assault on her fortress, her maids dusted off the battlements, thereby showing her disdain for the English.

Reading of this brave Scotswoman inspired my short scene during which Beth heads up to the crenellations while Lord Exford's forces are assaulting Dunleavy. She plans to show her lack of intimidation in the same manner that Black Agnes had. Of course, Alex appears at the top of the field just afterward and the story continues on its own trajectory from there, but Black Agnes's story provided the kernel of inspiration that sparked the scene.

While all this research was admittedly engrossing, none of it would have had any resonance for me without Alex and Beth's relationship to frame it. Though all my heroes seem to need a bit of redemption when I first meet them, Alex remains the only hero I've written thus far who had such a great distance to go. Taking a man who'd once abandoned his lover and child, and trying to find ways to show him growing and changing into a man worthy of honest, committed love, was a tall order for me to fill. In matching him with a passionate, intelligent, and practical woman like Beth, I found that the task became a little easier. In the end, Alex discovered in himself the kind of man embodied by all my favorite heroes: one who is selfless, strong, committed to those he loves, and willing to do that which is supremely difficult if it is also what is right and honest.

It is very difficult for me now to say good-bye to this series and to the characters who peopled it. Even with the struggles and seemingly insurmountable obstacles that can sometimes arise while writing a novel, the characters and their stories tend to live and breathe in my imagination long after I reach "The End." I have found that it is no different with *The Templar's Seduction*—only it is perhaps a little more pronounced, as my memory this time must include characters from the other two books in the trilogy as well. When all is said and done, however, I truly enjoyed every moment of time I spent following Alex and Beth to their well-earned happy-ever-after. I can only hope that you did too. As always, thanks for coming along on the journey.

—MRM

Avon Romantic Treasures

Unforgettable, enthralling love stories, sparkling with passion and adventure from Romance's bestselling authors